Rising From The Ashes

Copyright

Opening Quote

There was nothing in sight but memories left abandoned. There was nowhere to hide. The ashes fell like snow. And the ground caved in between where we were standing. And your voice was all I heard. That I get what I deserve. So, give me reason to prove me wrong, to wash this memory clean. Let the floods cross the distance in your eyes. Give me reason to fill this hole. Connect this space between. Let it be enough to reach the truth that lies across this new divide.

New Divide by Linkin Park

Chapter One

☙ Raleigh ☙

I sit as straight as possible behind the receptionist's desk in the lobby of Alex Lucinio's top floor office in the Lucinio Tech corporate building. I've been here for almost a half hour already. I've made it a point to get here at least a half hour before my boss. I want to make a good impression on him. I'm trying.

But the truth is, he hates me. I don't know why, but ever since he laid eyes on me, he's hated me. I can feel it in the cold glare he gives me with his icy blue eyes. I feel it every time he walks into the room and sees me. An instant chill runs from the back of my neck down my spine. I want to cry.

I won't, though. I won't let him see that weakness in me. I will never allow him to see it because he'll use it to his advantage. He'll pick up on it and throw more insults my way. Like how I'm just as cold and calculating as my father.

I swallow hard at the thought and force myself to breathe. My father. Alex killed him. He murdered the only person I've ever known as a father. At the very least, he had a hand in killing him. A very large hand.

Matthew Lucinio.

I dab at my eyes and shake my head with a sniffle. But that wasn't who he was to me. His name to me was Matthew Jennings. I wipe more furiously at my eyes.

No. Alex Lucinio doesn't get that power over me. He doesn't get to make me cry. My father would hate seeing me cry. He never could handle my tears. He always said they broke his heart. I don't want to break his heart.

I take another deep breath. Over the past six months since my father's murder, I have learned things about him that are devastating to me. My mind believes everything. My heart is another story. My heart shatters all over again with every word that is uttered about him.

The night of his death, I came home like I did every night after my walk on the beach. I didn't get out a lot. I spent most of my time studying. I'd been homeschooled for my entire life. My father had always believed it was for the best. He didn't like public or private schools. He said he didn't believe I could ever get a good education when all the school cares about is money, sports, and parties.

I had always understood. I even agreed with him. I had a goal. I wanted to attend the University of Oxford. I'd researched it. I'd studied so hard for it. I applied for it after I finished my studies nearly six months ahead of schedule. I'd done well on the SAT's and ACT's. I worked really hard on my application. I didn't apply to any other university. I knew I belonged at Oxford.

My dad encouraged me. He always said that if I wanted it, I could have it. All I had to do was set my mind to it and work hard. That's what I've always done. I worked my ass off to reach my goals. And just when it was in my grasp, it was ripped away.

I look at the clock on my desk impatiently. I start swinging the leg I have crossed over my other. It's nerves. The closer it gets to the time Alex is supposed to arrive, the more nervous I become. He's never late. Ever. I always dread the second he walks off the elevator. Even though my pulse picks up slightly. I hate that my heart always skips a beat when I look at him.

I chew on my bottom lip. I never used to do that, but lately I find myself doing it until I almost bleed. Sometimes, I do. I blame Alex. I blame him for making me a nervous wreck. Terrified of what he's going to say to me next. He already thinks I'm a liar and terrible person.

The truth is, I'm not. I haven't lied to him about anything. I've told him and his brother, Josh, everything I know. Matthew was a great father. He was gone a lot, but that was his business. He always checked in when he had to go away. He loved me. As hard as it is for them to believe, my father loved me.

I start to flick my nail as I wait. I look down at my clock. He should be here anytime now. And then I can, hopefully, start my day. As long as he doesn't throw things at me that are mundane just to keep me busy. It's not like he doesn't already give me enough to do.

I jump when the elevator door opens but recover quickly. Striding out of the elevator looking down at his phone is the object of my nightmares.

Though, I'd never admit it, he's also the object of my dreams. All six feet two of him. Alex is built well. He takes care of himself without looking bulky. His dark hair matches his dark and brooding features. Except his eyes. His eyes are a piercing blue. I've never seen him smile. Not once. I don't think he's capable. At least not when it comes to me.

"Did you get my reports?" His deep voice sends shockwaves through the air. My hair stands up on my arms. I have instant goosebumps, and things happen between my thighs that make me blush.

My heart sinks while it speeds up at his words. "R-reports?" I nearly whisper.

He lets out a sigh that sounds more like a low growl. He slowly looks at me as he puts his phone in his pocket. "Yes. Reports. From yesterday. You know. That thing with numbers on it that tells the CEO how things are going with his company?"

The glare he gives me brings tears to my eyes as I frantically try to remember him giving me that order. I think about every email or interoffice message he sent to me yesterday. I quietly and quickly glance at my sticky notes and to-do list.

"I… I didn't k-know you needed them." I choke back the sob threatening to escape. I won't let him see that. I refuse. I don't want him to know the effect he has on me, but especially in this way. I don't want to disappoint him. I don't want to upset him. Even though he hates me, I want to make his life easier.

Alex says nothing. Instead, he keeps his icy glare glued on me as he slowly stalks behind my desk. I dig my nails into my arms when I cross them over my chest and cower, though I try not to. I bite my lip and keep my eyes straight ahead, though my shoulders tense. By sheer force of will, I keep myself from trembling.

Alex forcefully rips a sticky note from the top of my computer screen. He puts one hand on the back of my chair as he slams his hand down on my calendar. I jump and let out a quiet squeak as I squeeze my eyes shut. He's so close to me that I can feel his body heat.

I hate that I like the way he smells. It's spicy. Fresh. Unique to him. I've never smelled anything quite like it. I don't like that I know him just by his scent. I despise that it makes me feel almost calm instead of terrified of him. I don't understand it. Just like I don't understand why he hates me.

"Right there, Raleigh. I made sure you could see it. I need to go over them before my meeting today."

I open my eyes slowly, taking a breath. His scent fills me. I nod. "I'll g-get them, Mr. Lucinio."

"Now, Raleigh."

"Yes, sir," I whisper.

Alex stands slowly and walks to his office without another word. His stride is cocky. Confident. Self-assured. Everything he is. He seems totally unbothered by the fact that he scared me as badly as he did. I shouldn't be surprised. I know how he feels about me.

I force myself to do what he asks. I quickly download the reports he's requested and print them. I bite my lip when I notice they all have to do with accounts. I love math and numbers. Math has always been my favorite subject. It comes so easy to me. So do patterns. It's like they just jump out of the page at me.

Which is why I suddenly find myself so much more nervous than I already was. I hadn't meant to really look, but it's glaringly obvious. So obvious that I'm sure Alex will see it right away. I should just keep my mouth shut.

I open my desk drawer to get a paperclip. Alex hates staples. I learned that my first day here when I made the mistake of stapling one of his reports. He threw the report back at me and told me to use a fucking paperclip. It's neater. He can take the paperclip off and read the report, and then use it to bind it when he's finished. When I saw him dividing the report into piles, I understood why. But I don't really get why he couldn't just explain it.

My fingers brush over a letter. A letter that breaks me every time I look at it. My hand trembles. The tears I fought so hard to keep at bay around Alex spill from my eyes. I quickly take the paperclip and slam my desk drawer. I swipe at my eyes and breathe deeply, shaking my head. I won't think about that. Not now. Not ever. I don't know why I keep the letter. I must be a masochist. It's caused me nothing but pain. Maybe it's because it's the only thing I have that physically ties me to the past that was ripped away from me.

I take a Kleenex and use it to dab my eyes. I take a drink of the water I have sitting on my desk and suddenly remember the mocha I ordered for Alex. I look at my clock.

"Shit…" It's late. Of all days to be late, why does it have to be today?

I shakily grab the stack of reports I just printed off and paperclip them all separately. I don't want to face his wrath for having his reports messed up. I can't handle anymore today. Not after last night and the nightmares I constantly have. I'm too exhausted.

I pick up the reports and stride as confidently as I can to Alex's office. I listen for a moment, making sure he's not on the phone. I quietly open his door when I hear silence. Alex is sitting behind his desk. He's taken off his jacket. It's ridiculous how comfortable he looks. How in control.

Sexy.

His white dress shirt fits him so perfectly. The top two buttons are undone. It's tucked into a pair of black slacks that only serves to show more of his perfectly sculpted body. If he didn't strike fear into God himself, he might be the most attractive man I've ever seen.

Who am I kidding? Myself? It's obvious how attractive he is. Everyone knows it. The girls he dates. Him. I'd be stupid to not admit that he's beyond my wildest dreams.

And just as untouchable.

I silently hand him the reports. He doesn't look up at me when he takes them. He says nothing as he quickly starts leafing through them. I bite my lip when I notice that he doesn't see what I noticed right away. He may have an issue with me, but this is my job. And no matter what he thinks, I'm grateful to his family. Even to him. I don't know where I'd be right now if his brother hadn't taken me in.

But when I see frustration and anger cross his features, I quietly leave the office and make my way to the relative safety of my desk. I sit down and try to compose myself. It's not easy, but I'm getting better and better at it as the days pass. It seems to be the only way to survive all of the hurt and pain.

Learning about the man I called my father my entire life hasn't been easy. I didn't know he was the leader of a mafia. I didn't even know his real last name. I thought he just traveled a lot for the company he worked for. He always told me he worked in finance. That's why he had so many different accounts and businesses to keep track of. I didn't know he lived a whole other life with a whole other family and an entirely different last name. I didn't know that he killed a lot of people. I didn't know any of the things he did. But it's difficult to argue with evidence.

Josh Lucinio, Alex's twin brother and leader of the Lucinio Mafia, spent hours with me explaining everything. How my father had spent years giving him a serum and brainwashing him. He beat him into submission so many different times. He forced him to do things that Josh isn't proud of and would never do otherwise. My father ruined his life. Or at least tried to.

Josh explained to me everything that had been going on over the past few years. He took me through ever since I was born. Everything that my father was doing. He explained to me what happened the night Matthew was killed.

I didn't know my father was involved in a sex trafficking ring. The thought makes me sick to my stomach. I had no idea he'd kidnapped anyone. The thought that he'd wired two women to blow up infuriated me. It still does.

The evil things he did over the years, though, is just not the man I knew. I've struggled over the months to come to terms with who he was, and who he was around me. There are so many stark contrasts. I'm having a hard time wrapping my head around it.

Josh was kind enough to take me in. He didn't have to. He could have kicked me out onto the street and made me fend for myself. I wouldn't have blamed him if he did. It must be difficult to look at me every day. I'm a living and breathing reminder of all he despises.

Instead, though, he's been very kind to me. He's treated me like family. Sort of like a little sister. Even though I'm the farthest thing from it. It was only a few days after that Josh found out my entire life really was nothing more than a lie. I really don't even know who I am.

I grew up believing that my biological father was Matthew Jennings. Or Lucinio as I know him now. He was all I knew. But just days after losing him and being told the truth about him, I found out that he's really not even my father. I have no relation to him at all. According to the DNA test that was run anyway.

The blow was just one more on top of the several I'd already received. It's not every day that a person finds out the man who raised them was nothing more than a heartless, cold-blooded killer. Or that they really were an orphan with no family.

If it weren't for my friendship with Dallas Cassidy, one of the girls my father kidnapped and wired to explode, I would have no one except Josh. Dallas and Josh are the only ones who really talk to me and listen to me. His friend's, the Crane family, are nice people, but I don't really spend a lot of time with them. They're all busy with their own lives.

Mostly, I just try to keep to myself. I've grown tired of explaining myself to everyone. Especially to Alex. He's so suspicious of me. He can't believe that my father, well, his father… I sigh to myself. I don't even know what to call Matthew anymore.

I slump a little when the elevator door opens. A young man in an apron walks out with a huge smile on his face. He could be cute if I was attracted to his type. Blond and spiky hair. Sort of tall. Taller than me anyway. Though, that's not hard. I'm hardly five feet two. The guy is probably close to my age. I just turned eighteen a few days ago. He's a little scrawny. Not a lot of muscle. He's definitely not as tall as Alex.

I plaster on a fake smile that I hope looks sincere. "Hi," I say quietly. A little quieter than I intended. I clear my throat.

"Hey, there." He smiles so brightly that his greasy face looks like it might break. I hadn't realized just how greasy it is until he got closer. He leans on my desk. His aftershave is overpowering. I fight to keep from coughing.

I put a hand up in front of my mouth and take a breath. It doesn't help. I cough anyway. Even with the large desk and high front that keeps me mostly hidden, it does nothing for his overpowering scent. Gross.

"Um… What can I do for you?" I ask after I finish coughing.

"Oh. Right. I was just blinded by your beauty. I forgot I have your order." He puts a carrier with Alex's mocha on the desk.

"Thank you."

"And you can give me your phone number. Because damn. Let me take you out. There's a concert tonight in one of the parks near the lake. You'd look great on my arm."

"Uh… No. No thank you." My mind races to think of an excuse.

"Oh, come on. I don't bite." He gives me a disgusting grin that makes me think he does. I don't know how anyone could find him attractive, though I am sure they do. Definitely not my type.

"I have to work, so…" I trail off hoping that will be enough. I reach for the cup, but he pulls it out of my reach.

"Come on. You can't tell me the big bad boss man doesn't let you out at night."

A shiver runs down my spine the more uncomfortable I get. "I work early in the morning." I once again reach for the cup.

He once again pulls it away. "Seriously. Come on. I'm a nice guy. You're hot. We could have a lot of fun together. And if you don't want to go to the concert, we could find a quiet place. Like my apartment."

"Really. No thank you." I try to be forceful, but even I hear the fear in my voice. I wouldn't go anywhere with this guy. "I don't want to. Thank you, but can I have my boss's order please?"

"What are you afraid of? Just come out with me." He puts the cup on the desk and starts to make his way around my desk.

My panic starts to rise. My throat feels like it's closing. I start backing away. My desk is in the middle of the room. I can escape either side if I need to. And that's just what I intend to do. Escape is all I can think of.

"What are you doing?" I practically whisper over the heart that's relocated into my throat. I back away further towards the other side of my desk.

He laughs. "I'm just giving you my number, sweetheart. In case you change your mind."

The need to flee is overpowering. But not as overpowering as the spicy and fresh scent that gives me butterflies. I can sense his presence just before I back right up into him. I collide with his hard body. I'm so relieved that I allow a couple of tears of relief to escape. He might hate me, but in this moment, I've never been so happy to have him around.

"She said no," Alex growls as his hands grip my waist. I know I'm trembling, but I can't stop myself. If his hands weren't on my hips, I'd be on the ground curled in a shaking ball.

The guy looks up at him. His hand is poised over a blank sticky note he was just about to start writing on. "What?" he asks, a little bewildered.

"No. She said no. You know what that means, right?" Alex lets me go but doesn't move. If I could crawl behind him and use him for a shield, I would. I still may.

"Yeah. I know what it means. I'm not stupid." He stands up and faces us.

"I'm not so sure about that. You're fired."

The guy's mouth drops at Alex's words. "You can't fire me! I work for Starbucks!"

"And I own the fucking building. By the time you get downstairs, you'll be terminated. You can hand in your apron. And if I catch you in the building again, you'll face me. You won't like the result. Now walk away."

The kid gawks at Alex. "But -"

"You might want to listen to him, kid," a deep, rich, and super powerful voice says from behind us.

"Josh," I whisper, closing my eyes. I've been so terrified, I didn't even know he'd stepped off the elevator.

The guy says nothing more. He grumbles the entire way to the elevator and shoots me a glare that could melt steel, but he doesn't say another word. I don't breathe until the elevator doors close. I quickly grab onto the corner of my desk when Alex moves. I nearly fall backwards.

He grabs his cup and walks back to his office. "Get me the financials for NDS," he says without looking back.

I clutch my chest and start hyperventilating as I make my way to my chair. "Oh God."

Josh is immediately at my side. He helps into my chair. "You okay? What the hell just happened?"

I shake my head and force several deep breaths. "I... have t-to get that r-report." I turn to my computer.

Josh grips the arms of my chair and turns me back to him as he kneels down. "Hey. Stop it. This is me. Not Alex. What just happened?"

I bite my lower lip. "I don't know." I shake my head. "He came up here to deliver Alex's mocha. I usually get it myself, but they opened late. I don't know why. Next thing I know he's saying he wants to take me to this concert in a park. But he wouldn't take no for an answer. Then he walked behind the desk and freaked me out." I start to relax as I look down at my hands. "I overreacted. I'm just not used to being flirted with."

Josh wraps me in a tight hug. "That wasn't flirting, and you didn't overreact. It made you uncomfortable. It was aggressive as hell. Unwarranted. Not something you should tolerate. I sure as hell won't tolerate anyone talking to you like that."

I relax completely in his arms. "Why do I think of you as kind of a big brother and Alex as…" I trail off, not being able to think of the words. I sniffle instead. "He still hates me."

"Alex doesn't hate you, Raleigh. He just refuses to allow himself to think that he might be wrong. Alex has been like that our whole life. He doesn't like being wrong. It leaves a bad taste in his mouth. I promise. He'll get over it."

"Report, Raleigh!" Alex barks.

I jump nearly a mile. "He hates me," I whisper. The dam bursts. The tears I fought so hard all morning flood out of me. I cry hard into Josh's shoulder.

"No, honey," Josh whispers back. "Alex is struggling in his own way. He's never wanted mafia life. When I took over, he stayed to help me. Now that I'm stable and Alex can do what he wants to, it's just… It's different. It's not something Alex has ever been able to do. It's a new life for him. He's dealing with that. He's dealing with the fact that he was wrong about you. And as much as it eats him, he hates the fact that he lives alone. He's always had people around him. His crew. Me. Ryan and his family. Now that things have calmed down in his life, he has a lot of time on his hands. And it's time that he's never had."

"But why take it out on me?" I ask quietly as the tears slowly subside.

"Because to him, you're sort of a project. A part of his past that he wants to let go but can't. He doesn't want mafia life, but it's all he's known, Raleigh. Figuring out your past is sort of his way of hanging on to a part that he wants to let go but is afraid to."

"That doesn't make sense. If he doesn't want it, then why hang onto it?" I slowly pull away and look at him.

He smiles and reaches up to wipe my tears. "It doesn't make sense. It's not something I think I have a chance at explaining. I won't even try." He reaches over to hand me a Kleenex. I take it and start wiping my puffy eyes. "How about you get me the NDS report he wants. Then head to the bathroom and compose yourself. I'll have Alec bring Dallas over after school. You two can do a girl's weekend. I'll make myself scarce."

I nod. "I'd like that," I say softly. "But..." I turn towards my computer. "But it's not the NDS reports he wants."

Josh stands and leans against the desk with his arms folded over his chest. "It's not?"

I shake my head. "The problem account is EXM. I saw it this morning. They have two different bank accounts. One of them is paying their bill. The other is taking it back out." I hand him the reports after I print them out.

He thumbs through them. "Holy shit, Raleigh. How the hell did you see this?"

I look up at him. "I don't really know. It just... sort of jumped out at me." I shrug. "I was always good at math, and with numbers. My father -" I cut myself off. "Um... Matthew. He... um... he always had me help with his business accounts." I say it quietly and look down. "I know how that makes me sound. It's just one more reason to make Alex suspicious."

Josh squeezes my shoulder. "I'll deal with Alex. This doesn't make you look more suspicious. At least not to me because I know if I asked you to explain what he made you do, you'd tell me."

I look up with a soft smile. "I don't want to keep anything from you. I wouldn't. If I can tell you anything that you want to know, I'll tell you."

"I know. You've already proven yourself to me. To all of us. Alex will come around." He glances towards Alex's office. "But if he ever treats you like he just did, tell me. I won't let that shit slide."

He pats me on the shoulder before he heads for Alex's office. I watch him disappear behind the doors. I won't tell him that Alex treats me like this every day. I don't like the idea of coming between two brothers. Especially brothers as close as him and Alex.

I make my way to the bathroom to clean up and, hopefully, make myself presentable. I don't want to make Alex look bad when the people for his meetings start showing up.

As I start reapplying the small amount of makeup I wear, I think about the protective tone in Alex's voice when he was telling that idiot guy off. How he didn't move until the guy was in the elevator, and the doors were closed.

My cheeks flush at the thought of his chest against my back. So strong and unyielding. Warm. Protective. Safe. The way Alex growled sent butterflies to my stomach. It wasn't just protective. It wasn't just powerful.

It was possessive.

His hands on my hips didn't feel like he was just steadying me. It was like he was showing the guy that he not only doesn't have a chance in hell, but that he needs to stay away from me. That I'm not his.

I blush darker because although I know how Alex feels about me, it hasn't stopped me from thinking very inappropriate things about him. It's like the meaner he is to me, the more attractive he becomes.

I push the thoughts aside because I know that Alex will never think of me as more than an annoyance. I'm not stupid. I know that the only reason I work here is so he can keep an eye on me until he figures out whatever it is he thinks I'm hiding.

That doesn't stop the undeniable attraction I have to him. I've never dated. I've had celebrity crushes, but I never had the time to really form relationships. I was too busy with my studies. I know now that my father kept me hidden away because of his real life. It wasn't just me buckling down and being a good girl. It wasn't just me wanting to reach my unattainable goals.

The realization hurts. It always hurts when I think of it.

I finish reapplying my makeup and slowly head back out of the bathroom. I sit back down behind my desk and tell myself for the millionth time how truly insane I am. How messed up. How can I have an attraction to a guy who I will never have a chance with, but who also hates me?

I groan. I can't stop thinking of the tone of his voice, and his hands on my hips. I wonder if maybe Alex Lucinio has a heart underneath his cold, hard exterior after all.

Chapter Two

☂ Alex ☂

I'm surprised when I look up and see my brother closing the door to my office instead of Raleigh. I narrow my eyes when I see a stack of papers in his hand as he strides purposefully towards my desk. He drops them in front of me.

"Raleigh too afraid to come in here herself?" I snatch the report and start leafing through it. I glare with a low growl as I stand. "I fucking said NDS. Not EXM! I don't have fucking time for this!"

"Sit down," Josh growls just as dangerously as I had moments before.

I shoot him a glare that could melt the strongest of steel. It has little to no effect on him. He sits down and crosses his arms over his chest as he watches me. While every fiber of my being is seething, I've learned one thing about Josh. There isn't a point in arguing with him.

It wasn't always like that. Growing up, Josh was usually timid. He didn't like to cause tension. I can't blame him. We usually ended up getting a beating for that. I took the brunt of them. I looked at it as being my responsibility as his big brother. Protect him at all costs.

Little did either of us know that our father's acts of treachery stemmed all the way to our birth certificates. It was less than a year ago that we found out Josh was the oldest brother. Thirty-four years. He kept the secret for thirty-four fucking years. And used it in his sick game to play us against each other.

I cross my arms over my chest and look down at him from behind my desk. "I have a meeting in thirty minutes. And a huge fucking problem on my hands. I don't have time for this. What do you want?"

He doesn't say a word. He watches me until I do what he says and sit down. "Thank you. I don't know exactly what's happening, but you have the right report."

I look at him exasperated. "Josh, what the fuck? You just said it yourself! You don't know what's going on. I have a huge problem with NDS. They haven't been making payments, but the CEO sent me bank statements. They are paying. But I'm not getting the payments. I need the reports for NDS!"

"Alex. Look at the fucking report. If you're convinced you need NDS, I'll get it for you. But look first."

I blink at him. How can he be calm in this situation? This is a disaster. This is multi-millions of dollars this company is losing. And if I don't find it, they are going to pull their account. They're account alone could pay the salaries of everyone who works in this building. Including me.

I sigh and look down at the report. After a few moments, I finally give up. "What the fuck am I looking at?"

Josh shakes his head and gets up. He walks to the door of my office. "You must have had a bad night or something. You're really off you're fucking game."

"Oh! Josh. Um… Can you give this to Alex? I found something else."

I raise an eyebrow at Raleigh's voice. I growl low when the blood rushes directly to my cock. Like it always does. I adjust myself. Fucking traitor. My breath catches when I see her walking in front of Josh.

I immediately focus on the papers in front of me. It's better than looking at her. Strands of her auburn hair falling from the messy bun she's piled her hair into have the same effect on me that the subtle scent of her perfume does. Or watching her ridiculously taut body moving underneath the white blouse I'd love nothing more than to rip off… with my teeth.

I force myself to think of all the reason's she's not to be trusted. She truly loved Matthew. I know what he's like. I know the evil, conniving motherfucker that he is. In order to love him, a person has to be just as fucked up. I know she's not being totally truthful. She has everyone else wrapped around her pretty finger. Not me.

When I have myself back in check, I look back up. She's standing in front of me. She hands me another stack of papers. "NDS," she says quietly.

I swallow to wet my dry throat. Fuck my reaction to her. "It's about fucking time."

She flinches. I feel bad, but only for a second. I look down at my reports and start searching for the information I know is there, but don't see. I blame her. I have never in my life had an issue seeing numbers. Patterns. Problems. It's like a superpower or something.

It's how I've gotten where I am. I'm observant. Seeing things that others can't or don't is how I've survived. My entire life has been spent figuring shit out and acting on it. The fact that I am not able to focus enough to see what I need only sets me more on edge.

Out of the corner of my eye, I watch as Josh sits. Raleigh doesn't move from the front of my desk. Josh shakes his head slightly at her when she looks at him. Ignoring them isn't helping me in the slightest. Not like I'd be able to ignore Raleigh anyway.

Steeling myself, I look up at her. I know I'm exuding a dangerously dark look, because she backs away slightly. Good. The less I can smell her, the better for all of us. I watch as she claps her hands in front of her.

"What? What am I missing?" I snap at both of them.

"Alex, for fuck's sake. Calm down." Apparently, my brother has had enough attitude today. He doesn't know what's at stake. Neither of them do. "We can talk about why the hell you're acting like a child when she's done explaining to you what you're missing." He nods to Raleigh and softens his voice. "Go ahead. Tell him what you saw."

She takes a deep breath and shakily walks around my desk. I move my chair back to give her room, but it's a mistake. I'd rather smell that subtle scent than have her perky little ass in front of me. So, I move my chair over so I'm next to her instead. Thank Hell she squats next to me as she starts leafing through the reports on my desk.

"This morning when I printed off the accounts report you wanted, I saw this," she says, barely above a whisper. She takes a yellow highlighter and starts neatly highlighting line after line of transactions. She takes a blue highlighter and starts highlighting line after line of withdrawals.

I shake my head, trying to follow along. It doesn't help that I can smell the strawberry scent of her shampoo. She takes the other stack of papers as I watch her and starts highlighting more lines in a green color.

"Raleigh," I finally say. "The highlighting is pretty, but what the fuck am I looking at?"

She takes a breath and looks up at me before standing. "EXM is paying on time every month with their account." She points at the seven-thousand-dollar monthly payment. "But they are pulling it back out. Or… someone is pulling it back out." She points to a seven-thousand-dollar withdrawal happening every month.

"Fuck…" My eyes widen as I quickly flip through the pages. "How did you see this?" I don't look up. Instead, I become more and more angry seeing how far back this shit goes. How the fuck did I miss this?

Ever since I took over this company, I've run across nothing but problems. Lucinio Tech is my baby. I have nurtured this company since it was born when I was barely eighteen. It was my way to show my father that I had what it took to run an international multi-billion-dollar company. I didn't need the mafia.

Granted, I was just about to begin college when I started it. I admittedly used my relationship with Ryan Crane, my best friend and leader of one of the most powerful mafias in the world, to my advantage. He helped get it off the ground. He put in staff. But he followed my business plan and kept me involved in every aspect. By the time I'd graduated college, I was all into the company.

But being in the mafia comes with a price. Shit tends to blow up. It didn't matter that I haven't technically been a part of it for many years. I always end up being dragged into situations somehow.

None of that matters right now. What matters is that my company is about to implode. Crumble around me in a supernova type of splendor. It took me a couple of months to really gain total control over Lucinio Tech. I'm not about to let all the work I did fall apart on me.

"Son of a bitch," I growl. "How the fuck did you see this?" If Raleigh answers, I don't hear her. I'm seething. This is the type of shit I spent weeks fixing when I took over. "How the hell did I miss this?"

The more I dig into the financial report for EXM, the sicker it makes me. My chest tightens. This is the kind of shit the NDS executives were talking about. This looks bad. Really, really bad.

"There's more," Raleigh whispers. She shakily moves the other report towards me. "NDS."

I glance up at her. She's nervously biting her lip. I look back down at the NDS account, focusing on what she's highlighted. After just a couple of seconds, it all hits me. Hard. I gasp out a breath. The money they've been paying to us hasn't been going into our account. It's been going into the account that EXM is making withdrawals from.

Josh stands and leans over the desk. "I texted Lance already," he says as he tilts his head to look at the numbers.

My chest constricts. It feels like the familiar hand of betrayal has gripped my heart and started squeezing. I stand quickly and gather the account information in front of me. I am trying not to hyperventilate.

"Alex?" Raleigh whispers. I can hear the alarm in her voice.

The panic immediately morphs. Suddenly, the intense and dark anger I've kept locked deep inside for a long-time bubbles to the surface. I can feel it in my veins. It fills me like venom. When I open my eyes, not even realizing I closed them, I see nothing but red.

I turn slowly towards her. "How long did you know?"

I see the exact moment the confusion in Raleigh's icy blue eyes turns to fear. "W-what?"

"Alex," Josh says in warning.

I grip Raleigh's hips and shove her against the window behind me. Raleigh screams as I hold her against the glass. "How fucking long did you know?"

"Alex! What the hell is wrong with you?" Josh shoves me back hard enough that I hit my desk and fall backwards over it.

I hit the floor hard but spring to my feet and glare at my brother. Raleigh has sunk to the floor and is hyperventilating. I breathe deeply a few times as I try to rein in my temper. But every time I look at her, I feel the anger rising again.

I look at Josh as I brush myself off. "She has you wrapped around her fucking finger. You don't even know what she just found, do you?"

"Do you?" Josh growls. He folds his arms over his chest and stands like a barrier between me and her.

"She's not that innocent. Those accounts? They're fucking hers."

He furrows his brows but doesn't move. "Fucking hell, Alex. Really?"

I glare down at Raleigh once more. She's managed to bring her knees up to her chest and make herself as small as humanly possible. My eyes flick back up to Josh. I can't help but feel a little bit of vindication. Everyone, including my own damn brother, has doubted me. But I knew. I knew Raleigh Jennings wasn't as innocent as she seemed.

"Top drawer. On the right." I'm tingling. "You think she's been forthcoming to you about everything? Take a look."

I watch him as he takes a folder out of my desk drawer. He opens it and scans it before looking down at the account numbers Raleigh highlighted. I watch as his face falls further and further. The tingling has turned into full on vibrating.

Finally, he looks up at me. "You and I need to talk." He turns to Raleigh and kneels in front of her. "Raleigh." He holds out a hand.

I watch in pure fascination when she takes his hand, and he pulls her to her feet. I can't help but feel a little bit of excitement because she's about to finally get what she deserves. Weaseling her way into this family ends now.

"I told you I'd figure you out, Raleigh. I told you that your lies and deceit wouldn't be tolerated. I knew it might take me time, but your games and whatever plans you're carrying out end today, sweetheart."

She looks at me. I can see she's terrified. A very small part of me feels a tiny twinge of empathy for her. But the ice in my veins cools any of the heat she sets off in me when Josh propels her to the door. I turn to follow, a small smirk of victory on my lips.

Josh turns and levels me with a cold glare he has never used on me. I actually shiver. "Sit the fuck down. You come out here, I'll throw you down the fucking elevator shaft."

I don't know why, but the tone of his voice makes me stop in my tracks. I narrow my eyes, but I stop. I fold my arms over my chest and wait for him to come back. He walks into my office moments later, his eyes on me.

"You should know better than anyone, I don't take orders. From anyone. Including you. I don't give a shit if you're my twin. Or some dangerous and scary mafia boss. I don't care that you're the older brother. Don't fucking give me orders."

"Sit down, Alex." His voice has lost the dangerous edge he tried using on me moments ago. He sounds almost tired.

"Where's Raleigh?"

"I have Alec coming for her. Sit down, Alex." He stands between me and the door.

"Josh, fucking hell. I'm not a fucking kid. She's been caught red-handed. She's been lying this whole time." I gesture angrily at the door.

Josh's almost demonic glare returns. "The only thing that girl has kept from you is that all her fucking dreams were shattered the night we took out Matthew! Including that she was rejected from Oxford University, which is the only college she wanted to attend! Now sit the fuck down!"

I don't know why, but his tone sends an uneasy feeling all through me. Something suddenly doesn't feel right. Like he knows more than what he's saying. Things that I don't. I eye him suspiciously as he waits for me to follow his command.

When I don't, Josh does something he's never done. He growls, grabs me by my arms before I have any time to react, and shoves me into a chair. He stalks to the other side of my desk and sits as he takes a few deep and calming breaths with his eyes closed.

The shock of him physically shoving me into a chair only manages to set me more at unease. It should piss me off. No one has ever dared do what he just did. "Why do I get the feeling you're keeping something from me?" I rub my arms where he gripped them.

The anger I should feel at him pushing me into a chair is non-existent. What scares the hell out of me is how freaked out I suddenly am. Like there's something huge he's not saying and has been keeping from me.

He watches me, like he's measuring what he wants to say. Finally, he sighs. "Those accounts aren't hers. Do you honestly think I didn't know about them?"

"What are you talking about?"

"The accounts you traced to her." He holds up the folder. "Had you said something to me about them, I would have fucking told you. Instead, you have this un-fucking-believable vendetta to systematically tear that girl to shreds. What the hell is wrong with you? I've never seen you put hands on a woman like you just did to her."

I close my eyes and scrub my hands down my face. "Because there's something wrong, Josh. Because I know it. I'm pissed you won't listen. There's so much shit I see that you seem to ignore. Do you know how fucking frustrating it is to not be able to get your own brother to believe you when you say something is wrong?"

He gives me a deadpan look. I know I fucked up immediately. Because he does know. He knows better than anyone. I can't count the number of times he tried to tell me something was wrong while we were growing up. While I was in college. When I fucking fled to Italy to escape everything in my life. Him. Our family. The woman I loved more than anything in my world. I ignored him because I was too wrapped up in myself and wanting to get the hell away from everything.

Josh stands before I have a chance to apologize. "Those accounts belong to one of Matthew's affiliates. He set it up under her name to throw off suspicion. At first glance, it looks like a trust fund. But if you look deeper, like I had Robby do when Lance brought those fucking accounts to me, there's no money in that account. At least none that can be used. Because the account is a front. It doesn't even have an actual routing number."

I shake my head. "What the hell are you on? The routing number goes to an offshore bank."

"Which doesn't fucking exist, Alex." Josh pinches the bridge of his nose. "I texted Lance. He'll help you deal with the money. He'll get Robby if he has to. You're on your own here. Hire another executive assistant. I'm not allowing Raleigh to come back here." He glances at the window. "Not after that."

It feels like I've been kicked by a horse. I rub my chest with a low groan as Josh walks towards my door. I don't bother to say anything because I know he's right. I was out of line. I might have problems with Raleigh. I don't trust the girl as far as I can throw her, but she didn't deserve me putting my hands on her. Not like that.

I wait for Josh to close my door and leave me to my thoughts. But my only thought is how much I fucked up. I seem to be doing that a lot lately. Raleigh may very well be the source of my latest mood swings, but I can't deny that she's a damn good executive assistant. I've been lucky.

I also can't deny that having her around just so I can keep an eye on her while I investigate my suspicions is a lie. I like having her near because it actually feels nice having a woman around who makes me feel things I haven't felt in years. I thought I was destined to be a bachelor for my whole life.

At first, I didn't have an issue with that. Getting my fill of a woman before sending her home was perfectly fine with me. But that life gets old very quickly. I'm thirty-five now. I'm the CEO of a very successful company. I'm out of mafia life. Technically. I don't have an excuse to keep women at a distance anymore.

Despite the many women I've been with, though, not a single one has made me feel what she does. I can't look at her. If I do, I fear my body will betray me. Just having her against me earlier when that douche was hitting on her threw my entire brain into a tailspin while my heart took a ride on a tilt-a-whirl.

I can't make sense of what her subtle scent is. Every time she walks by me, I smell something different. Sometimes, it's peach. Sometimes, I smell something like honey. It's not overpowering. It's sweet, but not so sweet it makes a person feel like they're going to be sick.

Just thinking of her does things to me that I haven't felt for a long time. Things I didn't know I was capable of feeling anymore. It's much easier to push that all aside and focus on all of the reasons I should hate her.

But the truth is, I don't hate her. Not at all. I just don't want to admit that I was wrong. I've been holding onto some preconceived notion that because she was closely affiliated with a man who has never shown any love to anyone but himself must mean that she is just as bad. Maybe it's time to admit that it's me who is the asshole.

Josh is right. I've never done to any woman what I've done to her. I've intentionally intimidated her. Scared her. I know how scary I can be if I want to be. Josh isn't the only one who inherited the ability to be terrifying.

I sigh as I stand. I have to apologize. The way I've acted over the past few months since I've known her is appalling. It's not who I am. I walk towards my door hoping that she hasn't left yet. But I'm not that lucky. Sitting behind her desk is my brother. Raleigh is nowhere in sight.

"She left already?"

Josh looks up at me. "You honestly think I'd let her stay after that? The girl couldn't catch her breath. I contemplated having Alec take her to the ER."

I let out a breath with a low groan. "Fucking hell." I rub my eyes. "I really fucked up."

"Yep. And now you're stuck with me for the day."

"What are you talking about?"

"You have meetings, don't you, Mr. CEO?"

I look down at him incredulously. He's not dressed to play executive assistant. Jeans and a black t-shirt. Not a chance. "No. Get out. Go home. I'll do this myself. I'll leave my door open so I can hear them come up."

He gives me a wry grin. "Come on. Don't want your big brother around?"

"Fuck you. You're older by like five minutes. Get out. I can't have important people seeing you in jeans and a t-shirt. You look like me. What if they think you are me?"

His grin widens. "Even better."

I shake my head and point to the elevator just as the doors open. I look at him, slightly panicked, as NDS' CEO walks off the elevator with two other impeccably dressed people. My heart ceases to beat when I realize they can clearly see Josh lounging behind Raleigh's desk.

"Mr. Lucinio," he says, less than amused as he watches Josh stand.

"Mr. Koda!" I say cheerfully as I stick out a hand.

He watches Josh a few more moments before taking my extended hand and focusing on me. I can see how disappointed he is to see Josh dressed so casually standing behind the desk of my executive assistant. It doesn't take much to see that it messes with the professional image I'm trying to portray.

Mr. Koda clears his throat. "I trust you found the problem. I have been a customer of Lucinio Tech for years, Mr. Lucinio. I would hate to pull all of my accounts. The idea of starting over with someone else gives me hives."

I watch Josh throw me a wink over his shoulder as he steps into the elevator with his hands in his pockets. He keeps his eyes on me as the elevator doors close. I realize with a start that he just exacted some kind of fucking revenge on me on behalf of Raleigh for my behavior towards her.

I'm both pissed off and impressed.

Well fucking played…

Chapter Three

☙ Raleigh ☙

I sniffle and wipe my eyes again. I curl up in an even tighter ball in the oversized white chair I've claimed as my own. Josh's home library is my sanctuary. When Alec Cassidy, Josh's best friend and leader of a motorcycle crew called the Viper's Venom, brought me home from the office, I beelined through the house right to this spot. I haven't moved since.

I've seen Alec poke his head in and check on me numerous times, but I haven't moved. I've tried to stop crying, but I can't. Every time I think of the cold hatred in Alex's eyes when he had me against the window in his office, I cry harder. I can't stop thinking about what would have happened if the glass broke. I felt like I hit it hard enough to shatter it. I doubt he would have stopped me from falling. The thought is chilling.

"Raleigh?" Alec calls from the door. I look up but say nothing. He looks so concerned that for a moment, I almost forget that he's only around out of obligation. Because Josh told him to be. He doesn't care about me. No one does. "I'm going to grab Dallas. Josh got tied up on his way home. You going to be okay? Do you want to come with?"

I shake my head. "No," I whisper.

Alec stands in the door for a couple of moments. I don't know what it is about him, but he's somehow a comfort. He shouldn't be. He's intimidating. He's covered in tattoos and looks like he could bench press Josh if he wanted to. He's around the same height as Josh. Maybe a little bit taller. He's definitely got more muscle tone. I'm fairly certain his arm is as large as my head.

Obviously, something is wrong with me. Not long ago, I was a happy young woman. I got along well with my accountant father's new wife, though she was barely older than me. I was on my way to a prestigious university. Now, I'm surrounded by the mafia and bikers. Somehow, I feel like I belong more here than I have anywhere. I must be certifiably insane. There's no other explanation.

I jump slightly when I feel Alec's arms wrap around me. I almost immediately melt when he pulls me close to him. I close my eyes and let the comfort he's offering seep into my tense muscles. I ignore that he's just doing this out of obligation. Right now, I'll take all I can get.

"Raleigh, I know how tough things are for you. I can't imagine how all of this shit makes you feel, but I know it's hard." He pulls back and looks down at me. I'm a little surprised to see concern in his dark brown eyes. "What Alex did was out of line, honey. I'm not making excuses for him, but his entire world is fucked up right now."

I nod and wipe my eyes. "There's some financial issues in the company."

"I know. But that's not what I meant. Alex is having a hard time coping with all of the changes this past year has brought. He's not thinking clearly. I doubt he even understands all of the shit he's going through. Alex isn't a bad guy. And as soon as he works through all of this shit, he'll realize that he's been wrong about you since the beginning."

I shake my head. "He's never going to like me. I remind him too much of everything he hates."

"Raleigh, you've always just been an innocent pawn in a fucked up game played by a very dangerous man. Alex will realize that. In the meantime, you have a life to live. You have some pieces that you need to put back together for yourself." He kisses my forehead. "I'm going to grab Dallas. We'll be back here in a little while. I know it might be fruitless, but I'll say it anyway. Don't think about Alex. Know that Josh will deal with him. Focus on yourself right now. Do what you need to do to come down. Read a book. Get lost in a movie."

I smile softly as I nod. I won't tell him, but there's no way that I won't be thinking of everything that happened. It's impossible not to. I watch as he leaves the library and snuggle back into my chair. I pull my favorite pink fleece blanket up and burrow into it.

A few months ago, I knew nothing of this world. I didn't know mafias still existed. I didn't know there were motorcycle crews. I guess I was sheltered. I was so focused on my studies and getting into the university that I wanted to. Everything else didn't seem important. I had a loving father. His wife was incredible.

Thinking back and knowing everything I know now, I feel so stupid. My father constantly brought work home with him. I am sure lots of people do that, but his accounts always seemed strange. They were always a maze of intricacy. It was a challenge to me, though, and I felt like helping him made me smarter somehow. I was so incredibly blind.

It's hard to deny that he was a bad man and Renza, his wife, was just as awful. The evidence was laid out before me. I saw everything. He spent his entire life trying to destroy people, especially the Crane Mafia, all because they had the power and control he craved.

My father wasn't the man I thought he was. It's time I start to realize that. He tried to kill Jessa Crane. She is the sister-in-law to Ryan Crane, leader of the Crane Mafia. He tried to kill everyone in the Crane Mafia at some point. He somehow succeeded in killing Ryan's parents. He may have succeeded in killing Ryan had Alec and his crew not been around.

It's difficult for me to know that just underneath the very floor I happily walked across was a bunker of sorts. A place he kept women who he planned on trading into the dark underworld for his own gain. I hate thinking of all the damage and destruction he caused. I despise him for nearly blowing up Jessa and Dallas, who is Alec's little sister and my best friend, though she is three years younger than I am.

The longer I sit and think, the more I know I need to figure out a way to get out of here. Knowing my father was a leader of his own mafia and knowing I am currently living under the roof of someone else who leads a mafia is something that scares me. It doesn't scare me because I fear what goes on behind closed doors. It scares me because I don't like that I feel so comfortable here surrounded by all of this.

What kind of person feels comfortable surrounded by people who aren't afraid to be violent? Who have been violent? What kind of person feels safe surrounded by people who carry weapons capable of taking out the military? It's a horrifying thought that I feel safer than I ever have.

But even as I think of all the reasons I should leave, including Alex and his uncontrolled rage aimed directly at me, I can think of so many more reasons to stay. Safety. Security. Not having to worry about anything at all because Josh takes care of it. It all makes me feel even more of a messed up person.

It makes sense when I think of it. Why shouldn't I feel like a messed up person? I don't even know who I am. I don't know if Raleigh Jennings is even my real name. I don't know who my parents are. I don't know my family. I don't even know where I was born. For all I know, my parents are drug addicts who knew they couldn't take care of me and gave me up for adoption. Or maybe I was taken away from them. Perhaps I was one of those poor kids who came out already high as hell on heroin and addicted to it because my mom couldn't leave it alone.

There are several scenarios that have run through my head since I've been told the truth about life. I'm not even sure I really want to know the details anymore. Maybe it's just best for me to move on and live my own life.

Which brings me back to the other idea I've had playing in my mind. Maybe I should leave. Figure out how to survive on my own. It's not like Josh wouldn't allow me to. I get a paycheck from Lucinio Tech that Josh has made me save most of. I have enough saved to start my own life.

I slump at the thought, though. Despite everything, I like it here. I like having a family around that cares so much about each other. I like having the Crane's so close. They are like an extended family. I know I could go to them if I ever need to.

"Raleigh?" Josh's voice rings out from somewhere in the hall just before he pops his head in the library. "How are you holding up?"

I shake my head and wipe my eyes. "Terrible, if I'm being honest. I'm confused. I feel a little lost."

He nods as he walks into the library. He takes a seat on the coffee table in front of me and folds his hands in his lap. "Want to talk about it?"

I shift a little so I'm sitting up more. "What happened with Alex?" I ask quietly.

"I told him I'm not letting you go back after what he did. He knows he was in the wrong. He wants to apologize, but I'd sent you home by that time."

I look down at the floor and nod slowly. I say nothing for a few moments as I compose myself. While what happened scared me beyond reason, I can understand why it happened. Alex is protective and feels like his family is being threatened. It's not an excuse, but at the forefront of my mind is my job. I really love my job. In my heart, I really don't think Alex would physically hurt me. I'm sure that's one more thing that makes me psychotic. I was technically assaulted.

I sigh and look up at Josh. "I don't know what to think. My mind has been all over the place since I left the office."

"Talk to me. Let me help you make sense of it."

"I don't know how." I chuckle and shake my head. "I feel like I don't have an identity. I don't know where I came from. I don't know where I belong. I don't know if I have a family out there somewhere that might be thinking of me. I feel like my whole entire world was a lie and came crashing down so epically it could go down in the history books. My parents. Who were they? Why did they give me up? I don't even know if my name is really Raleigh." I reach up and swipe my eyes.

"I get it. It wasn't exactly the same for me, but after we realized what my father was doing to me with the brainwashing and serum, I had an identity crisis myself. It took me a long time to figure out who the hell I was and where my place in this world is. But the truth is, you have to find that place for yourself. And know that you have a place right here to fall back on. That being said, I promised I'd help you. I've gotten side-tracked with a few things, but my full attention is back on figuring out where you came from. Okay? One less thing to worry about."

"It's not just where I came from. It's…" I pause as I think. "I guess it's more knowing. I'm scared of knowing and scared of not knowing." I sniffle and shake my head. "I'm a mess."

"How about this? I figure out your past. And when I do, you tell me if you still want to know. If you don't, it's okay. If you want to know later, I'll have the information. In the meantime, you have a family." He gestures around the library. "You have a home. We all care about you. And before you say anything, even Alex. He doesn't hate you."

I take a breath. "I love my job…"

Josh's gaze darkens as he sits back. "You're about to tell me that you don't want to leave your position."

I close my eyes a moment before opening them and holding his. "I can help him so much. If he'd just let me. I know it's insane, but I really love Lucinio Tech. I love being able to help Alex. I really think he could take that company to new heights."

"And you aren't afraid of him."

I shrug. "Should I be? I mean what he did scared me. I was terrified the glass would break and I'd fall. I question if he would have attempted to grab me before I did. But the more I think about it, I'm not afraid of him. Because I trust you. I trust this family. And you all trust and love him. To me, that means he's not the scary monster he tries to be…" I can feel myself blushing. I try to hide it.

Of course, Josh doesn't miss it. I've learned he doesn't miss anything. He grins. The asshole. "You like him."

My eyes widen. I blush darker. "No! No. I can't. No. I refuse!"

Josh laughs and stands when he hears a door open. "You fucking like him." He strides out of the library laughing.

"I don't!" I call after him. Just because I have an unprofessional reaction to him despite the chill I instantly feel around him doesn't mean I'll act on it.

"Yes, you do!" Josh yells as he walks away.

A few minutes later, the hurricane known as Dallas Cassidy explodes into the library in a flurry of flailing limbs and flushed cheeks. She says nothing. When she reaches me, she throws her arms around me before I have a chance to say or do anything. I relish in the hug and warmth of her embrace. Before I know it, I'm melting. It's like the earlier tension and confusion begin vanishing layer by layer until I feel a little more like myself.

"My God, what happened? Alec said you were upset and could use a friend. Something happened at work." Dallas pulls away slightly and looks at me. Her fingers are tangled in my hair.

"I'm okay. Now. It took a little while."

She takes my hand and sits next to me in the chair. "Tell me."

"I suppose since my mind feels a little less chaotic, I can talk about it," I say quietly. I take a deep breath. "You know how Alex has been treating me."

"How you think he hates you." Dallas nods and runs her fingers soothingly through my hair.

"Well, today, it sort of all came to a head." I look down and play with her fingers on the hand she's linked with mine.

"How…so…? Alec said it was something bad."

I sigh and look up slowly. I focus on the door as I chew on the inside of my lip. "There are accounts that my fa-" I cut myself off and shake my head. "Matthew. There are accounts that he set up in my name. I didn't know anything about them. At all. Nothing. Alex…" I trail off and sniffle.

Dallas leans her head against my shoulder. "It's okay. You can tell me."

I slump slightly. "I may as well just tell you everything." I wipe a stray tear away. "I don't know how to feel about him. Everything in me says run. Run far away. From all of this." I gesture around us. "Mafia. Motorcycle gangs. This isn't how I grew up. But then I think of you and Josh. Everyone in this family and how close they are. Even how close they are to the Crane family. They should be archrivals. They're both huge mafia factions. But I see the love everyone has for each other, and I want that." I look down again. "And then Alex. I… I just…"

"I feel like you're weighing your words because I'm only fifteen, but you don't need to. I really do understand. Maybe because it's how I grew up, but I've always been told I'm wise beyond my years."

I smile softly. Dallas really does seem more grown-up than her age suggests. When I'm talking to her, I don't see an age difference between us at all. Even though it's only three years anyway. Dallas is just a gorgeous woman. She's rather small, like I am. She has this pretty brown colored hair I'm so jealous of. She doesn't wear a lot of make-up, but the small amount she does makes her gorgeous blue-green eyes pop and look so much bigger than they are. She doesn't look all that tough, but she's been my anchor the entire time I've known her.

"I've had this weird attraction to him ever since I first saw him. Of course, that happened to be waking up after he put me in a sleeper hold." I shake my head.

The day my father and Renza were taken down and I arrived home, I was instantly attacked as soon as I got out of my car. I didn't know what was happening. All I knew was a giant arm was around my neck. I fought, but I had no chance. The person who had me was twice my size and a hundred times stronger. I tried elbowing, flailing, and stomping, but my world quickly went dark as a deep, very comforting voice whispered in my ear to go to sleep. It was like my body obeyed without any question, though my brain was screaming at me to fight.

When I came to, Alex was standing over me. As soon as I saw him, I had butterflies in my chest. My throat went dry. My whole body felt tingly. Things happened between my thighs that brought an instant blush to my cheeks and forced me to look away from him. I was beyond embarrassed at my reaction to him.

"I just don't understand how I feel about him. He's terrifying sometimes. Like today. Those accounts? Alex found them and assumed that I knew about them. It looked like Matthew was funneling money through it. It looks like there are fake companies set up that are putting money through Lucinio Tech then pulling it out. It's going through that account. I don't know much about money-laundering, but Josh explained it a little bit. He said it's going through that account into another one. And probably another. There is also money that is being taken from another huge account and being directly deposited into that account instead of Lucinio Tech's bank account."

Dallas watches me with wide eyes. "And… he thinks you're involved somehow."

I nod slowly. "He was so upset, Dallas. I was showing him a couple of things I found. I didn't know about the account then. I was just showing him that one of the companies was making their payment every month and then pulling it. It was being deposited into a different account. Then there was another company, the one that has such a huge account with us. That company was making their payments, but it was being directly deposited into that same account."

"Oh my God."

"I knew what I was seeing, but I didn't know the account was in my name. I just saw the numbers, and how they matched. I'm really good at that, you know?"

She nods. "I know."

"Alex had seen a few things like that when he took over the company and fixed it. But he missed that, I guess. It's obvious Matthew has been funneling money through Lucinio Tech. I know I can help him make sure there's no other accounts this is happening with, but after today…" I shiver. "He was pissed. His eyes got so cold I honestly felt like my blood was turning into icicles. Then… he… shoved me… against the window." I sniffle. "I was terrified it was going to break, and I was sure there would be no way in hell he'd try to save me from crashing through it."

"Oh, Raleigh." Dallas wraps herself around me and buries her face in my shoulder. "I'm so sorry." She tightens her grip on me. "You didn't need that. Not after everything you've been through."

"The thing is…" I take a deep breath as I sit up and pull away slightly. "It scared me in the moment. But the more and more I sit here and think about him and everything, the more I just go right back to fantasizing about him. Which makes me feel like a crazy person. How can I be terrified of him one second and obsessed with him the next?"

"Oh, Raleigh," Dallas whispers. She hugs me a few moments before pulling away. "I think… you need to talk to him. And if he gets all growly with you, make him listen. You're such a strong woman. I can see that. I just think…" It's her turn to weigh her words. "I feel like maybe you don't see it. But I know you have the ability to stand up to him. I watched you go toe to toe with Josh when you first got here. I've gotten to know him since the night he saved me and Jessa. I'd never want to be on the other end of his anger."

I chew on my lip a few moments as I think. "You think I should make him listen to me? Tell him that I'm not a bad person and can help him if he lets me?"

"And that he needs to start treating you better. And you won't tolerate his temper and loss of control. Although, I think he already knows just how much he completely messed up. I know Josh won't let him get away with that."

I lean my head against the chair. Most of me knows Dallas is right. It's time I stand up to Alex. Today was the last straw. It has to be. I don't deserve to live like this.

Chapter Four

🐓 Alex 🐓

I swirl the amber liquid in my shot glass around and stare at the wall in front of me. I haven't bothered to change out of the day's suit, but I have lost the tie and unbuttoned a few buttons. I even managed to roll up the sleeves before I slumped into the brown leather of the couch in my living room.

I take a drink of the whiskey and let it burn its way to my stomach. Ever since I had a second to think today, which was after all of my meetings and the tongue lashing I got from Mr. Koda, I've realized just how far out of fucking line I was with Raleigh. I've never in my life gone that far over the edge with a woman I didn't end up killing. I spent years as a mafia boss' son. I spent the rest of my life leading the mafia in some way. I've done a lot of shit I'm not proud of, but a lot more that I am.

Today is definitely not one of my finer moments. I refill my glass and go back to swirling the alcohol around. I'd say I don't know what's wrong with me, but I do. I know exactly what's going on. It makes me feel like an even bigger asshole.

I spent God only knows how fucking long thinking my father was dead. I watched my brother shoot him in the head. We burned down the house. My ex-girlfriend, Jessa Holloway, now Jessa Crane, was my father's obsession because she looked like a woman he'd fallen in love with and lost. He had decided in his warped mind that if he couldn't have her, Jessa would suffice. After we'd saved her from his evil clutches, we'd thought that was the end of it.

My brother, Josh, had also been another of his pawns. He'd been giving him serum that made it easier to brainwash him. He'd tried to turn Josh against me. When that didn't work, he'd made Josh believe the only way to save me was to pretend to be me in order to woo Jessa. By the time it was all said and done, Josh not only didn't know right from wrong, he also didn't even know who the fuck he was.

When we finally uncovered the shit he was doing and took him out, I spent the next couple of years helping Josh take his rightful place as the leader of the Lucinio Mafia, a position I never wanted, even though my father wanted me to. Josh thrived at the helm and has steered this family to an even more powerful position in the world than we'd ever had. He turned it into a legal operation by using Ryan Crane as a role-model.

We should have really known our fuck of a father wouldn't just die. His vendetta against the Crane Mafia, for being more powerful than he could dream, and us, for betraying him, only grew stronger. The guy we killed was a look-a-like. He'd paid the fucker to get plastic surgery to look like him. I'm not sure if the dude knew his role in my father's master plan was to die, or if Matthew fucking Lucinio told him a ton of lies to get him to cooperate. Either way, he went down for the crimes my father should have paid for.

Over the next few years, Matthew was building an army. He knew the Lucinio Mafia and Crane Mafia had aligned. He knew that he had no chance against us. So, he started aligning himself with smaller mafias while systematically trying to turn our allies against us. When everything failed, he finally came out of hiding.

It all came to a head a few months ago. Through contacts we had, Josh and I gathered a team and showed up at a house to take out an enemy Ryan had uncovered and asked us to deal with. We had no idea that the information had been dropped by Matthew. He also dropped information through Ryan's contacts that the enemy would be at the same house. Though he'd asked us to deal with it, he also thought acting on the information he had was imperative. Neither of us had time to communicate our intentions to each other. We needed to act. Our goal was to take down the enemy. When we both showed up with our teams at the same house, shooting commenced.

Josh and I didn't know then that our father was still alive. Ryan did but hadn't gotten a chance to tell us. That very night, Josh and Ryan joined all of the forces between both the Crane and Lucinio Mafias. All of our allies and theirs all around the world made us larger than the United States military. And we probably could have aligned with them, too, if we needed them.

After tracking a sex-trafficking ring, we found where the fucker was hiding out. We went in with a staggering number of men and took my father and his wife down once and for all. He'd managed to get his hooks into Jessa once more and kidnap Dallas. No one understood what the hell an innocent kid like Dallas had to do with anything, but we knew Matthew never does anything without a purpose.

It turned out Dallas is Jessa's sister. Jessa had been adopted when she was just a girl. Alec Cassidy, Dallas' older brother, is Jessa's brother, as well. Matthew had somehow connected the dots.

We'd managed to take out Matthew and his wife, but we'd almost lost Dallas and Jessa. He'd rigged them with explosives as a last-ditch effort to destroy Ryan and the Crane Mafia as well as me and Josh and the Lucinio Mafia. He knew taking out someone so important to all of us would cripple us at our very core. We'd saved them, but he did take out Ryan's parents. It was a blow all of us felt and are still recovering from.

I drink down my whiskey and refill it. I bring the glass to my temple as I swallow and close my eyes. The night we took out Matthew, we found Raleigh. According to her, she is his daughter. She believed him to be an accountant who was away on business a lot. She described him as some fucking doting and loving father. Exactly the opposite of what he actually was.

I've felt from the very beginning that she was hiding something. I've been right about everything about her so far. Starting with the fact that she wasn't even his legitimate daughter. According to some things we've found, she was adopted by him as a baby, but all of her records are faked. We have very good hackers on our team. They can't find anything about the adoption.

Josh has told me that means nothing. He feels like she's another victim in Matthew's overall plan. A plan that we could still be uncovering years from now.

And there is my problem. I'm waiting for my father to somehow jump out of his grave a second time and come after us. I'm suspicious of everything. Everyone. We took DNA. We know he's dead. But some small part of me feels like that fucker won't stay dead this time either. Like he'll find a way to wreak devastation on all of us once more.

I can't stop myself from thinking it will be through Raleigh. She's said it herself. She'll always love the guy. He was her fucking hero. Loving a man that fucked up has to mean that she's just as fucked up. At the very least, it means she's loyal. People loyal to Matthew Lucinio are dangerous.

"Alex?"

I look up to see my mom stepping quietly through my front door into the darkness surrounding me. I haven't turned on any lights since I've been home. It gets dark earlier in the fall. Somehow, though, it seems to get darker here. It's barely eight, according to my phone, and it looks like it's fucking midnight. I hadn't realized I'd lost so much light.

I sigh as I turn on the lamp next to me and down the shot glass. I grimace. It somehow burns just as much going down the third time as it does the first. I set the shot glass on the coffee table and watch as my mother sits next to me. She places a comforting hand on my arm.

One good thing came out of my father's bullshit. My mother, Rebekkah, found out her family never knew she was alive. Her father, Ryan's grandfather, made a deal with my grandfather to merge several of their companies and align the Crane and Lucinio Mafias. She was to marry my father.

My father, however, had married another woman out of defiance. His one true love. When his plan didn't work, his revenge and hatred for the Crane Mafia was born. Ethan, my mother's brother and Ryan's father, was told she was dead. His father had someone or something made to look just like her. Ethan saw her in her casket at her funeral and believed she was dead.

When we discovered my father was alive, Josh and I had our mother flown from Los Angeles, where we had lived, to Chicago, where we were at the time and planned to live. We wanted to be closer to the Crane's, as they are like our family.

39

Ethan and his wife, Jenny, were, at least, alive long enough to see my mother is alive. They were able to reunite. We found out that Ryan and the Crane's aren't just like our family. They really are. My mother has been able to get to know her nephews and their wives. She was even reunited with her own one true love, who is also the father of a child she never told her family she had. We gained a brother. She gained her entire life.

"Alex, talk to me. Josh said you really jumped off the edge today and did something you've never done and never would have if you had a clear head. What's going on?"

I sigh and lean back against the couch. I don't look at her. "Raleigh. I found out some shit today and slammed her against the glass in my office. In not so many words I called her a liar. I accused her of knowing things she didn't. At least according to Josh. I'm not totally convinced."

I don't need to look at my mother to know her blue eyes are exuding disappointment and sadness. She, like everyone else, thinks Raleigh is a completely innocent party in a very messed up man's scheme. Maybe she's right. I don't fucking know anymore.

My mom lets out a heavy sigh. I already know I'm in for it. "This has got to stop, Alexander." Whenever she uses my full first name, I know it's about to get bad for me. Her voice goes down at least an octave. She sounds dangerous as hell.

I wince. "Mom -" I close my mouth immediately when she stands and levels me with a glare. People think Josh and I get our mean streaks from our father. They're wrong. My mother has the ability to silence the most vicious of storms. At least when it comes to me and Josh. It's a power she rarely has to wield.

"You will not speak until I'm finished, young man. I do not want to hear another word out of your mouth about Raleigh being in on some stupid scheme Matthew cooked up."

"Mom -"

"Alexander! Enough!"

My eyes widen at her tone. I haven't heard it since I was just a kid. I glance at my door when I hear it open. Moments later, I see Ryan Crane in the fucking flesh. I sink into the couch. I know it's about to get much worse for me.

"You slammed her against the window in your fucking office," Ryan growls. "Tell me I didn't hear that right. Tell me that, for some reason, Josh lied to me." Ryan stops in front of me and stands next to my mother. He towers over as he crosses his arms over his broad chest and glares down at me.

"Slamming her against the window wasn't my best moment. I'll give both of you that." I stand and take a deep breath. I pace around the room a moment before turning to them both. "But for fuck's sake, you all just seem to trust this girl hands fucking down!"

"Do not take that tone with me, Alexander," my mother bites at me. "She has proven herself over and over again. You just refuse to see it because you can't see past the fact that she had a relationship with Matthew that none of us did."

It's my turn to cross my arms over my chest. "Is that not reason enough?"

"No!" Ryan finally yells.

"When the fuck did she prove herself, Ryan? You fucking give me one good example, and I'll shut my mouth."

"Okay. How about her seeing the shit you didn't today? She helped you save your fucking largest account because she was able to see through all of the bullshit you have going on."

"All that proves to me is that she's good with numbers, Ryan. It proves that she saw an account number that is tied to her that she claims to know nothing about."

Ryan scrubs his hands down his face. "I'm only going to say this to you one time and one time only. Whatever the hell you have against her is on you. But if you ever lay your fucking hands on her again, it's not fucking Josh you'll have to worry about. I'll throw you through the glass of your cozy top floor office and not bat an eye when you hit the ground. Got me?" He starts to walk angrily past me.

I grab his arm. "Renza Gregorson," I growl. My mom gasps. I can feel Ryan tense under my hold.

Renza had been the best friend of Ryan's wife, Arianna. She had also fallen under Matthew's spell. She disappeared just after trying to kill Arianna. We found out that she had married Matthew and been working as his little spy for months. She'd been giving him information on their whereabouts throughout their honeymoon. They thought they were running from Arianna's psychotic mafia boss father who had arranged for Arianna to marry the son of another mafia boss. Little did any of us know that they were all working for Matthew. And that Renza was the rat we had been looking for the entire time.

He slowly turns. "Doesn't have a goddamn thing to do with this." He levels a dangerous and dark glare at me.

I meet his with one of my own. "She almost succeeded in taking out not only Arianna, but our entire fucking family. So, tell me again why I should trust someone so connected to Matthew, but who we hardly know a damn thing about." I drop his arm as we stand face to face.

I can sense his fists clenching at his side, but I don't move. Just when I think he's about to throw a punch, my mom steps in between us. She gently shoves both of us apart and stands between us.

"Enough. Both of you," she says. Ryan and I both unclench our fists.

"Sorry, Aunt Rebekkah," Ryan says, his voice softening. He leans down and kisses her cheek before taking a breath and looking back up at me. "Look. I get it. Okay?"

"Do you?" I ask, sinking in a chair. "It doesn't seem like it. You're my best friend, Ry. You're like a brother to me. Cousin or not. We're closer than that. Something about her does not add up." I hold up a hand when he opens his mouth. "I know. I know. She's answered all of your questions. She's been very upfront and honest about everything she knows. None of you can sense she's lying. But I don't feel that way. I'm sorry. I don't."

Ryan sits down on the couch next to me and rubs his temple. "I get it. But I can't see any connection to Matthew or any of his factions. We've taken out so many of them already. Beyond a few stragglers. There's just…" He sighs. "There's nothing, Alex. We've asked her about shit like the accounts in her name. Then we verified it." He sits forward and rests his hands on his knees as my mom sits next to him. "I know what you're going to say. Nothing connected Renza either. But you're wrong. There were a lot of things connecting Renza to Matthew. We just didn't see them because we weren't looking for them. I hear your concerns, Alex. And you know I trust you and your instincts. So, talk to me. Tell me why the hell we're on such opposite ends of the spectrum on this."

"Okay. First and foremost is Renza." My mind circles to my other best friend, Gavin. "What about Gavin's wife? Marissa. Same fucking thing. They were married for how long? Years. And she was working for Matthew the entire time."

"But that is not shit we were looking for, Alex. When we dived into it, we saw accounts that tracked to him. We don't have that with her. We looked. Nothing tracks from him to her or vice versa."

"Ryan, I have account numbers. Accounts in her name somehow attached to my company." I just watch him in exasperation.

"I'll have Lance bring you everything he and Robby found about that account. It's been funneling money from Lucinio Tech ever since the company was first established. Different accounts. We'd catch it, deal with it. We'd find it again. Same fucking account number. Different names. This time, it happens to be set up in her name to look like a trust fund. But how many trust funds are you aware of that can take money whenever? I don't know about you, but I had to wait until I was eighteen for part of my trust fund. I had to wait until I was twenty-one for the second part of it. Then I didn't get the rest until I hit twenty-five. Raleigh is eighteen. Withdrawals and deposits are coming and going from that account every damn day and have been since you were a teenager, Alex."

"Ryan will get you what they found." My mom looks at Ryan, chastising. "You and Josh should have made sure he saw everything when you first found it."

Ryan holds his hands out and chuckles. "We just got a lot of this stuff totally tracked, Aunt Rebekkah. I'll get it to him. Promise."

"Why do you trust her so much, mom?" I ask her.

"Oh, honey. It's not that I am trusting blindly here. I have sat and talked with her. I've had long conversations with her about her life. She just doesn't strike me as a liar. She doesn't seem to be keeping things from any of us. Josh has asked her difficult questions. Questions you've been in the room to hear the answers to. She doesn't hesitate. Her answers don't appear to be thought up. She doesn't seem to want to hide things."

I stand, agitated. "Don't you guys think it's strange that she gravitated towards the people who are leaders? Those who have the biggest voices? You, mom. Ryan. Josh. Hell, even Arianna and Dallas."

Ryan raises an eyebrow. "How old is Arianna? How old is Dallas?"

I sigh. "Okay, fine. Close to her age, but that isn't the point. You're forty-one. Me and Josh are thirty-five. Why you? Why Josh?"

"If I had to guess, Alex, I'd say it's because we aren't dicks to her." Ryan leans over and kisses my mom on the cheek as he stands.

"I respect the hell out of you, man. You know that. But if you really want to talk about this, then one of my issues is who she's become close to. Arianna has your ear. Dallas has Alec's. Jessa's. Who also has yours and Josh's. Hell. Even mine. It just seems to me that she's picked her alliances well."

Ryan leans down and picks up my bottle of whiskey. He puts the cap back on and walks it to my bar. He puts it away and leans on the counter. "Okay. I'm not going to argue and invalidate how you feel about it. What else?"

"What about how in the dark she says she is about everything?" I ask. "She had to wonder about the money. She had to be curious about all of those accounts she said she helped with over the years. Balancing things. Finding anomalies. Come on. And then he's an accountant. Yet, he's gone for weeks on end?" I shake my head. "I just can't buy that."

"With all due respect, honey, she didn't grow up in a mafia family. At least not in the sense that you and Josh did. Or Ryan. Even Arianna and Dallas." My mom stands and walks to me. She hugs me and runs her hands soothingly up and down my back. Just like she used to do when I was a kid and throwing a tantrum.

And just like when I was a kid, I begrudgingly relax a little. I wrap my arms around her and rest my cheek on top of her head. "I just have a hard fucking time believing that she can be as clueless as she leads on. Like there were just no red flags. She blindly loved this man with all she is. She's a smart girl. I can't believe that."

My mom gives me a squeeze before she pulls back slowly. She tugs me down to her level and kisses my cheek. "I wish I knew how to help you, but I think the only thing that will ease your mind is if you talk to her on your own. Calmly. Rationally. I know you're capable of that. I know my son." She gives me a soft smile and lets me go. She quickly hugs Ryan before leaving.

I'm about to follow her and escort her home. We live in the safest part of Chicago in a secured compound built specifically for the Lucinio and Crane families. It doesn't mean I want my mom walking back to her house in the dark. I stop when I see one of our guards step out of the shadows to escort her, though. I nod to myself. We're a very well-oiled machine.

"My honest opinion, Alex, is you need to talk to her. You need to sit down and have a conversation with her. Talk to her about why you feel the way you do. She feels like you hate her. And maybe you do. But wouldn't you want the same courtesy from anyone if you were in her position? I mean, think about that for a second."

I sigh and nod slowly. "Okay. If I were in her shoes, maybe I'd feel that way." I sit on a stool on the other side of the bar. Ryan watches me. I scrub my hands down my face. "I don't hate her. Okay? I just don't trust her. At all."

"Talk to her, Alex. Give her a chance to at least prove herself. I can't explain to you why the rest of us feel differently. All I can tell you is the biggest difference here is that we've talked to her. You've done nothing but watch her. Investigate her."

"Someone has to," I grumble.

Ryan chuckles. "Like I said earlier. I am not going to invalidate how you feel about this. But you're letting your feelings about your father get in the way of you thinking rationally. The Alex I know, and have known for fucking nearly twenty years, would never have gone off half-cocked like that. Have a conversation. Let her prove to you whose side she's on. That's what we've been doing." Ryan stands and stretches. "You know what I asked her the other day?"

"What?"

"I left my laptop open next to her. It had all of my account balances on the screen for her. Then I watched her after I walked away. She had every opportunity in the world to look. When I got back, I finished transferring some funds to Arianna's charity. I asked her why she didn't look. I won't tell you her response, but I will say that it surprised the fuck out of me. In my opinion, it sealed the deal for me. She's honest. Trustworthy."

"Maybe she just knew you were watching."

Ryan shrugs as he starts heading for the door. "Maybe." He stops at the door and looks back at me. "You're asking me to trust you and your instincts. I do. I'll help you look into whatever you want me to. You know that. All you need to do is say the words. But on that same hand, Alex, I'm asking for your trust. I'm not asking you to abandon all your concerns. I am asking that you just trust in me enough to talk to her. What's that old saying? Something about holding your friends close and enemies closer?" He grins and winks as he walks out the door, closing it behind him.

I chuckle. "Fucking asshole," I say as I get up and head for my bedroom.

I doubt I'll be able to sleep, but Ryan is right. I may not be ready to trust her, but, at the very least, I can talk to her. Keep my friends close and enemies closer. I seem to be no closer to figuring out anything about Raleigh.

Maybe it's time to switch tactics.

Chapter Five

☙ Raleigh ☙

Crawling in my skin. These wounds, they will not heal. Fear is how I fall, confusing what is real. Discomfort endlessly has pulled itself upon me. Distracting, reacting. Against my will I stand beside my own reflection. It's haunting how I can't seem to find myself again. My walls are closing in.

Monday morning, a couple of days after my incident with Alex, I wake up to my alarm. I blink sleepily and sit up after shutting it off. I rub the sleep out of my eyes with a yawn and shake my head. The alarm tone is the perfect song to sum up my life. Linkin Park. Seriously. They're like the soundtrack to my life.

I slowly crawl out of my bed and trudge to my shower to wash off the sweat my latest nightmare caused. Josh told me that he's not allowing me to go back to Lucinio Tech, but after this weekend, I know I need to face Alex. I love my job. I refuse to allow him or anyone else to take away the one thing in my life I truly enjoy.

After talking with Dallas about everything this entire weekend, I know I'm a good person. I know that I'm not lying about anything. But I also know that Alex has seen more than I could ever imagine. I know that

47

Matthew has done a lot of terrible things to him and his entire family. I didn't see that side of him.

I've decided that I am going to go back to work. I'm going to face Alex. I'm going to make him talk to me. I'll answer anything he wants me to. I'll do whatever he wants me to as long as it proves to him that I'm not the monster he wants to believe I am.

I'm just as upset about the things I found out about him as Alex is. Maybe even more. He grew up with the demonic asshole side of Matthew that I never saw. I'm angry that he and his family had to deal with that, but I feel so betrayed and hurt that everything he was dealing with was going on behind my back. I know I couldn't have fixed anything for any of them, but at least I wouldn't have been kept in the dark.

At least I wouldn't have been lied to my entire life. At least things that didn't make sense throughout my entire life would make sense. Maybe things I didn't understand I would have been able to.

After I finish showering and getting dressed, I look over my reflection in the full-length mirror on the back of my door. I tie my hair up in my usual messy bun. I make sure my purple blouse is in place and check to make sure there isn't any lint on my black form-hugging slacks. Satisfied, I give myself a nod before grabbing my purse and phone.

It's still early. My intention is to get to the office, pick up Alex's coffee and, if they have it, his favorite strawberry cream cheese muffin. When he comes in, I'm going to tell him that we need to have a conversation. I'm going to stand up to him. I am a strong woman. I do not deserve to live in fear of my boss.

Though, even after he threw me against the window, I don't exactly fear him. I am, however, terrified of some of the thoughts he puts in my head. It makes me feel even more crazy because I shouldn't feel them. Not only is he my boss, but he's the brother of the greatest man I've ever known.

Josh is so beyond brave and kind. I would never want to come between him and his brother or family. I certainly don't want to let him down. He's done so much for me. He believed in me when no one else did. I doubt I'm exaggerating when I say I owe him my life.

I take a breath and make my way down to the kitchen. I have enough time to grab some fruit on my way out. I took a little longer in the shower, so I'm running later than I wanted to be. I'll have to hurry.

"Going somewhere?" Josh rumbles from behind me.

I let out a quiet squeak of surprise and nearly drop the fruit in my hand as I whirl around to face him. Josh is leaning against the wall in black gym shorts slung low over his hips and no shirt. He has his arms crossed over his chest. He must have just gone for his run in his downstairs gym.

"I thought I'd be gone before you were done with your workout."

Josh doesn't move. "Sorry to disappoint you."

I sigh and put my fruit down on the counter. "I'm not letting Alex take my job away."

"It wasn't Alex's decision to pull you from Lucinio Tech. It was mine."

"I know. But I love my job, Josh. I feel like I'm actually doing something worthwhile. Maybe people don't think an Executive Assistant does anything truly life-changing. But I enjoy what I do. I feel like I'm making a difference. And what's more is that I'm making my own way. I'm not totally dependent on you and your family."

He holds up a hand. "Stop, Raleigh. Stop it. You're doing it again." He pushes off the wall and walks to the counter. He pulls out a container and starts putting fruit into it. "I've told you over and over again that this is just as much your family now as it is mine. My mother already thinks of you as one of us. I think of you as a little sister. Don't let Alex make you feel like you don't belong or don't have a place here." He hands me the container.

I take it with a deep breath. "Okay. Wait. You're... letting me go?"

Josh turns to put the rest of the fruit away and chuckles. "I'm not here to control your life, Raleigh. I'm here to guide you, if you want me to. I'm here for you. But I'm not going to tell you that you can or can't do something. Unless, I think it will endanger your life or someone else's. Alex lost control, but I don't think for a second he'd do anything to physically hurt you. Scare you, yes. Not hurt you." He turns back to me. "If you want to go back, I won't stop you. But you'll need to tell the new Executive Assistant to go home. You don't need her. I called a temp agency to replace you."

I nod, determined. "Okay."

"And you'll need to talk to Alex. Stand up to him. Don't let him treat you like that. Call me if you need to, but I'd like to see you two actually have a real conversation. Make him listen to you. Air out your grievances, Raleigh. Both of you." He looks at the clock on the wall above my head. "You'd better get going."

"I won't let you down."

He shakes his head. "Don't worry about letting me down. Worry about not letting yourself down. Alex is really a good guy. If you really like him like I think you do, you're going to have to get under the tough guy asshole facade he's put up."

I blush and duck my head as I turn and hurry out of the kitchen with my fruit. I make my way to my black Maserati Ghibli and jump behind the wheel. I love my car, though, it was Josh's first. He gave it to me to get back and forth to work when I told him I wanted to save up to get a vehicle of my own so I didn't have to rely on him or anyone else to get me where I wanted to go. I didn't want to accept the car, but Josh does not take no for an answer. He refused to drive me or give me a way to take a cab or bus to work. In the end, it was walk or take the car. I'm glad I took the car.

After navigating the morning Chicago traffic, I arrive at Lucinio Tech. I drive through the secured parking garage thankful my badge still works to get me in. I find my parking place and sigh when I see the vehicle parked in my place. Well, the parking place for the CEO's Executive Assistant. It's right next to Alex's on the top floor of the five-story parking garage.

I wipe a stray tear. I knew there would be another car there. I don't know why I'm so upset about it. Maybe it's because I feel like I'm easily replaced in the company. A company I've grown to love so much. I choke down the thought of being replaced in Alex's life. I have no right to those thoughts. I'm not his. No matter how much the crazy part of me wants to be.

I find a parking place and quickly make my way to the building. I scan my badge and hurry inside. The security guard at the guard's desk eyes me with wide and very surprised eyes. It makes me feel worse. Obviously, he didn't expect to see me.

"Ms. Jennings!" the middle-aged guard exclaims. He's dressed as all of the guards here are. A suit and tie with a service weapon attached to his hip. "We got notice that you quit on Friday."

"Misunderstanding. Something happened. I needed to leave to regain my composure," I say as I slow. I didn't count on this, but I suspect they're about to throw me out. Or make me wait for Alex to show up.

The guard eyes me warily, but just when I think he might make good on the threat playing in my mind, his phone rings. He answers. After a few nods and 'yes, sirs,' he waves me by. I suppose I'll have Josh to thank for that.

I hurry to the elevator and hit the button for the ground floor. As soon as I step off, the smell of delicious coffee hits me. I'm glad I ate that fruit on the way here, or I'd be buying all of the delicious bakery items Nicole Reddick has stocked at her small location here. She's married to one of Alex's friends, Taylor. He's a Lieutenant with Chicago's Police Department, and she is the best baker I think I have ever come across.

I quickly order Alex's mocha vanilla cappuccino. While they're making it, I run to Nicole's bakery and order the strawberry cream cheese muffin for him. I splurge and buy myself the raspberry rose cookie I've become beyond obsessed with before hurrying back to Starbucks just as they are putting my order on the counter.

I look at my watch as I step onto the elevator. It's a simple, small watch with a leather band. I usually don't wear them, but Dallas got it for me when I turned eighteen. I love it and wear it all the time.

If I timed everything right today, Alex should have just gotten to the office. That gives me time to get rid of the person sent by the temp agency. Then I can take a few moments to compose myself and decide what I'm going to say to him when he steps off the elevator.

But as the door opens to the top floor where Alex's office is, I realize I never should have believed I'd be that lucky. Of course he'd already be here. Of all days I want him to show up at his usual time, he has to show up early.

"Mr. Lucinio, you can't expect to run this without a little help. That's what I'm here for!" a ridiculously perky and annoying female voice says. I can't see her, though. Alex is blocking my view, but she must be behind my desk.

"I have help. And as soon as I get her back, I won't need you," he growls. My heart stammers. He couldn't be talking about me. Could he?

I slowly step off the elevator, but don't make any attempt to get any closer. Some sick part of me really wants to know what he's about to do. The crazy part of me wants to know if I'm who he is talking about. Could he really want me back?

"But wouldn't you like someone to assist you while you're trying to get her back?" The girl's voice is squeaky, but what annoys me the most is I can hear the flirt in it. What kind of professional flirts like that with someone who is supposed to be her boss? Someone she's never met before. At least I hope she hasn't. Alex does have a bit of a reputation of being a ladies' man.

That's also not the only thing striking to me. It's Alex. His perfectly tailored black slacks are uncharacteristically wrinkled. The white shirt usually impeccably ironed and tucked into his slacks is slightly untucked in the back. He's not wearing a belt. He always wears a black leather belt. It's so he can carry his gun, which he is also not wearing. Like every other man in the Lucinio family, Alex is never without a weapon. He may not be in the mafia anymore, at least technically, but he is never without a weapon.

"I'll call the temp agency and make sure you're paid for the day," Alex says. He sounds a little more growly than usual, but there's something else. Exhaustion?

"Mr. Lucinio, really. You're a busy man. Let me make things easier on you."

"I said out. I don't need you. Go home." Without another word, Alex walks back to his office. I blink. He's not wearing shoes.

"What the hell is going on?" I whisper to myself.

The girl from the temp agency glares after him with what I'm sure she thinks is a sexy pout. She angrily gathers her things, not noticing me. I take a second to look her over. She's too skinny, in my opinion. She must be model height. She's all leg and sharp edges. Exactly the type of woman I'm sure Alex loves. Tall. Too sexy. Someone who looks high-class enough to be on his arm.

I snap myself out of my thoughts. The truth is, I've never seen him with anyone. I'm glad I haven't because it would probably break my heart. Which upsets me because I have no right to feel like I do about him. I really should just hate the guy and leave him to the temp agency. Damn me for being too loyal and loving my work.

"I don't know who you are or where you're from, but he's an asshole. Best of luck." The woman breezes by me and waits for the elevator, tapping her foot angrily.

I walk slowly towards my desk and force myself to breathe. I had been so confident this morning. I thought of everything I wanted to say. But that confidence is quickly waning. Alex doesn't seem to be in a great mood. He looks like he slept in his clothes. My heart is racing because I feel like I'm in for some kind of final showdown. I just hope I'm still standing after it's done.

I sit down and log into my computer. I know he has meetings today. I want to make sure I know when they are so I can keep him on schedule. Or at least cancel them if he's not feeling well. I'm not sure if he's sick or something, but I don't want him in meetings looking like he doesn't want to be in them. I've come to learn how important Lucinio Tech is to Alex. Even if he doesn't want to be in meetings, he's very good at acting like he does. I don't think he'll be capable of that today.

I get myself into his schedule and start writing down meetings. I always make sure that he gets reminders fifteen minutes before his meetings, but I also make sure to have them written down for him. He seems to like that he has his schedule in multiple places. He's never actually said anything about it, but I figured since he didn't yell at me about not doing it, that it's something he prefers.

Thinking about it, he's never actually screamed at me about my job. He gives me a ton of things to do during the day, but he's never told me I'm doing anything wrong. The only time he's yelled at me about anything related to my job was Friday when he got angry about me not seeing the note left about the NDS report he needed.

Everything else he's ever yelled about were things so simple I've always felt he was just nitpicking. He has yelled at me about having too many buttons unbuttoned on my shirt. The shirt was a V-neck and didn't have buttons on the top part of it. I stopped wearing it without a blazer.

He once told me my desk was unorganized and messy. I represent him. I need to be neater. I couldn't argue with him. My desk had been a mess that day, and he did have important people coming in. I hated the idea of making him look bad. I quickly cleaned everything up. I made sure to be neater from then on.

Every single time he's criticized me, though, he's been forceful. Angry. Like everything he's forced to say to me is painful for him. An annoyance. Like he wants nothing to do with me but doesn't have a choice because he needs to keep an eye on me.

I sigh and take my notepad as I stand. I grab Alex's cappuccino and muffin, sensing he probably needs it more than he'll ever lead on to me. It really looks like he's had a rough weekend. Maybe the guilt of the past few months has finally gotten to him. That's probably wishful thinking.

I take a deep breath and quietly walk to his office. I knock quietly. He doesn't answer. I'm not so sure I really expected him to. He probably thinks that girl from the temp agency hasn't left and is trying to talk to him again. I knock once more, a little louder this time.

"Go away!" he growls.

I blink and furrow my brows. Alex has his moments of being a complete asshole, but never when it comes to his job. I open the door quietly. I'm not entirely certain what I expect to see when I open the door. Alex throwing something across the room at me, maybe?

What I see is so far out of the scope of my expectations that I freeze in place. Takeout containers litter his office. Enough paper to make me believe he cut down an entire forest is scattered all over his desk. Stacks of paper. Paper on the floor. Plastic coffee cups are all over the place.

And in the middle of it all laying on his back on the black leather couch is Alex Lucinio. His arm is over his eyes. His other is over his middle. His hair looks more disheveled than it did when I saw him a few minutes ago.

I stand staring at him in shock and awe. I've never seen Alex anything less than put together. Seeing him like this makes my heart hurt. It's alarming because I don't know what could be so bad that the confident man who is more than intimidating and scary at times is reduced to whatever this is.

At the same time, seeing Alex obviously in such a vulnerable state makes it hard for me to breathe. He's the most beautiful man I've ever seen. Everything I came in here to say is gone. I don't remember any of it. All I want to do is make whatever is upsetting him go away.

Chapter Six

🍎 Alex 🍎

I've thought the same thing all fucking weekend. This can't be happening. It's not possible. I've worked way too hard for it all to end like this. Too fucking hard to get my company back out of the clutches of my father. Even with Ryan's help over the years, I didn't realize just how deeply he had his hands into it.

"So fucking stupid," I mumble.

I should have kept a closer eye on it. I knew with everything happening over the past several years that Lucinio Tech was getting left out. I was neglecting it. I knew my father had some type of control over it. I let it go. This is all on me. I let my baby down. Fucking stupid. And now I am paying the price. Tenfold.

"Alex?"

My heart stops beating before it quickens. Fucking traitor. I take a deep breath, but don't move. "What?"

"You… Are…? What's happening?"

"My entire life is imploding. Nothing to be concerned about." I hear something being set down on the table next to me before I hear things being moved. I move my arm from over my eyes. Raleigh is cleaning my office. "What are you doing?" I sit up.

"Cleaning up," she says quietly. I expect to hear judgment. Anger. Something. Instead, I hear nothing but quiet kindness.

It makes me sigh. "Raleigh, you don't need to clean up after me."

She shrugs but doesn't meet my eyes. "I know I don't need to. I want to."

All I can do is blink a few times. I've been nothing less than a complete dick to her ever since I've met her. I don't deserve her kindness. I certainly don't want it. But fuck if some part of me doesn't like it. I shake my head to drown that part of me out, but my eyes fall on the table in front of me. There's a fresh cup of coffee with my name on it from Starbucks and a muffin from Nicole's bakery.

I glance at Raleigh before my eyes fall back on the coffee and muffin. I reach for the muffin first and sink my teeth into it. I let my eyes close and savor the taste. I don't know when she started bringing me these, but I can't live without them now. I also have no idea when she figured out my favorite drink from Starbucks is a mocha with a shot of vanilla cappuccino, but she's had one waiting for me every single day since she's learned that little vice.

I quietly eat the muffin and take a drink of the coffee because I need it more than I'd ever let on. I intended to talk to Raleigh this weekend and beg her to come back to work. I may not trust her yet, but I know I at least owe it to my family to talk to her. Maybe I'll get some answers to questions I have but haven't bothered to ask.

My plans were shot to hell Friday night on my way up to bed. I hadn't even gotten changed when I got a call from our accountant. Mr. Koda and NDS had pulled all of their accounts with us. The issue with his money being stolen and laundered into the mafia, though I hadn't breathed a damn word about where it was going, had spooked him. I grabbed a gym bag, threw some clothes into it, and came right back to the office.

I've been trying to figure out how the hell he got tipped off about the mafia and my ties to it ever since. I've been tracking his money. I've gotten almost every single penny back. There was no reason at all for him to pull out on me. Especially after he'd given me his word that he wouldn't during our meeting Friday. I haven't slept. I've lived on takeout for two days. Thank fuck for the shower in my office bathroom.

I wanted to go home today before anyone got here, but on my way out, I heard someone step off the elevator. I was not happy at all to see it was a leggy blond with way too much fucking make-up. I'm capable of replacing Raleigh on my own. I do not need my brother calling temp agencies to do it for me. I stormed out of my office and told her to leave before she'd even had a chance to put her shit down.

The real issue is that I don't want to replace Raleigh. Issues I have aside, Raleigh is a hell of an Executive Assistant. I don't doubt for a second no one could measure up to her. She gets things done. She manages my schedule like no other. She doesn't complain when I give her some stupid task to do because I don't have the time. Like pick up my dry-cleaning for me.

I also, though I hate admitting it, like having her around. I gave her this job, well, probably forced this job on her is the better statement, because I wanted to keep an eye on her while I investigated her. Beyond that, she's nice to look at. I trusted that she wouldn't fuck up her job. Which is to assist me. She's made my life a lot easier.

"Raleigh," I say as she starts picking up my clothing.

She looks at me with watery eyes. "Hmm…?"

"Stop. Come here."

She sucks her lower lip into her mouth as she puts a pair of my sweats into my gym bag. She puts the bag on the end of the couch and hugs herself but doesn't come near me. I don't blame her. Not for a second.

She takes a breath. "Mr. Lucinio -"

"Alex, Raleigh."

She blinks at me a moment before taking a visible deep breath. "What's going on? I've never seen you like this. I know you probably don't believe it, but I'm concerned. I've been thinking I should call Josh because I don't know what to do, but I didn't want him to come in and see…" She pauses and looks around. "This."

I follow her eyes. My office has definitely seen better days. It's not just a mess. There's also an odor. Sweat and gym socks. It smells a little like Damon's bachelor pad did when we were in college. I hadn't noticed it until this moment, but now I'm hyperaware. I don't know how Raleigh hasn't started throwing up.

I stand and stretch. Raleigh takes a few steps back. I walk towards my desk. "I got a call from my accountant on Friday. Late. I was walking up the stairs to my bedroom at home. I knew I'd be here this weekend trying to figure some shit out. I grabbed that gym bag and didn't look back." I sit in my chair behind my desk.

Raleigh doesn't move closer. She's still hugging herself, but she has turned so she's facing me. I can see how confused she is. "What happened?"

"Mr. Koda pulled all of NDS' accounts. All of them. You've seen the reports. You know how much he brings in. It's not that we won't make it without NDS. But he's been my largest and was my first account. He's been with us for a long time. Somehow, he got tipped off that the issue with his accounts is tied to the mafia. He pulled everything."

A look of hurt crosses her face. I know what she's going to say before she does. "And… you think I had something to do with it."

"No… Raleigh, no. For -"

She shakes her head and wipes her eyes. "It's okay. I shouldn't be surprised at this point. I came here to talk to you about… everything, but I can see now there isn't a point, so I'll just leave." She turns and starts walking quickly to my door.

I almost leap out over my desk. The thought of her leaving does things to me I don't want to think about. "Raleigh!" I chase after her, crossing my office in a few hurried steps. "Raleigh, stop." I reach for her arm but think better of it. I'd likely make her scream in fear. Instead, I jump in front of her before she reaches my door. I hold my hands out in front of me, more to show her I mean no harm. "Just stop a second. Please?"

Her eyes widen. I'm sure it's because of the near begging tone of my voice. She sniffles. "Why? So you can berate me?"

"No. No, Raleigh. Just… please sit down. Let me explain. Okay? Thinking you had anything to do with this didn't even cross my mind, but I understand why you would think that."

She watches me a few moments before she takes a couple of steps back and turns. She slowly walks back towards my desk. I breathe a quiet sigh of relief. At least one thing is going right today. I can't help the surprise or stop the flutter I feel when she scoops my coffee from the table and sets it on my desk. After all I've put the girl through, she still cares enough to grab my coffee and put it on my desk.

When she's settled in one of the chairs in front of the desk, I make my way to my chair. I sit down and let out a long breath. "Koda and his company, NDS, are an international security intelligence company. As you know, Lucinio Tech does a variety of things, but one of them is security software. We pride ourselves on our ability to stay ahead of the new hacking programs. Being that he runs a company that is all about security and intelligence, he's constantly looking for premier software. He took a chance on us when we were just a baby company. He took the word of Ryan Crane himself and cashed in on it with us. He's never had an issue, and we've used his company to test new software. Our relationship has been very close for many years. Following so far?"

She nods. "I understand."

"When I took total control, I found several issues. Issues that have gone back to when I first started this company. My father was laundering money through here since close to the day I opened it. Ryan has some damn good people on his team and has helped me stop a lot of it. Over the years, though, while I've been chasing mafias around the fucking world and doing his bidding, he's gotten his claws deeper and deeper into this company. It was his way of controlling me, I'm sure. He's always been one step ahead. One of the accounts that I found out he was using to funnel that money was the account that you saw EXM pulling money from. I've found several fake companies over the past few months that are all connected to Matthew. And they all use that account. I traced it to you."

Her eyes widen. "But I didn't -"

"You didn't know anything about it. I know. I didn't on Friday, but I know now. That same account has been one that Ryan has been chasing for a long time. But I didn't know that. I stopped tracing it when I figured out who it went to. That was wrong of me, and I'm sorry for it. I allowed my suspicion of you to cloud my judgment. That's not who I am. It's not how I've ever been. I'm thorough. The truth is, Raleigh, I don't know what to think of you. I don't. I'm suspicious as hell of you because you're so fucking connected to Matthew, and with everything my family and the Crane's, who are also family, have been through with him, I can't be sure he's not going to fucking come back from the dead. Again. And I don't know if he's planning something through you. Or if you're so loyal to him that you're planning some kind of revenge. I realize that makes me sound like a paranoid fucking asshole, but it is what is."

I watch as she thinks of what to say to me. I don't at all like the fact that it hurts me a little bit to know I'm doing this to her. I'm hurting her. I'm putting her in the position she's in with me. I know she has to feel like she's walking on broken glass. I shouldn't feel one way or another. My job, at least from my standpoint, is to protect my family. It's not all on Josh. He may have taken total control of Lucinio Mafia, but one thing we've learned from Ryan over the years is when it comes to family, we all are responsible for taking care of everyone.

After a few moments, Raleigh meets my eyes. "I know you don't believe me. I even took the weekend to really try and understand why. And I get it. I understand. I don't know what I can do to gain your respect and trust, but I promise I will." She looks down. Her shoulders tremble slightly. It pisses me off that the thought of her crying cuts me. Raleigh steadies herself and looks back up at me. "I love my job, Alex. I feel like I can make a difference in the world in some small way. I'm not stupid, though. I know that me sitting here begging for you to let me keep working for you probably makes you even more suspicious of me. I guess there isn't anything I can do about that but prove to you through actions that I'm not trying to pull one over on you. I doubt my words will do anything to convince you, so I won't try. All I ask of you is to please treat me with respect. At least try." Her eyes fall to the window behind me before she looks down once more and reaches up to wipe away a tear.

I hate that my heart feels any emotion at all for her, but even I'm not that much of a dickhead to not feel remorse for my actions. "I was out of line, Raleigh. I'm sorry." I watch her as she nods. A few moments go by, but she says nothing. I stand slowly and sigh as I turn to my window. "Losing NDS has left a bad taste in my mouth. I don't like losing anyone, but them… It hurts. There's no other explanation for it. I want them back. I don't think I need to tell you how much they mean to this company. But to me, they mean the world. They were my first client. I don't like this."

"I'd like to help, Alex," she nearly whispers. "If you'll let me, I mean."

I won't pretend that I still don't trust her, but I'd be a fool to not accept the help she's offering. She does seem to have a skillset I could really find beneficial right now. I obviously have a lot more on my mind than I'm allowing myself to believe. I've missed shit that I shouldn't have and lost my largest and most favorite client.

I lock my hands behind my head as I stretch. I turn to her. "Okay. I won't lie to you. I know how lucky I am having you for an Executive Assistant. You're good at your job. I'd already planned to beg you to come back. And that's not something I do. Ever. But if you're serious about helping me, then cancel everything on my calendar and yours for the week. You and I are going to be spending a lot of time in this office. I'd suggest you go home, grab whatever you need for the week, and meet me back here. We're going through all of my accounts. Everything. We're finding anything that looks off that I've missed. And when it's done, we're getting Koda and NDS back here."

Her eyes widen slightly. She looks around the office and bites her lip. After a few moments, she nods slowly. "I'll do whatever you need me to do." She stands and gives me a wary look. I know she wants to say something else.

"We're going to be stuck in this office together for a few days. You may as well just get it all out."

She watches me for a moment. "Okay. If you really want me to. I know you're suspicious of me. But I will answer anything you ask of me. I have nothing to hide. I won't tolerate your vicious biting at me. I won't. I've already made the decision that if we can't get along, I'll leave. I don't want to come between you and your family. I would rather walk away and make my own way in the world than ever do that. But I don't deserve to be treated with anything less than respect. I realize that my… our…" She shakes her head in frustration as she sniffles. "Matthew. I know that he hurt you and a lot of others. I'm still trying to deal with that." She chokes down a sob. "I just want you to understand that I'm trying. Okay? I'm trying to…" She wipes her eyes. My chest physically aches. "I'm trying to adjust. I'm trying to figure out what to do with all of the information I've gotten about him."

I stand rooted to my place behind my desk. I watch as she flees my office but can't force myself to follow. The words were few, but she's managed to make me feel even worse about everything.

The asshole in me says she's a world-class little actress. Make everyone feel guilty and bad for her. I'd love to believe him. I'd love to keep on as we are. Me trying to figure out what the hell she's hiding. And her doing whatever the hell she does.

Unfortunately, it's not the asshole who has the biggest voice right now. I've never had a problem seeing a woman cry. There's a few I can't handle. My mother. Any of the women in my family. Jessa. She's the one woman I've been with that I saw a future with. Fate had other plans, but she's still one of my best friends to this day. Anyone else, though, and I could walk away without feeling an ounce of anything.

So why the fuck, do I feel like shit seeing the tears in her eyes? I scrub my hands down my face and start picking up my clothes. When I have them all gathered and in my gym bag, I leave my office. Raleigh isn't at her desk, but I can't even pretend that it surprises me. She's efficient. I don't doubt she's on her phone on the way home dealing with my cancellations.

I take the elevator to the first floor and hastily walk to the garage where I left my car Friday night, nodding at security on my way out. I raided Nicole's small bakery when I got here, knowing it would be a long night. I didn't want to come down to the ground floor after parking, then go back up to my office.

Exhaustion hits me. Maybe I should call Raleigh and tell her I'm taking a nap and will be in later. I get in my car. My fingers hover over my keypad. I sigh and put my phone down. I just want to get this done. I want to find all of the issues with Lucinio Tech and fix them. Maybe knowing Matthew is out of my hair forever will help me focus and get back to things that are important.

Like Raleigh.

Chapter Seven

❦ Raleigh ❦

I put my bag in my car just as Josh drives into the driveway. He gives me a confused look as he parks, but I don't have time to say anything when he gets out of the car because my phone rings. It's Alex.

I clear my throat. "H-hello?" I expect him to start yelling about something. Something I didn't do before I left. I don't have a clue what it would be, but I have little confidence in him not being upset with me about something.

"Hey, this is a reach, but I could use a ride back to the office. I'd call someone else, but there's not really a point to pulling anyone from whatever they're doing since you're already going back. Did you leave yet?"

"Oh. Um…" I look up at Josh as he walks over to me. "Y-Yes." I take a breath. "I can be there in a few minutes."

"Thanks." Alex hangs up. My heart starts hammering in my ribcage while I think of all the reasons he'd call me, of all people, for a ride.

"How did it go with Alex?" Josh asks.

"Um… I honestly don't know how to answer that. I'm not entirely certain he's really willing to trust me. Or even try to trust me. But he is allowing me to keep my job. And he did ask me to help him clean up the company once and for all." I shrug. "But that involves all day and night in the office and, apparently, me picking him up from his house."

Josh shakes his head and looks up when he sees Alex crossing the street. His house is only a couple down from Josh's. "He looks exhausted."

I nod. "Yeah. He spent the weekend in his office. I walked in and almost called you. It was bad. It was a mess. He looked like hell. Turns out, NDS pulled their account after assuring him they wouldn't. Something about getting tipped off that the mafia was involved in the entire thing behind their missing money."

Josh's eyebrows shoot up. "The fuck?" He looks down at me. "Who the hell tipped them?"

I shake my head and shrug. "I don't think Alex knows either. But I think he's pretty intent on figuring it out."

Alex yawns and rubs his eyes as he walks towards us. "I got in my car and sat there for five minutes. I don't know where the hell the time went or how I'd managed to back out of the garage and not remember. I'm chalking it up to being fucking exhausted." He tosses a bag in the backseat of my car.

"She said NDS pulled their accounts," Josh says. He leans his forearms on the roof of my car.

Alex growls low and mimics his brother's position. He rubs his eyes again. "I got a call Friday night from my accountant. NDS pulled their accounts and apparently gave a reason. It's the reason that's fucking with me."

"Mafia?"

"Yep. He somehow learned that the mafia was behind it. Got spooked. I called and left him several messages. He hasn't returned any of them. I don't exactly need him. The company will go on without him. But he's a huge account, and he's my first. He took a chance on me. I'm pissed because I feel like I let him down."

"No, Alex. You didn't let him down. There must be a reason. Lance is working with Robby and Ryan to track that account. They hit a wall." Josh moves aside and holds my door open for me so I can slide into the driver's seat. "I'll stay on it. You two find anything, let me know if I can do anything to help."

Josh closes the door behind me as Alex gets in. I close my eyes and keep my hands on the steering wheel. I grip it hard until my knuckles turn white. His scent is overpowering. Strong. Powerful. Spicy. Something I can't figure out. Something so uniquely Alex.

He's surrounding me. There's no space between us. He's a big guy. All muscle. All beautiful man. I can feel his body heat, though he's not touching me. This is going to be a terrible drive. And will probably take ten times longer just because it can.

"You okay?"

Why does his voice have to be so sexy? It's not as deep as Josh's. It's not as commanding. Powerful. Dominating. It's still all of that, though. Just on a whole other level, and holy Christ, it does things to me that I don't understand.

I take a breath, mistake, and push the button for my window to go down as I open my eyes and turn the key in the ignition. My car quietly purrs to life. If I didn't feel the barely there vibration of the powerful engine, I may not know it's even on.

I shift the car into gear and nod. "I'm fine." Though, I doubt he really cares. I'm sure he's just trying to be at least cordial.

He watches me as I pull out of the drive and start driving through the compound. I know I'm barely breathing. I wave to the security at the gate and put on a bright, very fake smile I don't feel as I drive by them. When I hit Chicago's sometimes stifling traffic, I let out a quiet, slow breath.

Alex finally takes his piercing blue eyes off me. "I hope you're prepared. I don't know what the hell you did with Matthew's accounts, but I sure as fuck hope it can help the predicament Lucinio Tech is in."

I take a moment to compose myself before daring to speak. "He sometimes took what I thought was work home with him. He said it was a teaching experience. He would just put printouts in front of me and tell me to tell him what was wrong. He did it from a very young age. I guess I just started to see things jump out at me that didn't look right. If I found something, like an errant account number that didn't seem to belong, he would have me track it. Not like a hacker. He would have me see if it was in other accounts. When I was finished, he'd tell me I did a good job. I passed the lesson. He'd reward me by taking me out to dinner at a fancy place. I always felt so special because I got to dress up. When I was little, he made me feel like a princess. He called me his little princess. When we got wherever we went, he always told everyone I was his special date for the evening." I blink back tears.

Alex doesn't speak for a long time. I hear him clear his throat quietly. "He was never like that with us. Not that I wanted him to call us his little princesses." He chuckles at his own joke, but I can hear the edge to his voice.

"I can't imagine what it was like for you," I nearly whisper.

He shrugs. "We just had two very different lives, I guess. I don't understand how you thought what he was doing was normal, though. The accounts and all that shit."

It's my turn to shrug. "You said it yourself. We lived two very different lives. I was homeschooled. It was passed off as a lesson. Maybe if he'd started doing it later, I would have thought differently. But he started doing it when I was young. I just never knew any better. He never let me go to public school. We didn't own a TV. I had a radio, but that's all. All of my time was spent reading textbooks and doing homework. He gave me extra lessons in life. That's what he called them. The accounts were one of them. Maybe it makes me stupid in your eyes, but to me, it was normal. It was my normal. I looked at it like something he was doing to help me in life. Preparing me for the real world."

"And you never questioned it when you got older? Never questioned why an accountant was gone for what must have been weeks at a time?"

I pull into the parking lot and start making my way up to the top floor of the parking garage to my parking place. "I won't lie and say I didn't find it annoying. But he always checked in. He explained it away. He told me when I got older that he owned the company and sometimes he had to go away to get new clients. Obviously, I know the truth now, but then, it was just normal. He checked in every night. He said goodnight. I had a nanny and tutor. Honestly, my day was filled with activities and homework. The times he was gone went quickly. I was never bored. I never wanted anything. I was even okay with not getting every single day and night with him until the last three or four years. He still went away, but it was never for as long. And by that time, I was working towards Oxford

University." I park my car and take another deep breath when I step out, thankful that he seems to have dropped it. I don't want to talk about Oxford.

The ride up to the hundred and second floor is silent. It gives me a chance to gather my thoughts, but that's not easy when Alex is in such close proximity. His masculine scent fills the elevator. I think he showered because he smells fresh. I've seen Alex in jeans and a t-shirt before, but something about the jeans he's wearing today makes him seem bigger. Taller. More CEO boss than even his suit does.

The plain black t-shirt makes him look like he stepped off the battlefield. It stretches across his muscles. I can't help but wonder why it isn't tearing. It's so tight. He looks like he's about to go to war. I suppose maybe we are. Even the sleeve tattoo of skulls all the way up his right arm looks more angry. Prepared to battle.

"Did you cancel everything?"

His voice makes me jump slightly, but only because he'd been stoically silent for so long. I nod but realize he's in front of me and can't see me. "I did it on the way home."

"Good." He shuts off the lights in the lobby where my desk is and opens his office door. He stands to the side waiting for me.

I hadn't realized I'd stopped at my desk. Instinct, I suppose. Or habit. I don't know. "I assumed you'd want me out here," I say quietly and more than a little unsure.

He chuckles. "Where do you think you'll be sleeping?"

I glance at my desk. "Um… Under my desk, I guess?"

"I may be an asshole, Raleigh, but not even I'm that cruel. Get in here."

I scurry into his office at his tone. I don't know what it is but disobeying him isn't an option. He doesn't leave any room for it anyway. He closes the door behind us and strides ahead of me. He drops his bag near his desk and opens a cabinet off to the right side of the room. It's where his filing cabinet is.

Alex doesn't leave anything to technology. Which I've always found odd because he runs a giant tech company. One of the things he sells to his clients is backup software so they don't need to worry about computers crashing and everything lost. Everyone who works here has the same software installed on our computers, but Alex still keeps paper file after paper file of information on clients dating all the way back to when he first opened the company.

At least certain ones. The largest and most special to him. I've never understood why, but I've never had the nerve to ask him. Right after I started working here, we had a system crash. The backup file system worked just fine to restore everything.

He pulls out a large box. I force my eyes away from the bulging of his biceps and forearms, the tattoos drive me crazy, but not before I notice all of the stupidly delicious veins running between all of his arm muscles. I try to focus on anything else. The clouds border the gray Chicago skyline. It looks like a storm is coming in. When looking at the sky fails, I focus on the bird crap on the window.

Nope. That doesn't work either. Especially when I can sense he's moving closer. Thunder rolls in my ears, but I can't be sure where it's coming from. Would I be able to hear thunder when the storm hasn't quite arrived? Or maybe it has.

Alex snaps his fingers in front of me. "Still with me?"

I truly hate that his voice cuts through the loudest of noises in my head. I shake my head to try and clear it. Not easy with him so close. "Sorry. I got lost in thought."

"Well, do you think maybe you can focus enough to hear my words? Or should I write them down for you?" Sarcasm drips from his voice, but it's the subtle hint of venom behind his words that brings the tears to my eyes.

I sniffle and lower my eyes, blinking to stop the tears from falling. "I'm fine, Mr. Lucinio."

"Alex."

I nod but say nothing as I step around him. I don't really know what to do with my stuff, so I put it on one of his leather chairs in front of his desk. I watch him take out a few more boxes before he walks behind his desk.

He picks up his phone. "Hey, I'm not taking meetings or seeing anyone this week. I'm here, but unless I give explicit orders to allow it, no one comes up." He pauses while he waits for whoever he's talking to, I assume the front desk security team, to speak. "Well, they'd be allowed. Let's just say if they ain't family, they ain't allowed up here. We'll have food delivery coming, but I don't want them up here. Take the food. Tip them. Bring it up yourself." He pauses again and nods before he hangs up and looks at me. "You can take the couch to sleep. There's a penthouse below us, but I doubt we'll be making it there. Not with all this work. You know there's a bathroom with a shower through that door." He points to the private bathroom door in his office. "I expect your full attention if you're going to help me right this ship. Got me?"

I nod. My heart skips a beat when I look into his beautifully icy blue eyes. At the same time, I feel a chill in the air. I hug myself knowing full well it isn't the air-conditioning kicking on. It's Alex. I can tell it's a struggle for him to have me near him, but at least he's not being mean. Well, too mean.

"So, what's the plan? What do you need me to do?"

He watches me for a few moments before he walks to the boxes he's arranged neatly against the wall. He picks one up and puts it on the table in front of the couch as he sits down. "This is EXM. I've been through these accounts myself when I first took over completely, but obviously, I had other things on my mind." He looks up at me. He doesn't need to say anything. I know he means me. Of course, he doesn't keep it hidden. "Like you."

I bite my lip and choose to ignore him as I sit on the floor across from where he's sitting. "The best thing to do is start from the beginning. Are these the files from when they first signed with Lucinio Tech?"

He nods. "At the risk of sounding like Matthew, look for anything unusual. EXM is a cover company now, but I don't think it was when they first signed. I think they aligned sometime with him and agreed to help him launder money. I want to know how far back it goes. I want to go through every single account all the way back to the beginning. When we're done, we'll have a paper trail. We'll have account numbers. I can get the information to Lance and let him do his thing. Then we can figure out what the hell we do from there. By the end of this, I want NDS back. I want a clean fucking company."

I nod, but I think of Lance Engle. He's one of Alex's close friends and the Lucinio Mafia's resident hacker. He's very good at what he does, so I've been told. Whatever he can't figure out he brings to Robby Massena, the hacker for the Crane Mafia. I've also been told they do work for the Government. They must be stellar at their skills because I can't believe the Government would allow them to do what they do without imprisoning them. Robby himself told me he once hacked into the Department of Defense and Department of State.

"What about Lance?" I ask quietly as I watch him lay folders out on the table. I notice they are by year. I'm sure when I open them, I'll see transactions by month.

"He's got other things going on. Josh has given him a few things. Including tracking the account in your name."

I shut my mouth immediately and open the folder without another word. I know Josh has been having Lance dig into my adoption in an effort to find my biological family. Or at least what happened to them. Like if they're alive or dead. Maybe if we find them or find someone from my biological family, I'll get answers I've been asking myself ever since the day I found out my entire life has been a bold-faced lie.

Do I have a family? Do they miss me? Have they been looking for me? Did they give up on me? Do they even know I exist? Why did they give me up? But the most important question of all…

Who am I?

Chapter Eight

☜ Alex ☜

"Mr. Koda. It's Alex Lucinio again." I pace behind my desk as the sun rises over the Chicago skyline. I've called NDS' CEO at different times throughout the day since I found out what happened on Friday night. He hasn't responded. I expect to get a harassment order slapped on me pretty soon. I pinch the bridge of my nose. "I know I've called you several times over the past five days, and you're probably sick of hearing my voice at this point, but we need to have a conversation about your decision to leave Lucinio Tech after our meeting Friday. Call me back, please, so we can figure all this out. I think there's been a misunderstanding. I'm available anytime."

I hang up and put my phone down. I scrub my hands down my face and choke back the groan of frustration about to escape. I check my watch and decide I need to get coffee. I'm running on such a small amount of sleep I'm barely functioning.

I quickly and quietly make my way out of my office to the elevator. I punch in the button for the ground floor and beeline for Starbucks. I notice Nicole's bakery is just opening and make a point to stop in and grab something to eat.

After I grab my cappuccino and something for Raleigh, I head for the bakery. I know what I want, but I don't have a clue what Raleigh would get. Now that I think of it, I don't think I've seen her eat anything while she works. Despite what we've ordered this week, Raleigh typically doesn't take breaks for lunch. She works right through. I hate that I've paid enough attention to know that.

After browsing the selection for what seems like hours, I finally give up. I don't know if I'm more upset that I don't know what Raleigh likes or if I'm upset because I care. I shake my head and finally give up.

"Hey, I'll take a strawberry cream cheese muffin," I say to the young blond behind the counter. I'd say she's in high school, but if that were the case, she'd be in class right now. I'm betting my billions that she's a college student in need of extra cash. Hopefully, this isn't her first day.

She wraps the muffin and puts it in a bag. She looks up at me, giving me a dazzling smile. Her green eyes shine. "Anything else, Mr. Lucinio?"

I'm not sure why it surprises me that she knows my name. This is my building. "Yeah. Uh… There's a girl who comes in here all the time. About a foot shorter than me. Small. Auburn hair. Really pretty." Son of a bitch. I need to shut-up. My dick twitches at the thought of Raleigh. I curse myself and force my cock to stand down.

"Oh. Your Executive Assistant?"

"That would be correct. Any idea what she gets?"

She tangles a strand of hair around her finger and looks up at me through her lashes. Normally, I'd be up for a little flirting. I haven't been with a girl in almost a year. But I'm not in the mood, and I'm a little bit pissed off that she's trying it with the CEO of the company who owns the building she's working in.

Above and beyond that, she's doing it on Nicole's dime. Nicole is nothing less than family to me, and I don't tolerate my family being fucked with. If she's brave enough to try it with me, I doubt she hasn't with others. It's not the type of image I want to portray.

"Raleigh usually gets a raspberry snickerdoodle cookie, or she likes the rose one. Otherwise, the vanilla rose muffin. We don't have the rose cookie she usually gravitates to today, but we have the muffin and the raspberry snickerdoodle."

"Get her both. And from now on, she's referred to as Ms. Jennings. She's my Executive Assistant. Show her some respect. Also, I don't want to catch you or hear about you flirting with anyone in this building. You not only represent my sister and her company in this bakery, but you also represent me." I pay her as she stares wide-eyed at me and take my items without another word. I can feel her eyes on my back, but I don't really give two shits.

I stride directly to the executive elevator, the one reserved just for me and my assistant and anyone who needs to get to my floor. If they aren't my family, me, Raleigh, or security, they get a security escort up to the floor. I used to allow security to use a key card and let whoever was going up to my floor do it on their own after being scanned in, but that all changed the day the Starbucks asshole scared Raleigh. I hadn't told her about the change because I'm still pissed off that I allowed that day to affect me at all.

When I get to my floor, I step off the elevator and hurry towards my office. Raleigh is dead asleep on the couch. She'd fallen asleep on the floor, but I couldn't bear to leave her there. Especially when I saw her shivering. The little blanket she'd brought with her obviously wasn't keeping her warm. Another thing I am currently pissed off at myself for noticing.

I picked her up and put her on the couch. I got a blanket out of the closet in my office, because I've been taught to prepare for everything, and put it over her. Then I sat there and watched her sleep, constantly berating myself for every thought running through my head about her. What her lips would taste like. What she'd feel like straddling me on the very couch she's laying on. The same thoughts that I've been fighting off ever since she drove into my fucking world.

It's so much easier for me to be a complete dick to her then it is for me to admit that no woman, not even Jessa, has stirred in me what she has. Feelings I've never in my life felt for anyone are constantly simmering at the surface whenever she's anywhere near me. Fuck. They're there when she isn't. She's always on my mind. Fixating on all of the reasons she can't be trusted is a much better option than opening up myself to her in any manner. I like my life the way it is.

I set her coffee and breakfast down on the table in front of her. I devour my muffin on the way to the bathroom to take a shower. I can't be in the same room with her when she looks so fucking peaceful like that. It does things to me it shouldn't.

I quickly strip and step in the shower. It does nothing to tone down my thoughts, though. It does even less to quench the raging hard on I've had all morning. After I put her to bed, I passed out not long after from straight up exhaustion. When I woke up, my head was on her hip. I don't know how the hell it happened, but I don't think I've ever moved so fast.

Thankfully, my movement didn't wake her up. It was something I was grateful for. Not only because it gave me a second to compose myself, but also because she needed the sleep. I have to give her credit. She didn't pass out like I thought she would on Monday night. She fought through Tuesday. It wasn't until around two this morning when I noticed she'd lost the battle.

It's barely after eight in the morning now. The sun is streaming through the window. It catches her hair perfectly. I can see the red undertones highlighted in the light. The girl is beyond beautiful, and I kick myself every single time I think those words about her.

Before I realize what I've been doing, my stomach tightens. I let out a quiet growly groan as I come hard against the shower wall. "Fuck…," I whisper, leaning my head against my forearm against the shower wall with my dick in my other hand. "Fuck, this can't happen. Not with her."

I quickly clean myself up and step out of the shower to dry off. It's not the first time I've jacked off in the shower to thoughts of her. Every time it happens, I make sure I'm extra snappy with her so she stays the hell away from me. It's bad enough I can't get her scent or her curves out of my head when she's not around me. The things she does when she is around me pisses me off even more.

When I finish drying off and brushing my teeth, I throw a bit of cologne on, telling myself it's routine and not for her. I reach for my clothes and realize I left them in the closet where we decided we'd store our stuff so there weren't clothes strewn all over the place. I've learned that Raleigh is really fucking organized. She hates clutter and messes. At first it came as a shock to me considering the state I've seen her desk in.

Truthfully, the more I think about it though. I think it was an off day for her. It's only happened one time. Matthew hated messes and disorganization just as much as Raleigh seems to. Josh and I both got our

74

fair share of beatings for having a messy room or leaving something out that we shouldn't have. Even spilling something on accident received Matthew's wrath. Even though I took the brunt of them and made Josh run, he still ended up with the worst of it when I left for college.

Thinking of all the beatings Josh took by Matthew and his fucked up guards makes my blood boil. And that is just the feeling I need right now. Anger. Anything to take my mind off her when I walk out this door.

With the towel wrapped around my waist, I quietly open the door. Of course, fate wouldn't be on my side. Fate seems to hate me as much as I hate her. Raleigh is sitting up on the couch and staring at me wide-eyed. I don't miss the way her eyes slowly travel down my body and back up before she clears her throat and quickly looks away.

With any other woman in the world, I'd make some kind of witty comment. Or ask her if she's enjoying the view. But not her. Not. Her. I quickly walk to the closet and grab my bag. I almost run back to the safety of the bathroom. Anywhere I can't feel her eyes. The heat they left in their wake.

I'm in trouble. I know it. I feel it deeper than I've ever felt anything. She's somehow chipping away the ice I've fortified my stone wall with. I can't let her. I know I can't. I just don't think I'll have much of a choice. Spending the past couple of days with her has been the biggest mistake of my life. I should be doing all of this myself.

But even I know that statement is stupid beyond belief. She's found things over the past couple of days that I had not only missed but never would have thought to look for. Matching account numbers for several different companies. Random accounts that were withdrawing money from Lucinio Tech's business account, but not enough to raise awareness. Money going into Lucinio Tech's business account from account numbers that never have and don't belong to any client we have. She's been invaluable.

Yet one more thing to piss me off. I quickly get dressed and steel myself before walking back into my office. Raleigh says nothing as she gets up and grabs her things. Seconds later, I hear the shower running.

I sigh and sit down. I grab my coffee and get back to work. The sooner we get this done, the sooner things can get back to normal. It's a lot harder to be an asshole when she's with me all fucking day. For the hundredth time in the past two days since I came up with this hair-brained idea, I curse myself.

"I really think we'd have better luck if we looked through Lucinio Tech's accounts better," Raleigh says as she yawns. She blinks adorably a few times and shakes her head. "I'm sorry. That was a stupid thing to say." She goes back to the accounts in front of her.

I shake my head. I don't know if it's exhaustion or me having a change of heart, but I'm not suspicious of that statement at all. I usually would be. I'd take that to mean she wants a better understanding of the company so she can figure out a way to report back to whoever she's working for. The problem is I'm starting to think maybe everyone else is right about her.

I scrub my hands down my face and rub my eyes. "I don't think you're stupid, Raleigh. I didn't take too well to you saying that in your car the other day." I say the words quietly, but I know she hears the edge in my voice. It's difficult to hide. I have my issues with her, but even I can see she's far from stupid. Raleigh just bites her lip and nods. I lean back on the couch and rub my head. "Maybe we need a break. What would you like for dinner?"

She looks up at me with the most hopeful expression I've ever seen. It's only then I realize neither of us have eaten anything since I brought up the pastries this morning. Right on cue, my stomach growls and makes me feel like a bigger jackass. I am absolutely not used to these feelings.

"Can we? Maybe some pasta tonight?" Her eyes sparkle with both exhaustion and something else. I can't place it, but with the moon and stars in the sky above us shining through the floor to ceiling glass behind my desk, I can't help but notice how pretty she is.

I mentally shake my head. "Yeah. Whatever you want."

After dinner, Raleigh dives right back into the work in front of us. I have no choice but to admire her effort and tenacity. She hasn't quit. It's gone a long way in starting the shift in my opinion of her.

"I still don't understand how someone as smart as you didn't pick up on the shit going on around you," I say.

She shrugs. "It was just normal for me. I don't know what else to say about it. I wish I could ease your fears about me."

"There's a lot of them, Raleigh. I can't deny you're good at your job. And you have been an invaluable help with this stuff. But you loved Matthew. I don't understand how. He was vicious and cruel. Calculating. But he also adapted really well to any situation. He was charming and charismatic. He could make friends anywhere. He was a lot like you."

It's the first time I've really aired out my grievances with her. As I watch her take it all in, an ache settles in my chest. It's taken me a little over six months to realize just how unfair I've been to her.

I would never want anyone to judge me based on knowing my father was a ruthless mafia leader. But I did that to her. So fucking hypocritical. Now I'm starting to see the reason everyone has been so pissed off at me over the way I've been treating her.

"Raleigh, I -"

"It's not easy for me, you know. At least you know where you came from. Who you came from. I don't even know my real name." She doesn't meet my eyes. Instead, she stares straight ahead. She stands and walks to the window. She hugs herself as she looks over the city. It takes her so long to continue, that I get up and start walking towards her just to make sure she's okay.

"Raleigh -"

She spins on me. There's a fiery fury that stops me so quickly in my tracks, I stumble. She glares a little more viciously, but I can see it. I can see it so clearly. She tries to cover it with cold anger, but the pain is more than prevalent.

"I don't know if I have a family out there looking for me. I don't know if I was adopted or kidnapped. I know nothing about who I am or where I come from. All I know is who I was told to be by a crazy man who tried to kill and did kill a lot of people. My entire life was a total and complete lie. Do you think that's easy to live with?" She swipes at her eyes as she moves around my desk and starts running for the door to my office.

I reach for her because I don't know what else to do. "Raleigh!" I manage to grip her arm.

She turns and yanks her arm away. "You act like I'm some cold-blooded murderer! You think that all I'm here to do is destroy your family just because that's what he was trying to do. But I'm not! I'm just trying to figure out who I am. In a matter of hours, my entire world was ripped away from me, Alex. I got a rejection letter from the only college I'd applied to. I was so sure I'd get in. I worked so hard for it! And do you know what I was told? I was told that I didn't meet their qualifications. I was homeschooled and passed my SATs and ACTs with a near perfect score. But because I didn't attend a public or private school, I wasn't good enough for them! Do you have any idea how much it hurt me? To know that I worked my entire life for that one moment only to have it ripped away from me? Do you know what that's like?"

I feel like I've been kicked in the chest. Watching the tears roll down her face as she screams at me makes it all hit home a lot harder. She hasn't deserved anything that I've done to her. She was already hurting on a far deeper level than I could ever imagine.

I reach once more for her, but this time she steps back. I let my arm fall as a lump forms in my throat. "I didn't know."

"No! You didn't. Because you never asked! I have the letter. I kept it. Do you want to see it? Just to prove I'm not lying to you?"

"Raleigh, I didn't -"

"Did you know Matthew called me a failure that night? He berated me for hours after I showed him the letter. I went to him for support. All I wanted was to feel loved. Just for a second. Like he'd done so many times before. But he told me that I should have applied to other places. I should have applied to UCLA. Berkeley. Yale. Harvard. I shouldn't have put all of my chips in one hat. He said Oxford was right to reject me. Because only a stupid woman would apply to just one university. He said he didn't raise a stupid woman. I ran. I thought it was because he'd had a bad day. I thought when I got home after my walk on the beach, he'd apologize to me. But I never got the chance to talk to him again. Do you know what it's like to not get to, at least, say goodbye? To ask if he meant what he said? Do you know how it feels to not have any closure at all?"

All I want to do right now is hug her, but I'm not sure I dare step any closer. She might actually slap me. I'd probably let her. "I'm -"

"You have no idea what it's like, Alex." She shakes her head. "You walk around like everything fits in this box you've created. Like every person is just exactly as you view them when you know absolutely nothing about them! I don't even have an identity!" She sobs and furiously swipes at her eyes again before she turns away from me once more. She runs for my door again.

I catch her just as she tries to yank the door open. "Raleigh, would you just listen to me for a second? Fucking hell!" I close the door and pull her back against me.

She turns towards me and tries to shove me away. Both of her fists hit my chest. "Let go! I am done! You win! I quit! I don't deserve this!"

I stagger back but grab her wrists and back her against the wall. "Knock it off! Stop fighting me and listen!"

"Let -"

I don't think of the consequences. I pin her wrists above her head and kiss her.

Long.

Hard.

She stares at me with wide eyes and stiffens. I let my tongue flick across her lower lip and give into the primal need I've been fighting for longer than I care to fucking admit. She lets out a whimper and relaxes against my hold but presses against me. She opens just enough for me to dart my tongue into her mouth.

She tastes better than I imagined. Sweet. A hint of banana and something I can't put my finger on. She moans quietly and closes her eyes. I let her wrists go and let my hands travel down her arms. She's so fucking silky and smooth. When she shivers, so do I. Her arms wrap around my shoulders. She presses against me harder. Her nails dig into my shoulders. Her tits press against my chest, driving me mad with need.

I wrap my arms around her and pull back slowly. We stare at each other enveloped tightly in one another's arms. Our breath comes out in heavy pants. She opens her eyes slowly and blushes a pretty shade of pink that has things stirring in me that haven't for a very long time.

I hold her against the wall. "I don't know what any of this has been like for you. I don't know what it's like to suddenly have everything ripped away from you." My voice is low and as calm as I can make it, though I can hear a slight tremor. "I'll admit that I had a pretty good heads up on what Matthew was really like. I may not have had my entire world ripped away from me, but I do know what it feels like to have your entire life flipped upside down with no preparation." I tighten my grip around her waist when she looks down. "I'm sorry, Raleigh. I'm sorry it took me this long to realize that just because you had a far different relationship with him than I did doesn't mean you're just like him. I'm sorry I made you feel stupid, scared, alone, and like I hated you. That was wrong of me. All of it. I know I can't undo it all, and that in itself is going to be a regret I'm going to have to live with."

She sniffles and bunches my t-shirt in her fists. "I'm sorry if I made you think I'm untrustworthy," she whispers.

I shake my head. "You haven't done a damn thing wrong. This is all on me. It's on my shoulders because I didn't want to think that Matthew was capable of showing love. To anyone. I didn't want to think that son of a bitch had a whole happy life going on behind mine, Josh's, and our mother's back. I didn't want to give you the time of day because, at least in my very fucked up mind, it meant that he was capable of raising a child who is everything me and Josh are not. We're both dark. We've got very little morals. We have very few lines that we won't cross. But you. You're this bright, vivacious woman full of life and dreams. By the time I was your age, he'd snuffed all of that light I had out. And you know how badly he fucked up Josh. It was very hard for me to believe that he was capable of leaving you to actually grow. To be happy."

"I'm... so... scared right now."

"Of what? Me?" She has no idea how terrified I am of her saying yes to that question.

She shakes her head. I breathe a quiet sigh of relief. "Of never knowing who I am. Who I really am. Where I come from. My history."

Her words cut me deeper than any injury I've ever had. And any physical damage I've ever had inflicted on me. It's not lost on me that my obsession with proving she's a bad girl has done nothing more than take away the resources we could have been using to get her the answers she needs. It's only made her feel more alone, even though she has so many surrounding her. It has to be difficult to fit in somewhere when she doesn't even feel like she has an identity.

I take a shaky breath and take her hand when I pull back. She's trembling, and I hate it. I just want to wrap her in my arms and replay the last six months. Maybe if I hadn't treated her like shit, she'd have the answers that she so badly needs.

I sit down on the couch and pull her down next to me. I lean back and put my arm around her, settling her into my side. My own abrupt turn around feels completely foreign to me, so I'm relying on instinct. I feel like what she needs right now is comfort, and an ear. I don't know if I'm right, but when she doesn't pull away, I feel like I might be on the right track. But I feel out of my element. I don't like that.

"How about I promise right now to help you?"

She looks up at me. "What?"

"What if, when you and I are finished with this account bullshit, I focus my attention on helping you more with finding out about your family and where you came from? I know Josh is helping you, but I also know his focus is split in a lot of different directions."

She sighs and tries to sit up, but I keep her firmly against me. She looks at me for a moment with furrowed brows. Like she has no idea what to make of me or my offer. I can't blame her. I don't know what to make of me either.

After a few moments, though, I finally get a nod out of her. I didn't realize just how much I needed her to agree to let me help, but as I sit hugging her, I can't stop berating myself for being such an asshole to her.

Chapter Nine

❦ Raleigh ❦

Five days.

Five days since my first kiss.

With Alex.

My boss, and the object of every single fantasy I've had.

I play with my pen as I stare blankly at the elevator doors in front of me. I can feel my cheeks heat with just the thought of his lips on mine. My entire body lights up. I get a warm and tingling feeling all over. Embarrassing liquid desire pools between my thighs.

I cross my legs and shake my head. I'm working. I shouldn't be thinking things like this. Not at work. It's inappropriate. No matter how sexy Alex is. I run my tongue over my lower lip and blush as I smile. God is he sexy. So sexy.

I lean back in my chair and force the thoughts from my head. If I'm being honest, I have no idea what's happening between us. We finished going through every single account Lucinio Tech holds. We only found a few other anomalies. They were taken care of immediately. Though, how exactly, I didn't dare ask. All I know is Josh and Alex took some of their guys and were gone all weekend.

I run my hands through my hair and sigh before going back to playing with my pen. I look down at my desk. Since the kiss, there hasn't been another one. Alex was incredibly sweet to me the entire night. But he hasn't tried to kiss me again. He really hasn't done anything since then. He hasn't hugged me. He hasn't even touched me.

I don't understand what happened. I thought we were making progress. He hasn't been an asshole at all. He's been very respectful. I just don't know exactly what I'm supposed to do now. Do I just… pretend it didn't happen?

I groan quietly. I wish I were brave enough to just ask him where we go from here. It would be nice to know if I'm to be relegated to the memory of his lips on mine and the feel of him against me, or if I'll get another taste.

I glance up when the elevator doors open. Alex is dressed in his usual business suit tailored to fit every single inch of him. I can't decide if he looks better in jeans and a t-shirt or a suit. He fills both out so well.

I smile and stand when he reaches my desk. "Hey, Alex." I put his coffee and muffin on the desk.

He doesn't look up from his phone. "I'm sure it will be a busy day. How many messages do I have?"

"Oh… um…" I can see he's looking at his email. He's probably super distracted. I shake my head and hand him his messages. "A lot of calls. A few of them I already dealt with. I crossed them off the list. I color coded them, though. Most important are in red. Yellow is the next most important. No color is the least important."

He nods and takes the list. He doesn't take the muffin or the coffee. "Thanks."

"Alex?"

He keeps walking like he doesn't hear me. I watch him walk towards his office. I grab the coffee and muffin and follow him. I smile to myself because the view from the back is just as nice as the front.

He brings his phone up to his ear as he walks through his door. "Alex Lucinio."

I watch him walk into his office and behind his desk. He launches into a conversation that sounds important. I quietly put his coffee and muffin on his desk as he starts taking off his jacket. I force myself to turn away so I'm not staring at his muscles rippling.

I quickly make my way back to my desk and take a breath, even more confused about what's going on between us. I don't know what exactly I expected, but on Thursday, the day after our kiss, he didn't make any mention of what happened. Friday, when we were finishing everything up, things seemed a little chaotic. I couldn't blame him for focusing on anything other than what we had going on in front of us.

Then they all disappeared for the weekend. I didn't have a chance to talk to him about what happened like I'd wanted to. I found ways to distract myself, but my mind always went back to Alex. I've never been kissed before. I've never had a reaction like that to anyone. I haven't really had many friends, though. Or many contacts outside of the people that Matthew brought home. He called them his associates. I just stayed out of the way.

I jump slightly when the phone rings but quickly pick it up. "Lucinio Tech. Alex Lucinio's office. How can I help?"

"Hey, Raleigh. It's Josh. Alex isn't answering his phone. Can you patch me through? Tell him it's about our problem account number."

"Oh. The one that money is being funneled through?"

"That would be the one. We think we found the origin. If we're right, we might have to look for a leak within Lucinio Tech."

I rub my chest at the sudden ache. Lucinio Tech has become important to me. I hate the thought of someone within these walls betraying our trust. But it makes sense. It has to be someone who has account access. It's a thought I've had ever since we started discovering money being taken out and deposited by accounts with different names but the same account numbers. I just didn't feel it was really my place to point that out. I don't want to accuse anyone of anything without proof.

"I'll have to put you on hold and transfer you. Just a sec." I place Josh on hold and take a breath. Alex has a lot going on today. I'm hoping I'm not about to interrupt a call he's already on using his cell phone or something. I push the button to his office. "Alex?"

It takes a minute, but he finally answers. "Yeah?"

"I know you have a lot of stuff happening, but Josh is on line one."

"He's gonna have to call back."

"He said it's important. It's about that account." I intentionally keep it vague just in case he's talking to someone else. I don't want to give too much away.

There's a pause. "Thank you for not saying any more than that. I owe you. Transfer him over."

I smile brightly and blush, happy that I made the right decision. "Coming through now." I quickly transfer Josh over then get to work on my own list of things to do.

Alex has several meetings happening today. I need to get refreshments set up in the conference room. I need to make sure he has the right things he needs for each meeting. It's important he has a heads up of what each meeting is going to be about and with who, so I need to make sure he's briefed. Just so he can keep everything straight.

I glance at the clock. It's getting close to his first meeting, so I quickly look at his schedule to see who it's with. Marketing. I print off the email I received with the Marketing Director's presentation notes and the email itself so I can read it and make sure he's prepared. Just as I'm about to get up, I shiver.

"Raleigh?" Alex's voice rumbles over the speaker of the phone on my desk.

"Yes?"

"I have a lunch meeting scheduled today with customer support. Move that back for me. Josh, Gavin, Damon, and Lance will be here to discuss our issue. Order something and set us up in the conference room."

"You got it."

I quickly set to work. I sent an interoffice message to the manager in customer support to move the meeting back. I then order sandwiches and a fruit tray to be delivered. I call down to the bakery to have pastries delivered.

Satisfied all the calls I need to do are done, I head to the kitchen to start making coffee. I love that this floor has its own kitchen, complete with a stove and oven. When Alex bought this building and set up his offices here, he spared no expense. On anything.

The security is top of the line. The executive suite is the entire top floor. It has a conference room that is just off the kitchen. It makes it easier for me to bring in the coffee and anything I order for his meetings. Alex likes to take care of anyone he has meetings with, so he spares no expense on snacks or drinks.

To bide my time while the coffee is being made, I clean out the refrigerator. I wrinkle my nose at the smell. Our leftovers from last week had been long forgotten until just this moment. Gross. I shiver as I start tying up the garbage bag. I change the bag and quickly take the full one to the garbage shoot. I giggle when it slides away. I'll never get tired of that. It's the little things that entertain me.

By the time I'm finished, though, I realize that everything I just did was to keep my mind off Alex's lips. Who am I kidding? I'm trying not to think of him at all. It just manages to confuse me more. It does nothing but make my heart hurt. I just wish I knew what we were to each other now. The fact that he hasn't mentioned the kiss or tried it again makes me feel like he didn't like it. Or maybe I didn't do it right. It was my first.

I hug myself and start walking back to my desk and shake the thoughts from my mind. I've been fighting it the entire week. The thought that he feels like it was a mistake. I could almost deal with him not liking it more than I could with him thinking it was all a mistake.

I sigh heavily as the elevator doors open. I glance at the clock above my desk as I come around the corner. Alex's morning meeting. Stepping off the elevator is the CEO of Shaw Incorporated himself. His swagger is just as confident as he is.

I smile. "Hey, Chase."

He grins. "Hey, honey. Is Alex ready for me yet?" He gives me a side hug.

I lean into it, not realizing how much I needed it. "I'll tell him you're here. How's Breetana?"

"She's good. I think she missed having you around this weekend, though. Where were you?"

"Oh. Dallas needed some help with her math homework. She stayed the weekend."

He smiles and lets me go. I lead him to the conference room. Chase Shaw is one of Ryan's brothers. Alex thinks of him like family, as well. I've gotten fairly close to his wife, Breetana. She has a garden behind their house that she just recently started. I love gardening. It's beyond relaxing.

I grab Chase a coffee and the caramel creamer he likes. I set it in front of him just as I hear the elevator ding. I hurry out of the conference room and am relieved to see the pastries I ordered are being delivered. Security waits by the elevator doors as I take them. I set them up in the conference room.

After, I head for Alex's office. I poke my head in and breathe a sigh of relief that he's not on the phone. "Alex?" I call quietly from the door.

"Yeah?" He doesn't look up.

I furrow my brows but quickly shake it off. I tell myself for the thousandth time that he's busy. "Chase is here."

"Set him up in the conference room and grab me his file. We need to upgrade his computer system and security software." He gets up and grabs his phone. He strides quickly towards the door.

I backtrack to my desk and grab Chase's file. I hand it to Alex as he walks past me. He flips it open and looks it over as he walks to the conference room. I sit down, bewildered, as I watch him. It's almost like he's completely ignoring the fact that we shared a bone melting kiss just a few days ago.

He hasn't said good morning to me. He's barely acknowledged my presence. At least when we were going through the accounts, he'd talk to me. Granted, he didn't mention this kiss. He even grew distant, but it wasn't like this.

I can't help but feel that he thinks it was a huge mistake and now he's pushing me away. I breathe out a sad sigh and slump in my chair. Maybe he's right. A workplace relationship is unethical. Especially when the relationship is between a subordinate and her boss. What the hell was I thinking? It's bad enough that I can't stop thinking about what he looks like under his suit.

I automatically start thinking of Alex when he came out of the bathroom after his shower. Water droplets dripped down his washboard abs. All I could think of was licking them off. He looks like he was chiseled out of marble. A stone statue designed from the depths of my own mind just for me. The muscles in his arms rippled just like those in his legs. And then that stupidly sexy strip of hair that snaked its way underneath his towel.

I groan and put my head down on my desk. It's completely hopeless. I'm hopeless. Alex is gorgeous. All man and more. So, so much more. He's so far out of my league that I have no hope of catching him.

Which is why I believe he feels our kiss was a huge mistake. The more I think about it, he's totally right. It's a mistake for anyone to daydream about their boss. It's an even bigger one to kiss him.

I shake my head when my phone rings. I hate that Alex has the ability to jumble my thoughts so completely. Maybe it was better for us both when he hated me and was on a mission to prove I'm a horrible person. Maybe I should tell him to go back to that. At least then I knew where I stood with him.

I pick up my phone after taking a breath. "Lucinio Tech. Alex Lucinio's office. How can I help you?"

"Ms. Jennings. It's Lane Koda."

My eyes widen. "Oh! Mr. Koda! We've been trying to reach you. I hope you're well." My heart starts racing as I look towards the conference room. I hate interrupting Alex's meetings.

"Yes. I've been out of town. You can't begin to imagine my confusion when I started listening to my voicemails."

My stomach clenches and I furrow my brows. Something isn't right. "Let me get Mr. Lucinio, Mr. Koda. He's in a meeting, but I know that he wants to speak with you right away."

"I'll hold."

I quickly put him on hold and dart for the conference room. I quietly slide into the room. Chase and Alex both stop talking as they watch me walk to the phone in the middle of the table. I would never do this if anyone else was in this room with him. But Chase is family.

"I'm sorry to interrupt," I say. I look at Alex as I push the button for the speaker. "Mr. Koda? I have Mr. Lucinio right here for you."

Alex's eyes widen as he leans forward and pulls the phone closer. "Mr. Koda! I'm happy you've been able to return my calls." He's trying to be calm, but I can see he's about to burst with all of his questions.

Chase grabs his coffee and quietly gets up. He gestures for me to follow. Alex gives me a wink and a grin as he listens to what Mr. Koda is saying. I quickly follow Chase out of the room, closing the door silently behind me.

Chase perches himself on my desk as I sit down in my chair. "Did Koda say anything?" he asks.

I shake my head. "Not much. Just that he had been out of town and just came back to all of Alex's messages. He said he was confused." I look up at him. "I don't think he knows what's going on."

"Which means… he has no idea that his company jumped ship with Lucinio Tech." Chase takes a drink of his coffee.

"That's the conclusion I came to."

"That means you have a leak within these walls, Raleigh. Or they have a leak within theirs, but instinct and intuition say it's here. I've been around the mafia enough to know when there's danger lurking."

I nod and take a breath. "Let's see what he says first."

But I know he's right. I feel it.

If NDS didn't pull their accounts, someone made it look like they did…

Chapter Ten

🐦 Alex 🐦

"I can't say I'm not happy to hear that this is all a misunderstanding, Mr. Koda. I assure you, I'll do my part to get to the bottom of it."

"I gave you my word, Mr. Lucinio. I know you know that means something. I won't lie and say that this doesn't reek of a mole, though. I just don't know if it's in my company or yours."

"I know. If you'll trust me, I'll definitely get to the bottom of it."

"I've trusted you for years. You have my support. You'll always have my business. I'll look into the background program you've set up for me. I'm sure I'll be able to match up my books that way. If I find anything, I'll take care of it and keep you apprised."

I nod. "I'll do the same, Mr. Koda." My heart does a little backflip of both relief and anticipation. "Thank you for getting back to me." I stand after we say our goodbyes and hang up. I swiftly walk out of the conference room. "Raleigh!" I round the corner to the lobby and head directly for my office as I scroll through my calendar on my phone. "Cancel everything for today and reschedule it except for my meeting with Josh." I glance up to make sure she heard me and see Chase sitting on her desk. "Oh, shit. Chase, I completely forgot we were in the middle of a meeting."

Chase holds up a hand. "Don't worry about it. You know what I want. I know you'll get it done."

"I'll send someone out tomorrow morning to get started on the upgrades to the computer system."

Chase stands and shakes my hand before pulling me into a hug. "We're here for you. Don't forget that."

I return the hug before letting him go. He shoots Raleigh a wink. A pang of jealousy shoots through me, but I tamp it down with a low growl at myself. First of all, the guy is like family. He's also married. I know he's not the type of guy who would try and steal her away. And second, I don't know what the hell Raleigh and I are, but whatever it is doesn't give me the right to feel jealousy towards anyone. She's not my girlfriend. She's nothing but my Executive Assistant.

I'm completely lying to myself. I haven't been able to stop myself from thinking of that kiss. Her pinned against the wall in my office with her body pressed against mine threw me into a territory with her I never wanted to be in. With anyone. Now all I want is her lips on mine again. I want her body against mine again. But the one thing that I want more than anything is all of her. Just her.

When the door closes to the elevator, I retreat to my office. I have a lot of work to do, but it's a way to hide from her. I realize just how much of a dick that makes me, but until I can figure out what the hell to do about her, hiding is my best option.

I lean against the door of my office after I close it behind me and scrub my hands down my face. "This is wrong, Lucinio. So fucking wrong." I push off the door and walk to my chair. I drop down, suddenly exhausted.

I'm her boss. It doesn't matter that she's living with my brother, or that she's friends with any member of my family. She's my subordinate. Plain and simple. She's proven that she's not out to get me. I've even managed to get past all of that and realize that she's actually a good girl.

But that is where it ends. I can't allow myself to want her. It's against every single part of every ethical rule in the world. How awkward would it be if it didn't work? She said it herself. She loves her job. Fuck, she's good at it, too. I can't imagine having another person in her place in this office. Even when I was being a legitimate asshole, she still did her job better than fucking anyone. I was with a temp for twenty minutes last week and already felt lost. I can't risk losing her.

I stand with a deep rumbly growl and lean against my window with my head resting on my forearms. I don't know why, but this view has been my calming force ever since we moved Lucinio Tech into this building. Through the entire remodel and everything else that comes with stepping into the position I should have been in years ago, this view has been my center.

Like a charm, it works to put my mind right back where it needs to be. On my job and not the perky tits and far too kissable lips of my Executive Assistant. It's back on the issue at hand. A very obvious inside problem with Lucinio Tech. At least, that's what my instincts are telling me.

I sit back down in my chair and pull up the program I had designed that runs in the background of my accounting. It captures everything. It's the entire reason I discovered the issues I had when I first took over and why I pulled originals of all accounts. I knew my father would somehow get his hands into this company. Even with Ryan's help through the years, I knew he'd manage to touch the one thing in my life he hadn't fucked up. It's why I had the program designed. It took time to perfect, but with the help of NDS and Mr. Koda agreeing to be my test subject, I'd managed to get it done.

I start pulling up NDS' records and rub my eyes. I haven't recovered from the week spent here in this office. Or from that fucking kiss. I force the thoughts away with a shake of my head. I can't think about it.

After we found all of the problem accounts, I gave all of our information to Lance. By the end of the night, we had all of the information we needed. They were all fake accounts. All were being funneled through Lucinio Tech by three different mafias all affiliated with Matthew. We sent teams out and took off the very next day to deal with all of them. By the time we got home early this morning, I was exhausted but satisfied my issues with all of that shit was over. I thought it was pretty fucking brazen of them to continue funneling money through here knowing Matthew bit the dust. Especially knowing that my brother and I were more than partially responsible for the son of a bitch's demise.

The last thing I expected was to get a call from Mr. Koda saying he had just gotten back from a vacation where he'd totally unplugged from the outside world. No phone. No laptop. No work. Just him, his wife, and their kids out on his yacht in the middle of the Indian Ocean. He had no idea what I was talking about in any of my messages.

When he'd left Friday afternoon after our meeting, he was under the impression that everything was running smoothly. I'd found the issue with his account. His system was still being protected by high-tech security software. Everything was just fine. He didn't know anything about his company pulling their accounts from us.

I immediately got the sick feeling that my accountant, the man Ryan hired when this company first started, was behind it. We both trusted him. He'd brought a couple of problems to us over the years that we were able to deal with. He never hid anything from us.

Which is why the feeling I have makes me sick. The guy is a good guy. He's near retirement age. He has a nice family. I've met his kids and his wife. I'm hoping I'm wrong. I'm hoping that, somehow, I've made a mistake like I did with Raleigh. Unfortunately, I've lived for too many years being forced to rely on my instincts. Not trusting my gut was liable to get me killed.

I suppose my biggest issue is that ever since my focus became Lucinio Tech, I don't know if I can trust myself. I'm out of my usual element. I fucked up with Raleigh. Who's to say I'm not making the same mistake here? I don't even know if I can trust my instincts anymore.

As my program pulls the information I need, I decide there's one thing I can do to help get things back to how they should be. It's not something I want to do. My body and heart are arguing with me at every turn about it, but I need to do it. I can't mess up what Raleigh and I have. Relationships only manage to complicate things. Not only that, she hasn't said anything at all about our kiss anyway. I'm hoping that's because she realizes that it was something that can't ever happen again.

I force my finger to push the button that gets me to Raleigh. It's not an easy task because every part of my being hates everything about what I'm going to do. But I know better. I know that we really need to keep things professional. If I expect to be able to keep her as my assistant, I can't mix business with pleasure.

"Yes?" Her sweet voice makes me close my eyes and relish in it. My body instantaneously responds. For a second, I can't speak. "Alex?"

I shake my head. I have to do this. It's the right thing. "Can you come in here a minute?"

"Sure."

I take a breath and steel myself. I tell myself that I have no feelings for her. That the kiss was in the heat of the moment. When my chest clenches at the lie, I know I won't be able to get the words out of my mouth.

I look up when Raleigh quietly enters my office. She's beyond beautiful. Even when she wears simple black slacks and a sweater like she is right now, she's stunning. It was one of the first things I noticed about her. She's got the kind of looks that a person doesn't need to try to accomplish. It's just there. She could wake up in the morning with no makeup on and be stunning. I know all too well how beautiful she is when the sun hits her face in the morning.

I ignore the fire coursing through my body. It's dangerous to allow myself to feel it. It will make me back down. The only way I can get back to thinking clearly is if our relationship goes back to what it was. At least for the most part.

She smiles when she stops in front of my desk. "Did you need something?"

"Raleigh, uh… That kiss the other day." My stomach clenches at the words I'm about to utter. I look down at the pen in my hand. Anything to keep the fact that her beautiful smile just fell into a frown out of my head. "It can't happen again." It takes me a few moments, but I make myself look up at her.

She's wringing her hands in front of her. My heart clenches. She nods slowly. "You feel like it was a mistake," she whispers. She doesn't meet my eyes. I'm grateful because she'd see my own emotional turmoil over this. It's tearing me apart far more than I thought it would.

I stand and slowly walk around my desk. I lean on it in front of her. "Raleigh, it's not that I don't want to. I do. But it was a mistake. It is a mistake. You're my Executive Assistant. I don't want to ruin that. I already felt lost not having you for twenty minutes last week." I grip the edge of my desk so I don't reach out and touch her. "Above and beyond that, you and I both have a lot going on. I said I'd help you figure out where you came from. And I have my hands full with this transition from mafia to CEO."

She nods and sniffles. "It's not the right time…"

"Not the right time at all. Besides, you deserve someone far better than me."

She hugs herself and keeps her head down. "I'm sorry. I understand." She turns and walks towards my door. She reaches up to her face. I know she's wiping away a tear.

It's that motion that breaks me. I let go of my desk and follow her. "Raleigh -" But my words are broken when she opens the door, and I see Josh. "Fuck," I whisper to myself. I was hoping she'd agree with me. Maybe tell me she wasn't interested in me. It would have made everything better for both of us.

"What was that all about?" Josh asks with narrowed eyes.

I shake my head. "Nothing. I'll take care of it. We have shit to do." I swallow hard to keep my own tears from falling. What the fuck is wrong with me?

I lead Josh, Damon, Lance, and Gavin to the conference room. Damon Knight has been my friend since we both were kids. He spent more time at my house than he did at his own. Not like his parents gave a shit where he went. If not for me and him joining my crew, he probably would have ended up in prison long ago. Me being in the mafia gave him an outlet for his anger.

Gavin Vandenberg has also been around for most of my life. We met around the same time I'd met Damon, and the three of us became inseparable. Gavin didn't have a bad homelife, but his father wanted him to follow in his footsteps. Gavin couldn't see himself keeping banker's hours behind a desk. I couldn't either. When he refused to follow his dad into his family's business, he was completely cut off. Not like it mattered all that much. He was making more in a month with me than he would've been the entire year had he rolled over and did what his father wanted.

That's not to say they aren't just as close to Josh as they are to me. They are. They are as much brothers to him as I am. Before we took out our father, it was harder for Josh to join us. It didn't help that Jessa had no idea who Josh was or that I had a twin so he couldn't hang out with us when she was around. Which was a lot more often than she wasn't. He wasn't able to celebrate Damon's birthday with us because Jessa was there. They hung out after, but I know he felt distanced from us because of it.

Lance Engle joined my crew later on in college. I needed a hacker. He knew Gavin from college. Gavin recommended him. He fit in well with us. The three of us became close. They've run almost every mission I've ever done with me. When Josh took full reign of Lucinio Mafia, they seamlessly made the move with everyone else and accepted Josh as their boss. It made my transition out a lot easier, too. I didn't have to worry if they'd be okay.

Josh sits next to me at the conference table and pins me with a glare. I should have known he wouldn't let that go. "What happened?" he asks.

I sit down with a sigh as everyone settles. "Really. It was nothing."

"Alex. I know you're fucking tells. You're upset. She's upset. What the fuck happened?" Josh leans back in his chair. He doesn't take his eyes off me.

Gavin glances towards the door. "I thought you two were getting along. All happy and hunky-dory or whatever the fuck."

"I would chuckle, but I feel like my heart is broken." I lean forward as the room falls silent. Everyone's eyes are on me. "Can we just get to the reason you wanted to come in here?"

"Not a chance in hell," Damon says. His elbow is resting against Lance's arm. I've questioned several times if those two have something going on, but it's between them. I figure they'll tell me one day.

Just as I'm about to tell him that hell is where he can go, Raleigh quietly comes in with lunch. Whatever it is smells delicious, but not as good as she does. She doesn't even have to be near me, and I already can smell her scent. Honey. Vanilla. Something as sweet as she is.

I may have made a grave mistake. I say nothing as I watch her walk out of the room, but I'm fighting myself on every single level not to chase her. I don't know what she's done to me, but now that I've moved on from accusing her of being a vindictive and evil liar, all I want is her near me. All the damn time. I can't stop thinking of her silky hair tangled around my fingers.

"Raleigh, stay and eat something," Josh says.

Raleigh stops at the door leading back out of the conference room. I silently thank my brother. "No. It's okay. I'm not really hungry," she says quietly. "I'll grab your drinks." She slips out without another word.

"Alright. Spill." Lance crosses his arms over his chest. Each of my friends is pinning me with the same intense glare Josh is.

I sigh. I know they won't drop it. "I kissed her last week. I told you all she laid into me. I realized a few things. We moved on from it. But what I didn't tell you is that I pinned her against the wall before she could walk out the door and kissed her."

"Christ, Alex," Josh growls.

I put up a hand to ward off the lecture. "I know. Okay. I know. I haven't been able to stop fucking thinking about it. So, today, I told her it can't happen again. I told her it isn't that I don't want it to. It just can't."

Gavin shakes his head. "Man, have I taught you nothing about women over the years?"

"Just tell me what's going on with that fucking account," I growl between gritted teeth. I don't want to talk about Raleigh.

"Okay, okay. The account. You know it's gone back for a while. Different companies, same accounts. The companies we know are cover companies. Not legit," Josh starts.

Lance leans forward and picks up where he left off. "We found the origin. Well, Robby found the origin. I just stood back and watched. He traced it to an L.A. mob. I say mob because these guys act more like gang members than an organized crime unit. They have a lot of territory, though. And it's all territory that was Lucinio Mafia's. When your father was running it."

I narrow my eyes. "So, it's pretty clear whoever this is was working for him."

Josh nods. "I don't think they know Matthew is dead, though. I don't think it's reached them yet. They act like they've been pretty sheltered and protected from the law. I have Cole asking a few of his contacts with LAPD if they've heard of these guys since Matthew was taken out and not protecting them anymore."

Cole Westwood is a guy I met during college. He was friends with Jessa. She even lived with him after we broke up. They may have dated a while, but it's not something I cared to really ask about. He was an integral part in helping me save Jessa from Matthew's clutches back then. He's been a part of my crew since and also made a seamless transition to Josh. When we all decided to move to Chicago, he made the move with us and transferred to Chicago Police Department.

I look up when Raleigh comes back in with our drinks but continue on with the conversation, hoping that my body will follow suit and ignore her as well. Of course, it doesn't. It's never listened to me when it comes to her. I'm hyper-aware to every move she makes.

I take a breath. "So, who is it?"

Josh smiles. "Vacello." He watches as my eyes shoot open wide. "I know what you're thinking. That was one of the first gangs he had us take out. Looks like he took out the leaders. Maybe they didn't want to cooperate. Then he rebuilt them with people who would fall to his whims."

My eyes follow Raleigh as she quietly leaves the room again. "I hate to say this, but it makes sense." I reach for the food and start building a sandwich, suddenly needing to do anything but think about Raleigh.

"We're going to see what Cole finds out, then I'll grab a crew to deal with it," Josh says. He follows my lead and begins building a sandwich.

I take a bite and choke back the moan. The ham is fucking delicious. "So, it all leads back -"

"Alex!" Raleigh's scream cuts through the entire top floor. It seems to bounce off the windows and walls. We all jump up and sprint to the door. "Josh! Alex! Help!"

Josh is the first one out, but I've pushed past everyone else and almost reach him when I see Raleigh. She turns her terrified eyes on me as someone pulls her into the elevator.

"Raleigh!" I yell. My heart has stopped beating in my chest. I don't know how I'm still moving.

Josh and I reach the elevator just as the doors close. We both slam into them. Gavin, Lance, and Damon reach us as we're turning. I can't think. I can't speak. I feel like my ribs are going to crack with how fast I'm breathing. I'm sure my lungs can't keep up with me.

"Alex!" she screams again as the elevator starts its descent.

I run to her desk and dial security. When I hear them pick up, I don't wait for an answer. "Stop the Executive elevator now!" I'm panting as I watch the numbers above the doors keep ticking down. "Fucking stop it!"

"We're trying, sir," he says as calmly as he can. He's trained for that. Just like I am. Be calm in an intense situation. "Stopped. Floor sixty-two."

"Send everyone you've got up here right now!" I drop the phone and run to the stairs that Gavin, Lance, Damon, and Josh are already running down. All I can hear echoing through my ears is Raleigh's screams.

Chapter Eleven

☙ Raleigh ❧

"Alex!" I scream as a hand clamps over my mouth again.

"Stop screaming! I'm not going to fucking hurt you! Fuck!"

But I don't listen. "Alex!" I fight and push at my attacker. I bite the hand he has covering my mouth.

"Fuck! You bitch!" He yanks my hair and throws me against the elevator wall.

"Alex!" Tears are streaming down my face, but I do all I can to keep the attacker away from me.

"Your dick boss isn't going to save you, so stop screaming for him!"

I recognize his voice. I know I've heard it before. I know I've seen his greasy face before. And the cologne. It's overpowering. I recognize it from somewhere. I just wish I could remember where.

The elevator jolts to a stop. I fall back against the wall. The railing hits my lower back. I whimper as I sink to the ground. I curl up into the corner because it's the farthest I can get away from where he fell.

He glares at me. "What did you do?"

"Nothing!"

When he scrambles to his feet, I do the same. There's no way I'm going to put myself at a disadvantage to him. His glare turns more vicious, but then I see something else. Something more... visceral. My eyes widen when I realize who he is.

He looks at the buttons on the elevator and starts pushing them. When the elevator doesn't move, he turns his sickening eyes on me once more. He stalks towards me. I duck out of his reach, but I know he'll catch me eventually. This elevator isn't that big. There's only so many places I can go.

"You're that guy from Starbucks. I thought you were fired. How did you get access to the elevator?" I narrow my eyes at him.

He grins. "I have my sources. I guess since we're stuck here, I might as well have a little fun." He lunges for me.

I step out of the way, prepared to fight. I wipe my eyes and pray with all I am that someone monitoring the cameras has seen what's happening. I may not understand what happened with me and Alex, but I trust that he runs a tight ship. Someone will have seen what's happening. There are cameras all over the place.

I'm sure Alex alerted them even if they haven't seen what's happening. He saw me. He got to the elevator just as the doors closed. I could hear him and Josh both pound on the doors as the car started to move.

"Stay away from me. I'm warning you." I try to make myself appear tougher and braver. It doesn't work. Even I can hear the quiver in my voice.

He laughs. "Please. I'm bigger than you in every way. If you'd just shut-up and come with me, we wouldn't be in this situation."

"I'm not going anywhere with you."

He looks around the elevator. "Looks to me like you already are." He lunges again, but I kick my leg out. My foot meets his shin, and I dive to the side again. "Ow!" He grips his shin and collapses against the side of the elevator.

"Stay away from me!" I scream.

"Raleigh!" I jump almost a mile when Alex slams his fists against the doors of the elevator. "Raleigh, I'm coming!"

"Alex!" I jump towards the elevator doors, but Starbucks guy catches me around the waist. He slams me against the wall of the elevator.

I scream and try to push away, but he has me pinned. His chest is against my back. "Alex! Help!" I push back with all my might.

We both tumble backwards and hit the floor. I struggle to get away, but his grip is strong. I don't give up. I struggle and claw my way away from him. I can see the elevator doors are being pried open. I scramble towards it. Before they are even all the way open, I crawl through them and launch myself at Alex.

"I got you. I got you. You're safe," he whispers in my ear.

I can feel all of the fight I just had in me evaporate. I sink down his body until my knees hit the floor. Alex sits on the floor and pulls me in his lap. He wraps his arms around me as I cry and sways gently with me.

I grip his shirt hard and bury my face in his shoulder. "H-he tr-tried t-to -" A sob cuts me off.

"Ssh… Ssh… I got you. I got you now. You're okay. You're safe." He tangles his fingers in my hair and holds me close and tight to him. "Go back to work," he growls. "Now."

I don't look up, but I know he's talking to the people on this floor. They must have gathered around when they heard and saw the commotion. I instinctively know I'll be the talk of the entire company.

I wipe my eyes. "I want to go home," I whisper.

"I know. I know, baby." I feel his lips on my neck, but don't dare read too much into it. He's just comforting me.

"Want us to take her with us?" I feel Josh's hand on my back.

"No. I don't want her out of my sight. Go. Deal with him. I'll take care of her."

I feel Josh put an arm around me. He kisses my head and stands. I don't know how long Alex holds me on the floor, but I'm not really sure I care. I feel safe. I don't want him to let me go for anything in the world.

"I want to go home," I whisper into his neck using his sexy and intoxicating scent to calm me.

"I know, baby." He pulls away, but only slightly. "We need to get up, okay?"

I nod, but don't let go of him. "Okay."

"Good girl." He shifts and stands, picking me up with him. He lifts me easily in his arms.

I bury my face in his neck and wrap my arms around his shoulders. I close my eyes and let him take me wherever he's taking me. I feel weak.

The adrenaline is gone. Left in its wake is a bone deep exhaustion that makes me just want to sleep and forget about everything.

"I just want to go home. I'm not cut out for this."

"Ssh…" He kisses my cheek. "You're safe, honey. I got you." He steps off the elevator and carries me a few moments. I hear a door lock and am suddenly surrounded by his masculine scent. There's only one place I know that smells completely like him.

His office.

I open my eyes and pull back slightly as he sits down on the couch. I blink at him, slightly confused, but give up trying to understand. I'm not sure I care enough to question why we're in his office and not in his car on the way home. So, instead, I bury my head back into his shoulder and let him soothe my racing heart.

He tangles his hand in my hair and presses his lips against my neck. "I'm sorry. I'm sorry for what I said. I was sitting in that meeting with Josh thinking about you. While nothing has changed about my opinion on all of the reasons we can't do this, Raleigh, I…" He takes a deep shaky breath. My grip on him tightens, afraid of what he's going to say and anticipating it just as much. "I want to try."

My fingers curl around the barely there hair at the nape of his neck. "What does that mean?" I whisper.

"It means I'm afraid that if I fuck up, I'll not only lose you as my girl, but also my Executive Assistant. I don't think I can handle either of those scenarios. I haven't opened myself up to any woman except one. I know now that we weren't meant to be, but when I lost her, I ran as far as I could. All the way to Italy. Things worked out with me and Jessa. She's an incredible friend. She's like family to me now, but then? It was a devastating loss I barely survived. As soon as I saw that son of a bitch with his arm around your neck dragging you into the elevator, I knew right then that losing you will destroy me. I'm not even going to try and deny my feelings for you. They've been simmering under the surface. I've tried to shove them away, but I can't. Not anymore. I don't want to. I just want you."

Butterflies take flight in my heart and stomach. His words are words I've wanted to hear for so long. Now that he's said them, I don't know what to do with them. So, I just nod and swallow down the lump forming in my throat.

I snuggle myself closer to him and cling to him. I'm afraid if I let go, I'll wake up and it will have just been my worst nightmare turned into the most beautiful dream. I don't want to wake up. I want to hear those words forever.

He wants me.

Alex stays quiet as I listen to the steady beat of his heart.

When I open my eyes again, the office is dark, and I don't feel Alex. My heart leaps into my throat. I make a strangled sound I don't recognize and sit up quickly. My eyes fight to adjust to the dark while I struggle to keep the panic under control.

"Alex?" I squeak.

"I'm right here, honey." Like magic, his arms wrap around me again.

I instantly relax and melt into him. "I'm sorry."

"Don't. Don't be. You went through a fuck of an ordeal. I don't blame you at all for being on edge." He runs his fingers through my hair and hugs me close.

"I was afraid you'd left."

"Not a chance in hell. I had to finish running the background program I have for accounting and pull the records. It took a little longer than I thought. That's all. I just finished. I'm going to bring what I discovered home. Josh wants to speak with both of us about what he found out."

"It was that kid from Starbucks that you fired…"

"I know, honey. I recognized him right away."

I feel tears sting my eyes. "I didn't… It took me time. I knew I recognized him, but I couldn't place him. Maybe if I had -"

"Raleigh, no. Stop it, baby. We're not doing this. You didn't do a damn thing wrong. Judging from the crying heap we pulled from the elevator, I'd say you handled yourself well."

I shake my head and sniffle. "I just kicked him in the leg. He… hurt me worse."

Alex takes a shaky breath but lets out a dangerous growl that sends shivers down my spine. "I saw the bruises. And I assure you, he will never ever have the opportunity to touch you again."

I nod slowly at the words. The threat behind them should make me fear him and run, but it has the exact opposite effect on me. They make me fall more in love with him.

Love. It's the first time I've really allowed myself to think of that word in relation to Alex, but there's no other word to describe what I feel for him. It's never been lust with me. There's always been something about him that was beyond what I understood and could describe.

After a few moments of allowing myself to feel nothing but Alex, I pull back just enough to look up at him. Even in the dark, his blue eyes shimmer. I reach up and run my fingers through the stubble on his chin before placing my hand over his heart.

"What did you find out with the program you ran?" I ask quietly.

"Uh… I don't know, actually. If what I'm thinking is anything to go off, though, I think we have a very large inside problem on our hands."

I nod and let out a sad sigh. "I was really hoping that wouldn't be the case."

"So was I. My accountant has been with this company since it first started. It's hard for me to believe he'd do something like this."

"Maybe he didn't…" I say the words, but my heart sinks because I don't know if I believe the words myself. Though, I want to.

Alex leans in and brushes my hair back from my face. He tangles his fingers in the locks and tugs gently as his lips meet mine. My insides melt, just like the first time, except this time everything feels different. Less hurried.

When his tongue teases my lips open, I close my eyes and let him take me to the place only he can. Somewhere higher than the clouds. I tangle my fingers in the fabric of his shirt when he pulls me closer and give into the feeling I've wanted since he first rocked my world with his heated kiss only days ago. So much has happened that it feels like a lifetime ago.

Alex pulls away slowly. "How do you feel?" He cups my cheek.

I lean into his hand as I open my eyes. "Okay… I still want to go home."

"I know, honey. I would have let you go with Josh, but I couldn't make myself leave your side."

I shake my head. "I wouldn't have wanted you to."

"Let's get home. I'm done here. I canceled everything for tomorrow. It's going to make more work for us. We still need to catch up on what we were already working to catch up on, but you're more important."

I blush as he stands. He takes my hand and grabs the things he needs. I follow him out of his office and wait for him to lock up. He keeps me close to his side when we step in the elevator and doesn't push me away when I close my eyes and turn into him, burying my face in his chest to avoid the visuals being in here brings to the very forefront of my mind. He sweetly kisses the top of my head and leads me to his car.

I pause next to mine when I realize I drove. "Alex…"

He shakes his head. "I'll send someone for the car, baby. I'm not letting you out of my sight."

I nod, grateful. I didn't want to drive home by myself. I feel a hundred years older and frail. It's a strange feeling. My mind is all over the place. I'm still not certain if I'm dreaming or not. I feel like I'm hovering above my own body.

"Nothing feels real," I whisper when Alex starts driving. I hug myself.

He reaches over and lays a hand on my thigh. He squeezes gently. "It's a natural reaction to processing trauma, honey. I remember you felt the same way after we took out Matthew."

I'm both surprised he even knows that and upset he can say that so casually. But we've made so much progress, so I say nothing. I sniffle and look out the window. The city flies by as Alex speeds through the streets. I'm hoping he's oblivious to my mood change.

I know there's a deep-rooted hatred of Matthew throughout the Lucinio family. Even the Crane's. Alex's mother, Rebekkah, was taken from her family, the Crane's, and spent most of her life under his control. When they thought they'd killed Matthew the first time, she never bothered contacting her family because she didn't think they cared about her at all. She had no idea they had all been told she was dead.

I know all of the terrible things he did, but I keep going back and forth. My heart hurts at the fact that the only man I've ever known as my father is gone. It hurts even more because I have no family to speak of.

Of course, I go back to being angry again. How dare he do that to me? Did he kidnap me? What did he do to my parents? Did he kill them? How could he lie to me my whole life? Is that why he homeschooled me? Because he knew my adoption wasn't legal? Did he change my name? Who am I? Is my name even Raleigh?

I squeeze my eyes shut to the tears and try to focus on Alex. His scent surrounds me. His hand on my thigh is comforting. He's gently rubbing it with his thumb. And he wants to be with me. He said he did. No more avoiding. No more dancing around it. At least, I hope.

"Hey," Alex says quietly. I open my eyes slowly and realize we're parked in front of Josh's house. I look over at him. He leaves his hand on my thigh and leans over. He kisses me softly. "I thought I lost you there."

I shake my head and sniffle. "Please don't ever lose me," I whisper, fighting the tears.

He squeezes my thigh and kisses me softly. He runs his thumb over my lower lip. "Never happening." He slowly lets go of my thigh and gets out of the car. I take a breath before opening my door. He's at my side before I even stand. "Ready?"

"I don't know." I close my door and take the hand he offers. He leads me inside the house. I follow like a lost puppy unable to function without him. It's not a typical feeling, but I don't have the energy to be strong.

Alex leads me into the living room and sits in a chair. I panic slightly because I really don't want to be away from him. I'm still feeling vulnerable, and while I feel safe with every single person in this room, he calms me. He makes me feel safest.

Thankfully, Alex pulls me into his lap. It takes me a moment of warring with myself. I'm not sure if either of us are ready to be so open about something so new. In the end, I decide I don't care. If a person can't be honest in front of their family, then who can they be honest in front of? At least Alex has a family to share it with.

I forcefully push all thoughts like that out of my head. I know that his family has accepted me as one of their own. It's just something I struggle with. No one here is related to me by blood. I fight with myself every single day because I really do like all of them. I'm glad they accept me. But I feel like a burden to them. Just another girl they've saved from a tough situation. It's an everyday battle I know I shouldn't be having.

"First off," Josh says as he sits on the couch nearest to us. "Are you doing okay, Raleigh?"

I lay my head on Alex's shoulder. "I'm trying to be. I'm struggling with what happened and why," I say honestly and quietly.

"I have those answers. I can't say either of you will like it, but it's something to go on." Josh reaches over and pats my thigh.

Damon leans back and kicks his stockinged feet up on the table. Lance sits next to him. He looks just as tired as me. Gavin stays standing, though. He has his fingers locked behind his head as he stretches.

"How did someone I fired end up with access to our floor?" Alex asks. It's a question I've been wondering since I first realized who he was.

"Good question," Gavin answers. "According to him, it was given to him. He doesn't know by who, but it's someone who goes to the coffee shop he works at across the street from Lucinio Tech at the same time every day."

"I can look at the security footage," Lance says. "But I don't know who I'm looking for. I thought you and I could do that. See if you recognize anyone. We know he was given the card between nine and ten this morning and was given a grand upfront. Upon delivery, he was to get another grand."

"Wait," I say sitting up. Fear clenches my heart as my eyes widen. "That means he was supposed to deliver me to someone."

Damon nods. "We're pretty sure it was to the guy who gave him the card. Which is why we've decided until we figure out who this guy is, you won't be going into the office."

I take a deep breath as my heart races out of control. My eyes dart around the room. "I can't leave Alex to -"

"Baby, don't. Stop." Alex pulls me against him again. "I'm with them. I don't want you going in either."

I look at him. "But you -"

He shakes his head and puts one finger on my lips to silence me. "There is no negotiation on this. Hopefully, we'll be able to figure it out quickly and you can come back right away. We have tomorrow to deal with it. If we can't figure it out, then I'm absolutely not letting you step foot in that office. All of my security measures were completely walked through. That's something right there that pisses me off beyond belief, and I need to deal with that. Until I'm positive you'll be safe, I'm not allowing you to come back. I'm sorry if that makes me an asshole, but I'm not letting you in that building unless I know you're safe."

I don't bother arguing with him. I know there isn't a point. And I trust him. I know he doesn't want me in harm's way. Hell. I feel better about not being in the office anyway. Not until whoever tried to kidnap me is no longer employed there.

What angers me is that I don't know why I suddenly became a target. "Why is this happening?" I ask. "I haven't done anything to anyone."

"Another good question," Josh's deep baritone voice answers. "We don't have a full answer, but we do have an idea. While Gavin was…" He glances at me then Alex before standing. "While Gavin was coercing him into giving answers, he said that all he knew was that he was supposed to take you and bring you to the person who hired him so that he could gather information from you. He didn't know what kind of information, but Damon thinks it might have to do with your week-long look into Lucinio Tech's accounts. I don't know if that's what it is. I'm not going to sit here and pretend that's exactly what it is for certain. But I will say it makes sense. Until we figure out who the person behind it is, though, I can't know for sure."

I just nod as I hug myself and tuck my feet into the chair. Alex keeps a firm hold on me as he starts talking to everyone in the room about next steps. I try to listen because part of me wants to know what they're planning, but I can't.

A few months ago, I was a normal seventeen-year-old who was looking forward to her eighteenth birthday and going to the university of her dreams. In such a short amount of time, everything was taken away from me, including my identity.

Now, I'm sitting on my boss' lap in the middle of a mafia boss' living room discussing an attempt on my life. Or rather an attempt at kidnapping me. Not like I wasn't technically already kidnapped. By the same people in this room.

What is that called? Stockholm syndrome? When you start feeling safe with your captors and fall in love with one of them? Yeah. I'm a fucking mess.

Though, if I'm being honest, I wasn't exactly kidnapped. After Josh had all of the information he wanted from me, he said I was free to go. It was my choice to stay because I didn't have anywhere to go. I no longer had a family and don't know if I even have a biological one anyway. At the time, it seemed like staying was the best option.

Now all I want is to stay.

Chapter Twelve

🍎 Alex 🍎

"This is the timeframe we'd be looking for," Lance says quietly.

I squint at the screen of his laptop. "It's lunchtime. A lot of people leave around that time."

Damon yawns. "What about outside cameras? Do they give us a wide enough view to look across the street towards that coffee shop?"

Lance glances at him. "Let me check." He pushes a few keys and brings up another angle for the camera view.

"Realistically, how many people go to that coffee shop anyway? It's a pretty popular place." Gavin takes a drink of his imported bottle of beer.

"It has to be someone who knew we were looking at accounts," I mumble.

Josh leans against the mantle. "Who knew?"

I look up at him. "My security. My accountant."

"And of those people, who has access to the Executive elevator?" Josh asks.

"All of them. Security does. My accountant does. He's had it since we first transferred our offices to Chicago because he was running the company while I transitioned."

I look down at Raleigh when she stirs. She crashed about an hour ago with her head in my lap. I give the girl credit for wanting to help, but I knew she wouldn't last. Not after an adrenaline dump like she had. I run my fingers soothingly through her hair. She stills once more.

"There's a lot of people coming and going," Damon says as he leans back. "This is looking pretty fucking oblique." He starts rubbing Lance's back when he stretches.

"Maybe we should revisit this after we've had a little sleep," Gavin mumbles with his eyes closed.

I chuckle. "Too bad we don't have coffee shop boy to identify the fucker. Should have waited a bit before you killed him."

Gavin grins, but doesn't open his eyes. "Who said I killed him?"

I look up at him a little surprised. "You mean you didn't?"

"Not yet. Even was nice enough to patch him up so he didn't bleed out on us. I thought we might need him."

"You are a sick son of bitch. Why the hell are we friends?" I smile widely.

Gavin opens his eyes and sets his beer down. "Please. Like you haven't had a little fun fucking some people up. He's still downstairs in the dungeon of torture."

Josh lets out a quiet burst of laughter. "Asshole. It's a basement that ain't finished yet. And the only reason we took him down there is because Ryan has something big going on, and he's using my shed to keep everyone he captured separated."

I shake my head. "You both are a fucking match made in Hell." I glance down at Raleigh. "Let me put her to bed. Then we'll go down there and ask questions."

"Best thing I heard all night," Gavin drawls.

Damon snorts. "You ain't even a little Southern. That sounded like a dude from L.A. trying to be all tough and sexy at the same time. You failed."

Gavin laughs. "Works on the ladies."

"You all are a bunch of idiots. I'm the only sane one. It's a fact I've known for a long time and only now decided to admit. My whole fucking family is nothing but lunatics." I grin as they all quietly laugh.

I gently shift Raleigh, careful not to wake her. I breathe a quiet sigh of relief when I get her in my arms without her waking up. I kiss her forehead when she subconsciously wraps her arms around my neck. I carry her up the stairs to her room. She's beautiful all the time, but something about the soft, peaceful smile on her lips right now catapults her to the next level. She's the most gorgeous woman I've ever seen.

I gently lay her down in her bed and pull the covers up. I can't imagine she's too comfortable sleeping in the clothing she's wearing, but I don't think we're to the point in our relationship where stripping her down would be appropriate. Although, seeing what she's wearing underneath the top layers wouldn't upset me in the slightest.

"Alex?" she asks quietly as I tuck the blankets around her.

"Yeah, honey?"

"Thank you for saving me today."

I chuckle and sit on the edge of her bed. I lean down and kiss her softly as I push her hair out of her face. "I don't think I did much saving. All I did was have the elevator stopped. Seemed like you did the rest with your well-timed and well-placed kick."

She smiles as she sits up slowly. Her blankets fall to her waist and I'm keenly aware that she's taking off her pants. She's mostly covered, but with the light from her window, I can't stop myself from seeing a glimpse of silk and black. I clear my throat and turn away, but I can't bring myself to stand and walk to her door like I should.

Out of the corner of my eye, I can see her pull the blankets up higher and hide herself while she removes her shirt and her bra. She lets everything fall to the floor and holds the blanket close to her with one hand while she points to a t-shirt draped over the back of the chair by her desk.

"Can you grab that t-shirt for me?"

I don't dare say anything. I just stand and grab the t-shirt. I hand it to her, thankful it's dark. I'm all too aware of my dick trying to stand straight out and rubbing very painfully against the front of my pants. I don't need her seeing that.

She puts the t-shirt on behind her covers. My breath quickens because I can just make out the outline of the side of her tits just before she pulls the t-shirt down. I chastise myself because I shouldn't be looking, but holy hell. It's hard not to.

I sit back on the edge of her bed and adjust myself as discreetly as I can. My hard cock is painful, but it's way too soon for any of the very improper thoughts speeding through my mind to become a reality. Instead, I lean over when she's settled and tuck her back in again. I kiss her, tangling my fingers in her hair, because I need to touch her.

When she lets out a quiet moan into my mouth, though, I know it was a terrible mistake. My brain tries to stop my hand from moving down her neck to her collarbone. It tries to keep my lips on her mouth instead of trailing down her jaw to her throat. When she swallows and quietly whimpers, I'm gone.

My thumb flicks across her already hardened nipple over her shirt. She arches up and gasps. I groan when my dick twitches, begging for the release I've denied it for too long. I kiss along her jaw to her neck and tug her hair as I squeeze her tit gently, running my palm over her nipple.

She arches into me with another gasp again and spears her fingers into my hair. I'm dizzy. My mind goes fuzzy with delirium. A primal need that makes my entire body buzz. I don't know how I manage it, but I pull away slowly. We're both breathing heavily. I keep my hand tangled in her hair and shakily move my other one up her body.

I run my thumb over her lip. "You're going to be so much trouble for me."

She smiles and brazenly nips my thumb before sucking it into her mouth. She looks up through hooded eyes when she lets it go. I shake my head with a smile and lean down once more. My lips meet hers again, but I force the kiss to be slow and sweet. I pull away just as slowly as I'd kissed her.

She moans quietly and lets her hands trail from my hair down my shoulders and neck. She rests them on my chest. "Maybe I'm tired of being the good girl."

I grin and shake my head. "Maybe it's time for you to close your eyes and go to sleep." I kiss the tip of her nose and make myself stand.

I can hear the strangled pout. "Fine."

"I'm not done with you, Raleigh." My voice is hoarse. "But I'm taking my time. We're both going to enjoy this ride."

She smiles and pulls the blanket up further so it covers the lower half of her face as she turns to her side. I groan and don't try to hide the adjustment I make to myself as I turn. Her giggling as I close the door is damn near my undoing. I lean against the wall and will my dick to behave before I go back down there and make a fool out of myself.

After a few minutes of forcing my blood to return to all parts of my body instead of just my dick, I finally make my way downstairs. Gavin, Damon, and Lance are all waiting for me, but Josh seems to be MIA.

I raise an eyebrow. "Where's the boss?"

"Security called. He didn't say what was going on. Just rolled his eyes and said to start without him." Gavin starts heading for the stairs that lead to the basement.

We all follow. Gavin flips on a light. Laying on a cot in the middle of the room is the kid from the coffee shop. For a moment, I'm a little baffled he's allowed to run free in the basement. Then I see he's handcuffed to the cot, which is bolted to the floor. Clever.

I'm not at all surprised to see the beating he took. Gavin does not and has never fucked around when it came to getting information. The kid's eye is swelling shut. His lip is bleeding. There are scratches all over his arm. His clothes are torn.

I cross my arms over my chest and grin. "Damn. What the fuck did you do?"

Gavin laughs. "Just had some fun. He thought he could fight his way out." Gavin takes out his switchblade and kneels in front of the kid. "He found out pretty quick he couldn't." He runs the blade down his arm, leaving a scratch that doesn't bleed.

The kid whimpers. "Just let me go."

"No chance of that happening," Gavin growls. "You fucked up, pretty boy. Messed with the wrong girl. Got in with the wrong crowd."

The kid pulls hard on the cuffs and lets out a guttural cry. "You can't do this!"

"I do really like when they still have fight left." Gavin gives him a maniacal grin. "You help us out, we'll talk about what we can do for you. Fair?"

The kid gives him a hopeful look. It quickly falls from his face when Josh starts coming down the stairs. He slumps when he sees my brother. I'm pretty sure he starts crying. It makes me wonder what the fuck happened when I was with Raleigh.

"I'm done fucking around, kid. We're showing you some video. You're telling us who paid you off. The lead turns out?" Josh crosses his arms over his chest and shrugs. "I let you live. I can't say you'll see the sunrise, but your blood won't be on my hands. But you jerk us around, they'll never find your body. You understand me?"

The kid sputters. "You gotta protect me! They'll kill me!"

Josh shrugs again. "That's on you. It ain't on me. You're the one who made the decision to get involved in something obviously bigger than you."

"Why the hell would I tell you anything if you're not going to protect me?"

"Because if you don't…" Josh glances at Gavin. "I won't stop Mr. Vandenberg from finishing you off. And you know how much he'll enjoy it." Josh's voice is low and dangerous.

The kid very wisely sits up. He's hunched because his wrist is attached to the leg of the cot, but he looks at us. "The guy works for someone. He said if I didn't do what he said and take the money, his boss would just make me do what he wanted and dispose of me after. He said by doing what he says, I'll at least have some protection."

"Now we're getting somewhere." Josh kneels and signals for Lance.

Lance kneels and turns his laptop. "Tell me who you recognize. Don't lie to me. I'll know."

The kid watches the screen for several minutes. I'm starting to think he isn't going to say anything. I'm having a hard time thinking that the person who gave him the access card and hired him took that long to leave the building.

Finally, he points. "Him."

Lance pauses the screen. "Show me."

He points. "That one."

Lance turns the computer to me. "Recognize him?"

My heart both sinks and speeds up at the same time. "Yep." I turn and start walking up the stairs. I don't really give a shit what happens to him anymore. I'm not involved in that aspect of things. Not anymore.

If Josh lets him go and leaves him to his own devices, the kid will be dead by morning. And it won't be on our hands. It will be on the hands of whoever hired him. If he kills him, it will be a mercy kill. Either way, unless Josh chooses to protect him, there's no fucking way he's getting out of this alive.

"Hey, hold up," Josh says behind me.

I turn and wait for him to meet me in the kitchen. He closes the basement door behind him. I lean against the counter. He grabs a bottle of water and hands it to me. I twist the cap off and take a long drink. My heart starts to calm.

"Fucking accountant's assistant," I tell him. "He doesn't have an access badge. He had to have gotten it from Samson."

"The accountant."

"Yep."

"Which means he stole it or it was given to him."

"Samson wouldn't do that."

"I think we need to have a conversation with him."

"I agree." I take out my phone and start to dial. But I'm cut off by a blood-curdling scream that doesn't sound human. I look towards the basement. "The hell?"

"That was female," Josh says. "And it came from upstairs."

"Raleigh."

Josh and I both take off running up the stairs. We pull our guns as we run. When we get to the top, Josh holds up an arm to stop me. Years of training kicks in, and I stop in my tracks. We silently walk to Raleigh's door. I fight every part of me to bust open the door. I, instead, force myself to rely on my training.

Josh puts one hand on the door knob. The other readies his weapon. I raise my Glock, preparing to not only cover him but also to defend Raleigh. Just as Josh starts to push the door, it flies open. Raleigh, dressed in just the skimpy t-shirt and panties I left her in, streaks through the door.

I catch her as Josh scans the room, his Glock at the ready. She starts to talk, but I put a finger to my mouth and push her down the hall towards Josh's room. I pray to Hell she knows what I want her to do and does it without fighting or asking questions while I keep an eye on my brother and gun trained to back him up.

Thankfully, Raleigh does exactly what I want her to and makes a dash for Josh's room. I watch her out of the corner of my eye as I start following Josh into her room. When she's safely behind the door and it's securely closed, my attention is solely on her bedroom and any shadow that might start moving.

Josh and I check every nook and cranny, including under her bed. We check her closet. Her private bathroom. There's no one in the room, but the glass of the sliding door leading to her balcony is shattered. The cold Chicago breeze is blowing her curtains in the wind.

"What the fuck happened?" I growl.

Josh steps onto the balcony and sweeps the yard. "Security called me because they thought they'd seen someone sneaking onto the property. When I looked at the cameras, it looked like a black shadow at the bottom of the screen." He takes out his phone and dials a number. "I told them to be alert." He ducks back into Raleigh's room. "Ry, it's Josh. Get your ass over. Get guards on everyone. Security breach." He hangs up without saying another word.

I'm still amazed that my brother speaks the way he does to Ryan Crane. No one, including myself, has ever given Ryan an order. My brother seems to take no issue with it. Maybe that's why he was and always has been the one who was meant to take over Lucinio Mafia. Josh Lucinio fears no fucking one.

I follow him inside after seeing no one out there. "What the hell, Josh?"

"Go get Raleigh." He has his phone to his ear once more and is barking orders.

I close her door and beeline for Josh's room. I reach for the door knob. Locked. Good girl. "Raleigh. It's me, baby. Open up."

It takes her a few moments, but I eventually hear the door open. She only opens it a crack so she can see it's really me. When she does, she opens it wider and wipes her eyes as she steps into my arms. I wrap her as tightly as I can against my body and sway gently with her until I feel her racing heart start to steady.

"What happened?" she whispers.

I tangle my fingers in her hair. "I wish I knew." I kiss her neck. "Let's get you some clothes. I'm not leaving you alone."

"Alex!" Ryan calls from the foot of the stairs. Raleigh jumps.

"Yeah?"

"Pack her a bag. We're going into lockdown."

"What does lockdown mean?" She looks up at me both curiously and fearfully.

"It means there's a breach. You're going to the safest place on the property."

"And… where's that…?"

I take a deep breath. "With Ryan. We haven't finished all of the construction for the compound, but we're eventually going to have a safe room in every single house. Right now, it wasn't feasible to do that. We needed to get everyone's houses built."

"So… he has a safe room…?"

"All of the Crane's do right now. They were all installed when the rest of the construction was going on. The next phase is the safe rooms and an underground bunker accessible from each house. It might seem like overkill, but we're two very powerful mafia families. We constantly have someone chasing us."

She takes a deep breath and pulls slowly away. "Okay…" She squares her shoulders and walks slowly to her room.

I gently take her wrist before she opens the door, though. "Let me." I take out my Glock once more. She obediently steps back and waits for me.

I feel a stabbing pain spread through my chest. She's resigned herself to this being her life now. Seeing how sad it makes her breaks me.

I'll never be able to force this life on her. No matter how I feel about her. I don't know that I'll ever be able to fully leave it behind me.

Which means if I truly love her like I think I do, I may have to let her go…

Chapter Thirteen

❦ Raleigh ❦

I sigh for the umpteenth time and burrow deeper into the giant quilt I've wrapped myself in. I throw my book and let out something between another sigh and a groan. I pick up my phone and scroll through random videos on social media before finally giving that up, too. Dallas is in school. Alex is God knows where. I'm bored.

Damon chuckles across from me. "I've never seen anyone so restless. Are you really that bored?"

I shoot him what I hope is a withering glare. "I'm not restless."

He barks out a laugh. "I call bullshit."

I whine and stand up. I pace the library in Josh's house. My place of solitude has become a prison. "I don't like not being able to do anything. Why can't I go to work, at least?"

Damon calmly and patiently puts his own book down on the table. "Because you're a target, Raleigh. They've already gotten to you once while at work."

I narrow my eyes. "They got me here, too. At Fort Knox."

Damon chuckles. "This is more like Camp David. Ryan's house is Fort Knox." He stands and comes to stand next to me at the window I'm whimsically looking out. "Look. I know you ain't used to this. This has been my life. It's all I've ever known. And I mean that. I was basically raised a Lucinio. I spent more time with Josh and Alex and their mother than I ever did at home. Matthew, despite how truly fucked up he was, was more of a father to me than my own father was. So, I'm used to this shit. I know you aren't. It's hard. I get it. But you have to trust us. I get how difficult that is. It's not unlike what happened to Josh's ex-girlfriend. She was very quickly and very much thrown into a world unfamiliar to her."

"Josh's ex-girlfriend? He's mentioned her a couple of times, I think. Was that the one at Robby and Luke's party? Just after I got here? They're still good friends, right?"

"They are. Her name is Lyric. She's like a little sister to all of us. They broke up because they just felt they were better friends. But they're still very close. We all are. We have a memorial every single year for the child they lost to a miscarriage."

"Oh my Gosh." My heart breaks for the woman I've only met briefly, and the man who I'm quickly starting to consider my own family. "That's awful." I clutch my heart.

"As Josh always says. It's painful. But they'll never forget him. They have a memorial every single year for him. They have a garden that's dedicated to him. He's laid to rest right with Ryan's parents."

I nod. "So, that's what that garden is. I've never been brave enough to ask."

Damon smiles. "The point is, you're not alone. You have people willing to talk to you about what's going on right now. Lyric has been through it. Whether you or I or anyone else like it or not, you are a target. Of who? Don't have a fucking clue right now."

"Yes we do. Alex's accountant's assistant."

"Partially. But we don't know if he's working for someone. All we know is that Alex's accountant is dead. We know that he was killed in his office. And we know that his assistant is gone. He's had a one-week head start on us. He could be anywhere. We know he was the one who broke in because we caught him on camera. Other than that? We don't have any idea. Maybe he's working alone. Maybe he's got back-up. Maybe he has a boss. Maybe he lied. We have a lot of questions that we don't have answers to."

"What about the coffee guy?" I know they questioned him, but I don't know where he went. Maybe they didn't ask the right questions. "Maybe I could talk to him."

"That's not only something that would never happen -"

"Why?" I look up at him. "I could talk to him. If I had back-up and knew he wouldn't hurt me."

Damon smiles. "I admire the tenacity, but no. You'll never find him."

My eyes widen at the threat of his tone. "Oh."

"We let him go. But whoever he was working with didn't need him anymore and thought he needed to be silenced."

I wrap my arms around myself. "That's... He didn't deserve that."

"He made his bed, Raleigh. He got involved with dangerous people. I realize that you don't think he deserved it. Honestly, though, there's no telling what he would've done with you had you not fought him off and had we not gotten there when we did."

I open my mouth to argue, but I know he's right. I really don't know what would have happened if things hadn't gone exactly as they had. If one small detail had changed, things could have gone so differently. What if I hadn't thought to kick him? Or what if Alex hadn't thought to tell security to stop the elevator?

All of these thoughts are thoughts I've already had. And they upset me even more about the entire situation. What if I'd just gone with him and not fought? Would Alex's accountant still be alive? I know they were close. He ran the company in Alex's absence. Would his life have been spared if I'd just gone along?

I guess it's all answers I might never get. It makes me no less restless anyway. I really just wish I could somehow go back in time and stop it all from happening in the first place. Just like I wish I could have gone back and stopped Matthew from adopting me. I suppose, had he not, I may have never met Alex. Maybe fate had a hand in it. Maybe all of everything that's happened has some kind of larger meaning in some kind of grand master plan.

I sigh and turn away from the window. "I'm bored. I'm angry. I feel like a prisoner. Alex is keeping me at a distance. I thought we were past that. I just want to..." I gesture grandly. "Go outside."

"That isn't how it works, Raleigh."

I turn to him. He's leaning against the wall watching me. I sigh again. "I feel like I'm being an immature child ranting and raving when there are things larger than my understanding happening. But I'm really just... upset." I plop in my chair.

"You're going stir crazy. You aren't used to not at least being able to go outside for a walk. I get it. But that puts you at risk. We learned our lesson a few years ago. Granted, things were a little different, but we thought Jason's property was safe. It was covered with guards. Jessa was going crazy. She wanted to go outside and just walk around the property. The guards we had on her agreed to let her do it. What harm could possibly come from allowing her a breather on their own property? They were wrong. We all were. They let her go for her walk. She strayed a bit too far. She didn't have any guards with her. They all had eyes on her, but no one was with her. Matthew's guys got to her. Had she not been thrown into a shed with Josh, who was coming down from the serum he'd been injected with and starting to think clearly, she might be dead. We were lucky. We'll never make that mistake again. Not with you. Not with anyone. My job is to keep you safe."

"Okay... I get that, but why can't that be Alex's job?"

"Because he has a job."

I shrug. "So do I. He is my job. Literally."

Damon chuckles as he strides across the room. "Come with me."

"What?"

"Now. Before I change my mind." He turns down the hall.

I jump up and run after him. I find him in the kitchen near the door that leads to Josh's garage. He's strapping on a bulletproof vest and a shoulder holster. He checks that his gun is loaded and points to the counter.

My eyes fall on a much smaller vest. "What am I doing?"

"Put it on. You want to get out of the house, right?"

I nod and quickly put it on. When Damon has everything in place, he makes sure my vest is where and how it should be. He leads me out to the garage and helps me into an SUV with tinted windows I'm sure aren't legal. One more thing I suppose I'll have to adjust to. I climb in and say nothing. I don't want him to change his mind. I just want to get air. I don't even care where we're going, as long as it's somewhere outside.

I watch as he backs out and takes out his phone. He dials a number. Seconds later, I can hear it ringing through the speakers of the SUV. Damon puts his phone in the cup holder and turns onto the street.

"Hey. Everything okay?" a deep voice says surrounding me. It takes me a second to realize it's Josh.

"We're good. I'm taking her to the yacht before she tears the house apart."

Josh chuckles. "Have her back by six. Alex misses her and he's driving me fucking crazy."

"I'd argue, but I can't deny it," Alex says in the background. Just his voice brightens my mood. He may be being a little distant, but I'm smart enough to know that this situation hasn't been easy on any of us. I can't really blame him.

"Be careful out there. Check the boat. Take someone else with you," Josh commands.

"You got it, boss."

Josh growls as he hangs up. It makes me giggle. I've learned he hates being called boss, but the guys really enjoy razzing him and doing it anyway. I won't deny that it makes for some very fun entertainment.

Damon stops at the giant guard's house on the property and rolls down his window. After talking to one of them for a moment, the guard runs to the house. He returns moments later and slides in the backseat.

"Raleigh. Meet Jim. Jim. Raleigh. Jim has been a guard with the Lucinio Mafia for God only knows how long."

Jim's laugh is rich and easygoing, instantly settling me. "Raleigh. It's nice to meet you. I'm not upset about skipping some training to hang out on the water for a little while, so thanks for letting me out."

"No problem." I nod with a huge smile. "Glad to be of service."

I can hear Damon chuckle behind me as he steers the yacht further out into Lake Michigan. I'm standing in front of him on the bow of the ship with my eyes closed and my arms out like Rose in Titanic. The only thing missing is Alex behind me singing "Come Josephine" in my ear. The very thought makes me giggle because there's no way Alex Lucinio would ever do that.

I smile even more as I grab onto the railing and feel the cold mist from the water spraying on my face. I needed this. I needed the relaxing feel of the air hitting my face and the water all around me.

When Damon starts slowing down, I climb down from the railing, smiling. "Okay, I admit. I needed that."

Damon grins and starts to turn the boat. "You look a lot more carefree."

I sit in the chair next to him. "So, when do you think I'll be let out of house arrest?"

Damon laughs. "I have been thinking a little bit about it. I think I can convince Alex to ease up on you a little bit, but you'll have to agree to having guards on you all the time. And I mean at work, too. Like up on the Executive floor. Off to the side so they don't interfere with you and your work, but they need to be on that floor with you. I'm sure Alex can be talked into taking you to and from the office, but the part he's worried about is when he's in meetings or in his office doing CEO shit."

I nod. "Done. All of that. Absolutely done."

He looks over at me. "I think one of your biggest problems is that you think Alex is over his head at work." Damon starts guiding the yacht back towards shore. We're a ways out yet, and he's taking it leisurely.

"I know he is. I've kind of been fighting a little with myself about why he's become as distant as he has since my room was broken into."

Damon glances at me. "He's smitten completely with you. I've known him a long time. He's never been smitten with anyone. Not even Jessa, and he was with her for almost five years."

"Smitten?" I laugh. "That seems like such a floofy word for such a large man."

Damon grins. "There's no other word. The guy is fucking heels over ass for you. He has been since he first laid eyes on you."

I snort. "Yeah right. Alex hated me."

Damon shakes his head. "No. Most of his problem with you stemmed completely from the fact that he didn't want to admit he felt so strongly for you. We all knew it. He was the only one who had to catch up."

I blush and hide my face behind my hand as I smile. It's a very sexy thought knowing that Alex feels the same way about me as I do about him. Thinking of the six feet two-inch muscular man as smitten, though, is something else entirely. It makes the butterflies in my stomach take flight. I want to giggle, but I hold it back and keep the smile hidden.

"What was Alex like as a kid?" I ask. It's something I've been super curious about because it really seems like we grew up on two different planets.

"Well, he was sunshine and rainbows."

I laugh. "Come on. Be serious. I really want to know. He's told me a little of how he grew up. And Josh told me the rest. But what was he like? Was he really the hero that Josh makes him out to be?"

Damon chuckles. "Honestly?"

I nod. "Honestly."

"Alex was definitely Josh's superhero. They grew up thinking Alex was the oldest. They knew from a very young age that Alex was the heir to Lucinio Mafia. Matthew treated Alex like a king. For the most part. He got beatings, but most of them were the beatings he took for Josh. Josh, in Matthew's eyes, was the weaker one. He was born with an umbilical cord around his neck. He came out barely breathing. He wasn't crying. Alex came out screaming and reaching for his brother. It was like he intuitively knew that his brother was in danger. And that's how they grew up. Alex was always the one standing up for Josh. Defending him. Fighting for him."

"That's so sad…"

"Matthew switched their birth certificates. He paid off some people. As far as anyone knew, Josh was the youngest. Alex was the oldest. It wasn't until just a little while ago when Rebekkah came clean about it all."

I fall silent for a few moments. Alex really does seem like the hero, but Josh has truly stepped into his role as leader. I never would have guessed for a second that it wasn't the other way around. That Josh was the one defending Alex their whole lives.

"Alex and Josh went through so much," I say quietly.

"Yeah, but it shaped them. When I met Alex, I was a pissed off kid. My parents were both crack dealers and crack addicts. I had a lot of pent-up anger. I took it out on smaller kids. One day, Alex stuck up for one of those smaller kids. But instead of kicking my ass, like he damn well could have, he took me home for dinner. I think he saw something in me that I didn't. Potential or something. Alex stood up to his dad when I sat down at the dinner table. His dad didn't want company. Especially a poor kid from the rough part of L.A. Right then is when we became friends. Rebekkah became like a mom to me. And since Alex kept bringing me around, Matthew became like a father to me. He gave me an outlet for that anger."

I tilt my head. "You mean he took you on missions with Alex and Josh?"

He nods. "He started them young and let me tag along. I turned out to be a damn good asset to him. Eventually, Gavin joined in. We were three badasses. Throughout high school, Josh sort of ran with us, but he had his own friends. We ruled the school. Alex, though. He was always the leader. He was always the one we looked to for guidance, and we followed him without question. When he decided to go against his father's wishes and not take over Lucinio Mafia, Gavin and I followed him without question. Alex is and always has been a natural leader. What you see today is how he's always been. He has a mean streak. I'll give you that. He was admittedly an asshole to you. But that's really not typical of him. He can be an asshole, he can be really mean, but he usually has a good reason."

"Well, after talking to him, I understand where he was coming from. I can see how he got where he did in his conclusions of me. I'm not even really sure I wouldn't have come to the same conclusions and acted the same way if I were him."

"We all were suspicious of you, but Alex fixated on it. We all had a conversation with him about it, but another thing about him is he's always been stubborn. Once he gets something in his head, it's hard to change it. I'm not sure what you did to make him see reason or if he just finally saw it himself, but I think you both are good for each other." He smiles. "Just my two cents."

I smile as he guides the yacht back to the dock. "I feel a little bit lighter. Maybe I needed your two cents. Or blessing in some way." I blush and look down shyly at my hands.

He parks the yacht as Jim jumps down and starts tying the ropes. After everything is shut down and steady he smiles and kisses the top of my head as he stands. "You have it." He offers his hand and guides me to the ramp. He helps me down as he and Jim both look around.

Very suddenly, all of the tension I felt at home comes back. The entire purpose I wanted to get out in the first place is because I've been forced into seclusion due to some jackass' dick move to break in and go after me. Not knowing who he is, though, is something I don't like.

Except for Jim's whistling, the ride home is quiet. I have a feeling we're all lost in our own thoughts. I might have dragged up some uncomfortable memories for Damon. I'm just about to say something when we arrive home. Damon drops Jim off and drives to Josh's house near the end of the compound.

"I'm sorry if I gave you some uncomfortable memories," I say quietly.

Damon smiles. "You didn't." He parks the SUV. "The past is the past. I got myself out of that mess. I have my own house now. I'm part of an incredible family. And I'll never have to worry for a second about money. I won't need to wonder if my parent's next hit is going to send us to the streets again. I worked my ass off to get here. I barely think about them. And when I do, it's barely more than a fleeting thought."

I smile. As I start to get out of the SUV, Josh pulls in next to us. My smile turns into a grin so large, my face could crack. Where there is Josh, there will be Alex. I haven't seen him since last night when he said goodnight before he went to his own house. They left before I was even awake.

Josh opens my door for me. I'm sure he expects a hug, but my sights are one-hundred percent on the man behind him. Alex smiles when he sees me. Before he has a chance to really open his arms, though, I'm jumping in them.

Alex's arms lock around me. Our lips press together in a toe-curling kiss that melts my insides. I'm not sure if the growly groan comes from me or him, but it vibrates through my being. My legs and arms are wrapped so tightly around him that when he drops his arms to grab something from Josh, I don't move.

Alex's lips never leave mine as he walks me inside. His tongue meets mine in a furious tango. I don't know where he's taking me, and I don't really care as long as it's with him.

Chapter Fourteen

☙ Alex ❧

"I really just want answers. I couldn't give a crap what the fuck you've been doing over the last month and why the hell you haven't been able to get those answers for me," I growl into my phone as I lean back in my chair.

"Mr. Lucinio, I have other clients," the private investigator I hired to track down any of Raleigh's relatives says to me.

I put my feet up on my desk and shake my head. "You work for me, Mark. Let's not forget that." I glance up at Raleigh as she quietly enters my office and closes the door silently behind her.

Mark sighs. "I thank you for the help in getting me my own firm, but I can't drop everything for you. I'm doing my best."

I eye Raleigh as she walks behind me and hugs herself while she looks out the window. I don't like my girlfriend looking so melancholy, but seeing her makes me smile. I never thought I'd use the word girlfriend about anyone again, but fuck me, I love the way it sounds when it comes to her.

"Do better. You need to remember that just because the company is yours, I own a stake in it. I'm not trying to be your boss. You know that.

But I did you a favor when I pulled you out of the fucking gutter you came from. What has been given can just as easily be taken away."

Mark sighs again. I don't need to see him to know he's rubbing his head in consternation. "I have a missing girl, an unsolved murder, and a cheating husband. Now, I can put the fucking cheater on hold, but in the grand scheme of my cases, the location of family just doesn't seem as important."

I growl low as I put my feet down and sit forward. I really can't argue, but he's managed to piss me off for the last time. He's been putting me off for the last month. I don't do well with anyone putting me off, but I really don't do well with it when it's my girl who is stuck in the middle. The longer this shit takes, the more it affects her. And the more upset she becomes at not having answers, the more pissed off I get at not being able to give them to her.

"Look. I'll get you help from the LAPD. I'm guessing the reason you got hired is because they were slacking. I'll get someone put on the case. One of my contacts. That is the stuff they get paid for, and they have more resources than you. You put everything you have behind doing what I said, Mark. I'm sick of being put off. I get the cases are important, but you know I don't like to wait. You should have asked me for the fucking help long ago." I hang up the phone without waiting for him to say another word.

"What was that about?" Raleigh asks quietly.

I turn in my chair and hold up a hand for her. She takes it, and I pull her into my lap. I wrap her in my arms and pull her close. "The private investigator I hired to gather some information for Robby and Lance to work with to find your parents has been putting me off. He has some other cases that take priority, and while I agree with him, I don't like being put off. He was hired on the other cases because LAPD constantly has a high caseload. Things get swept under the rug a lot down there."

"Oh." She looks down at her hands.

I draw my eyebrows together and use two fingers to raise her chin so she's looking at me. "What happened? When I came in here less than an hour ago after lunch, you were all bubby and smiley."

She sighs. "I got a text from Dallas. She's upset with me. She needs help with her math homework tonight."

"Okay. Why is that upsetting?"

She bites her lip and snuggles into me. I drop my hand back to her hip. "Because she doesn't concentrate…"

I rub my thumb in a slow circle on her thigh. "What does that mean?"

She lets out a breath before standing and pacing in front of the window. I watch her. Finally, she turns back to me. "Don't get me wrong. I love her to death. She's my best friend. Really. I don't mean to speak badly about her, but when she comes over to get help with math, she doesn't need it. She's so smart. The reason she likes coming over so much is because of Josh. She doesn't know I know, but she has a super serious crush on him. She totally can't take her eyes away. I don't have a problem dropping everything and helping her. I don't. But she isn't there for the help. And who she likes isn't my business. Josh is incredible. And they do have chemistry, I guess. But I haven't gotten to spend time with you in a week since we went to that movie." She looks down again with an adorable pout. I almost chuckle. "I was really looking forward to some time with you."

"Honey, come here." I hold out my hand for her again. She takes a deep breath and takes it. She squeaks in surprise and widens her eyes when I set her on my desk in front of me. I scoot myself forward and position myself between her legs. I wrap my arms around her waist. "I won't pretend I don't see it. I know she has a thing for him. And I know he's been talking to Ryan about it because Ryan and Arianna had a similar type of relationship."

"I really don't have an issue with that. It's not like he'd ever act on it until she's of age, but -"

"You're upset because you want to spend time with me tonight, but I also think it might have a little to do with you thinking maybe she's just using you to spend time with him."

She blinks at me for a few moments. "That makes me a terrible friend."

I chuckle and shake my head. "No. That makes you human. I can't imagine anyone is going to be upset with you for wanting to spend time with your boyfriend when you haven't gotten the opportunity to in a week. You've sacrificed it quite a bit to help her out. That being said, though. I think you need to talk to her about this. I highly doubt she even understands how you feel. And she won't unless you talk to her. In the meantime, Josh is a grown man capable of figuring out ways to spend time with Dallas that isn't going to be problematic. Ryan did it with Arianna for years in the public eye. I can't even begin to tell you the things you'd find about him if you searched him. And that's even with the fact that he threatened and paid literally everyone off to shut the hell up about him."

"I don't want her to be upset with me, though." She sighs. "She's the only friend I have. Everyone is so busy with their lives and things. Dallas has always been there for me. She was my sounding board and my shoulder to cry on when it came to all things you and how confusing you were. She still is. It's just…" She slumps when the words won't come to her.

I can't help but smile. "All things me, huh?" I let my hands slowly slide up to her sides. I tickle her.

She lets out an adorable squeak as she jumps. "Alex!"

But I don't let up. "What kind of things?"

She laughs and tries to push me away. "Alex!"

I grin even wider as I tickle her more. She squirms. "Tell me. What things?"

"Ack!" She laughs harder as I keep tickling her. Her smile is so bright that it lifts my spirits. "Okay! Okay!" She squirms even more. "I'll tell you!"

I keep my arms firmly around her and kiss her chest. "Good. Talk."

She giggles. "Mostly about how big of an asshole you were, but how I hated the fact that I still thought you were my person."

I raise an eyebrow. "Your person?"

"You know…" She flails her arms a little, as if that will tell me exactly what she means. "My person. Like… the one I know that no matter what, I can turn to if I needed help."

"Huh. I was pretty sure I struck the fear of Satan himself into you."

"Well, you did. It's why I was so mixed up and confused. Because I knew you hated me."

"I have never hated you, baby. I just didn't trust you. There is a very large difference. Though, I can understand how you'd get there."

"I mean, just the way you were around me. Yet, I still felt like I could always go to you if I needed to. And I've always had this… this…"

She closes her eyes and tilts her head before opening them again and looking down at me. "Insane and very unexplainable attraction to you."

I grin because she knows damn well I've felt the same way. I've told her many times already. "Is that why you jump me every chance you get?"

Her mouth drops and she slaps my shoulder. "I'm trying to be serious!" She giggles.

I laugh and squeeze her hips. "Okay. I'll give you serious. Tell her that you have plans. You can't help her tonight. But it's the weekend. You can help tomorrow. I'll swing by and save you. Maybe even help you out in the teaching quest. I'm not too bad at math myself. Numbers have always been my thing."

Her eyes widen in the most adorable way. "You'd really just give up your whole day to come be with me while I help her?"

"Baby, come on. You have to know by now that I'd do just about anything you asked me to." I pull her a little closer to the edge of the desk and kiss her neck.

I feel her release a breath as her arms wrap around my shoulders. She rests her cheek on top of my head. I let her take some time feeling me because it seems to be what she needs right now. I'm content having her in my arms.

Everything between us has been smooth sailing since I got my head out of my ass and we started this whole thing. She's a very easy person to please. She hates fancy dinners out. She doesn't like all of the dating nonsense where it feels like the entire goal is to impress the other person. Raleigh prefers home-cooked meals, movies at home, and snacks to go with the movie. She likes walks along the water. A perfect day to her is curled up in my lap reading a book.

The past month we've spent as an actual couple has been the best of my life. I've never been with anyone I feel like I don't need to hide anything from. She's seen me at my darkest. She knows where I come from. She knows that no matter how legal I portray myself and this company, the mafia is right behind me.

The mafia has been something I've hid from everyone I've been with unless they somehow knew. The more legit Josh became over the past few years, the more out there the Lucinio name became. My father was famous for who he had on his arm. No one really mentioned his connections. Josh is famous for following in Ryan's footsteps. He molded the Lucinio Mafia after the Crane Mafia. His connections to Ryan makes this family instantly interesting to everyone and their damn grandmother.

Which has catapulted me to a fame I really had enjoyed avoiding. Being with Raleigh has been the first real thing I've ever had. I don't need to hide half of myself from her. She already knows about me and my connections.

It's made connecting with her a lot easier. When I disappear in the middle of the night, and she wakes up with only a note on my pillow instead of me, she doesn't ask questions about where I've gone or accuse me of being with someone else. She knows Josh needed me to help him out with something. Though, he's been keeping his word and only pulling me in when he needs me, so I don't disappear often.

I can't complain about her experimentation with me either. I've taken everything with her at her pace. We've never done anything she hasn't been comfortable with, but holy fuck. She's taken things a lot farther with me than I thought she would have at this point. We've had some very hot and heavy make out sessions that ended with an adorable pink flush to her cheeks while she was swallowing my come. But my favorite is the noises she makes when she finally hits her release. She's only let me touch her, but I'm more than happy about it. I crave her in any way I can get her.

Raleigh is also not at all shy about what she wants when it comes to me. There have been times when I've gotten lost in work and forgotten completely about lunch. Since lunch has become something important to her, she likes spending that hour a day with me, she'll walk into my office, move things aside and sit on my desk right in front of me just to tell me it's time for us. It's one of the sexiest things I've ever seen. Not many people would dare do it.

After a few minutes of hugging her tightly and feeling her tension melt away piece by piece, I slowly let her go. I kiss her softly and rub my hands up and down from her hips to her thighs and back. She hates wearing skirts, but the things I could be doing right now if she were.

She glances towards the closed office door when we hear a knock and sighs. "Can today be over yet?"

I chuckle and kiss her chest, right between her tits, once more. "Come in," I call towards the door as I help her down from the desk.

I hear someone clear their throat and look up to one of the guards we have on Raleigh. Chance. He's standing by the door in a military type stance. Feet are shoulder width apart. His hands are clasped in front of him instead of to his sides, but it looks like it might be a strain. One of the reasons that we have him specifically with Raleigh is because he is a former Marine. Very fit. No nonsense. Not many can or have ever gotten by him.

"Sorry to interrupt, sir, but your sixteen hundred hours meeting is here."

I smile. It's hard to break the military from a man, let alone the lingo. "Thank you."

He nods. "Yes, sir." He turns and leaves the office in the efficient way he came in.

Raleigh smiles a little bit as I stand. "I guess that's my cue."

I lean down and kiss her long and deeply until she gives me the quiet moan I want. I pull away slowly and cup her cheek. "I'll make it up to you later. I think you just need to regroup. It's been a long as hell week."

She nods. "So long. I feel just bone-tired."

"Have Chance take you home and stay with you until I get there. Take a nap, but get an overnight bag for yourself to stay with me."

She shakes her head. "I can stay. I'll grab the coffee for you both."

"Raleigh." I let my voice lower. Her eyes widen at my tone just like they always do when she knows I'm serious. "That wasn't a suggestion. I'll take care of the coffee. Have Chance take you home, or I'll set you in the car myself. Unceremoniously. I'll throw you over my shoulder and haul you to the elevator right past anyone who may be in that lobby right now."

She nods and lowers her eyes. "Yes, sir."

"Good girl."

Walking into Josh's house after work isn't exactly what I want to be doing, but we've learned our lessons well. Until we get this entire situation under control with whoever went after Raleigh, precautions need to be taken. We've heightened security not only with her, but everyone.

We know that when something happens to one family, Lucinio's or Crane's, it's only a matter of time before the other family is somehow pulled into it.

We aren't taking chances with anyone's lives. Our compound should be impossible to penetrate, but it's happened more times than we care to count. Until all construction is completed, we'll need to combat our weakest points. Right now, that point seems to be the lake. We've already started putting a stone barrier up, but that barrier wasn't completed. It became top priority. All other projects were put on hold. Thank fuck the barrier is nearly completed. With the extra security enforcement and the barrier, at least no one will feel like a prisoner.

I chuckle because those are the exact words my mother used a couple of weeks ago, right before Raleigh uttered them herself. It was comical to me then and still is now. They say a man marries a woman like his mother. I never believed that until Raleigh. She's a lot like my mom. Tenacious. Strong as hell. She has to be to withstand all of the bullshit I put her through for no reason other than I wanted to keep her at a distance.

I poke my head into the library expecting to see Raleigh. Instead, I see Josh reading with Dallas' head on his thigh and her math book next to her. I raise an eyebrow but turn to leave. I shake my head and turn back.

"She's upstairs grabbing her overnight bag," Josh says. Dallas squeaks and quickly sits up, but Josh drops a hand on her shoulder before she gets too far. "Friends can hang out and read together. Alex is my brother. He's not going to run off and tell everyone you had your head on my leg."

I chuckle when she blushes a furious shade of red and settles again with her nose in her book. "I'm not one to judge, Dallas. Even if I were, I can't. My best friend comes to mind."

Josh chuckles. "He's talking about Ryan and Arianna." He shoots me a glare. "Need anything else?"

I hold my hands in front of me in surrender and smile with a shake of my head as I leave. Josh doesn't spend a lot of time relaxing. When he actually gets the opportunity to do it, he hates conversation. He doesn't mind the company, but he likes quiet so he can read. His guilty pleasure is historical non-fiction. He loves anything about the wars. Any of them in any country during any era.

Just as I turn the corner towards the stairs that lead up to Raleigh's bedroom, I see her. She constantly takes my breath away. It doesn't matter what she's wearing or what she isn't. She's wearing jeans and an oversized t-shirt right now. All I can think is she's the most beautiful woman in the world.

I take the bag she's carrying over her shoulder and put it over mine instead. I pull her close and hug her. I just saw her less than two hours ago and already I missed the fuck out of her. Who would have thought someone who was so hardened against this girl could have done such a turn around and fallen to his knees with just a look? I certainly never thought it would be me. I was perfectly content denying my feelings for her.

Of course, now, looking back, I realize what a complete lie that is. I hate myself for how I acted. It was so unlike me. I was never content denying my feelings for her either. I just refused to admit it.

"I want to try out a new chicken recipe," she says into my chest as she breathes me in.

I smile because I love when she does that. My heart swells with a strange sense of pride when she inhales my scent and relaxes. "Chicken, huh?"

She nods and looks up at me but keeps her arms firmly around my waist. "Yeah, it's baked chicken, but it's supposed to taste fried. I don't know if it will work, so we'll have to have takeout on stand-by." Her eyes light up with a sparkle she only gets when she's happy.

She's never been allowed to cook. Matthew always had housekeepers and cooks who did that for her. She always thought it was because he wanted to make sure she ate well. But the longer she's out of his clutches she's started to realize what I knew the very second she told me she'd never cooked anything for herself a day in her life until she came here.

He had no intention of letting her out of his sight. He never would have allowed her to go off to the University she wanted to go to. Even if she had been accepted. I'm still on the fence about that one. While investigating after Josh told me about the denial letter she'd received, I saw her test scores. They're almost perfect. There is no way any University worth giving a damn about would have sent her a denial letter. I'd dropped it, but I have every intention of digging back into it as soon as we get more information of where she actually came from.

I laugh at the humor in her voice about the takeout and the smirk she gives me. "Anything you want."

She blushes as I kiss her. I smile and take her hand. She could burn my house down with this new recipe, and I'd still let her try it over and over again if it puts that sexy sparkle in her eyes. Anything to make her happy.

Chapter Fifteen

❦ Raleigh ❦

I giggle and swat at Alex when he tickles my neck with the scruff on his face while I'm trying to finish washing the dishes. He grabs my wrists and crosses his arms and mine over my chest. He kisses my neck and growls low against it while he sways gently with me.

"I can't do these without hands," I say giggling even more.

He smiles against my neck. "I think I'm done cleaning up." He kisses across the back of my neck to the other side and tickles me again with his scruff, making me erupt in another fit of giggles.

"Alex!" I try to break free of his hold, but he only holds me tighter. He pushes against me. I gasp at the feel of his unbelievably impressive length against my backside. I'm so much smaller than him that it's against my lower back, but I still feel an instant heat between my thighs. "God…"

"How about we finish these later?" he whispers low and huskily. "I promised I'd take some of that stress of the week away."

"But if we finish now… we won't need to do them later…"

He pauses and rests his chin on my shoulder with a groan. "Fucking logic."

I giggle again. "And if you help…"

He sighs dramatically. "Fine." He lets go and nudges me to his side with a sexy grin so he can finish washing, and I can rinse.

We're both smiling as we work side by side. When he finally hands me the last dish, I look up at him with a devilish smirk. I've been waiting to do this since I first started the dishes. He raises an eyebrow and watches me cautiously.

I dip my hand in the draining rinse water and splash him, successfully drenching his t-shirt in water. His mouth drops in complete shock, but before he has any chance to react, I take off running with a squeal.

"Oh, you're going to regret every second of that."

I don't dare look back. "You have to catch me first!"

I hear nothing but silence behind me. That's perfectly fine with me. My intention is to run upstairs and lock myself in his bedroom while I quickly change into the tank top I sleep in so we can settle and watch the movie we picked out for the night.

My plans do not go as I thought. I squeak when Alex's arms encircle my waist just as I reach the second step. He hauls me back hard against his steel body. The shock of his chest against my back takes my breath away and sends an electrical current through my body and straight to my core. I don't know how he does it. It's simply not fair.

"Time to pay your debt," he growls against my neck.

I would flail, but he has my arms pinned against my sides. I laugh as he drags me to the couch. "Alex! What are you doing?"

"You're about to find out." He somehow effortlessly flips me around and tosses me onto the couch.

I laugh as I bounce, but he's almost instantly on top of me and pinning me to the cushions. I smile up at him. The pure and raw heat that darkens his eyes makes me shiver in anticipation of whatever he is about to do.

I moan as soon as his lips hit my neck. "Alex…"

He nips. I jerk against his hips. He grinds down against me. His hardness hits perfectly against me. I nearly start panting as I push up against him. I close my eyes and relish in the feel of him.

He's stripped his shirt. The feel of his skin beneath my hands when I trail them up the hard planes of his abs to the steel ridges of his chest drives me even more crazy with need for something only he can give me. Something primal and deliciously naughty.

I open my eyes just as he pulls up my shirt. I sit up enough for him to pull it off and toss it. His mouth lands on my nipple. One of his hands pinches the other. I start tearing at my bra. I want to feel him. His tongue. His teeth. The thin satin is too much.

He chuckles and grabs my wrist. "I said you're going to pay for that. Did you honestly think for a second I wouldn't torture you for a while before I give you pleasure?" He pins my wrists above my head.

"Alex… please…" I push against his hand but get nowhere. He's far too strong.

He kisses down my collarbone. "No," he rumbles. When he gets back to my hardened peaks, he nips them both.

"Ah!" I arch into him, but he uses his other hand to push my hips down.

I writhe under him and moan. My eyes roll back in my head. I pant. His beautifully hard cock molds to me harder. I try to grind against him, but he's managed to render me motionless. The only relief he lets me have is what he gives me.

He rubs himself against me as he lavishes both of my nipples in turn. My panties are soaked. I can feel them getting wetter and wetter the more needy and hot he makes me. My bra is just as wet from his mouth. His teeth scrape over the fabric and tug lightly.

"Alex… you're driving me crazy," I whimper.

"That's the whole point." He smiles and starts a long, torturous path down my stomach to the waistband of my jeans. He undoes the button and pulls the zipper down with his teeth.

"Oh my God…"

"I'm going to let go of your wrists. You're going to be a good girl and not touch yourself or try to remove clothing. Because if you do, the torture is going to get far more intense." He looks up at me. His intensely blue eyes glitter with a dare he knows I won't take. "Am I clear?"

My mouth goes completely dry. All I can do is nod and pant, waiting for him to take me to the heights I'm pleading for. He lets go of my wrists and lets his hands wander slowly and unabashedly down my body. He stops on my breasts and squeezes. My body naturally responds by arching into him. I have no control.

He reaches behind me and unhooks the bra with such ease, I'm briefly intimidated. I force myself to push it aside, though, and enjoy every moment of him. He pulls the bra off and tosses it. His mouth is instantly on me once more. I sigh in both relief and pleasure.

His tongue is magical. It does things I haven't even had the courage to dream of. He licks my nipples and sucks them into his mouth, one after the other, until I'm so delirious I can't think. I shake my head back and forth moaning and gripping the cushions beneath me.

Just when I think I'm going to die, I feel Alex's hand slowly making its way down my side. My eyes widen, but I can't speak anymore. I'm not even certain I remember my own name. All I can do is let my body talk for me.

He nips and sucks my nipples while his hand slides slowly down my waist to my thigh. He gradually moves it up my inner thigh but stops right before where I want him, plead for him. I try to maneuver myself lower so he has to touch me, but he nips my nipple harder in reproach.

"Do you want me to prolong this?" he rumbles deeply against me, sending the vibration through every single nerve ending in my body.

I shake my head. "No. No. God, no."

He smiles against me and continues his languid torment of my boobs. The licking and kissing. The biting and nipping. His teeth scrape lightly over my skin. He starts kissing down my body again.

His hand lightly grazes my pussy. It's so soft, but the sensation shoots right through me. Every part of me tingles. I claw at the cushions. I want to scream but no sound leaves my mouth except whimpers and moans.

"You make the sexiest fucking sounds." He kisses my belly button and tucks his fingertips in the waistband of my jeans.

I blush a deep shade of red. My vision blurs with ecstasy. "Alex… I don't… know…" I can't finish the sentence. My eyes tear up. I'm going to cry with how much I need him.

"Patience," he whispers. "I'll make it worth the wait, baby."

He tugs my jeans down and throws them into the haphazard pile that has become my clothing. He kisses up my leg, then follows with the other one. His licks and nips along the way bring me closer and closer to the point of no return. I'm trembling. I try to clench my thighs together, but he doesn't let me.

When he finally reaches my pussy, I think the unending journey to my pleasure is over. But that is simply not what Alex wants. He pushes his nose against my center above my thin black satin panties and takes his sweet time making his way to my clit, inhaling me along the way and letting out a low growl of obvious appreciation.

"Oh… God…" I don't know if it's possible to blush darker than I had been already, but when I realize he's smelling me, I feel my cheeks getting hotter. My eyes grow wider. My panties feel damper.

"Shit, baby." Alex's tongue darts out and puts pressure against my clit.

I buck into him. "Ah!" My pussy tightens instantly and vibrates deep inside me. It's like a buzz going through me and straight to my clit.

Alex pushes my panties aside. I close my eyes, dizzy with desire. I expect his fingers. He's never used anything else on me. Instead, I feel something wet and unrelenting. I look down in shock and arch into him. His eyes are on mine as his tongue darts in and out of my pussy.

"Mmm… Fucking delicious." His voice is deep and rumbles through my pussy.

My head falls back. My eyes roll back in my head. I scream and come hard. "Alex!" My pussy pulses and clenches erratically around his tongue. "Ah! Alex! Ah!"

"Oh my fucking sweet Jesus," he moans as he laps everything I give him up.

I tremble under him and fight to catch my breath. I take in lungsful of air as my body quakes and spasms under him. He's masterful. He knows exactly what to do to make my body sing for him. His tongue slows its pace, helping me come down until I collapse on the couch totally exhausted. I continue shivering.

Alex crawls on top of me and wraps me in his arms. He leans down and kisses me so passionately and lovingly, I melt into him. I blush when I realize the tangy, sweet taste on his tongue is me. I've tasted him before, but I've never tasted myself. I've never done anything with anyone except him. He was my first kiss. He's been my first for everything. I don't want anyone else. I only want him. I want him to be my first and only everything.

He pulls away slowly, but stays on top of me with his arms protectively and possessively wrapped around me. He kisses my neck softly. "You okay?" he asks me with his lips against my neck.

"I c-couldn't h-hold on," I whisper, my chest suddenly constricting.

Alex has made me come a few times over the past month since we've been together, but he's always made me wait until he's told me to come. It's never been something I've minded. I love when he tells me to come and my body obeys.

He chuckles against my neck. "It's okay. Seeing you lose control like that was the sexiest thing I've ever fucking seen."

"My God," I whisper. "Your t-tongue…" My arms finally find the strength to wrap around him. I hug him so tightly, I question if he can breathe.

He kisses my neck and hugs me tighter. "Fuck, you taste better than I dreamed in all of my dirtiest fantasies."

I close my eyes and bury my face shyly in his shoulder. "Alex…"

He smiles and kisses up my neck to my jaw until he finally reaches my lips. He kisses me softly and pulls away gently. "Look at me."

I open my eyes slowly and am unable to stop the words on the tip of my tongue. "I love you," I whisper. I feel my face redden immediately, but before I can say anything further, he leans down and kisses me again. It's like he knows I was about to apologize for the words being said so soon.

"I love you, too."

My breath catches. "You do?" I barely get the words out.

He grins, but it's the love I feel in my heart reflected in his eyes that sends the butterflies in my stomach on a flight through my body. His eyes sparkle with all of the feelings I can't put into words.

"I do."

I bite my lip and look at him shyly as he gets up and pulls me up with him. My eyes fall to the incredible sized bulge in the gray sweats that ride low on his hips. They really leave nothing to the imagination about Alex's size.

I reach out and run my hand along his length on the outside of his sweats. He groans and sits. Something I've come to love about him so much is that he isn't shy about taking what he wants and never makes me feel embarrassed about taking what I do. He always makes me feel like the most sexy thing he's ever laid his eyes on. It gives me the confidence I need sometimes to take what I want.

What I want right now is him. I shift to my knees next to him while he pushes his sweats down his hips. I hold myself back from completely pouncing on him, but I can't stop myself from taking his length in my hands.

I love the way he feels. I've always imagined a man's cock felt like the rest of him. Most men I'd come across, including my father, had rough hands. Their skin doesn't feel like a woman's. It's not soft. It's thicker. I've always felt like it was more oily. I thought all of him would feel the exact same way.

I was very wrong. Alex's dick is large and thick. It's longer than both of my hands fisted one on top of the other. He's so thick, I'm not certain he'll be able to fit inside me. I can't get him all in my mouth. By the time his tip touches the back of my throat, he's not even halfway in. Smooth and very silky skin encases a hard, rock-solid shaft. The vein that runs on the underside of his dick is the only soft part of him. It's also one of the most sensitive.

Alex is well-groomed. The only hair in his middle region is the sexy treasure trail that runs from his navel to just below his waistband. I've run my tongue along that strip of hair enough times to know it's another of the only soft parts of Alex's titanium-like body.

I lean down and lick his tip while I use both hands to stroke him from his balls up to his tip. The low growl of appreciation he emits vibrates through his whole body. But it's the salty and tangy liquid I'm languidly lapping up that really spurs me on. Alex is close, and I've barely touched him.

I use one hand to lightly scratch along the vein under his balls while I use the other to pump his dick. I take him in my mouth and suck while I slowly bob my head up and down, taking him as deeply in my mouth as I can. When he touches the back of my throat, I swallow with a quiet moan. I've learned the moan sends vibrations down his dick. The swallow drives him crazy.

When he jerks into me, I know I'm doing it right. His fingers tangle in my hair and tug lightly. My eyes want to close in pleasure, but I don't let them. I love watching him. I love watching his eyes close when I flick my tongue into the dimple just below his tip. I love watching his dick jerk when I hit just the right spot under his balls. I love watching him arch into me when I palm his balls and roll them in my hand. I love everything about Alex.

"Fuck, your mouth is the definition of sin, baby." His head drops back on a moan of satisfaction. "I'm so close already. Your moans when I was licking you drove me to the brink."

I smile around him, delighted that I have the ability to drive him just as crazy as he does me. I lavish his tip with my tongue and tug on his balls lightly as I scratch just under them. He pushes my head down a little. I feel his arm shake, and that's how I know he's ready for his release. I stroke his length faster and take him as far into my mouth as possible. I hold him there.

I keep flicking my tongue over his cock and moan while I stroke faster and faster. I feel his balls tighten in my hand. He tightens his grip on my hair. I watch as his stomach muscles tighten. He arches. His dick jerks.

"Oh my…" His head falls back once more before it falls forward. Jets of come start spilling on my tongue. "Fuck, Raleigh!"

"Mmm…" I swallow all he gives me, savoring the taste as he did me just a few minutes ago. I watch his head fall back against the back of the couch again as he catches his breath. I lick him clean then lick my lips as I slowly sit back up on my knees.

His hand falls from my hair and trails down my back as he smiles. He snakes his arm around my waist and pulls me to him just as his phone rings. I wrap my arms around his waist and cuddle into him, not caring at all that I'm still naked. Maybe I should, but it's Alex. I've never been more content than I am in this moment.

"Shit. I have to take this." Alex puts the phone to his ear. "Hey, Damon, what's up?" His thumb makes circles on my hip. I lay my head on his shoulder but instantly tense when he does. "What? What happened?" He sits up slowly and lets me go. I furrow my brows and hug myself as I watch his back. He lowers his head into his hand and sighs deeply as he nods and rubs his temple. "Okay. I'll be right there, bro. Don't worry about it. Raleigh will understand." A couple of seconds later he hangs up and looks over his shoulder at me. The blissed out look in his eyes moments ago is replaced with a storm I can't decipher.

"What happened?" I ask.

"Damon got some bad news. All he said was he needs his family and begged me to meet him at Josh's."

I nod, my heart breaking for him. I don't know what happened, and it's a little shocking to feel such pain for him when I can hardly be considered close to him or family, but I feel it anyway. I sit up and shift, reaching for my t-shirt Alex threw on the table.

"Of course, I understand." I smile softly at him. "I… guess… I'm not really sure what my role is right now," I say hesitantly. "Should I wait here for you? Or do you want me to go home…?

"Raleigh…," he whispers. He reaches for my hand and draws it to his lips after interlocking our fingers. He kisses it softly. "He said family. You and I are together. You're mine, honey. In this family, that means you belong to them just as much. They're as much your family as they are mine. So, to answer your question…" He shakes his head and leans into me. He kisses me lovingly and pulls away slowly. "You're coming with me."

I don't intend to smile as brightly as I do, but even I can feel my cheeks struggle to contain my happiness. I suppose I knew that the family I've begun to consider mine also felt like I belonged with them, but hearing Alex say the words fills me with so much joy, I feel like I might burst.

What really has me exploding with merriment, though, is Alex calling me his. Ever since I first laid eyes on him, being his was all I wanted to be. Now that the words have left his beautiful lips, I can't contain the cheer erupting from my heart.

I quickly wrap my arms around him and hug him so hard that the muscles in my arms strain. Feeling his arms wrap just as tightly around me, though, is all my heart needs. I can feel it exploding in a crazy display of fireworks in my chest.

I'm his.

All his.

I never want to be anyone else's.

Chapter Sixteen

☙ Alex ☙

My heart skips a beat when Raleigh's head pops through the top of my Chelsea F.C. soccer hoodie. I'm a not-so-closeted fan. A few years ago, I, like a fucking groupie, followed them around to every game they played and rooted them straight to a FA Cup victory. I don't care what anyone says. I'm telling everyone they won because I was cheering them on from the front row.

Raleigh wearing one of my prized Chelsea clothing items, though, does things to me I never dreamed possible. She drowns in it. It's far too big for her. It drops past her ass and hits her mid-thigh. She really doesn't need to wear the jeans. The hoodie could almost be a dress for her. Fucking hell if it doesn't make my dick hard.

My hoodie.

My girl.

Mine.

She smiles up at me. "I'm ready."

My throat has long ago gone dry. "Okay." I don't know how I managed to get those words out, but even I can hear the deepness in my voice. Far raspier. Enough of a difference to make her eyes widen.

I smile and take her hand before I forget the entire purpose of putting clothes in the first place. Fuck. I've already forgotten my damn name. Not something I'm used to, but it happens more and more frequently with her. She's intoxicating.

I lead her out of the house and lock the door behind me. Josh's house is only a couple of houses down at the end of the cul-de-sac. It seems too close. I've been meaning to ask Raleigh something, but I don't know if I have enough time to get the words out.

I take a deep breath and decide to just go for it. "Raleigh, I've been meaning to ask you, uh…" I squeeze her hand and scrub my hand down my face as we walk.

She looks up at me. "Ask me… what?" There's a tremor in her voice. I hate that I put it there. With everything I've put her through, it doesn't surprise me. She's probably waiting for a blow that will destroy her.

But that's not what this is. "Well…" I trail off and look down at her. I squeeze her hand again before slowing our pace. We're almost to Josh's. "You spend most of your time with me now. Not just at the office. Here." I gesture around the complex. "I know you like Josh's library, but what if you moved in with me? I can turn my study into a full library if you want me to. You can stock it with whatever you want." I pause outside Josh's house. My heart feels like it's going to relocate to my throat as I wait for her answer.

She looks up at me with the biggest smile I've ever seen. "Alex…," she whispers. She takes my other hand in hers. My heart is literally pounding so fast, I can hear it in my ears. "I'd love to move in with you… but do you think we're ready for that?" Her beautiful smile fades slightly. I can see the worry cloud her eyes.

I move my thumbs in a circle on the top of her hands. "I know we started off rocky, baby, but yes. I've never been more ready for anything in my life. I love having you around me. I want you with me all the time. I'll understand if you aren't to that point yet, but if you aren't, just know that I'm ready whenever you are."

She watches me with a soft smile. I know damn well what's going on in her mind. It breaks me because I am the one who made her so distrustful of my intentions. Sometimes, I think I've busted through it, but then, times like this shove me violently back to reality. I have a long, long way to go. As my heartbeat quickens impossibly more, I just hope she'll give me the chance to prove all of that shit is over. We're not going back.

Finally, when I'm fairly certain I'm going to pass out from lack of oxygen, or maybe too much, she slowly and shakily wraps her arms around my waist. She nods against my chest, but it's her whispered words that send me flying to the moon.

"Yes. I'd love to move in with you."

I let out a whoop and wrap her in my arms. I lift her off her feet and kiss her deeply, swallowing her squeals of surprise and turning them into moans of delight. "Fuck, Raleigh. I thought you were going to say no," I rumble against her neck.

She adjusts to my grip and wraps her arms around my shoulders. She rubs her nose against mine. "I wasn't sure you were serious."

I grin. "Dead serious."

Her bright smile returns. "When?"

I laugh. "How about this weekend? We made a commitment for tomorrow, but Josh and I can knock out moving your stuff into my place in a couple hours. I could probably even convince Gavin, Lance, and Damon to help."

She giggles before biting her lip. "Speaking of Damon…"

I look up at the house as I slowly let her down. The reason for standing out here suddenly slams into me again.

Damon.

Something about his tone when I talked to him threw me off. I've never heard Damon sound like that. He sounded like he was trying to keep it together. Broken. All he said was something happened. He needs his family. I don't even have to know what it is. I already feel for him. He might not be my brother by blood. Like Ryan, though, he's my brother by heart.

I sigh and take Raleigh's hand. "Yeah. I'm hoping he's here already. He sounded pretty upset."

She squeezes my hand. "Then we should get to him. He needs us. He needs his family."

I smile. Despite whatever we're about to walk into, hearing her include herself in that statement instead of excluding herself lightens the heaviness I feel surrounding me. It's a fuck of a feeling being totally honored to have someone at my side through anything, but the fact that it's her is something else on an entirely different level.

I know I'm still beating myself up for treating her the way I did. I have a lot of making up to do for all of that. But it's the fact that I lost myself and pushed her against the window in my office. I know I didn't do it hard enough to hurt her. I'd never do that. But the fact that I lost control in the first place is enough to make me sick. I'll never forgive myself for that. No amount of making it up to her will ever be enough.

I lead her inside Josh's house listening for voices. Hearing none, I lead Raleigh to the pool. It's one of Josh's favorite places. It overlooks the lake, but it's also enclosed and completely private. This house is one of Josh's biggest splurges. He spared no expense with the pool.

As I thought, Josh has gathered everyone outside. Damon is sitting next to Lance. Their heads are together. Lance is rubbing his back. Gavin is talking in hushed voices with Josh. Dane and Cole are leaning against the house watching everyone.

"What's going on?" I ask them, keeping my voice low. "Do we know?"

Cole shakes his head. Cole Westwood has become a really good friend since he joined us, but I think one of his proudest moments was making Sergeant when he agreed to work under Dane.

Dane Michaels is a Lieutenant with Chicago P.D. and the commander for a specialized unit that works with major crimes. He also works directly under Josh and is our contact within Chicago's department. Dane has the ability to tip us off to unusual spikes in crime. Josh is only more than happy to pull in people to help. He loves having a legal mafia, but doesn't shy away from protecting others and crossing lines when he needs to. Josh takes out bad guys Chicago P.D. can't. Chicago P.D. turns the other way. In the end, it's in their best interest. They get credit for taking down terrible people. Josh remains the dark and mysterious force behind them.

"We're just waiting for mom," Josh says when he sees me. "She was walking over with Kent. Dane asked her to be here, too."

I nod and quietly pull Raleigh to a pool chair as we wait. I sit and tug her between my legs before wrapping my arms around her and burying my face in her hair. I kiss her neck to try and make the tightness in my chest subside. It's obvious this is serious.

"What do you think is happening?" Raleigh asks me as she settles.

I take a breath. "I honestly don't know, baby. But Damon looks really upset. Kind of has me a little bit on edge."

She wraps her arms around mine. "Whatever it is, we'll help him get through it."

I smile as my mom walks in with Kent. Kent is Dane's father. He's also my mother's long-lost love. Dane is my mother's son. She didn't know if Kent or Dane were still alive after she was traded to the Lucinio Mafia in a business alliance years ago. Even when the alliance ended, my father's clutches in her was only just beginning. She just found out Dane was alive when we were helping the Crane Mafia take Matthew down.

Kent and mom have been completely inseparable. I don't blame them. They're making up for lost time. She's been able to get to know Dane as her son. Josh and I have enjoyed the fact that he's our brother. It's been some light from a very dark past. My mother's much deserved happily ever after.

When everyone is settled, Damon takes a deep breath. He doesn't stand, but he does look up at all of us. He looks like he went through Hell and barely made it out. It puts me even more on edge, but when his eyes fall on Raleigh, I inadvertently tighten my grip.

Damon makes a strangled choking noise. "I'm sorry, Raleigh," he whispers, raspily. "I didn't know."

"Didn't… know what…?" Raleigh asks. Her voice quivers, though. She's more scared than confused.

Damon is quiet for a few moments while he tries to gather himself. He carefully gets to his feet, but he's shaky. I've never seen him like this. Not even when he's drunk. The guy can hold his liquor better than anyone I've ever met.

He hands both of us a box and sits on the pool chair next to ours. Raleigh puts it on her thighs as everyone moves closer. It's a shoebox decorated in some kind of quilted, satin cloth that is a shimmery pink. Almost like a magenta, but slightly darker. Raleigh looks back at me quizzically. I nod, giving her the support she's seeking, and lean forward. For the second time tonight, my heart feels like it's going to palpate right out of my chest.

She slowly removes the cover and sets it aside. Everyone looks in the box and at each other, but no one really knows exactly what they're looking at. On the surface, it's nothing but papers. It doesn't seem significant.

Raleigh, though, sniffles. "Oh God…"

"What?" I ask.

With shaky hands, she pulls out a square of fabric that looks to be about the size a quilter would use to quilt with. It's the same color as the fabric surrounding the box. She clutches it to her chest and bursts into tears.

My only instinct is to hug her as close to me as I can. I don't hesitate. I wrap her in my arms and shift her so she can bury her head in my chest as she sobs. Her body shakes with the effort to control herself, but with every breath she takes, she cries harder. I tangle my fingers in her hair and hug her closer.

I look at Damon. "What's happening?"

Damon reaches into the box and pulls out something on very old paper and hands it to me. Josh glances at him and walks behind the chair to look at it with me. Lance sits next to Damon and starts to soothingly rub Damon's back once more. Gavin comes behind the chair to stand next to Josh.

"Shit…," Josh murmurs. "Is this what I think it is?"

"A birth certificate?" I shake my head. "I don't get it."

Josh points to the name. "Raleigh Knight."

I don't know if my heart starts beating so fast I can't feel it anymore, or if it's simply stopped all together. I look up at Damon. "Where did you get this? How do you know it's her?"

Damon takes a breath. "I got a call a few weeks ago. My parents both died of a drug overdose."

I nod. "You mentioned that." He'd told us as soon as he got the call that his parents were dead. He didn't seem all that upset. None of us did. He was raised more by my parents anyway.

Damon reaches up and wipes his eyes. "Raleigh… I didn't know. If I had, I would have done something."

Raleigh just nods. It's like the two of them have some kind of unspoken communication going on that I'm failing to understand. Looking up at my mother, though, I'm not the only one. Dane and Cole seem to be a little baffled, as well.

Gavin reaches over and takes the box. "I still don't get it. How did you know this is our Raleigh?" He digs through the box looking for something we've all missed.

Damon holds his hand out for the box. Gavin gives it to him. "Because of this." Damon takes out an envelope. It's white, but it's bedazzled and glitter-glued. "My mom, when she wasn't high, was really into arts and crafts." Damon smiles softly. He hands the envelope to a still teary Raleigh.

She takes it shakily with one hand. The other is still clutching the fabric to her chest. She sits up slowly. I make sure my contact with her isn't broken. I don't need to ask. I know I'm grounding her right now. I watch her as she starts to pull something out of the open envelope that has her name on it.

She sniffles as she unfolds a letter. "Dearest Raleigh," she starts. I tighten my grip and rest my chin on her shoulder. "To begin, I want you to know that we never wanted to give you up." She lets out a strangled sob and grips the letter tighter.

I reach around her and gently take her wrists. "Let me," I whisper, gripping the letter. She lets go and covers her face with her hands. I rub her back soothingly as I read. "Times were very difficult for us when we realized we were pregnant. We weren't in a position to care for you. We couldn't even care for Damon. He's your older brother." I look up as Damon lets out a strangled sob of his own.

"I'm so fucking sorry, Raleigh," he whispers.

I take a breath and start reading again. "We knew Damon had a friend who was well-to-do. His friend's family had practically raised him as their own. We thought if we contacted them, they'd help us." I take a breath. "Fuck," I whisper. I lean down and kiss Raleigh's shoulder and continue reading with my lips against her skin. "He did, but the payment he required was so very high. It meant that we would never be allowed to see you again."

Raleigh cries harder. She's starting to hyperventilate. I hand the letter to Josh and wrap my arms tightly around my girl. I don't know what the rest of it says, but I can only guess. My stomach hurts for her. My chest. My heart. I sway gently with her.

Josh sits in the pool chair on the other side of us. "We wanted you to have a good life. We didn't want to tell Damon about you because we knew he would have taken you. We didn't want that for him. He was so young. I hope you understand that. He was only a kid himself." Josh pauses. I glance at him. I can see my own anger reflected in his eyes. "So, we agreed to allow Matthew Lucinio to adopt you."

"Son of a bitch," Dane whispers.

Josh growls low in his throat. "A few years ago, we'd heard that Matthew was killed in a fire. Right before it happened, he told us that you were safe, but that things were escalating. He wouldn't tell us where you were, but that you were okay. We trusted that. After the fire, we did try to find you, but we knew that his family didn't know about you. He'd told us when he first adopted you that you would be well-cared for, but that he'd be taking you somewhere else. Somewhere far from L.A., where you were born."

"Cozumel," Raleigh whispers.

"Is that where you grew up?" Cole asks.

Raleigh nods. "I never kn-knew anywhere e-else as h-home…"

I run my fingers through her hair and kiss her neck. "Ssh…," I whisper.

Josh leans forward. "We tried to reach you. We regretted our actions in giving you up. We wanted to see you. At least to meet you to see how you were doing. We gave you up because we were too into drugs, but we got clean and wanted to know how you were doing. Matthew wouldn't allow that. He said that you were doing just fine without us and that if we attempted to contact you, he'd kill Damon." Josh pauses. "Like hell." He chuckles dangerously. "We believed him. We didn't realize how dangerous he was, but we also didn't want to lose Damon as we had you. We've never forgotten you."

Raleigh's sobs turn into full blown hysteria. She tries to pull away from me with an angry scream I know isn't directed at me, but I hug her tighter. I can't blame her. I'm angry for her. She was dropped right into a bear's den all because her parents were too fucked up to give up the drugs. While I commend them for being lucid enough to give her up, giving her to Matthew was so fucking stupid. And keeping Damon out of it? He had a right to know he had a sister.

"Enclosed in this box is your original birth certificate, a baby picture of you with us, and a placard we had made with your feet and hands. You don't have any family left, except Damon. If you're receiving this, then you already know him. He must have saved you from Matthew's clutches. We're so thankful for that. Matthew wouldn't allow us to give you any of this stuff. Just your baby blanket. We'd had it engraved with your initials, but he cut that square off and wouldn't allow you to have that. He said that it was because it would give away that you were adopted, and that wasn't the purpose of his help. I've written many letters to you over the years, and I've included them with this box. They were never sent since we didn't know where you were. We're both sorry, Raleigh. We're sorry we never got to meet you and love you the way you deserved. Love, your mother and father."

"I'm sorry, Raleigh," Damon whispers as she screams and cries. "If I knew…"

"Why would they do that?" she cries. "Why would they give me up?"

Raleigh breaks in my arms. She deflates completely and lets out such anguished and pained cries, I'm certain everyone in the complex can hear her. There's not a single person around her who isn't just as heartbroken for her as me.

She's been lied to her entire life. Now, all hope of her ever getting to meet her parents is ripped to shreds right in front of her. She'll never be able to ask them why they gave her up. She'll never get the closure she's confided in me that she desperately wants. Needs.

And as she loses her grasp on reality, I painfully come to realize that, though I want to be, I'm not the one she needs right now. She needs to be able to ask questions and get answers to things I don't have a prayer of helping her with.

She needs Damon.

She needs her brother.

Judging from the look on Damon's face, he needs her, too. It doesn't take a genius to see that he's having just as difficult of a time with this. He just found out he has a sister he knew nothing about who was raised by a man we all hate. I know him, and I have no doubt that he is pissed he didn't know about her. He would have stepped in in a heartbeat and taken Raleigh from his parents. Young and just starting college when she was born or not. He never would have allowed Matthew to get his hands on her.

I take a deep and steadying breath. "Raleigh," I whisper. I keep her securely in my arms and do all I can to soothe her and quiet her. "Sweetheart, I think you and Damon need to talk," I say against her ear. I look at Damon. He looks just as broken as she does. She nods as she takes deep breaths. "Why don't you take him inside into the library and talk?" I tug her hair gently. I don't want to let her go, but they need each other.

She looks up at me. "Why did they do this?" she whispers.

I shake my head slowly. "I don't know, baby. I don't. I wish I had those answers. I wish I could make all the pain you feel right now go away, but I can't." I lean in and kiss her softly. "But I think maybe Damon can." I put my head against her forehead and keep my voice low. "I think maybe you can help him, too." I intentionally flick my eyes towards him. He's hunched over. I can see by the slight tremor in his shoulders that he's crying.

Raleigh nods and wipes her eyes as she slowly gets up. I force myself to let her go, though, it might be the most painful thing I've ever done. I hate the idea of her not being near me while she's hurting like she is, but I also know I can't help her. Only Damon can do that.

She puts her hand lightly on his shoulder. "Let's go inside," she whispers.

It takes Damon a few moments to compose himself long enough to get up. Lance pats him on the back. Raleigh and Damon both wipe their eyes as they walk towards the house and disappear inside.

Josh pats my arm and goes back to leaning his elbows on his knees. "We may have solved the mystery of Raleigh's parentage, but I have a feeling our troubles are just beginning."

"Why do you say that?" I ask, tearing my eyes away from the door and looking at him.

Cole sighs and locks his fingers behind his head. "I don't know, but I'm with you, man."

I raise an eyebrow. "What am I missing?"

Josh chuckles and pats my shoulder as he gets up. "You aren't in the mafia anymore, Mr. CEO." He shoots me a smirk.

I laugh. "Fuck you. What's going on?"

Dane grins and takes his own seat. "Can't walk away, can you?"

"The mafia has been his life," my mother says. She kisses my head. "Kent and I are going to go for a walk. But we'll be around when Raleigh and Damon are done talking."

"Okay, mom," I say. I wait for her and Kent to walk away holding hands before I sit up. "It's a hard thing to completely leave. Now, what's going on?"

Dane glances at his parents, making sure they're out of ear shot. "We have a pretty high body count coming in. Seems to be a lot of similarities between them all."

"Looks like something we should be concerned about," Josh says. "Dane and Cole are keeping an eye on it."

"A mafia?" I ask. It's a little fucked up how I actually want him to say yes.

Josh shrugs. "Not entirely certain yet. But I will say it's not looking good."

I lean back in the pool chair. I've wanted to get out of the mafia completely for a long time. When I finally got the chance, I didn't think I'd miss it. Maybe it was just leading it that I didn't want. Or maybe I'm just fucking insane. Maybe I need the mafia to complete me or something ridiculous like that.

I'll step up if Josh needs me, but right now, my main concern is Raleigh. I can't imagine how devastating it must be for her to not get the closure she's dreamt of ever since she found out the truth about Matthew.

My job, above and beyond everything else, is to be here to support her and prove to her that she can always count on me to be her shoulder to cry on.

Her home.

Chapter Seventeen

❦ Raleigh ❦

I sit down in my favorite chair in the library and smile softly up at Damon as I wipe the tears threatening to fall. I haven't known Damon long. I haven't known anyone here that long, but I do know that Damon isn't one to cry. The usually tough, both physically and emotionally, man standing in front of me is struggling to hold it together.

"Raleigh," he whispers as he sits on the couch next to me. "I really didn't know. If I had, I wouldn't have let them give you to him."

I sniffle and reach over to take his hands in mine. They're large. Not quite like Alex's, but they are still very manly hands. Rough enough to know that he doesn't shy away from working hard, but gentle enough to know he won't hurt those he loves.

"My life wasn't bad, Damon." My voice cracks with tears. I swallow hard, but I am telling the truth. "I know how difficult it is to believe, considering you all know a different side of him."

"He was a cruel and very calculating man." Damon swallows hard himself and rubs his thumbs over the top of my hands.

I take a breath and nod slowly. "I know now. But... he... really didn't give me a bad life. I never wanted anything. I had everything I could want. The only thing I would have liked to have had was a television. He said he didn't believe in them. He wanted me to use my mind for more important things. I read a lot. And I didn't miss TV, honestly. I was too busy preparing myself for my college career. I believed that everything he had ever done was to help me reach my goals and succeed. He came off very supportive. At least until the last…" I close my eyes and take another breath before opening them and looking back at him. "The last couple of days."

"I know you feel like he was kind, Raleigh, but…" He shakes his head.

"I don't anymore," I say quietly. I let go of his hands slowly and stand. I pace a few moments as Damon watches me. "The longer I'm away, the more things start making sense. Like a different kind of sense, though. Not like the sense it made when it was happening." I sit on the arm of the couch across from him while I try to explain. "Before, everything just seemed…" I squint at him. "Normal? It was all my normal. All of it. No TV. Normal. Only music to keep me company or books. Normal. Having a nanny and tutor. Normal. His business associates coming for dinner all the time when he was home. Normal. Him disappearing for weeks. Normal. I never felt alone. I never felt like anything was off because it was how I grew up. I guess it's sort of like Alex and Josh. Even you. They grew up in a mafia family. So, everything mafia is totally normal. The tint on their windows that would probably get anyone else pulled over is normal for them. But that's not normal to me." I bite my lip as I look down.

Damon stands. "I guess I get it. Everything you've said to me wouldn't be my normal. I had TV to keep me company while my… our… parents were getting high." He starts pacing a little. "When Matthew disappeared for weeks at a time, we thought it was because he was taking care of one of our factions or enemies." He grips the back of the couch he was just sitting in. "But I suppose he was probably with you then."

I nod slowly. "I guess I'm not sure he was that whole time. I'm sure he probably was off doing mafia things during some of that. But I was never with him. Truthfully, I lived a rather privileged life, Damon. I had credit cards without a limit, just like Alex and Josh. Granted, I never really used them, but I did have moments of splurging. I went to spas. I just didn't go with friends because I didn't have any. I went with my nanny. She was the closest thing to a mother I had. Matthew told me my mother died during birth. He'd raised me as a single father, but he was a busy man. He needed help. He always told me he wanted the best for me. I wanted to go to Oxford. That was my goal since I was old enough to know what college was. He'd set me up with the best tutors to help me with that."

Damon stretches his arms over his head then locks his fingers behind his neck. "So why aren't you there? Why didn't you go?"

I look down again. "Um… I guess because my application wasn't what they were looking for. I did very well on the SAT's and ACT's. I worked really hard on the entrance exam and the application essay." I shrug and look up at him. "The night you all went after Matthew, I got my rejection letter."

Damon shakes his head and drops his arms. His features mimic the shock I felt when I read the letter. "What? How? I've witnessed how smart you are when you're helping Dallas with her studies."

I shrug again and swipe at my eyes. "I don't know. I went to Matthew after I got the letter. It was the first time in my whole life that he didn't pull me in his arms and hug me when I was upset. He told me I was stupid for only applying to Oxford. I should have had a second and third choice. Renza, up until that point, had also always been super supportive of me. When Matthew married her, she and I got along very well. We went shopping together. We were close in age. She was my first friend. I loved having her around. But she also snapped at me. She told me I was an idiot for thinking Oxford would accept a homeschooled girl with no life experience."

A dark cloud passes over Damon's face. I'm not sure I recognize the look that crosses over his face, but it quickly passes. He drops into the couch and puts his feet up on the table. "So, what now? Is Oxford still what you want?"

I smile softly. "I don't know, honestly. This is the first time in my entire life I'm actually living my life. I've never had freedom. I've never worked. I've never had people I can call and text when I want to talk. I've never really felt…" I stand as I think of the words. I pace a few moments before turning back to him. "I've felt loved, but I think what I feel here with all of you and Alex is really what true love is. The longer I'm away from it, the more I realize that everything about my life, including the love I thought I had, was fake. If Matthew really loved me as I thought he did, then he wouldn't have treated me like he had that last night. I feel like he knew it was coming to an end. I don't know if he knew you were coming, but I feel like he had to have known, and he knew he wouldn't survive. And, I guess that's where things have always been confusing for me. I replay that night and always go back and forth about it."

"Why?" He furrows his brow in confusion. "Seems pretty obvious he showed who he really was that night. Same with Renza."

I smile a little as I sit back in my chair. "Yeah… I can understand how you'd come to that conclusion. To me, though, I kind of wonder if he knew being cruel would make me run away to my favorite hiding place on the beach. It was one of the few places he allowed me to go on my own. It was a mile or so away from the house, but it was a quiet place. Private. He owned that part of the beach. I wondered if maybe he knew what was going to happen and didn't want me to be a part of it. I guess it's something I've held onto this whole time to justify to myself that he wasn't all bad."

Damon is quiet for a few minutes. Finally, he leans forward and rests his elbows on his knees. He makes a steeple symbol out of his fingers and taps the tips of them together as he looks at me. "He had some good qualities. Nowhere near redeeming, but they were there."

I tuck my legs underneath me and watch him. "He had to have some if he raised you, Alex, and Josh."

Damon gives me a soft smile. "I don't know that he really had a hand in it. It was mostly Rebekkah. She couldn't stand to see me starve. Alex was the only one who knew about what my life was like at home. He told his mom. Matthew wasn't all that agreeable at first, but he realized pretty damn fast that I was willing to do whatever I needed to in order to make my own way in life. I think that was always the one thing he admired about me. He could send me out with his kids on a mission to do something, and I didn't ask questions. Eventually, he came to trust me as one of his own. Of course, it had always been Alex I was loyal to, so when he walked, so did I. I followed his orders to stay and keep an eye on Jessa after he left. I traveled back and forth between here and Italy a lot. And I was always around for Rebekkah if she needed anything. My contact with my parents, though, was very limited. Especially after I started college. I had no idea she was even pregnant. I'd gone for many months at a time without seeing them. I was okay with that. To be honest, I'm pretty sure they were, too."

"That's so sad… I was always really happy when he came home. He called me every single night when he wasn't there just to check in. And he never seemed distracted or anything. He always seemed to make me a priority. I think now I'm seeing it was all an act. I'm not sure that he really ever truly loved me." I look down at my hands.

"I wish I could say that I think he did, but I can't. I really think that you were just a pawn. You were a way for him to control my parents. I don't know why. Maybe he was supplying them. That's what I think. He probably told them that he'll take their supply if they say shit to me. Kill me. They've been drug addicts my entire life and before. Mom had some moments of being sober. I assume the letter and the box of stuff was probably one of those moments. And I can say that, in their own way, they loved me. And you. They wouldn't want to see harm come to either of us."

I hug myself and keep my eyes lowered. "What were they like?" I ask quietly.

Damon chuckles. "Well, when they were sober they were actually pretty great. They were loving parents. They made sure I had everything I needed. Dad, even though he was almost always high, had a fairly good job. Growing up, I always questioned how the hell he managed to pull off a full-time job because most of the time when he was home, they were shooting up. But he'd pull it off. It was like he lived a double life. By day he was Mr. Marketing. Came up with really good ads and slogans. By night, he was a different person."

"Unless he was sober…"

Damon nods. "When he was sober, I never had to worry about food. Hell, he'd blow a grand on new school clothes for me. But those times were few and far between. Actually, about the time mom would have been pregnant with you, it was my senior year of high school. Alex and I were trying to figure out college. He wanted to go. Gavin was going. I didn't have the funding. That was when Alex started paying me for the work I did with him and his family. Up until then, I wasn't taking money. I didn't look at it like a job. And what the fuck was I going to do with money anyway? The Lucinio's were already taking pretty good care of me. If I wasn't with them, Alex made sure I had lunch at school. And when mom and dad were back on the needle, I wasn't with them anyway. I stayed with Alex. My senior year was when things blew up with them. I walked away. Mom had called a few times to check in. Just to see how I was. But she never mentioned being pregnant. Just said that they were trying to get clean. Sometimes, she thought they'd do it. Then they ended up going back."

I wipe a tear away. It's hard knowing how much my birth parents struggled. "It's a vicious cycle."

"Yeah. Yeah, with them it always was. I may have had my issues with them, but I can assure you that what they did by giving you up, they thought it was the best option."

I look up at him with a watery smile. "They probably didn't know what he was really like…"

Damon holds out a shaky hand to me. I stare at it a few moments before taking it. When he gently pulls me into his arms for a hug, I let loose the flood of tears I wasn't entirely certain I needed to let out. When he pulls me next to him, I cry into his shoulder. I'm not sure how long we stay like that, but when I feel his tears on my neck, I know he needed it just as much as me.

After a long while, Damon finally takes a breath. "I'm really sorry, Raleigh. If I'd known, I would have done something about it. By the time you were born, I had enough money. And if I'd talked to Alex and Gavin, we'd have figured it out. Gavin's mom would have been happy to help. Alex, at that time, was already really close to Ryan. Ryan would have helped. We were a very tight circle. Just like we are now. I wouldn't have just given you up. I could've saved you from all of this shit you've been through. The pain and confusion. All the shock with finding out who he really is. I would've saved you from that."

I sniffle and nod. "It's not your fault. You didn't even know."

"If I hadn't walked away, though, I would have."

I shake my head. "You had to do what you had to do for yourself. You had to survive. I don't blame you. There's nothing to forgive you for. You didn't do anything wrong. You can't feel guilty about it because you didn't know. Despite everything I've found out about him over the last few months, my life wasn't bad. He did take care of me. No matter what his ulterior motives were, he took care of me. And it might seem a little bit crazy or even stupid, but I really believe that his cruelty that night, while it may have been who he truly is, was his way of getting me to leave so I was safe. The more and more I play it over in my mind, I really believe that. That behavior may have been normal for him to you, but to me, it was out of character. I feel like he did it because he knew you were coming for him. Which would make sense. He did have Jessa and Dallas."

"You may not get anyone else to understand that, but I do. I understand holding onto the good things over the bad. I choose to look at the good things my… our… parents did over the bad. Even over the drugs, I know they loved me. I'm pretty sure that they felt like they were getting a sweet deal with Matthew. I can't prove it, but I don't doubt Matthew was supplying them to buy their silence on how things with you went down. Your adoption was never legal."

I sigh because it's a conclusion I've come to myself. "I figured that."

He pulls back slightly but keeps me in the hug. "Lance has been looking. He asked Robby to help. Neither of them has been able to find anything. As soon as I gave him that birth certificate, though, he was able to find a lot of things that didn't make a whole lot of sense."

My eyes widen. "Like what…?" My heart starts hammering in my chest.

"Well, Raleigh Jennings doesn't exist. You have no birth certificate. Nothing."

"But I have a driver's license. I needed a birth certificate to get that. And my passport."

"Honey, I don't know what Matthew did to get you that stuff. That's not my expertise. All I can tell you is that you do not exist in the State Department."

I slump, confused, and look up at him. "But my license. It's from the States…"

Damon shakes his head. "It's from Florida, but there is no DMV record. This is part of the reason that Alex was so suspicious at first. Because you really are a ghost, honey. Or at least you were. With that birth certificate we can actually get you real identification. We think he probably faked it. Or he paid someone to get you legit identification but keep you off the books. I guess it's a good thing you were never pulled over, or his entire ruse would have been exposed."

I shift and sigh again. I lean back against the couch. "I just don't understand a lot of this stuff. It's so upsetting. I feel like I don't have an identity. My whole life has just been a complete lie."

Damon leans back against the couch. "Well, you have an identity. You're a kind woman who landed one of the world's most eligible billionaire bachelors." He gives me a teasing smile and elbows me gently.

I can't help but laugh. "Alex is pretty amazing."

Damon grins. "Seriously, though. You're a good person. Identity isn't tied to a name. It's who you are. You're a hardworking woman. You're smart. You've made a name for yourself among the family. We don't look at you as a girl without a name tied to a ruthless man. We look at you as a young woman who has worked very hard to move past what she came from and make a life for herself. On her own terms. There isn't a lot of women in this world who would not only go up against Alex Lucinio, but also win his heart. But beyond that, you have a name. You're Raleigh Knight. You're my sister. Your parents may not have been that great of people. We may not have any surviving relatives, but we have each other." He pauses to look at me. "If you'll have me that is."

I smile and sniffle. I try to wipe my eyes before the tears fall as I nod. But when Damon wraps me in his arms, they start. I have no hope of stopping them, and I don't even want to make an attempt.

I'm Raleigh Knight. I have an incredible brother. An amazing boyfriend. And I'm part of such a strong and loving family. I am making a name for myself. I love my job. I love helping people. I might not know what the future holds, but I do know one thing.

Raleigh Knight belongs right here.

Chapter Eighteen

☙ Alex ☙

"I don't know how the hell I thought I could be CEO and accountant at the same time," I grumble at my computer screen. Like it listens to me anyway.

"Talking to inanimate objects?" Ryan asks as he closes the door to my office.

I look up at him. "Whoever let you in is fired."

He chuckles as he strides towards my desk like he owns the damn building. "That would be your girlfriend. I'm not sure how she'd take being fired for that." He plops in a chair and unbuttons his suit jacket.

I raise an eyebrow. "Did I forget about something?" I look him up and down. "Why are you wearing a suit?"

He chuckles again. "I'm sure you don't remember, but I'm not just a mafia boss. I do actually run companies that require attention sometimes." His smirk makes me shake my head.

"You're an asshole."

"I get that a lot."

"A six feet five-inch asshole," I grumble.

"Mmhmm. Get that a lot, too. My wife called me that just this morning." He crosses his arms over his chest. "What's got you all pissy?"

I lean back in my chair and yawn. "I bit off more than I can chew. I admit it. I thought I could do the CEO thing and all of the accounting, too. I'm a fucking whiz with numbers. Raleigh helps a lot. But I was wrong. Accounting is more than a full-time job. I'm in over my head."

Ryan shakes his head. "First of all, why the fuck are you doing the accounting?"

I look at him incredulously. "Are you so old you forgot what happened just two months ago? You know. My accountant shot and killed. His assistant disappearing in the wind. My girlfriend kidnapped, and then almost kidnapped a second time from her fucking bedroom?"

Ryan barks out a laugh. "No. I didn't forget, you fucker. I'm asking why you didn't hire someone else."

"Uh…" I rub the back of my neck sheepishly. I should have hired someone else. "Because I don't trust anyone."

"Then you should have come to me. I've been putting accountants in all of Lucinio's companies since Josh took over. Had I known you didn't hire anyone for that reason, I would have been happy to help. You know that. We've been friends for how long? You're like my little brother. You know that."

I don't know why, but the dressing down makes me feel better. I've been fighting to take control of Lucinio Tech on my own for a while now. I've completely ignored the fact that three of the people closest to me have run their own companies for years. I can lean on them without being judged and told I'm failing.

"You know, I think it goes back to Matthew." I glare. I hate saying his name. Just his name on my tongue pisses me off. "I fucking hate to admit it, but I feel like me failing with this company is proving him right about me. That's why I've been working my ass off to deal with everything on my own."

"If you think I didn't know that, you aren't as smart as I thought."

I chuckle and grab a pen from my desk. I start flicking it just to give my hands something to do. "I don't know, man. I think I'm having a difficult time giving up any control because I'm afraid I'm going to get stabbed in the back."

Ryan shrugs. "You might. But if you do, you deal with it. Lucinio Tech is a multi-billion-dollar international company. You can't expect to deal with all of the finances on your own, Alex. You need a CFO. Not just an accountant."

I stare blankly at the wall as I think. "That's giving another person too much power," I finally say. I lean forward and put my elbows on my desk. "I can't do that."

"How much power do you think a CFO has? You pay him or her well. They deal with the finances of the company. Everything, and I do mean everything, is approved by you. It's how Jason runs his company. Chase does it the same way. I do. Josh does. Granted, I have CEOs to work in my place. So does Josh. We step in when we need to or to check in. But you. You don't need that."

I sigh because I know he's right. It's been an idea I've been playing with for a while. "I guess I should really start looking, huh?"

"Have Raleigh do an ad and run it. I'll step into the interviews with you if you want my opinion on the candidates."

I nod, determined. "Fuck. It needs to be done. I'll get it taken care of. In the meantime, why are you here? Did I miss a meeting with you?"

Ryan shakes his head and laughs "I'm your five o'clock. Remember?"

I look down at my calendar and see his name. I shake my head. "Sorry. I've been lost in numbers for the last three hours."

"It's fine. Raleigh just told me to come in because she knew you'd probably still be looking things over."

"Yeah. Well, you got me now." I grin, teasingly. "What can I do for you, Mr. Crane?"

He smiles. "Crane Enterprise needs an upgrade. I told Jas I'd just let you know since I needed to come here anyway."

"I'll get it taken care of."

"As for me, I just acquired a new company. Superior Central Outlet."

I raise an eyebrow. "The fuck? You bought a clothing outlet?" Superior Central Outlet is one of Chicago's and the central part of the United States' largest clothing chain.

Ryan holds up his hands and shakes his head as he laughs. "It's not like that." He puts his hands down. "One of my guards came to me a month or so ago. Just about the time Raleigh found out who her parents were. He said his sister was in trouble. Well, her husband was. He ended up with a large amount in gambling debts after his sister was killed in a domestic violence incident. He didn't take it well. Started drinking and placing drunken bets that he lost. He realized his fuck up, but by that time it was far too late. He had loan sharks breathing down his neck and threatening his wife. The guard told me what was going on. I bought out the company and paid off his debts. When I make my investment back, I'll give it back."

I nod. "That sounds more like you."

"I own enough useless companies. I don't need a clothing chain added onto it. But while it's mine, I'm upgrading a lot of shit. Their systems are completely out of date, and I need something protecting customer's privacy. They've already had some credit card information stolen."

Putting on my CEO hat, I start taking notes. "How many stores?"

"Eighty-three, but two are re-opening after being closed due to his missteps and one more was in the process of opening before they halted everything. So, eighty-three now. Three more over the next few months."

"Got it. You want a full-on system overhaul?"

"I want it all, Alex. Whatever you feel like we'll need, but I also need something on the back end to stop the credit card theft issues."

"I can install a program to deal with that. In the meantime, what are you doing about physical employee and customer theft? You'll have to deal with that in retail."

"My hope is the owner knows how to deal with that shit and will just tell me what he needs."

"I'd suggest upgrading store security. I don't deal with things like metal detectors and alarm systems, but if you need any of that, I work with another company I contract out for those things."

"Set it up."

I make a note for it and to set up the time for techs to install the security software. "I'll get them out this week. Just need a list of the locations and where the headquarters is located."

"I'll get it emailed to you. What else do you need?"

"Jason's timeline, but I can call him and see when he wants the techs to do the install. For his system, it needs to be from the ground. My techs try to do it remotely, it will backfire in rapid succession and take my whole damn company down for a day."

Ryan laughs heartily. "Your security program is that good, it could take you out?"

I laugh because he knows the answer. "If it detects any kind of anomaly, yes. Obviously, my techs have code to get through it, you asshole."

"I'm fucking with you." Ryan grins as he stands. "Alright. Aria wants my undivided attention tonight. I promised her dinner and a movie. Time for me to go so she doesn't kick my ass." He winks.

I laugh. "It's funny a woman half your size and age can bring you to your knees."

He smiles as he heads for the door. "I think you know the feeling. Raleigh sure has a hold on you." The asshole doesn't bother to look back before he walks out of my office.

I laugh because he's absolutely right. She's only eighteen. That's seventeen years younger than I am, but if she asked me to, I'd chop off my own legs and fall at her feet. I wouldn't even question it. I shake my head as I stand. I have fallen far and fucking deep with this one.

I quickly cross my office to the door and open it. After looking at my schedule and seeing no more meetings, I only have one thing on my mind. And none of it involves accounting or hiring CFO's.

I grin when I see the back of Raleigh's head. At the end of the day, she gets tired of having her long, beautiful auburn hair piled on top of her head or held back with a ribbon hair tie. She literally lets her hair down, and I think it's one of the most beautiful things I've ever seen.

I put my arms on both sides of her and lean my hands on her desk. She squeaks as I kiss her neck. Chance, her guard, laughs from the corner he's standing in. My smile grows even wider as I nibble on her neck. She moans. I don't need to see her to know she's closed her eyes as she leans into me.

"Take off, Chance. I'll take it from here." I don't look up at him. I pull Raleigh's chair back and turn her towards me as I stand to my full height. I hold out my hands.

Chance laughs again. "You got it, sir." He immediately heads for the elevator.

She smiles shyly and takes my hands. "What are we doing?"

"I'm starving," I say with a smirk.

She tilts her head as I pull her up. "Want to order in?"

I smile wider and walk backwards towards my office, still holding her hands. "In a manner of speaking, sure."

Her adorable, confused look gets even more beautiful when she furrows her brows. "I could order Chinese."

I shake my head. "Nope. Not in the mood for Chinese." I back through my door and pull her into my office.

"Oh. Okay. Um… what about steaks? I hear the new chef at Eleven is really good and makes a mean filet."

"Nope. Not in the mood for steak either. Something… sweet." I fight to not look down at her body and ignore the fact that my dick is already straining against the zipper of my slacks.

"Something sweet." She chews the inside of her cheek as she thinks, and I damn near come undone.

Since she moved in with me last month, just after finding out who her parents are and that Damon is her brother, I've become obsessed with each and every one of her looks. When she's concentrating hard, she always bites the inside of her cheek. When she's lost in a book, she gets this faraway look in her eye.

One of my favorites is when she is laser focused on cooking me dinner, though I tell her she doesn't need to. Her tongue darts out of her mouth just slightly enough to make me want to suck on it. Her eyes narrow into adorable slits. I can't resist the look and am instantly hard.

But my favorite is when she's underneath me while I'm teasing her to her climax. Her eyes roll back just before she closes them, and the blissed out peaceful look that crosses her face is everything to me.

"Oh! I got it. How about gelato? Eleven is starting to make it for dessert."

I smile at how cutely clueless she is as I stop in front of the black leather couch. "I love Arianna to death, but I have absolutely no desire for gelato from her beloved restaurant. At least not right now. I have something much sweeter and far more delicious on my mind." It's then I give into the completely selfish need to look her up and down.

Her eyes widen in realization. "Oh!"

Without another word, I step closer and drop her hands in favor of putting one arm around her waist to pull her into me while I tangle the other in her hair and tug so she's looking up at me. Her eyes darken with the intense desire I feel as I kiss her long and hard.

She moans, and my dick twitches as it grows impossibly harder. I ignore it because while it may want her mouth wrapped around it, I want my mouth between her thighs. Ever since the first time I went down on her, I crave her taste. I'd happily deprive myself of all my favorite foods if it meant licking her sweet come when she releases it on my tongue for me.

I guide her down on the couch and prop a pillow underneath her head while I continue ravishing her mouth in much the same way I'm about to ravish her pussy. I nip her tongue lightly and suck on it before pulling away slowly.

I hook my fingers into the waistband of her pants and begin slowly tugging them down. She lets out another squeak and grips my forearms as she sits up. She looks around the office then back up at me.

"Here? Alex, what if someone comes?"

I grin and continue pulling her pants and panties down. "The only person who will be coming is you."

She blushes a furious shade of red and slaps a hand over mouth. "Alex…"

"Something you'll be screaming in a few minutes."

I drop her pants and panties on the floor. I waste no time taking what I want. I slide my middle finger slowly and deeply into her soaking wet pussy. She arches into me and closes her eyes when my finger slides deeper.

"Oh… yes…" She grips my wrist as I slowly thrust.

"You're soaked. Always so wet for me." I watch her pussy while I thrust. She coats my finger with everything I want from her.

Her thighs start to tremble. "Only for you. Only ever for you."

"Damn right. No one touches you but me."

I let her ride my finger. Her breathing quickens. She opens her eyes only to let them fall closed again. Her pussy tightens and clenches as I thrust. I twist my finger and crook it. I bend and take her clit in my mouth.

"Alex!" she screams, bucking her hips into me. "Oh my God!" She tangles her other hand in my hair and tugs. She keeps the one she had on my wrist firmly gripping it.

"Fuck, you taste like Heaven." I say the words low and deeply, letting the vibration from my voice reverberate against her clit.

"Ah!" She jerks her hips into me.

I lavish my tongue from her pussy to her clit and suck, repeating the motion again and again. I add another finger slowly and thrust, quickening the pace. Her pussy pulses and grips my fingers so tightly, I know she's going to come soon.

Her thighs tremble against my shoulders. She tries to close them as the pleasure from her release gets closer. I reach down and adjust myself. My cock is straining so hard against my pants that it physically hurts. I'm not a small guy. Even a semi-erection causes a painful problem.

I groan against her clit with relief when my cock cooperates and moves to the side where it can grow without hurting. While I thrust my fingers into her, I give myself a couple of squeezes to relieve some of the pressure. It does nothing. Her moans and sweet fucking scent of her sex drives me insane.

"Alex! I'm -" She doesn't finish the sentence before her hips arch off the couch. "Ah!"

"Come?" I slow my thrusts, helping her through as she releases. "Fuck, so sweet." I lick her clean as she jerks and writhes under me.

When she comes down, I pull her into my lap. I've noticed that after any kind of sexual activity, Raleigh likes being held. She likes the closeness, almost like she doesn't want to let the euphoric feeling go right away.

I'm perfectly content giving her all she needs from me. I used to think my life-long dream was to be out of the mafia. I was wrong.

My dream, my only dream, is her.

Chapter Nineteen

❦ Raleigh ❦

"So, as you can see, we need help," Alex says gesturing at the computer screen in his office.

I shift a little on his lap where he pulled me when he started explaining the accounting. "I thought we were handling it."

"Well, we were, baby, but we need someone who specifically focuses on just that aspect of things. I've pushed back a lot of meetings this week already because I've been focused on this. We need an accountant for this branch of Lucinio Tech. And we need a Chief Financial Officer who can handle the finances for the entire company. I can't do all of that, and I'd never expect you to. It took Ryan coming in here and telling me that earlier."

I reach for the last slice of pizza Alex ordered after ravishing me on the couch just over an hour ago. "I can create an ad for an accountant and a CFO if you'd like me to, but I think we need to be careful on where it goes. I know you said the job sites, but I'm not so sure I trust them. I think we need to specifically look in certain places, but I'm not really sure where."

"I just need you to create it. I'll take care of the rest. I can talk to Jason and Chase about it."

"Thank you. It's something I would like to do, but I can't do all that myself. I'm working three positions. The way I'm going, I'll never sleep."

I frown and look at him with the pizza halfway to my mouth. "That's not funny. You've already been working so much that it makes me worry."

He chuckles and smiles before kissing me. "You worrying about me is adorable."

I blush. "I mean it." Before he can answer, I hear the phone ring at my desk. I hit a button on Alex's desk phone to answer it. "Lucinio Tech. Alex Lucinio's office."

"Hey, Raleigh. It's Josh. Is he available?"

"Yeah, he's right here."

"What's up, Josh?" Alex asks. He nibbles on my neck and shoulder and tightens his grip around my waist.

"I'm thinking steaks and vegetable skewers," Josh says. "But you have nothing in your damn fridge. Do you two even eat?"

Alex laughs. "We just did. What are you doing at my house?"

"Construction. I need to be out for a couple of weeks. What did you eat?"

"Pizza and Raleigh." I feel him smile against my neck.

"Alex!" I squeak and slap his arm, feeling the heat creep into my cheeks while simultaneously making me wet.

Josh is cracking up. The bastard. "Come home and pick up steaks. I'm fucking bored."

"You're bored?" Alex shakes his head. "Aren't you the one always complaining you're always busy and have no time to relax?"

"I relaxed two days. Now I'm looking for action. Anything. But Lance has nothing on your missing assistant. Alec has something going on outside of the city. Dallas is busy with some huge fucking project that I don't understand."

"Why don't you go join Alec? I'm sure he'd love the Lucinio Mafia to help him decimate whatever poor fool pissed him off."

"Nah. He said it's already an unfair fight."

It's my turn to shake my head. "I'm surrounded by crazy people. But if you're so bored, you can help us find a new accountant and CFO."

"Done. Just bring home food. I'm fucking starving." Josh hangs up.

I look back at Alex. "Seriously. I've only lived with you for a month, but I'd already forgotten how insane he is sometimes."

Alex laughs. "Josh has never been good about sitting around. He needs to be doing something. It's been fairly quiet lately. That's why he's been going off to help some of his other teams with things that he really doesn't need to be around for."

"I can understand that. I sometimes feel bored if I don't have something to do. That's why I'm always asking you if you need anything."

He smiles. "And here I thought it was just because you love me."

I giggle and lower my eyes. "I do love you," I whisper.

He tangles his fingers in my hair and tugs just enough so that I'm looking into his perfect blue eyes. "And I love you." He kisses me until my toes curl. I'm breathless, but I cling to him like he's my air.

🍒🍒🍒

I laugh when Alex swats my ass on the way in the house.

Our house.

We put the groceries on the counter in the kitchen. Before we even get any of them out of the bags, though, Josh appears. He says nothing as he dives into the bags searching for his dinner. I watch him in pure amusement.

"Can I help you with something?" Alex asks, grinning.

"I can't even get to my kitchen. It's torn apart." Josh shakes his head. "I thought all they were doing was attaching my kitchen to the safehouse underneath. I didn't realize they were going to move everything out and demo the fucking the thing." He looks up at us. "You realize they threw everything in the fridge out?"

"Well, I don't think Ry would want rotting food in his garage while your kitchen is being demoed." Alex bites his lip to keep from smiling.

Josh growls low and goes back to digging through the bags. "I'm staying with Dane. He's not so much of a dick."

"I'd be okay with that, but Dane's house is in the same predicament as yours." Alex opens one bag and finds the steaks. He hands them to Josh.

Josh moans in appreciation. "Fuck me, I'm starving."

"Why didn't you just order something?" I ask, unable to hold in the laugh.

He looks at me like I'm the crazy one. "When have you ever known me to order out? Seriously. In eight months, have I ever ordered takeout?"

I tilt my head. "Come to think of it... no. Not once. Why?"

"Oh, here we go." Alex rolls his eyes and starts putting the groceries away.

"Do you think I look this way by chance? How the hell do you think I got this way?" He gestures down his body. "By eating takeout?"

I snort laugh. "No. I've seen how much time you spent in the gym. Which is how I know you can afford takeout." I turn my back and start helping Alex put away groceries. "You're one of those people who could eat takeout every single day for the rest of your life and never gain an ounce."

Josh laughs. "Maybe, but I'm not putting shit like that in my body. If I want a pizza, I'll make it myself." He starts walking out of the kitchen, but turns back. "Hey, I invited Gavin over. He's been moping."

"Aww..." I turn towards him while I hand Alex a bag of lettuce. "Is he okay?"

"Considering Gavin has a different woman in his bed every week, I doubt it's a woman. I'm going with the fact that he hasn't seen any action to keep him entertained, just like me." Josh grins and walks out to the back of the house where the grill is.

I look up at Alex while I hand him a bag of cheese. "I'm so confused."

Alex laughs. "Ever since Gavin's wife was killed, he's gone back to his old playboy ways. Gavin lives for women and mafia life. If he doesn't have a woman underneath him or he's not on a mission or... uh... persuading someone to give him information, he's not happy."

"You mean, if he's not beating someone up?" I smile but have no idea why.

Alex laughs. "We don't like to call it torture, but something close to that. We always tease him about how fucked up he has to be to get off on shit like that. He doesn't actually get off on it, but you know what I mean."

"I get it. Why it doesn't bother me, though, is something that freaks me out."

Alex closes the refrigerator door and pulls me gently into his arms. "Hey, now. Get out of your head. There's nothing wrong with you."

I take a deep breath and breathe him in. I love the way he smells. Spicy. Strong. "Shouldn't knowing that all happens be bothersome to me? What kind of person isn't bothered that her boyfriend's best friend likes torturing people?"

He keeps one arm firmly around me. The other snakes up to my hair. He loves my hair. "Baby, it takes a very special kind of woman to be involved with someone in the mafia. I don't think it doesn't bother you at all. If you didn't feel something, it would mean you have no heart. And I know better. I've been doing this a very long time, and even I still feel emotion when I'm about to make a kill. We all do. It's one of the many things that make us so different from other mafias."

I look up at him, keeping my arms locked around his waist. "So, I'm not crazy?"

"Well…" He grins. "I didn't say that. We're all a little insane."

I giggle and try to push away. It doesn't work. He holds me closer and tighter. Instead, I stand on my tiptoes and kiss his jaw. "I love you. I know I say it a lot since I first said it, but I can't stop."

"Good. I don't want you to." He leans down and gives me the kiss I want.

I close my eyes and melt into him with a quiet moan. I love when he takes control of everything, but when he dominates the kiss, all I want to do is stay inside his arms with his lips locked to mine and never leave.

He pulls away slowly when he hears the front door open. "That would be Gavin." He runs his thumb along my lower lip.

"Maybe we could just stay in here and let them have their fun outside," I say as seductively as I can, looking up at him through my lashes and letting my hands wander down to his perfectly sculpted ass. I squeeze.

He lets out a low growl. His eyes burn into mine. His grin turns a little dangerous. He leans down and kisses me with a quiet moan. I close my eyes and smile, thinking I may be getting my way, and he'll carry me upstairs to the bedroom. Instead, he slaps my bottom as he pulls away. I jump as my eyes fly open.

His sexy grin is far more teasing than dangerous. "Maybe if you're a good girl, I'll teach you all about the number sixty-nine."

Gavin chooses that moment to walk into the kitchen. I blush furiously as he laughs. "Am I interrupting?" He grins because he knows the answer.

I glare. "Yes. Go away."

He laughs again. "My apologies. Let me just grab a beer and he can go back to ravishing you and teaching you all about the number sixty-nine. Which is my favorite number, by the way."

Alex laughs as he pulls away. "You've always had the worst timing. You know that, right?" He grabs a beer from the fridge and tosses it to Gavin.

"I have impeccable timing. I'm sure she'd rather you fuck her on the bed and not the counter." Gavin winks at me as he opens the beer.

"Oh my God!" I throw a roll of paper towels at him. "Josh needs those. Get out."

Gavin cracks up. "I fucking love her. She doesn't take shit from anyone."

Alex drops an arm around my waist and laughs. "Damn right. Least of all you. Better do what she says before she makes me kick your ass. I'll have no choice if I want my dessert later."

I can feel the flames from my face scorching my entire body as I pull away from him, laughing. I grab a platter for the steaks on my way out of the kitchen. "I hate both of you," I call over my shoulder.

"No you don't! Your life wouldn't be the same without me to entertain you!" Gavin calls after me.

I can't help but laugh again, but the truth is he's absolutely right. I love how we've fallen into this easy banter, but my life really wouldn't be the same without him. Without any of them. I don't know where I'd be if they hadn't caught Matthew that night.

It's often something I think about. Would I have gotten into another college? Would I have gotten a job? Would he have let me leave to start my own life? I have always believed in soulmates. Even though I've never dated anyone or been with anyone in any manner before Alex, I've always believed there is someone out there for me. I know that's Alex, but I wonder if we would have met somehow if Matthew wasn't the way he was.

Being that Damon is my brother and one of his best friends, I know we would have met that way, but I wonder if my parents had done a legal adoption. Would I have still found out Damon is my brother? Would I have met Alex?

I know I can't possibly ever get those questions answered, so I refuse to let them bother me or keep me up at night. I can't help but wonder, though. How different would my life be today if certain things that happened throughout it had changed?

Just before I walk outside to the backyard, I hear the front door open. I turn and see Lance and Damon walking through the door. Damon closes it behind him and puts a hand on Lance's shoulder to keep him from walking into a wall.

I can't stop the smile that lights up my face. "Hey, Damon! Hi, Lance."

Damon shakes his head when Lance mumbles something neither of us can understand. "Hey, sweetie. Where's the boss?" Damon asks.

"Grilling out back." I cock my head. "Everything okay?"

Lance looks up at me. "Uh… Not exactly. Is Alex here? Or did he stay at work?"

I furrow my brows, suddenly a little uneasy. "He's in the kitchen with Gavin. What's wrong?"

Damon and Lance share a look with each other before looking back at me. Lance heads for the door to the backyard. Damon reaches up to rub the back of his neck. I watch him cautiously, growing more and more nervous.

"Head outside. I'll grab the guys," he finally says.

I tilt my head a little but do as he says. "Okay…" I glance over my shoulder and see him heading for the kitchen. I slide the door closed and hand Josh the platters. "That was weird," I mumble.

He takes the platters. "What was weird?"

I glance at Lance. He's already claimed a pool chair and has his nose buried in his laptop. I sigh and shake my head. "Did he say anything when he came out?" I ask quietly, looking up at Josh.

"Nope." He removes the steaks from the grill. "Why?"

"Well, Damon and Lance showed up asking for you and Alex. And they gave me a weird look. I don't know how to explain it."

"I'm sure he'll explain, sweetheart. Is Alex coming out with plates?"

"Yeah." I look towards the door as Alex and Gavin come out with Damon trailing behind. "And some other things."

"Good. Go take a seat. Relax. I got this."

I nibble on my lower lip and do as Josh says. I take a seat next to Lance, but before I can settle, Alex grips my waist and sits down, pulling me into his lap. I giggle when he nibbles my shoulder and kisses his way up to my neck.

"So, what's up, Engle?" Alex asks with his lips against my neck.

Lance looks up at him then shakes his head. "Wait until Gav and J sit."

"That bad?" I ask.

Lance chuckles. "I'll say this. You're going to be pissed off, Raleigh. And not a single one of us are going to blame you."

"Uh oh…" I snuggle back into Alex.

Josh leads Gavin and Damon over to us. He hands Lance a plate. Everyone settles and waits. Lance sets his laptop down long enough to cut his steak up so he can eat while he talks. I can't help but notice how calm everyone is.

Exactly the opposite of me. My heart is racing and sounds like an 808 drum set. Had I not already eaten, I wouldn't be able to. I'm already regretting the pizza Alex and I ordered. It feels like it could come up at any moment.

"Alright, Lance. I think you've made us wait long enough," Josh says. "What the hell is going on?"

He sighs and looks at me. "Well, Alex was really bothered by Oxford and you not getting in. So was Damon." He glances at Alex then back to me. "They asked me to do some digging."

I'm suddenly very uncomfortable. My heart no longer sounds like an 808. It sounds like a F-18 fighter jet. "Okay…"

Alex's arms tighten around me. "What did you find out?"

He lets out a breath. "That letter you received as a rejection? It's not the kind of rejection letter they send." He reaches in his back pocket and hands me a folded-up form letter. "They sent me a copy of an example rejection letter."

I take it with shaky hands and a sniffle. The letter looks totally different from the rejection letter I received. My head knows what happened, but my heart, which I can hear very clearly in my ears, refuses to allow me to speak. The tears I hadn't realized were falling hit the paper I'm trying so hard to hold still.

"Fuck, baby, I'm sorry." Alex hugs me tightly to him and gently takes the paper from my hands.

"He…" I start uncontrollably sobbing. I turn my face into his chest and tremble. "Why…?"

Alex runs his fingers through my hair as I cough and try to catch my breath. "I'm so sorry, beautiful. So, so fucking sorry."

Lance clears his throat. "There's more," he says quietly.

"Just get it out," Josh says. I feel him sit next to Alex and start rubbing my back lightly.

"Well, I dug pretty deep into their application records. They received an application from you and sent you a letter." Lance pauses as I try to compose myself enough to look up at him. He says nothing, but turns his laptop towards me.

"Jesus Christ," Alex whispers. He hugs me tighter.

I burst into a fresh wave of tears. "I don't understand why he would do that! To hurt me? To control me?"

"There's no rhyme or reason to why he does what he does," Josh says. "But if you want my opinion, it's a way to control you."

Lance clears his throat again. "Actually… I have an answer for that."

I rub my chest as I tremble. "I c-can't handle anymore."

"I really think you need to hear this…," Lance says.

Alex sighs. "What?"

"I have an ID on your accountant's assistant," Lance says.

"Damn. I didn't see that one coming," Gavin whispers.

I wipe my eyes and try to stay strong. "Who?"

"We know who he is. I have an employment record," Alex says.

"Oh, I know. I ran it. Franklin Edwards isn't his real name. Close, though. Edward Franklin," Lance says.

Something hits me and I inhale sharply. "Oh… my… God. Oh my God!" I sit up so fast, I hit my head on Alex's chin. I rub my head. "Ow. Edward Franklin. That was Matthew's partner! He was over at the house all the time!" My mind races so fast, I can hardly keep up.

"What?" Alex asks.

I reach for Lance's laptop and turn it towards me. "Yes! That's him!" I point to the image on the left that he has next to another image of a clean-shaven male with glasses and short hair. "I didn't recognize him because he looks so different, but now looking at them, I see it. It's the same guy. Mr. Franklin was Matthew's age. Um… Somewhere around sixty? He had a full beard. I never ever saw him without it. And there's something else. His smell. It always made me so sick. I hated when I had to have dinner with him at the table. I always gagged. He smelled like vanilla and cigars. It was so gross. I couldn't handle it." My eyes widen. "And he was the one who broke into my room!"

"Hey. Slow down, honey," Alex says. "I thought you couldn't see the one who broke in?"

"I couldn't! But there was something about him that made me think I knew him. I said that. When he heard you running up the stairs after I screamed, he ran. But I smelled him. I was so scared, it just didn't sink in. But it was him! It was that smell. He's the one who broke in!" I'm vibrating with anger and so many other emotions, I don't know how to handle them. So, I stand and pace. "I'm sure of it." I look directly at Josh. "Josh, I swear. I know it's the same guy."

"Okay. Okay." Josh nods. "Okay. Good. That helps. We know who we're going after. It makes it far easier. We aren't chasing a damn phantom."

"As soon as I found his real name, I found a shit ton of other stuff on him," Lance continues. "Bank records. Homes. And my personal favorite. His connection to Matthew. Matthew kept meticulous records. But you all know that. What you didn't know is just how tightly Matthew and Edward Franklin were. Business partners right down to the word partner. Partner in everything. In fact, to seal their merger, Matthew had planned some nuptials."

"The fuck?" Damon asks.

I stare blankly, a little lost. "I knew they were partners, but nuptials?"

Lance nods. "To his only daughter. Raleigh Jennings."

"Like fucking hell," Alex growls.

"Not happening so long as I'm breathing," Damon growls just as viciously.

"Not a chance," Josh says as he stands. "If that's what this shit is all about, he has another thing coming."

"When did your accountant take on the assistant?" Gavin asks.

"According to the records?" Alex asks. "Just before I took over. Which was just after we took that fucker down."

Lance types a few things on his laptop before looking up. "His hire date is just after we took Matthew out."

"Which means he knew. He fucking knew." Alex scrubs his hands down his face. "Finding him has to be top priority."

"Agreed," Josh says. "I'll take care of it. If I have to, I'll pull in Ryan."

I shake my head. "No. Pull in Ryan. Please, Josh. I haven't been around long, but even I know that the Lucinio's and Crane's are unstoppable when they work together."

Josh nods. "Okay. You're absolutely right. I'll call him now."

I nod and glare into the night as I fold my arms over my chest in resignation.

I'm done.

I'm done letting Matthew control my world even from the grave. From now on, I'm not going to be the meek girl I was. I'm going to be the girl I've become.

Strong.

Fearless.

With a loving and dominant man and family by my side, nothing will ever stop me.

Chapter Twenty

☆ Alex ☆

"Don't quit on me now, Lucinio," Ryan chuckles from his seat next to me.

I groan and keep my head firmly down on my arms, which are resting on the long conference room table. "I need a bottle of Aspirin and a six-pack of Alpha Pale Ale."

Josh laughs. The asshole. "I'll gladly buy it for you. But we have one more applicant."

"Fuck him," I whine. "Tell him I filled the position. He's free to go."

Chase chuckles. "I haven't seen anyone who can fill the position yet. You better pray this guy is your saving grace, or we'll be going through another day of interviews."

"You're a fucking dick," I growl, but still refuse to lift my head. My head is pounding. I want to go into my office and shut the shades. I want to turn the lights off and lay on my couch with Raleigh wrapped in my arms laying on top of me.

Jason laughs. "You're acting like my two-year-old."

That gets a smile out of me. I lift my head. "Jackson is a pretty smart kid."

"He is," Jason agrees. "But he has his moments of whiny ass tyranny." He grins. "Kinda like you."

I laugh but regret it instantly. I rub my temples and close my eyes. "Seriously, though. Thank you all for coming, but I'm convinced that having a table full of a bunch of CEOs who are self-proclaimed giant pains in the ass probably is scaring everyone."

"Well," Josh begins as he stretches in his chair. "I guess if they can't handle us, they can't handle the company. An accountant is an important position. Especially since he or she will be controlling your books. We need to find one like who you had before this Franklin fucker got his hands into it."

"What the hell is the deal with the lack of good candidates?" I ask, looking down at the applications in front of me. "The resumes look fucking incredible."

"Everyone beefs up their resume," Raleigh says quietly, handing me two pills and some water. "Excedrin from your desk drawer. I totally stole some myself."

I snake an arm around her waist and pull her close. She leans down and kisses me. I moan a little before pulling her back and letting her go. "I didn't realize I needed that." I take the Excedrin.

Raleigh rubs her eyes. "The last interview is the one I had to reschedule from this morning."

"The one who missed the L-Train?" Ryan asks. "He's already low on my list. We need someone dependable and able to get here when he needs to be."

Raleigh pats him on the shoulder. "I know. But I really liked this guy's application. And the mishap wasn't really his fault. He lives in a bad part of town. His car was lit on fire last night. He's never ridden the public transportation system, and there were no cabs available to get him here in time."

"Still." Ryan shrugs. "Need to prove dependability."

She smiles softly and turns before disappearing into the kitchen attached to the conference room. "Give him a chance. Really. I think you all will be super impressed." She slips into the kitchen, I'm sure to refill our drinks.

Jason looks at his watch. "Well, he has a couple of minutes, but I'm with Ry."

Chase nods. "I have to agree. Punctuality is huge. If you can't get to your interview on time, how can I be assured you'll get there for your job?"

I lean back in the chair and lock my fingers behind my head. "I'm inclined to agree, but I trust Raleigh. We should at least give him a fair shot."

"If he takes responsibility for his actions, it'll go a long way," Josh says.

Raleigh comes out with our drinks and places them in front of us. "I really think he'll impress you."

"This is a young kid, honey," I say as I lean forward. "I trust you, but are you sure about this?"

She sucks on her lower lip for a moment before looking back at me. "Really. I think you'll be surprised. Have you looked at his file?"

"We've looked at it," I say. "I'll agree he looks good on paper."

"I know he was late," Raleigh says. "But it wasn't his fault. I think you need to give him a pass on that and not hold it against him."

Chase raises an eyebrow. "You're really pushing this kid."

She nods. "I know. Because I believe in him. I thought he was the best one in all of the applications we had. And I know he's young, but he has experience with big corporations." She looks up when she hears the elevator chime with a triumphant smile. "I bet you that's him. Right on time."

I chuckle as she walks out of the conference room. "The guy does look like the best."

"Yeah, I'll concede to that at least," Chase says leaning forward.

"I'll grab you that water," Raleigh says, leading my interview into the conference room. "Take a seat." She smiles and vanishes into the kitchen.

We all look the guy up and down while we wait for him to choose a seat. He's dressed impeccably. I like that. Given the issues he had getting here, the fact that there isn't a wrinkle in his suit is definitely something that gives him points.

Instead of sitting, though, he surprises us all by walking around the table and offering his hand. "Austin Winters." He shakes each of our hands as we stand. "I apologize for having to reschedule. I need to figure out this public transit system. It's a lot different than New York!" He grins respectfully and acknowledges Raleigh when she sets his water down and slides into a chair at the end of the table to take notes.

"Yeah, it takes some time," I say. I really wouldn't know. I've never been near it.

"You're telling me. I thought it'd be easy. Car gets vandalized and burns up. I jump on a bus. Turns out that is not how Chicago works." He walks around to the other side of the table and takes a seat in the center facing us all.

I nod in satisfaction as he sits. "Mr. Winters. I'm Alex Lucinio. CEO of Lucinio Tech." I'm seated in the middle of the table directly across from Austin. I gesture to my right. "Next to me is Ryan Crane. He owns several companies worldwide. Next to him is Chase Shaw. You might recognize him as the CEO of Shaw Incorporated." I gesture to my left. "Josh Lucinio is an owner of several different companies worldwide. Next to him is Jason Crane. He's CEO of Crane Enterprises. The reason you're sitting in front of all of us today is because Lucinio Tech is a very large company. The four men next to me are the largest accounts we have. We have several other large accounts, including the Government, but the four men next to me are not only like family, but also our most important clients."

Austin nods. "Understood. It's a pleasure sitting in front of you all. I appreciate the opportunity."

Jason leans forward slightly and rests his elbows on the table. "Why did you choose that place out of all the open seats at this table?"

Austin meets Jason's eyes. "Because this chair allows me to see you all equally, while also showing you that I'm confident in both my abilities as well as being in a room with five powerful men."

I can't help but grin. "Good answer. Best we've had all day. Also the only person to choose that seat."

Austin smiles and leans forward himself. He sits straight, just as Jason is and all of us are, and looks me directly in my eyes. All I see is confidence. I like it. "Look. Mr. Lucinio. I'm not going to waste your time. I know I'm young. I know the issue this morning was a mark against me. I take full responsibility. I don't live in the best neighborhood. I shouldn't have left my car on the street last night. I'd had a long day of job searching. I was lazy. I admit it. When I walked outside this morning, my car was on fire and the fire department was arriving. I'd already woken up late. It led to one hell of a chain of events, but it all started because of my actions. There's been a lot of gang activity in that area lately. I should have known better. But I'm good at what I do."

Josh clears his throat and glances at Ryan. "What kind of gang activity?"

Austin, damn I give the kid credit, looks directly at Josh. "A lot of things. Vandalism. Burglaries. People getting beat up. Pick-pocketing. Flat out assaults. Sexual and otherwise. I won't let my sister walk alone in the area. She lives with me right now."

Ryan and Josh share another look. I know they're thinking they're going to be checking into it. I have no doubt it's tied to the increase in crime Dane has been tracking. I'm positive they're on the same page.

Ryan looks down at his folder. "It says here you had very high test scores for the aptitude test you were asked to take. Highest we've seen. You graduated with honors from Berkeley University. You've worked in accounting firms for three years after you graduated, then two years with…" Ryan chuckles and shows me Austin's resume.

I smile. "Well, that's interesting."

Ryan nods and looks up at Austin again. "PM Imagery. That's a marketing firm in New York, right?"

Austin smiles. "Yeah. I loved it. Great job. I was in charge of all the accounts there. I worked under Robert Guthery. He was the lead accountant in charge of the entire company's accounts. He was a great boss."

Ryan nods. "He's a great man. One of the best accountants I have working at any of my companies. I'm sure if I called him right now, he'd give you glowing reviews."

"He would. He was like a father to me. He took me under his wing. I hated having to leave, but opportunities arose that I couldn't pass up."

"What opportunities?" Josh asks.

"Well, I was offered a job here in Chicago. The company offered to pay my moving expenses. They said they had an apartment set up for me. The salary was doubled. I did a lot of research on the company. It was a great fit." Austin frowns. "But appearances aren't always what they seem. When I got here, the job fell through in a spectacular fashion. The company folded. I had sold my condo in New York. My position had been filled. I didn't have much choice but to adapt."

"And the company, they got you an apartment in a bad neighborhood?" Chase asks.

"Nope. They didn't get me an apartment at all. I was living in a motel for about two months before I got the apartment I did. The lease was month to month. I'd been looking for a job, but hadn't been lucky. I pulled a stint as a bartender for about a week. I was fired because I didn't like the way the manager was treating his daughter. I spoke up. Got a broken rib out of the deal, but the daughter, as far as I know moved away with her boyfriend. So, not all bad."

Raleigh was right. This kid is the most impressive we've had. I'm astonished because he's only twenty-seven. He not only worked at a very difficult and large corporate company, but he's also managed to survive for what looks like four months in one of the toughest parts of the city. Even more in his favor is that he's apparently done it while protecting his sister.

"Look, Mr. Winters," I begin. "I'm not going to sit here and mess around with you. Your tests are off the charts. You scored very high on the entrance exam we gave to every applicant. You breezed through all of the other interviews you've been through with some of my managers. You come very highly recommended by a few of those managers. You're the best candidate we've had all day." I glance at Raleigh's quiet smirk out of the corner of my eye and fight to hold in the laugh. "I'd appreciate if you stepped out for a few minutes to let us have a discussion."

"Sure thing." Austin stands and strides very confidently out of the room, politely closing the door behind him.

"I saw that," I say to Raleigh with a smile.

She smiles wider. "I can't help it. I saw the scores. I just knew it. He's a good fit."

I chuckle and look at Ryan. "What are you doing?"

He sets his phone down. "Getting that reference. Which is glowing, by the way. I just looked into his employment record and background. He's good."

Josh laughs. "You? You mean you texted Robby, and he did all of that for you."

Ryan grins. "Fuck right. You think I can do that shit that fast?"

We all laugh. "No fucking way!" Chase says.

"Okay, okay," I say, holding up a hand. "I like the guy. And if he's already gone through a background check with Ryan, Lance will have a lot less work to do, but I want to know what you all think. That's why you're here."

"We know Raleigh's opinion," Jason says with a wink in her direction. "He owned the need to reschedule. But what I liked is the guy's confidence. No one else we've seen today sat in the middle seat. No one else walked around the table to shake our hands. Not one looked us directly in the eyes."

Chase nods. "Truth be told, I was fucking impressed he sat in the middle, but he blew me away when he shook our hands after walking over here to us."

"His marks are incredible," Josh says. "That was pretty good in my book, but I think the fact that he worked for PM Imagery is what got me. I know that company is notoriously difficult. And not because of Ry."

Ryan nods. "All of that was great, but Robby's check is what's pushing me. He was very well-liked at PM. And his background shows no anomalies. Everything checks out. Including his address and the issue with his car."

"I'd say we're all in agreement," I say. "He's hired."

"One thing," Raleigh says, hesitantly.

I raise an eyebrow. "What, baby girl?"

"Well, it's bothering me. The neighborhood he lives in. I know the penthouse below this floor is vacant and has only been used by you when you were here before the move…"

I smile because I know where she's going with this. "You want me to offer the penthouse as part of his salary."

"Well, just until he's able to find something in a better part of the city…" She looks down. "I hate the idea of anyone living in an area of the city that's run by a gang that gets off on destruction and hurting people."

I chuckle. "One of the things I've come to love about you is your heart. Go call him back in here."

"You'll give him the penthouse?" she asks quietly.

"Yes, baby. I will."

She smiles at me as she stands and hurries out of the conference room. She doesn't know it, but I planned to include the penthouse in the hiring package anyway. I'm like her in a lot of ways. I hate the idea of anyone living in a shit part of town overrun by gangs myself.

Unlike her, though, I also know that part of town is about to go through a major overhaul because Ryan and Josh are going to join forces. No innocent soul should be a part of that. While I know they'll take care to make sure no one who doesn't deserve to be hurt will be, removing a couple of people so they don't need to worry about them is one way I can help.

We all watch in silence as Raleigh leads Austin back into the room and takes her seat. Austin smiles at us as he takes his as well. I can't help the smile that crosses my face when I see Raleigh beaming. The girl is far too beautiful for her own good.

"Mr. Winters, I'd be crazy not to hire you." I pass him the notepad I've been using to take notes. "The first number is your salary, if you accept it. We'll start you at a hundred grand a year with a three percent raise each year you're with us."

"Wow. That's very generous, Mr. Lucinio," he says, staring at the number. I'm sure he's calculating in his head how much his raise will be each year. Somewhere around three thousand. It's nothing to scoff at.

"You'll be in charge of accounting for the entire company. Not just the Chicago location. Your position will be what Mr. Guthery's is with PM Imagery," I continue. "That's a lot of responsibility, and one I don't give lightly. We've had a lot of problems with our accounts over the years. It's something I won't tolerate. I need to know you're up for the challenge."

"Yes, sir. I can handle it. I won't let you down."

Ryan slides his phone over to me. I quickly read the email before looking back up at Austin. "Mr. Guthery gives you very high praise. Since I trust him, I'm trusting in you to stick to your word and not let me down. Questions?"

"Just one." Austin nods. "Uh… Living arrangements. You've written on here that it's company provided. I'm almost afraid to get my hopes up, but what does that mean?"

I chuckle. "I have a penthouse suite just below this floor. I used to use it when I came here for business, but since I live here now, it's vacant. We discussed it and are offering it to you. Keep it off your taxes. No need to include it as part of your salary. I own the building, so there's no rent. I pay the utilities, so you don't need to worry about that. We'll consider it you and your sister taking care of it for me in my absence, but it's yours."

"Wow. I don't know what to say, Mr. Lucinio. It's a huge upgrade."

"We'll also be including a company vehicle. I need you to be able to attend meetings if I need you there. Sometimes they're off site. I don't trust the transit system, and I'm not a fan of cabs. Your vehicle will have assigned parking on the fifth floor of the parking garage where all of those I work closely with park. I'll have that dealt with by tomorrow morning." I nod to Raleigh. "Ms. Knight will take you to security. They'll get all of your identification done. In order to get into the penthouse, you'll need a palm print scanned as well as a retina scan and a key card. Your sister will need to go through the same identification process. I would suggest calling her and having her meet you here because the process takes time."

Austin nods. "Thank you, Mr. Lucinio."

"As for your personal belongings," Josh begins. "It's going to sound like I'm being a dick, but we'll need that taken care of today."

That gets an eye raise from Austin, but before he says anything, I step in. "I'll send you with security and get some people together. We take care of our own here, Mr. Winters. Ms. Knight doesn't like anything about your neighborhood. Frankly, none of us do. We'd like you out of it as soon as possible. So, we'll take care of it. You'll be moved into the penthouse tonight."

Austin clears his throat and nods slowly. It doesn't take a fool to see he's overwhelmed. Not a single person here would blame him. "My sister. She's at home right now. I don't…"

Ryan stands as his phone rings. "I'll take care of it." He glances at Josh with a nod and back to Austin. "Just give her a call. Tell her two men named Ryan Crane and Luke Massena will be there to pick her up within the hour. We'll ID ourselves and be driving a black Ford Escape with tinted windows."

"I feel like I'm missing something," he mumbles. "But okay. I'll text her."

I watch as Ryan leaves the room. Josh starts to stand. Chase and Jason both begin gathering their things. Austin takes his phone out and starts texting, but his eyes are on all of us. I like him. He's observant.

"I know it doesn't make a lot of sense now, but it will. Let's just get your clearance dealt with. For now."

Austin looks up at me. "Excuse the language, but you don't fuck around, do you?"

I laugh. "No. I don't. Something I'm sure you'll learn quickly. I think you'll be a good fit here, though. I hope you stick around."

He smiles as he stands. "I plan to."

I wait for Raleigh to lead Austin out before looking at Jason. "Now all we need is the CFO."

"Easier said than done," he says. "I haven't looked through all of the applications, but you have a very small pool to pick from."

Chase chuckles. "I've seen a couple I think might be good candidates."

"I'm not looking forward to it," I grumble. "The past couple of weeks have been long."

"Mr. Lucinio, I don't mean for it to seem like I'm eavesdropping, but my sister was a CFO for her last company," Austin says, poking his head back in the conference room. "I know she applied here. Her name is Skyla Winters."

"I recognize her name," Chase says. "She worked for…" He looks down at his notes. "I have it written down here. I liked her application. T-Rac Merc." Chase looks up. "That's a pretty large company. She's worked for them for quite a while. Looks like she moved up from Junior Accountant."

Austin nods, but none of us miss the dark look that crosses his face. "Yeah. She, uh… She had an opportunity at the same company I did."

"The one that fell through," Jason says. "What was that company's name?"

The look is gone as quickly as it appeared, making me think I may have imagined it. "Kinpire Enterprises."

I nod. "I've heard of them. Financial investment company. Their CEO was embezzling money. Clients lost trust and pulled their accounts." I leave out the part about most of them fleeing to Chase's company. Their downfall was his gain.

Austin nods again with a smile. "Anyway. I didn't mean to interrupt. I just heard you were looking for a CFO. Couldn't help myself from recommending her." He nods and turns, following Raleigh once more.

I wait a few moments before standing and looking at Josh. "You and Ry aren't hitting that neighborhood tonight, are you?"

Josh shakes his head. "No. But we are sending in surveillance. Things are probably going to get ugly. If they're as bad as he says…" He nods his head towards the door Austin just left. "Well, our guys aren't going to sit around and let people get jumped. If women can't even walk alone in that neighborhood, I doubt it's much better for men who aren't in the gang that is terrorizing that neighborhood."

"Isn't that the area Dane said was getting hit with a lot of major crimes?" I ask.

Josh nods. "I think Taylor has heard grumblings about gang activity in the area, too, but he hasn't been able to catch them. Ryan has had him going in a different direction anyway. We're pretty much all hands-on deck finding Franklin."

"Well, I can't say I don't appreciate that." I grab my folder with a yawn I can't stop.

"How is Raleigh anyway?" Jason asks, leaning against the conference room table and folding his arms over his chest. He's a solid six feet six, an inch taller than his brother and built the same damn way. The Crane brothers definitely got the same genes. Tall, dark, muscular, and brooding.

"Uh… She's trying. Some days are a struggle. It's not every day you find out the man who raised you wasn't your real father, but it sure as fuck is a shock to realize all of the shit he did. The nightmares she was having have subsided considerably. Funnily enough, though, I think she's more pissed off about the fake rejection letter from Oxford than she is about the arranged marriage bullshit."

"Well, I'm sure it's because she trusts the family to deal with that," Chase says. "There isn't a whole hell of a lot anyone can do about Oxford. It's been too long at this point. She'll have to reapply."

I'm not certain I should spill everything Raleigh has divulged to me over the last couple of months, Oxford and her future with them being one of them. Instead, I choose to say my goodbyes and head for my office.

Raleigh, efficient as she fucking is, already has Austin's hiring package waiting for me on my desk to sign off on. I smile and glance through everything, signing my name on the last page without really reading it. There's no point. I wouldn't care if she raised his salary by fifty thousand. I trust that she'd run that by me before she did it, but if it's what she wanted, I'd give in.

I'd give that girl the entire world if she asked for it.

Chapter Twenty One

☙ Raleigh ❧

I open my eyes when the couch cushion above my head presses down expecting to see Alex. I'm surprised to see Ryan.

"I didn't really realize how tall you are in real life," I say, closing my eyes again. I keep my hands firmly on my stomach but shift only a little so the feet I'd had dangling over the arm of the couch are tucked underneath me when I bend my knees and turn my legs to the side.

Ryan laughs. "How many times have you seen me over the last, what? Eight months? Nine?"

I carefully put one finger to my lips, knowing sudden movements might kill me. "Shh… There's a band of monkeys in my head," I whisper, keeping my eyes firmly closed. "They were putting on a show with their drums to thirty thousand people, but they've taken an intermission."

"Is that your way of saying the headache you had earlier has turned into a migraine?"

"Yes," I hiss. I feel him shift before his fingers are deftly massaging my temples. My eyes are closed, but they roll back into my head anyway when I moan. "If you stop, I'll die."

"Then I promise not to. Where's Alex?"

"Shower. He slipped in the mud after we got home when he went to grab the mail. He was a mess. Very unhappy. He invented curse words I've never heard before. I'm fairly certain he put a hex on the construction workers."

Ryan chuckles. "Did he forget they were extending the tunnel today?"

"I think he forgot what they're even doing at all. But I'm not sure I blame him. We've been so busy with finding a new accountant and a good CFO, I'm not certain either of us even know what day it is anymore."

"Friday. You have an entire weekend to regroup."

"I really like the sound of that. You'll have to forgive me, though, because I don't quite believe you."

Ryan moves to the back of my head and massages to my temples. "How come?"

"Well, I caught the way you and Josh were looking at each other. I'm pretty sure I know you both well enough to know you are going after that gang."

"You'd be correct, but that has nothing to do with you or Alex."

I sigh and slowly open my eyes, looking up at him. Ryan's dark eyes are calm. He always manages to set me at ease. It's one of the things I like about him. But I know my boyfriend. He may say he's always wanted out of the mafia, but he's lost without it. I'd be crazy not to notice how restless he gets. Maybe not like Josh or Gavin, but he definitely gets edgy.

"Alex will be going with for the raid or whatever you call it."

Ryan chuckles and shakes his head, pressing his thumbs behind my ears. The motion relieves all of the pressure. I melt into him. "He won't be. Josh only takes him when we have something big going on. This gang is small-time. And we aren't doing shit this weekend but surveillance. Which Josh and I have teams for. If we need to go in, we will, but we won't be pulling Alex for that."

I smile softly as more tension leaves my body. "I'd like that."

Ryan looks up when he hears Alex coming down the stairs, but he doesn't stop rubbing. I silently thank him because seeing Alex walking towards us wearing gray sweats low on his hips is enough to render me speechless. His perfectly sculpted six-pack and each of his hard ridges and planes make my mouth water.

But it's the tattoos that make my body tingle. I'll never tell another soul that. I didn't even know I was the kind of woman who thought tattoos were sexy until Alex walked into my life. Maybe it's just *his* tattoos, but I always get weak in the knees when I see them.

Alex smiles when he sees me. "Stealing my girl, Crane?"

Ryan laughs quietly. "I like them young, but I got my own." He winks at me.

I giggle. "He's making my headache go away. I didn't know he had magic fingers."

Alex laughs just as quietly as I slowly sit up. "He's had a lot of practice. Breetana gets migraines that I swear have to be worse than childbirth. And before anyone says anything, Jessa had a baby and agrees with me a hundred percent."

Alex sits on the couch next to Ryan and helps me into his lap. He takes over the massage, but instead of just working on my head, he also works my neck and shoulders. The nausea I'd felt when I first laid down on the couch is dissipating little by little.

Ryan grins. "Arianna is also in agreement. And her labor and birth were hard and painful, so if that's what she says, I'll go with it. She knows pain."

"So, what's up?" Alex asks while he rubs.

"I just came by to let you know Austin and his sister are settled."

"Good," I say softly. "I've been kind of worried about that neighborhood. And his car being lit on fire seems so random."

"If you saw the neighborhood, you wouldn't think that," Ryan says. "It's overrun with gang activity. There's graffiti all over the place. Even their place has been tagged."

I wrinkle my nose. "Ick."

"What about their stuff?" Alex asks. "Did the guys get everything moved okay?"

"Well, they did get all of the personal belongings. They left all of the furniture and bedding. The furniture didn't need to go, but it all looked pretty beaten up anyway. I asked about it, and they said they'd just gone to the Salvation Army and picked it up second-hand. They didn't want to blow through their savings when they hadn't planned on staying there long anyway."

"Don't blame them," Alex says, kissing my shoulder. "The penthouse is fully furnished anyway."

"Luke and I took her grocery shopping on the way over. Luke put everything away while I got her through security and dealt with her access." Ryan leans forward and looks over his shoulder at us. "She threw me a little, though. Two guys show up at her house. I know she was expecting us, but as soon as she ID'd us, she did everything we said without question."

I furrow my brows. "Well, wouldn't she? Her brother sent you. She would know that. I'm sure she trusts him."

Ryan nods. "Maybe. It just seemed…" He shrugs. "Off. Very off. And I'm not the only one who thought so. Luke picked up on it, too."

"Hmm…," Alex hums. "He did get a pretty dark expression on his face earlier when Chase was asking about his sister's job. It was gone so fast, I thought my mind was fucking with me."

Ryan shakes his head as he stands. "I don't know. Probably nothing to worry about, but Luke is looking into it. Anyway, I just came to let you know they're settled and both have the access they need to the penthouse. Austin had just finished getting his security badges and everything else when we got there."

I nod. "Good."

"I left a copy of his hiring package on the counter in the kitchen of the penthouse before Raleigh and I left."

Ryan stretches as he heads for the door. "He saw it. Said he'll look it over tomorrow. I ordered them both dinner so they could relax. Which is where I'm heading. I miss my girl."

Alex laughs. "Not your son?"

Ryan throws his head back and laughs. "No. He's in the terrible two stage of his life and hates me already. All he wants is Ari. I so much as look at him the wrong way, and he starts screaming."

I can't help the giggle that escapes my throat because I've seen Christopher throw a tantrum at Ryan when all he did was walk into the room and hug Arianna. "I think maybe he's being protective of his mama."

Ryan grins. "You want the truth? I couldn't be more proud of him. He's already showing those protective qualities I was at his age. And yes, Lucinio. I miss my son." Ryan walks out the door with a smile as Alex and I laugh.

"You know he's going to go home and cuddle them both," Alex says against my neck. His thumbs dig into a spot just below my skull that sends waves of relief through every nerve ending in my head.

I smile. "I know. I never would have pictured a man who is that intimidating to love his family as much as he does. I doubt Christopher will stay in this stage of hating his dad for long."

"Couldn't agree more." He kisses between my shoulder blades. "How's the headache?"

I lean back against him and melt when he wraps his arms around me. He puts his feet on the table in front of us, effectively trapping me between his legs. It's like I'm completely engulfed by him. I close my eyes with a content sigh. He tightens his grip and holds me close.

"Better. I guess I needed that massage more than I thought."

"What a hot shower does for my tension, a massage seems to do for you. I'm happy to oblige." Alex hugs me as tightly as he can and kisses my shoulder. "What do you want to do tonight?"

I'm quiet because I don't really know how to answer that question. I want to do a lot of things, but none of them are things I'm quite sure how to approach. Since we've been together, Alex has taken my pleasure to levels I didn't know existed, but I've never once told him what to do. All I've ever done is consented. From there, Alex has taken the lead and control.

We've been together for close to three months, though, and I'm feeling like I'm ready for things to go all the way. It's something I'd never really thought about. I've never had a boyfriend before Alex. My virginity had always just been a thing I hadn't given the time of day.

Since Alex and I started doing the things we do, though, I've thought more and more about it. Giving myself to him feels like the logical next step. It's more than that, though. I really feel like I don't want to give myself to anyone else. All I want is him. My heart knows it. All of me knows it with every cell of my being. I just don't know how to tell him.

"Baby?" Alex rumbles against my neck. I close my eyes with a quiet moan. His voice always sends shivers down my spine and directly to my clit. He kisses my shoulder. "Where did you go just then?"

I take a breath because I still don't know what to say. Instead, I sit up slowly and shift so I'm straddling him. I sit back on his thighs and trace his muscles. From his stomach up to his shoulders. He watches me with a soft smile and his hands on my hips. His eyes don't leave mine. I know he knows I'm deep in thought, but Alex stays quiet.

I start tracing the dark tribal markings on his right arm. "What does this tattoo mean?"

He chuckles while I focus completely on tracing the lines and intricate design. "To me? I liked the design. It was my first tattoo. It seemed easy for a first timer and looked cool."

"How long have you had it?" I love the feel of his skin under my fingertips. A little rougher than mine. His muscles flex under my touch. I smile because I know it's not intentional, and I love his reaction to me.

"I got it just after we thought we were free of Matthew. Josh had been bugging me to get one, but I hadn't. He got one at the same time as me, though he'd already had one."

I smile softly and trail the fingers of my other hand up his left arm. His grip on my hips tightens. "What about this one?" The sleeve tattoo starts at his shoulder and tells a story down his entire arm. "I want to know the story behind it."

He looks at his arm. "Well, the top is a broken compass. But if you look closely, you'll see inside the back of the compass at the top is a person with an AR-15 next to him. That represents me many years ago. I didn't want to be where I was. I felt like it was killing me, but I couldn't leave that small circle. That was my world, and it was all controlled by my father."

"That's so sad…" I knew all of that, but seeing it inked as a permanent reminder on his skin is heartbreaking.

He pulls me a little closer and kisses my chest just above the mounds of my breasts. His fingers grip my ass over the thin shorts I have on. "It's not a sad story. It has a happy ending."

I smile and kiss his jaw moving down his arm with my fingertips. "What about this next part?"

"The chains represent Matthew and being forced into a life I didn't want. Being chained to it. There is the face of the compass. It's to represent that I was starting to find my way. Even though my compass was broken, it still functioned. Still points me the right way. Inside the face of it is a person hunched over at the top of the circle. The hands of the compass are swords. I still couldn't leave that circle. My future, those swords if I could only reach out for them, was within my grasp, but the crushing weight of my obligations and family, those chains, made that impossible. I was finding myself, moving around and exploring, but not able to really escape that circle."

I move my fingertips down a little more. The lower I go, the deeper I feel myself fall for this amazing and strong man. "What about the tree?" I tilt my head and trace the empty branches. "It looks dead."

He chuckles and wraps his arms around me, pulling me closer. He kisses each of my nipples over the thin cotton of my tank top. "The tree is a new beginning. Damaged. Doesn't look too beautiful, but still living."

I trace the links of the chains. "But there's still chains around it." My voice quivers. I hate the idea he still feels chained to Matthew.

He nips my nipples and scrapes his teeth over them. I sigh and close my eyes with a shiver and moan. He smiles against my chest and kisses up to my neck. "I'll always be chained to my past in some way. At least I'm living the way I want to now." He kisses my jaw and gently nips. "What else do you want to know?"

I let my head fall back when he kisses down my throat and hums. "Mmm… The skulls," I whisper.

"They represent the darkness within me," he says against my throat. "The people's lives I've taken and will take to protect others. Like you." His hands snake up my tank top. As he moves up my back, he pulls the tank top with him until my breasts are exposed to him.

My nipples, already hardened from his skillful mouth, turn into pebbled peaks. "What about the roses?" I ask. Of the entire tattoo that spans from his shoulder down to his wrist and covering his whole arm front to back, it's the roses sprinkled throughout that look the freshest. Like he just had them done.

I feel him smile against my tits. He licks each nipple before answering. "You. You're the life in all of the chaos and darkness that I came from and still deal with. You're the little bit of sweet in all of the bitter."

I wouldn't be able to stop the tears that spring to my eyes from falling even if my life depended on it. "Alex…"

His lips meet mine in a torturous dance I feel in my toes. I grind down against him, begging him with my body to give me what I don't have the words to say. The emotion is so thick, it's stuck in my throat. So, I rub against him and tangle my fingers in his hair.

Alex's hands slide down my back and cup my ass. He lifts me effortlessly as he stands, not breaking the kiss for a second. I whimper needily and wrap my arms around his shoulders and legs around his waist. Alex carries me up the stairs to the bedroom, all the while tangling his tongue with mine.

He groans as I pull him down with me when he drops me on the bed. "Fuck, you have no idea what you're doing to me." To prove his point, he presses his hips against mine.

I gasp. It's difficult to miss how his beautifully large, hard dick is pressed against my already wet and wanting center. I keep my legs firmly locked around his waist and arch into him, trembling and gripping his shoulders.

"Alex…" My eyes fall closed when his lips meet mine once more. The kiss is hotter. Like he can't get enough of me. "Alex, please… Please…"

I'm breathless.

Writhing.

His lips blaze a scorching trail down my jaw and throat. He tries to go further, but as soon as his hips move and I can't feel his cock anymore, I pull him back to me as my eyes fly open. I know I'm panting, but I need him.

All of him.

He smiles. "Hey…" He kisses me softly. "Slow down."

I shake my head. "Alex, I… I'm ready. I am. I feel like if I don't have you, all of you, I'm going to explode."

His eyes widen slightly in shock, but he covers it quickly. His easy, sexy smile falls back into place, but I don't miss my own desire mirrored in the depths of his eyes. "First and foremost, baby, I'm not rushing it. I feel like I've waited my entire life for you. I'm going to savor every second."

"But -"

He cuts me off with a deep and lingering kiss. He pulls back slowly after I moan. "Second, we are both still wearing clothes. If you want what you're asking of me, I'm doing it right."

I whimper. "Alex… I don't know how much more I can take. I need to feel you."

"And you will. But the right way."

He forces his way up so he's between my legs on his knees and crooks his finger at me slowly, telling me to sit up. I do as I'm told. I still want him, but I'm suddenly very shy. The promise in his words sends heat all over me, but now that I'm close to having what I want, him, it's a little scary. I'm about to experience something I never have before with the man I've loved ever since I laid eyes on him.

The way he looks at me as he lifts my tank top over my head, like he wants to devour me, makes me want to come for him now and here. I blush and lose myself in his touch. He's everywhere all at once, and it's still not enough. His large hands cup my breasts and squeeze lightly. His fingers play with my nipples and tug while they twist enough to make me gasp and arch into him.

They move down my sides to my hips while he guides me back on the bed. His soft, warm lips kiss me deeply. He nips my tongue when my back hits the mattress. His fingers slide inside the waistband of my shorts. He tugs them down while he's kissing lower and lower down my body. I've learned something about Alex. When it comes to me, he never hurries things. Even when I'm on fire underneath him, he always takes his time.

His tongue swipes across my nipples in turn just before his teeth scrape them. I grip the sheets. Or blanket. Or him. I don't even know. My entire body short circuits as soon as his tongue hits my clit.

"Ah! Alex!" I arch off the bed into his mouth and slide myself over his tongue.

Alex grips my hips and pins me to the bed. He nips my clit. "Patience, baby." The contrast between his warm breath as he speaks and the cool air around us sends an entirely different kind of pleasure through my body.

Alex's tongue is just as talented as his fingers are. He languidly licks from my pussy to my clit. I feel like I might spontaneously combust, but I force myself to calm down and enjoy him. Enjoy everything. Alex is always so attentive to my needs and pleasure. I quickly came to trust that he not only knows what I need and when I need it, but also what I'm ready for and how far to take me. Just like every other time he's been between my legs, I'm confident he'll give me all I need and beg for.

He smiles against me and sucks my clit into his mouth. I'd arch into him again, but his grip is strong. My thighs start to tremble. My insides feel like they're shaking. When I feel him slide one finger inside me, my walls feel like they could collapse. I feel like my stomach is already going through aftershocks, and the earthquake hasn't happened yet.

Lavishing my clit with his tongue, he coaxes another finger inside me. "My God, I'll never get over how tight you are." His deep voice makes my clit vibrate.

"Alex. I…" I try to close my legs while pulling him closer to me. I'm going to break. I'm so close. The ability to talk seems to be fleeting. I'm quickly losing control.

Just as I'm about to find that incredible peak and jump off it, Alex pulls not only his mouth away, but his fingers out of me, too. I grip the blankets under me, nearly giving into the urge to cry. The release was just within my grasp. It feels like it was viciously pulled away, though there was nothing vicious about the way Alex moved back.

It takes time to come out of the euphoric induced fog enough to realize that Alex has stripped and is leaning on his elbows over me. His crystal-clear blue eyes are glittering. The look of pure lust all over his face is unnerving and exhilarating.

"Are you sure about this?" His deep voice is dripping with sexiness.

I nod. "I'm sure." I take a deep breath, not knowing what to expect but trusting he'll be gentle. I let my hands find their way up his arms and snake them around his shoulders. "I'm ready. I don't want anyone but you. I just want to be all yours." I may not be sure about how any of it will feel, but I am sure of how I feel about him.

He leans down and kisses me tenderly. Lovingly. "You are all mine. With or without this." The tip of his dick stands at attention against my opening, but when I arch, Alex pulls back slightly. His hand wanders down my body to my thigh. He gently starts to rub while he pulls away from my lips slowly. "I don't want to scare you, but I want you to be prepared."

"Oh, Alex…" I cup his cheek. His concern for me is so touching. I'm overcome with as much emotion as I was when he told me the roses on his arm represent me.

"It's going to hurt. I know I'm big."

"I'm ready." I say the words as confidently as I can, but the longer he makes me wait, the more nervous I become.

He shifts a little so his tip is touching me again. I gasp when he reaches between us and grips his dick. He slowly rubs the hard shaft between my folds, soaking it with my wetness. The motion makes me shiver in anticipation while my blood suddenly feels like it's on fire. I can't help that my fingertips scrape across his shoulders lightly.

He moans and drops his head. He kisses my neck and positions himself at my entrance once again. "Ready?" His voice is low with huskiness and cracks.

I nod and run my fingers through his hair. "Ready," I whisper.

He slowly slides his tip into me. I moan and squeeze my eyes closed. He runs his hand slowly up and down my side. "Fuck… You're so tight…" He kisses my neck and across my jaw to my lips.

I grip his arms tight, clenching around him. "Alex…"

"Open your eyes," he whispers.

I do as I'm told, breathing heavily. Panicking. "What if you don't like it?" The words tumble from my mouth nervously. I hadn't meant to say them.

"That isn't remotely close to possible," he says against my lips. "Relax, baby."

My body obeys him of its own accord. I start to relax under his touch and soft kisses. He thrusts slowly, but he only allows his tip in and out of me. He smiles when he feels me relax more and more.

He moves his hand up my stomach to my tits and gently squeezes them while he rubs my nipples with his thumb. I keep my eyes focused on his and moan slightly when he thrusts a little deeper.

"Oh… God…" My pussy feels like it's pinching and squeezing around him. I've had him in my mouth; in my hands. But having him inside me makes him feel twice the size he is, which is already ten inches and thick. "You're not going to fit." My head falls back against the pillow on a moan.

He smiles at me so lovingly, I melt. "Baby… relax. I'll fit. I promise."

He never stops the sensual caresses. The tender kisses. His thrusts are slow and unforced. Before I know it, he's filling me completely. He's nestled deeply within my walls. I tighten around him before relaxing even more. I can't stop my eyes from rolling back into my head.

"Oh… my God…" I've always considered myself a fairly intelligent person. Uttering the same words over and over seem to be all I can do.

My mind is completely focused on him. His arms. His spicy scent. His lips moving from my chest up my collarbone to my neck and back down. His body over mine. Connected in the most intimate way. My senses are in total overload.

Alex groans when he starts moving inside me. He runs his fingers through my hair when I moan. "You're so beautiful." His thumb runs across my lower lip. He leans down and kisses me when I blush.

He keeps his pace slow and deep. The more he moves, the better he feels. I thought it would hurt worse and worse the more he thrusted. I was wrong. He only feels more like Heaven. He's so hard, yet so gentle. Every time his dick slides into me, it feels deeper and deeper.

"Alex…" I clamp around him. "I… I'm…" My stomach clenches. I feel like I'm in the clouds.

"Not yet, honey. Hang on for me."

I pant and wrap my legs around his waist. We both moan when he pushes into me deeper. He thrusts a little faster, breathing against my neck while he kisses it. I can feel his body tense. He gets impossibly harder inside me. It's when he thickens, though, that I grip him tighter. I arch into him, meeting his thrusts with moans and groans.

"Alex!" I feel like every part of me collapses around him. "Ah!" I arch into him again and again, my pussy clenches and tightens around him. My stomach starts to spasm.

"Fuck, Raleigh. Oh… holy fuck." He reaches down and touches his thumb to my clit. He presses down just enough to make me scream and starts rubbing.

"Ah!" I can't hold back, though I try to. I try so hard to wait for him. I come so hard for him, I tremble. My pussy pulses and spasms uncontrollably around him while my hips jerk into his.

"Raleigh!" Alex spills his hot liquid into me. He continues rubbing my clit, sending me into another orgasm while his cock jerks into me.

After we both come down, Alex slowly pulls out of me. I don't know how long we lay in the bed wrapped in each other's arms before I realize that he's running his hand slowly and soothingly up and down my back.

"Mmm…," I murmur against his chest.

"How's my girl?" He kisses my head and hugs me close, cradling me against him like I'm the most cherished thing in the world to him.

"Perfect," I whisper. "So, so perfect."

Chapter Twenty Two

☙ Alex ❧

I rub my temples, trying to catch up. "Gavin, stop. What the fuck? Go back."

"How far?" he smirks.

"The beginning, you fucker." I lean back in my office chair and loosen my tie. The sun is just setting over the city behind me. "What the fuck is happening?"

Gavin laughs. "We found Franklin."

"Yeah. I got that part. Why aren't you going after him?"

"Because we don't know where he is."

I blink confused. "You just said… you…" I shake my head.

Gavin leans forward. "We know he's in South Africa. We don't know where."

"Okay. Okay." I nod. "I got that far. Now what about this Jake's Diner?"

"Really good food. Hot waitress. Won't give me the time of day."

"What does that have to do with Franklin?"

"We chased Franklin to that diner."

"You said he's in South Africa. How the hell is he in South Africa and at the diner?"

"Is that what got you hung up?" Gavin grins. I know he's fucking with me.

"Asshole."

He leans back and stretches his legs in front of him. He locks his hands behind his head as his face grows serious. "Alright. Franklin is in South Africa. We tracked him there, but after he was picked up from the airport, the trail goes cold. Lance is on it. I'm sure we'll have him soon. The diner. Jake's Diner is near the Chicago PD's fourth district."

I nod. "South Chicago. Got it. What does that have to do with Franklin?"

"South Chicago, Alex. That's where your new accountant and his sister are from."

"Yeah? What do they have to do with Franklin?" My irritation level is rising. "Gavin. Look. I don't know where you're going with this, but it's been a long fucking week, and I'm only halfway through. This has literally been the Wednesday from fucking Hell. The only reason I haven't left and said fuck the entire day is because Raleigh keeps giving me kisses and coffee. My location in Tokyo is dangerously close to facing my wrath. I've told Raleigh to book the jet four times today just so I can punch the person in charge of the location for being stupid. She won't because she's more level-headed than I am, so I'm contemplating doing it myself. Just tell me what the fuck is going on."

Gavin watches me a few moments before sighing. "The gang is affiliated with Franklin. We took out the gang last night, but the leader and the dude under him were missing."

It takes a couple of moments for my brain to figure out what he's telling me. I cross my arms over my chest. "You think they're with Franklin."

"Yes."

"What does the diner have to do with anything?"

"The gang was shaking down a lot of businesses. The diner was one of them. We asked them to give us a call if they heard from the leaders. All of the businesses in the area."

"Okay. Following so far."

"About an hour ago, the very hot waitress that I have been hung up on for the past couple of weeks called me and told me the leader called her dad and scared the hell out of him. Something about burning the diner down and killing his daughter if he didn't give him the money he owes. Apparently, it's a very significant amount. More than just shake down totals. She doesn't know anything about it, but she said she thought she heard something around five hundred large."

I almost choke. "What the fuck?"

"That's what I said."

"And this is that waitress you met and hooked up with?"

"Yes." He scrubs his hands down his face.

"And she won't give you a second night." I can't help but grin.

"Now who's being the asshole?" he growls. He sits up. "She won't take my calls, but I'm hung up on her. I thought I felt something for Marissa, but it's nothing like this."

Seeing the anguish all over Gavin's face when he rests his elbows on his knees and looks down at his hands pulls at the softer side of me. "I'm sorry, Gav." I lean forward and rest my own elbows on my knees.

"Don't worry about it. Serves me right, I guess. I've gone through a lot of women over the past few months. Not one got a second night."

"You ghosted them all."

"Yep. I'm starting to regret that now because I realize how much it actually fucking hurts."

"She didn't necessarily ghost you, though."

"Well, she did. Until she had to call. She was pretty scared. Ask me if she'll take any of my calls otherwise."

I chuckle. "Give her time. Maybe if you're persistent enough and woo her, she'll come around."

"Yeah. Maybe."

Deciding to change the subject to put him out of his misery, I circle back to the biggest problem. "So, Franklin. South Africa. What's he got there?"

"Uh… Lance thinks a family."

I raise an eyebrow. "Okay. I didn't see that one coming. A family as in wife and kids? Because last I knew, he wanted Raleigh."

Gavin shrugs. "We don't know if that's still his plan. We intended to grab the leader and his underpart to question them. We hadn't counted on losing them." He smiles and shakes his head. "Josh was pissed. He threatened to shoot everyone."

I chuckle. "I'm not sure I blame him. Letting the leader go is a big fucking mistake."

"Still don't know how it happened. There was a bit of chaos. Cops showed up. Dane and Taylor didn't know anything about a gang unit going in until Josh called Dane from jail."

I laugh. "Wait. How did I miss that part?"

Gavin grins. "It was pretty epic. Cops showed up. Josh told them they can back off. He's got it handled. Talk to their boss. He thought their boss was Taylor. Turns out their boss is some hot shot Sergeant trying to make it up the ranks. Arrested Josh, me, and a few guards."

I laugh again. "Last time Josh was in a jail cell was with me just after we took down a gang in the outskirts of L.A. I think we were both like eighteen. I'm sure he didn't take that shit well."

"He wasn't happy. Fuck, neither was I. There was a dude in the cell that wouldn't stop fucking talking."

"So, Dane got you out. How did I not know about any of this until now? It's the end of the day."

Gavin stands and stretches. "Dane just got us out a little while ago. I came here. Josh went to sleep it off. On my command." He shoots me a wink. "I was pretty sure if he didn't, he'd kill us all."

I shake my head with a grin. "So, what's the plan?"

"The plan is we wait until Lance tracks him. We don't have another choice. Then I think Josh intends on going and taking a team with him." We both glance at the door when we hear the quiet knock. Gavin heads for it. "We're getting closer," he says over his shoulder. He opens the door and drops a kiss on Raleigh's head as he walks out.

She smiles up at him and steps in. "I didn't mean for him to leave."

"He was on his way out anyway." I smile and look her up and down. Gray slacks with a black blazer and a hint of a pale-yellow underneath. Simple, yet so elegant. "Have I told you today how beautiful you are?"

She blushes and nervously touches her hair. It's up in a messy bun. She's barely wearing any makeup, but the strawberry lip gloss she wears gives her lips a very warm and red glow. She's beyond gorgeous.

When she reaches me, I stand. She walks into my arms and wraps hers around my waist. She instantly relaxes with a content sigh. I hold her close for a few moments until she finally looks up at me.

I lean down and kiss her. "How's my girl?"

"Ready to go home. I need a bubble bath. With lots of bubbles." She tilts her head. "And a book."

I laugh. "No dinner, or me?" I put one hand against my heart. "I'm hurt."

She giggles. "I always want you, but you're dessert." She stands on her tiptoes and licks my jaw just before she slips out of my arms. She looks back over her shoulder and sucks on the tip of her thumb while she walks to my door. "Yummy."

I groan and reach down to adjust myself. "That was fucking ruthless."

She giggles again when she reaches the door. "Austin is here for your meeting. Do you want me to send him to the conference room?"

I laugh and point to my obvious hard on. "No. I'm not walking anywhere with this. He comes in here." I make a show of sitting down as she leaves my office laughing.

"Fucking brat," I mumble with a grin. She's my brat. All mine.

"Hey, Mr. Lucinio. You wanted to see me?" Austin says as he strides into my office.

"Yeah, take a seat." I gesture to the black leather chairs in front of my desk. My carefully crafted CEO persona slides back into place. I fold my hands on my desk as he settles. "How are things going?"

"Good. I'm settling in well. I've already gotten a pretty good grasp of things."

"That's what I like to hear. Do you have any concerns so far?"

"Well…" He hesitates and looks behind him towards the door.

"You don't need to be nervous. Tell me what's going on."

"Well, whoever was the accountant before had some… uh… hidden files… I found… in a secret compartment under the desk. They were on a flash drive." He holds it up.

I make no motion to take it. I don't want to let my excitement show. I'm pretty sure the guy is suspicious of me as it is. "Did you look to see what was on it?"

"It's a lot of encrypted shit. But I could see it's files." He leans forward and puts it on the desk. "Look. Mr. Lucinio, I don't want to cause any problems. I know who you are. I know who your family is. But there's something on there that someone has taken a lot of care to hide."

I raise an eyebrow. I suspected he had an idea where I come from. "How do you know who I am?"

"It doesn't take a lot. Ryan Crane is all over the news. Usually, for something good he's done for some area charity, but everyone knows he's the leader of one of the two largest mafias in the world. Your brother is the leader of the other." He leans back and holds his hands in front of him before putting them in his lap. "I know you're legal and everything, but judging from how quickly everything happened from me being hired to us both getting settled into the penthouse, I'm sure there's still other things going on that's bigger than me and my job."

I take a moment to weigh my words. I figured he'd figured it out already. He's a smart guy. "Well, yes. There are things that go on outside the scope of these walls -"

He chuckles. "Mr. Lucinio, you don't need to explain whatever it is you do outside these walls. My concern is what happens inside them. I'm smart enough to know that whatever you all do beyond Lucinio Tech is part of the good fight. I know that gang terrorizing South Chicago went down pretty hard."

"You remind me a little of the person I had in your position. He was a good guy. Knew a lot of what we do, but it wasn't a concern to him. He loved the company, and the work."

"I love the work. I'm already loving the company, and the atmosphere." He watches me like he's gauging my reaction to what he said.

I chuckle. "I like you." I smile and take the flash drive. "I'll get it to someone. How's everything else going?"

"Good. My sister is settled in and feels a lot more comfortable in this neighborhood. So, she's doing a lot more job searching." He smiles. "She's been getting a lot of interviews. Someone is going to snatch her up."

I laugh. "She's in the running. We have a lot of interviews on Friday. She's one of them."

He smiles. "Yeah?"

I nod. "Yes. A lot of people would call me crazy for even entertaining the idea of putting her in as CFO when her younger brother is the accountant for the same company, but I'm not everyone. If I do hire her, though, don't make me regret it."

His smile widens. "Looks like you've already made your decision."

I shake my head with a smile. "I can't deny she looks good on paper. We'll see how she does in the interview."

"She'll blow you away. And if you do hire her, she won't let you down. She was made for a company like this."

"I'm not making promises." I glance at my desktop and swallow a yawn. "Listen, I'm doing a company barbecue Saturday to introduce the new CFO. The reason I called this meeting is because I need someone to help out Ral-" I cut myself off. "Ms. Knight with a couple of things. Everything is pretty much all set up, but she has a list of things that needs to be done on Saturday. I have a business brunch. I'll be sending her with security, but I'd appreciate if they could focus on the protection part of it without being distracted by her assigning them tasks. She doesn't quite understand they aren't there to work for her. They're there to protect her. I'm sure you understand why a CEO of a huge company needs protection on his significant other. Add in the mafia…" I trail off, letting him finish the thought.

"I understand. Tell me where to be, I'll be there."

I glance at the desktop again and let out a sigh of relief. I turn to shut down. I refuse to be here a minute more. "Millennium Park. We'll be in front of the Bean. I'll send a car for you. Be ready at eight in the morning. Not a second later. That's already cutting it close since the party will be starting at eleven. I'm pretty sure Ms. Knight will be there earlier than that whether I want her to be or not." I stand after everything is shut down and grab my suit jacket. "Questions?"

Austin stands with me. "In a hurry to get out of here?" He smiles teasingly.

"You have no idea. I'm near flying to Tokyo and firing everyone. Or punching them. I haven't decided yet."

"Well, just think. If you hire my sister, you won't have to fly off anywhere." He winks as I grab the flash drive. "One minute with her in the building, they'll be flailing around like chickens with their heads cut off to correct all of their mistakes. The girl may be small, but damn. She's fierce."

I laugh. "She's looking better and better." I follow him out of my office and turn to lock the door. "Eight on Saturday. They'll pick you up out front." I turn and look at him. "If you need anything in the meantime, Ms. Knight will make time for you to see me. She knows how important your position is to me, so if I can do anything to help, or if you need anything, let me know."

"So far, so good, Mr. Lucinio. I'll be ready at eight."

I lean against the wall and watch Raleigh get ready while Austin gets on the elevator. Chance is quietly standing in the corner. I don't know how the hell we lucked out with him, but I'm glad the Marine decided to join us. He's one of the best guards we have. I trust very few with Raleigh's life. None of them are outside my circle. My close friends. My family. He's the only other person I trust enough to let near her.

"Ready to go?" Raleigh asks, smiling up at me.

I lean down and kiss her. "Definitely ready to go. I've had enough today."

She hugs me. "Want to just get take out?"

I kiss her head. "No. I'll cook while you're in the bath. Or I'll make Josh come over and do it."

She giggles. "How did he get so good at cooking?"

I laugh. "Well, he'll tell you he had to learn to survive. But the real story is Ryan taught him." I take her hand and lead her to the elevator. Chance follows.

"Really? That makes sense because Ryan is an incredible cook. I've never had chicken parmigiana the way he makes it. It's mouthwatering."

I chuckle and pull her close when we all step in the elevator. "Ry went to school to be a chef."

Her eyes widen adorably. "Seriously?"

I nod. "Yep."

"What did you go for?"

"I went for business. So, I could run my own company and show Matthew up. I didn't realize how fucking treacherous he was then, though. I didn't think he'd figure out a way to interject his way into my company. At least not for a few years. I knew he was running money through it, but I

218

didn't realize just how deep he went. At least not until I was able to fully take control."

"I hate him." She snuggles closer to me.

I hug her a little tighter. "We all hate him." I kiss the top of her head. "Have you made your final decision about college?" It's something she's been struggling with. She goes back and forth about wanting to go and not.

She takes a breath. "I know I'm supposed to go. But…" She looks down at her feet. "I really don't want to, and I feel like it makes me a terrible person. I think my priorities have changed. But I feel kind of bad because everyone I know went to college. You. Ryan. Gavin. Damon. Jessa. Bree. Chase. I could literally keep going all night."

I chuckle as the door opens. I lead her out. "That's not true."

"I didn't go," Chance says.

She looks up at him in total shock. "Seriously?"

"Yep. I enlisted in the Marine Corps at eighteen. I was in for fourteen years. I took a job as Head of Security for Lucinio Tech in L.A. when I got out. I worked for about a year before Josh approached me about moving up. I became one of his personal guards three years ago. Haven't looked back since." He leans against his SUV and crosses his arms. "I'd never tell you not to go to college, but I will say if you're happy where you are, college will always be there. I don't know the Crane's all that well, but I do know Arianna just started college. And she does it online."

"He's right. She waited a couple of years. Also, Josh never went, and he's one of the smartest people I've ever met. Fucker is a full-fledged, genius nerd. But you'd never guess it by the way he looks. Not a lot of nerds out there who can bench press you."

Chance laughs. "Fuck bench pressing her. She's easy. He could bench press me. I'm two-forty and six feet four. Solid muscle."

I laugh. "He could probably bench press us both at the same time."

She chews on the inside of her cheek. "So, what you're both saying is I shouldn't feel bad."

I lean down and kiss her as I open her door. "That's exactly what I'm saying."

She smiles as she gets into my black Lamborghini Aventador. I lean down and kiss her again before closing the door. Chance gets into his

SUV after I get into the driver's seat of my car. He follows me out of the garage and towards home.

I glance over at Raleigh. I'd be a fool to not see that she's stressed. I know it's because she's thinking of Franklin. I haven't had a chance to tell her what Gavin said. I'm not entirely certain I want to.

When I see her close her eyes with a soft smile, I reach over to take her hand. That conversation can wait until tomorrow. Tonight, my job is to make sure she gets to relax and worry about nothing.

I kiss her fingertips as I drive. Her grip softens more and more until the steady rise and fall of her chest tells me she's asleep.

I smile at her peace. A peace I know only I can bring. That I'll always give her.

Chapter Twenty Three

🍂 Raleigh 🍂

I swat at Alex's hand with a giggle when he slides it across my ass. "Would you quit that? You're making it difficult to concentrate."

He grins and pulls me close, dropping a sweet kiss to my nose as people walk by us. "No. Because I love touching you, and you flustered while you're trying to concentrate is adorable as hell."

I laugh. "I didn't know Hell was adorable."

Alex barks out a laugh of his own. "Where does that statement even come from? It's been said by men for years, but I've never really thought about it."

I smile up at him. "A mystery for sure. But for another time. We need to finish looking for the decorations I want."

"Isn't that what the caterer does?"

"Alex! No." I shake my head. "The caterer cooks. They don't set everything up. It's why I made you rent tables and chairs and a tent."

"Okay. So, the people who bring all that shit. Don't they set it up?"

I sigh in exasperation and cross my arms over my chest. "Has your mother never planned a party while you were growing up?"

He smiles and shakes his head. "Nope. My father was a dick. He kept her nice and locked up."

I swat his arm because I know he's lying. "Josh said she planned a lot of parties."

He laughs. "Okay, okay. She did. But we didn't have a lot of guests. It was all associates of Matthew. He never let her do any of the actual decorating. He hired a decorator for it. Which is the entire reason I don't know why you're doing this. It's not like I can't afford a decorator, and you have full access to all of the business credit cards."

I take his hand and pull him into the store I want to go in. "Because it's fun."

He groans. "I can think of a lot of other things more fun than shopping."

His suggestive tone sends heat between my thighs. I squeeze his hand. "Not fair."

"I've never played fair in my life, beautiful." He looks around the store. The horrified and lost expression that settles on his face makes me laugh. "This is torture."

I let go of his hand and start piling things in his arms. "It's not. I assure you. It's therapeutic."

"Shopping is therapeutic? Like hell. This is what women do to men as a punishment for things they've done and things they might do in the future. It's anything but relaxing."

I giggle and add silver confetti to the growing pile in his arms. "That's how I feel about bra shopping."

"Bra shopping? I can get behind bra shopping."

I giggle again and turn to him. "Did you know that clothing companies change women's measurements every single year? Like an example. Your pant size. What is it?"

"I'm a thirty-five waist and thirty-four inseam in jeans."

I nod. "And how long has that been your size?"

"Uh…" He raises an eyebrow as he thinks. "I guess probably since college. I haven't grown anymore. I'm still just as muscular and toned."

"So, almost eighteen years?"

"Yeah. Something like that?" He gives me a killer smile that makes me weak everywhere.

"Well, that's not how women's sizes work. Some companies use the waist measurement like they do for men, but most use a whole other system that makes no sense at all. I've been close to the same height and weight, for the most part, since I was fourteen. I lost maybe fifteen pounds due to stress and…" I gesture to him with a frown, not wanting to remember how things were between us for so many months. "You. But I have gone from a size zero to a size four to a six. Now I'm an eight. I don't weigh much more. No one can tell me that fourteen-year-old one-hundred-eleven pound me and eighteen-year-old one-hundred-nineteen pound me can go up eight sizes. This is the reason women have complexes."

"Wait a second. You're telling me your jean size has gone up eight sizes in four years and you've only gained eight pounds? So that's a size per pound. That seems ridiculous."

I tilt my head at a banner and stand back to look at it. "Yep. And let's not talk about my bra size. I have to get measured every single time I buy a bra because they change, too. One company says I'm a B-cup. The other says D-cup. Depending on where I go and the type of bra I decide to buy, the size literally changes." I nod at the silver banner with pink lettering, deciding to get it. I'm glad this store customizes them.

"I'm sorry, baby. I didn't realize shopping for a woman was so difficult."

I smile and scan the store for pink confetti and silver tablecloths to go with my new color scheme. "Not a lot of men do. But now you know." I look up at him and put a hand on his arm. "Thank you for coming with me. I know shopping isn't your thing. I was just teasing you."

He leans down and kisses me, impressively not dropping anything I've piled in his arms. "I know. I understand. Though, I'm glad whenever I need a new suit, I can just call the tailor, and he'll deal with it."

I laugh. Alex wouldn't be able to live without his tailor. I'm fairly confident that if he had to shop for a suit and get fitted for it all the time, he'd refuse to wear suits all together. As it is, most of his closest is full of tailored shirts, jackets, and slacks. He has an entire drawer filled with different colored ties, another filled with black boxer-briefs, and another filled with black socks. He has a shoe rack with polished black shoes. The rest of it is jeans and t-shirts with a couple of hoodies and sweatpants thrown in.

I still haven't figured out where he keeps his shorts and sneakers or the SWAT boots he wears when he goes out on a mission. I have no clue where he keeps any of that gear. I'm sure if I asked, he'd tell me. I just haven't because I don't feel like I need to.

I find the pink confetti I want and grab a few other things I think I might need before leading Alex to the counter. I laugh when he attempts to dump everything on the counter, and the cashier, who must be in her seventies, glares at him. I am pretty sure it is in his best interest to stop and let me pluck everything out of his arms. I put it all down on the counter. The cashier smiles at my semblance of some order.

"The silver banner with the pink lettering…" I begin as I turn and point at the one I like.

The nice older woman smiles. "Oh my. One of our most popular. Do you like that one?"

"I do." I turn. "I wonder if I can get it customized and have it ready by tomorrow evening? About this time?"

She nods enthusiastically. "Absolutely, sweetie." She hands me an order form. "You just write what you'd like on there and fill out the information."

I nod and take the form. "I also saw some silver and pink foil balloons that say congratulations on them. The ones with the fire and ice flowers on them."

"Sure. Just check the balloon box. Say how many, and I'll grab that balloon so we know which one you like." She scurries towards the balloons while I fill out the form.

"So…" Alex wraps his arms around me and kisses my neck. "What's next?"

"Well, I need a dress."

Alex groans. "You hate dresses."

"I know… but I wanted to look nice."

"Baby, you could wear a garbage bag and make it look like a prom dress. Besides, this is Chicago. It could be eighty degrees in the morning and suddenly drop to twelve an hour later. It'll be sunny and perfect, then snow the next second."

I laugh and turn in his arms after finishing the form. I reach up and touch his scruff. "I love this. Not the typical clean-shaven look of a CEO."

"Thank you. You're changing the subject."

I smile and wrap my arms around his shoulders. I stand on my tiptoes and kiss his Adam's apple. I love that he tightens his grip when he swallows and smiles down at me with a low groan meant just for me. I'll never get tired of the effect I have on him.

"I just want to match you. I really like that blue shirt you have with a black tie. It brings out your eyes. And I don't have anything that matches that."

His smile turns to a grin. "See, this is how it starts. We begin this beautiful relationship. All of the sudden you're dressing me. Next thing I know, I'm waiting for you at the altar."

My heart skips a beat at the thought of him waiting for me at the end of the aisle, but I don't get a chance to say anything because the woman comes back to finish our transaction. She bags our stuff up after Alex pays. Alex takes my hand and leads me out of the store, carrying all of the bags.

I'm silent as my mind wanders while we walk. I only shake my head when he points to a store with vintage dresses in the window asking me if I want to get my dress there. All I can think of is walking down the aisle to him.

He squeezes my hand. "What's got my girl so quiet?"

"Um…" I don't have a clue how to broach that subject. "I…" I blush. "I don't know."

I feel him smile. I'm not surprised to see the grin when I glance up at him. "Hmm… Could it have something to do with a statement made earlier about me at the end of an aisle?"

My eyes widen. I duck my head to hide the fact that my cheeks are on fire. I bite my lip. He's so incredibly intuitive. I can't keep anything from him. He always figures it out. Even if I don't know exactly what I'm feeling.

"Maybe," I say quietly. I veer into the store I had been looking for.

He chuckles as he follows me. "Is that something you think about?"

I blush even deeper as I nod. Tears sting my eyes, but I blink them away. I know there isn't a point to denying it. Alex will get it out of me somehow. He always does. It's one of the things I love so much about him. Sometimes, I don't even have to talk. He just knows what I'm thinking and feeling.

I look up at him and take a breath. "I… have." I look down because the glittering look of amusement all over his face and sparkling from his eyes is enough to make me melt. "It's silly."

"It's not silly. It's a big step. There's nothing silly about it."

I nod as I turn and beeline for the dresses near the back of the store. Alex follows. He puts the bags down on a bench and watches me peruse the racks. I keep glancing towards the front of the store, though.

There's a dress in the window that I really liked. It's what drew me into this store, but I also saw the price tag. I can't afford it. I make good money, but the dress costs half of what I make in a month.

Alex sits on a bench as I pull a dress off the rack. I'm not sure about the style, but the color is really pretty and will match his shirt perfectly. I find two more, though they are not blue. One is white and a little short. The other is black, and while I'm comfortable with the length, I think it will show more skin up top than I'm used to.

"I'm just going to try these on."

Alex watches me. "Okay."

I slip into a dressing room and sit down on the chair in the corner, taking quiet, deep breaths. My relationship with Alex is so incredibly new. I don't want to rush it by talking about all of my fantasies of marrying him that I've had. So many of them being before we were ever even together.

How crazy does that make me? Fantasizing of a man who hated me for so long has to make me certifiably insane. Now, when we've only been together for a few months, I want to ruin it by talking about marriage. Even I know that's the number one way to make a man run.

I wipe my eyes and sniffle softly. I don't want him to hear how emotional I am. I shake my head at how silly I'm being and start trying on the dresses I chose. I know I could talk to Alex about the way I'm feeling. I know in my heart he wouldn't judge me. But it doesn't stop me from being insecure about it. Maybe it just shows how immature I am compared to him.

I turn in front of the mirror and sigh. As I thought, the cut of the blue dress doesn't work with me. The left side of the dress comes up mid-thigh. The dress tapers off to a longer length on the right side. There's a weird cinch above my waist and the sleeves, which I don't like at all, are weirdly ruffled.

"How is this even in fashion?" I grumble to myself. I quickly remove it and throw it up so it's hanging over the door.

"Not a fan? That one matches my shirt," Alex says from outside the door.

"No… I'm trying on the white one. I liked the style better, but it doesn't match you."

"White matches everything."

I scrunch my nose as I start stepping into the dress. "No. No, it doesn't."

He laughs. "I can't think of anything white doesn't go with."

"Pastels. All of them. It looks awful."

"Don't they use white a lot with pastels?"

"They do. And they're wrong."

"Whatever you say, baby. I am not about to argue fashion with you. I know nothing about it, and you always look gorgeous."

I giggle and blush. "So do you."

I sigh after getting the dress on. The length is better, but still too short. It's also too light. The skirt reminds me of a crocheted potholder or something with silk underneath to keep it from being see through. Though, I'm pretty certain it's thin enough to be seen through anyway. The top is exactly the same. Gross.

"Are you going to come out and show me what these look like? Or do you want me to go off the sigh and say you hate it?"

I shake my head. "I'm not coming out there. I hate it. It looks terrible. I can't even describe what the top part looks like, but the bottom is a huge turn off anyway."

I shrug it off and throw it over the blue one. I guess the little black dress will just have to do. At least I know the cut will look okay. I just hate that it will show too much skin. But, unlike white, black really does go with everything. It's just not the color I wanted.

I check myself out in the mirror and let out another sad sigh. I was right when I thought the strapless dress would be the best option. It fits the top nicely, even though it dips a bit too low. It hugs my figure. The skirt is light and perfectly flowy.

"Still not the right one?" Alex asks. He's closer now. He's probably standing outside the door.

"No. It's so… It just shows too much. I'm uncomfortable in it. The other ones are sort of okay, but I don't like the style."

"Well, take that one off. I have one for you to try."

I start to take the dress off. "What do you mean?"

"I mean I have one here I am pretty confident you'll like. Throw that one up here with the rest, and try this one. I'll slide it through the door."

I bite my lip curiously and put the dress with the others. I open the door a crack. Alex keeps his hand on the door. Someone, I assume a sales clerk, slides the dresses off the door and thanks him, calling him Mr. Lucinio. Moments later, Alex slips inside the room with one hand behind his back.

"What are you doing?" I ask quietly.

"If you think I didn't notice you eying this dress since we came in, you don't know me very well, beautiful." He pulls the dress out from behind his back that I'd seen in the window.

I look up at him, both surprised and sad. "Alex… I can't afford that dress."

He raises an eyebrow. "Raleigh, do you want the dress?"

I swallow hard. "Yes, but I -"

"Do you know how much money I make?"

"I -"

"That's a yes or no question."

I swallow hard again over the lump in my throat. I want the dress, but I'd never ask him to buy it for me. Why I'm near tears, though, is something I have no words for. Alex's eyes are filled with such love and adoration. There's a soft smile on his lips. His voice, though the words were commanding, is nothing but sweet.

I nod. "I know you make a lot."

"Raleigh. Baby, I'm a billionaire. I run a multi-billion-dollar company. My brother runs a huge mafia. My family name drips with more money than any of us know what to do with. I have a private plane that's mine sitting in a private hangar. I have a car that's more expensive than most people's homes. My house itself costs three times more than the most expensive celebrity home in L.A. does. I'm not saying any of that to brag. I just want you to know that buying the woman I love a dress that she loves isn't going to break me. Money means nothing to me. Your happiness and keeping that beautiful smile on your face means something to me. You. You mean everything to me."

"Alex…"

"So, if this dress…" He holds it up with a smile. He never breaks eye contact with me. "If this is the one you want, say the word. I'd do anything for you, beautiful." He reaches out and rests his palm on my cheek. I lean into it. "All you need to do is ask. It's yours."

I smile softly and step into him. I wrap my arms around him and rest my cheek against his rock-solid chest. "I don't care about the dress. I just want you."

His arm comes around me. He holds me close and tight, tangling his fingers in my hair. He kisses the top of my head. "You have me. You never have to worry about that." He grips my chin gently and tilts my head up. He leans down and kisses me. "Now, about this dress." He holds it up. "I think you have a good eye. I also think that no dress you try on is going to compare, and I refuse to allow my girl to settle."

I smile and reach up to cover my flushed cheeks. "I do love it."

"Then try it on. See if you still love it when it's on you. If you do, it's yours. If you don't, we'll find something else. But for fuck's sake, Raleigh, stop thinking about money being a barrier. It's not."

"But I don't want you to ever think I'm just using you for your money," I say quietly. I take the dress and slowly start to put it on.

"I don't. I never would. You've never asked me for anything, baby. Don't think I haven't noticed how hard you work. I know you save everything you make. I know why. I know you want to make your own way in life. I'm behind you. I'll support you in that. But don't try and stop me from splurging on you a little bit."

I pull the dress up and turn to the mirror. Alex turns me a little so he can zip it. I could do it on my own, but I let him. His warm hands on my back while he slowly raises the zipper is intimate. Romantic even. Him simply dress shopping with me is romantic in my book. Knowing he's willing to do this with me only makes me fall more in love with him.

"Thank you," I whisper. "It's… perfect."

The dress is simple. The material is soft. Like the black dress, it hugs the top part of me to perfection. It doesn't dip so low that half my breasts are showing. There are straps that are so thin I question why they are there at all. The bottom flows around my thighs and just grazes my knees. I don't fear bending over and showing things I've only ever shown Alex.

Alex slips his arms around me from behind and bends to rest his chin on my shoulder. He sways gently with me and looks at my reflection. "Beautiful."

I smile shyly as Alex and I stand in front of the mirror. I love the dress. I know it will look perfect next to him.

But I can't stop thinking of another dress.

A pretty long and flowing white dress.

One I've seen in my dreams many times.

A beautiful dress I don't want to wear for anyone but Alex.

Chapter Twenty Four

❦ Alex ❦

"Jesus Christ, Raleigh," I growl into her neck. I thrust into her sweet, wet, tight pussy while holding her against the wall in my office. I have an interview with Austin's sister for the CFO position soon, but I've been dreaming of Raleigh in this position ever since I kissed her with her back against this wall in this exact spot.

Raleigh tightens her legs around my waist and bites down on my shoulder. "Alex," she moans, letting her head fall back. Her grip tightens around my shoulders. I feel her nails dig into my back. She clenches around my dick as I pump into her.

My eyes roll back in my head. I thrust harder. "Fuck…"

"Yes…" She buries her face in my neck.

I grip her ass and thrust harder, deeper and slightly faster, though still slowly. I want to enjoy the feel of her gripping my cock with all she's worth. I can't get enough of her. I crave her unlike I've ever needed anything in my life.

I roll my hips against hers and thrust as deeply as I can. The motion makes her gasp and shiver. She starts to tremble. The grip her legs have around my waist starts to slacken. The walls surrounding me begin to pulse uncontrollably. It's almost like she's sucking me deeper into her.

"Holy fuck, Raleigh," I whisper into her hair. I lift her and drop her down onto my dick.

"Ah!" she screams into my shoulder, muffling the sound. It's the final move to send her over the edge. She comes so hard, she rockets herself harder against the wall. Her pussy collapses and pulses around me. Her hips jerk against mine.

"Fuck me… Good girl…" I kiss her neck and bury myself in her pussy, waiting for her to start to come down.

"Oh, Alex…" She pants against my neck.

I push her a little harder against the wall and close my eyes as I come hard deep inside her. "Mmm… my favorite place to release." I smile into her neck as my hips jerk against hers while I spill myself into her. "Fuck, baby."

"I love that feeling," she whispers.

I smile. "So do I."

"But I can't help thinking of the consequences of us doing this unprotected."

I chuckle and pull back a little as I slowly let my dick slip from inside her warmth. "I probably should have told you so you didn't worry. I've never wanted kids. Neither has Gavin or Damon or Cole. The four of us got a vasectomy on our thirtieth birthday. To celebrate I don't know what, but that was how we decided to do it."

She blinks a few times as I let her slide down until her feet touch the floor. After a few moments, she cracks up. She doubles over laughing with her hand on the wall behind her for support. I grin because the humor in it isn't lost on me. It never has been.

"A vasectomy. On your birthday!" She laughs harder and drops to her knees. "For no other reason than to celebrate being thirty!" She wipes her eyes as she laughs.

I pull up my slacks and tuck myself away as I laugh. "Yes. It happened. To be fair, we were all drunk when we made that pact, but we stuck to it for the simple reason that we never wanted kids."

Still laughing, just not as hard, Raleigh stands and pulls her panties back on. "It's kind of funny, but I really don't want them either. Matthew was always talking about grandkids, but the more he talked about them, the more I decided I just didn't want kids. I used to feel really bad about it because I knew that decision would disappoint him, but now…" She shakes her head as she pulls up her own pants and looks up at me. "Now I don't feel bad at all. I have never gotten along with kids. And some of the dinners he had with business associates were also with their wives and kids. I always got stuck taking care of them and never really knew why. We had a whole house full of staff for that."

I finish tucking in my shirt and buckle my belt. "It was because he was trying to give you that maternal instinct. Train you for when he married you off." I cup her cheek when she frowns. "I'm never allowing that, baby. That Franklin fucker isn't getting anywhere near you."

She closes her eyes and leans into my hand as she takes a deep breath. "I know. I know you'll never let him get to me."

"Not just me. You have one hell of a wall in front of you. Me. Josh. Gavin. Damon. Lance. Cole. All of the Lucinio Mafia. You have the Crane Mafia. We're tracking him. He's not getting anywhere near you."

I watch the tension fade. She finishes adjusting her clothes and smoothing everything down. She runs her fingers through the hair that not long ago I let loose. I smile and put my jacket on while she puts her hair back up in that sexy as fuck messy bun that drives me insane.

"How do I look?" she asks me, clasping her hands in front of her.

"Beautiful. Your lip gloss is a little smugged, though."

She blushes. "I should fix that." She darts to the in-suite bathroom as I chuckle.

I glance at my watch when I hear people in my lobby. "Baby, take your time," I call. "I'll be in the conference room."

"Okay! I won't be long."

I glance at my clothing once before heading out of my office just to make sure I look presentable and don't have anything on me that will cause me to have to make a quick change. Satisfied I won't be razzed by my brothers or anyone else, I open my office door and walk to the lobby. Ryan, Josh, Chase, and Jason are all standing in a circle waiting for me.

"Man, am I grateful you guys are helping me with this," I say as I join them.

"That's what family is for," Chase says, clapping me on the shoulder and looking at his watch.

"I don't even know where to start," I confess.

"That's what you have us for," Jason says, smiling. "Let's head to the conference room. I have a couple things for you to look at. A scenario to run her through."

I follow Jason. "People do that shit? Run interviewees through scenarios? Why didn't we do that with the candidate this morning?"

"Because no one liked that stuck-up pompous motherfucker," Josh says from behind me.

I laugh. Leave it to my brother to not mince words. "I'll agree with that." I sit down and scrub my hands down my face. "Fuck, this can't get over fast enough."

"Eager to be back inside Raleigh?" Ryan asks with a grin, sitting next to me.

I punch his arm, half playful and half in warning, as I glare at him with a grin. "Fucking asshole."

Ryan laughs as we all settle. "This is an important position. You need someone with experience. That piece of shit couldn't find his head if it was stuck in his own ass."

Josh leans forward. "Jas came up with this scenario in the car on the way back here from his office. Genius."

I smile. I really hope this girl is all she appears to be because if I have to go through one more interview with a man older than I am who starts giving me advice on how to run my own damn company, I might shoot him. Apparently, the fact that I'm thirty-five and a CEO is a big deal. Considering how long I've known Ryan and his family, it's not unusual. Jason became a CEO of his own company when he was in his twenties. Ryan became one when he turned Crane Mafia legit. That was in his twenties. Even Chase was in his twenties when he started his company.

We'd had three interviews this morning before the one I consider a complete disaster. I'd cut the other three short as soon as they started acting more like they wanted to be a mentor. I'm sure if I'd let them go on, Jason would have thrown them all through a scenario of some sort.

I'd already been put in a bad mood, though, by the time our last interview came in, but I kept myself in check. It really wasn't until he told me that he has studied my company and can already tell me where I can save money. It involved the layoff of half my tech team and pay cuts for just about everyone else. I'd let that go, for the most part, already making my decision to not hire him.

I've never been all about money. My company is doing perfectly fine without firing thirty thousand people. I'd never allow a pay cut across the board. People have families. My job as their employer is to make sure they can put food on the table and keep a roof over their heads. If anyone thinks my goal is to save as much money while making a fuck of it myself has absolutely no idea who the fuck I am or what this company stands for.

After looking over my interview questions and Jason's scenario, it's finally time. Everyone has a drink of some sort. Raleigh walks in right on time with our candidate and disappears in the kitchen to get her drink.

The woman isn't that tall. Maybe five feet three. She's petite. There isn't a lot to her, but she is dressed impeccably, which I appreciate. She's wearing a conservative black skirt that hits her knees and a light blue shirt underneath a black blazer.

Just like her brother, she exudes confidence. She walks around the table to shake each of our hands. "I'm Skyla Winters," she says clearly and concisely with a nod to each one of us. She's also fairly young.

After we all shake her hand and introduce ourselves, we sit back down and settle. Raleigh comes out with whatever drink Skyla asked for. She settles at the end of the table to take notes. Her laptop is open on the table. She's very good about blending in and making people forget she's in the room. Like that would ever happen with me. I'm far too in tune to her to ever be unaware she's near.

I clasp my hands over my folder. "Ms. Winters. Before we begin, I want to get this out of the way. I'm not going to sit here and listen to any talk about how you want to tighten the belt at Lucinio Tech. I don't care about saving money. I won't entertain the idea of laying people off or cutting their pay. If you've done any research on this company, you'll know that none of this stuff is remotely close to what I stand for as the CEO or what this company stands for. Understood?"

The surprise she masks at my bluntness doesn't get past me. "Yes, sir." She gets points for not sounding weak. I like that she remains confident.

"This interview isn't going to be typical," I continue. "I'm not going to waste either of our time by asking you questions about your background. I can read. Your resume speaks for itself. Your background and education are all impeccable. On paper, you are what I'm looking for.

But I don't care about what the paper says. I care about your answers and attitude to the questions I will be asking." My eyes don't leave hers.

The blonde and blue-eyed girl in front of me holds her own. "Understood, Mr. Lucinio."

I nod. "To my left is Ryan Crane. He's -"

"The leader of the most powerful mafia in the world," Skyla says.

I blink in surprise. "Uh… yeah."

She looks from me to him. "Also, technically, the CEO of several different companies, though you mostly just check in and only intervene when you must." She looks at Josh. "Josh Lucinio. You're the leader of the other most powerful mafia in the world. Like Ryan, you are the CEO of several different companies and only step in when it's needed." She looks to Jason, sitting next to Josh while we all stare at her in shock. "Jason Crane. You started your own company just after college. Though you used what you considered dirty money, you quickly rose from the shadows of the Crane Mafia and created a name for yourself." Her eyes fall to Chase. "And you're Chase Shaw. You own the largest financial investment company in the world. Like Jason, you started it yourself. You grew it on your own. You reluctantly took a loan from your mother and paid her back very quickly." She smiles when her eyes fall back on me. "You're Alex Lucinio. You started this company when you were still in college. With the help of Mr. Crane, you grew it exponentially. Until recently, when you took the reins, Lucinio Tech was run by him."

"Well, damn," Josh rumbles, recovering before any of us. "You did your research."

"I like to know what I'm getting into," she responds. "I know this company was started specifically to help people with identity theft. With the help of Mr. Crane, though, you developed security software that could be used in his companies and other companies of many different kinds. You now develop security software for everyone, including the Federal Government and the regular person at home. I've studied your mission statement. You and your company stand solely on integrity. You truly believe in helping people, no matter how young or old or what their status is."

Ryan chuckles. "No further questions, Your Honor. The State rests."

I can't help but laugh. So does everyone else, including Skyla. I smile and open my folder. "I know we've put you through a lot of tests and things to get to this point. Which you did very well on, by the way. But I do have another test for you. A scenario. I want you to tell me what you'd do in this situation."

"Okay." She nods and politely folds her hands on the table.

I look up at her after reading the question. "We've hit hard times. We're losing a lot of money from our bottom line. Our fourth quarter looks like we'll be in the red. The rest of the year we've barely squeaked by. Christmas is coming up. Bonuses don't look like they'll be happening. We're in a budget crisis, but you know there's no reason for it. Our business hasn't declined. Talk me through what you do to fix it."

We all watch her curiously. The question insinuates that we have a money laundering problem. It's specific to the issue Lucinio Tech had when I took over and had for years. Now that we've discovered what was happening and where it came from, we haven't seen any other issues. What I want to know is what she'd do if the situation arises again.

"First thing I would do is start working closely with the accounting staff and management. I'd want to pull financials for each and every account. I'd want to know where the anomalies are because either someone is embezzling or there is a much larger problem. I'd want to dig deep to figure out what's happening."

"You pull financials," Ryan begins. "Nothing seems off."

Skyla nods. "Well, seeming off and being off are two different things. There would have to be something off somewhere because if the company is hemorrhaging money when they shouldn't be, it has to be coming from somewhere. I'd be looking at financials for us and our accounts."

Jason leans back in his chair. "Okay. You find something off. One of the accounts looks to be paying their bill, but you notice that the money is being deposited into another account that doesn't belong to Lucinio Tech."

"I'd bring that straight to the CEO and figure it out," Skyla says.

Josh clears his throat. "You bring it to the CEO. Mr. Lucinio says the account it's being deposited into doesn't belong to the company. It's discovered that the account is an offshore account. The money is being funneled back into the United States through several different accounts. It ends with the Lead Accountant here at Lucinio Tech."

We all watch her like a hawk. She sits tall. "If the Lead Accountant was anyone other than my brother, I might believe that there was embezzling going on. Given that it is my brother, though, I wouldn't believe for a second that he could do something like that. I would ask that you pull him and talk to him. I hope that you would give me the respect of trusting my instincts when I say Austin wouldn't be involved in embezzlement. That's not who he is."

I nod and give an almost imperceptible smile. I lean back and cross my arms over my chest. "Two-part question. It turns out Mr. Winters is embezzling. He admits it. He gives you the proof. He knows he's caught." I wait for her to process the unsaid question and answer me.

She takes a deep breath. "I'm a super honest person, Mr. Lucinio." For the first time, her voice wavers. "I'm not sure I'd ever truly believe he'd do something like that, but I wouldn't do something like try and get him into a country where he wouldn't have to face the consequences of his actions. It would break me. I'm sure. I'd need time to process it. But I would allow the justice system to do what they do. Whether I'd be able to come back here and pretend like it was all okay, I guess I don't have that answer for you." She lowers her eyes.

I don't give her a chance to recover, though I'd like to. "Second part of the question. Opposite scenario. You know he's innocent. You come to me. It's discovered there is more to the story. He's caught in the crossfire."

She looks up slowly and blinks a few times. The tears I see threatening to fall throw me off. It's a question. Personal, yes, but nothing she should get that upset about. Unless she's an empath or something, something like this has happened to her. My background check didn't uncover anything like this when it came to her or where she came from. Her reaction, however, makes me feel like I need to call in the big guns, and have Lance dig deeper.

She clears her throat and takes a breath. "That seems more plausible. And in that situation," she says quietly. Her eyes meet Josh's for a moment before resting back on mine. "I would truly hope that I can trust you and your family to do whatever they need to do to figure it out."

I smile and lean forward, clasping my hands once more. *Good girl*, I think to myself. The second part of my question was specifically aimed at figuring out how she would feel if the mafia was to get involved in something with this company. More so how she'd handle her own brother being caught in the middle.

"Do you understand the reason I asked that question?" I ask, not breaking eye contact.

Giving my own directness right back to me. "Yes. I fully understand. You want to know if I have an issue with you not technically being part of the mafia, but still being closely associated with them." She leans back in her chair and crosses her arms over her chest. "Since I've seen you all at work and know from personal experience that you're the good guys, I'll be honest and as direct with you as you were with me. I don't have a problem with the good guys." She holds all of our gazes.

After a few moments, I break the silence. "I'll be honest. I'm fucking impressed as hell, Ms. Winters." I slide the folder across the table with an offer I've already figured out. "Starting salary, upon your acceptance of being hired, is three hundred fifty thousand. You'll have paid vacation totaling four weeks throughout the year. You'll see a raise of one percent each year. Bonuses. It's all laid out for you there. Ms. Knight." I nod my head towards Raleigh. She smiles. "She'll grab your official hiring package. If you accept, of course."

"This… is…" She wipes her eye and blinks a few times before she dares look back up at me. "This is a very generous offer. Of course, I accept."

"Lucinio Tech only employs the best, Ms. Winters," I say. "And it's because of that reason that our salaries are competitive. Generous. We can afford it. We know that we wouldn't be where we are without the hard work of our employees. It's the sole reason I will never allow pay cuts or layoffs. I would never be where I am without all of them. We're glad to have you on board."

Josh clears his throat and stands, looking down at his phone. "I apologize." He gives a curt nod. "I have to take this."

"I'll get the hiring package," Raleigh says with a smile, following him out.

I let out a breath of relief. Fuck me, I'm thankful this hiring shit is over.

Chapter Twenty Five

🐦 Raleigh 🐦

I slip out of the conference room as Alex is asking Skyla if she has any questions or comments. I knew he'd already made his decision about her after he'd gone through all of her testing and previous interview results. Just like he had Austin, Alex became more and more impressed with her.

I really couldn't blame him. I liked her right away. I also thought it would be amazing to have a female Chief Financial Officer. There are far more males in positions of power like that. Maybe it's because I'm young, but it's nice for females who dream of being executives for large companies to be able to look up to a woman who has done just that.

I slide into my desk chair just as Josh, who is perched on my desk, hangs up his phone. I look up at him. "What was that all about?"

"Remember that flash drive Austin found?"

"Yeah." I turn to my computer and pull up Skyla's hiring contract.

"I was waiting for Lance to finish with it. He just did. Turns out it was emails sent from the accounting department. Franklin's email to be exact. I don't know how the Lead Accountant got them, but he encrypted them. He also had files that prove Franklin was taking money. Lance said it also proves his theory about a few things, but mostly we know now that he does have a family in South Africa and is connected to that gang we took out. The leader of the gang is his brother."

I furrow my brows. "Are you sure? I specifically remember one dinner he was there and said he had no siblings."

"Yeah, Lance is sure. He said the emails kept saying he needed to contact his brother for a bunch of different things. Lance verified it. Franklin does have one brother. A Gregory Franklin."

I think hard to all of the times I met the disgusting man. After a few moments, I shake my head. "Not once did he ever mention a Gregory. I would have remembered because I always thought that name was lame. Greg." I make a face.

Josh laughs. "What else can you remember about Franklin?"

I shiver and hit print. I lean back in my chair and sigh. "Just that he always gave me the creeps. He leered at me constantly. I trusted Matthew at that time. I told him everything. Including how I didn't like the way his partner looked at me." I hug myself.

"What did he say to that?"

"Just that I didn't need to worry about him. He was harmless. He said he had a wife and kids at home that he adored, just like he adored me."

Josh chuckles and shakes his. "It never ceases to amaze me how fucking thick he laid it on you."

I smile softly. "You know what really annoys me?"

"What?"

"That not only was my entire life a complete lie, but that he had planned this whole thing with Franklin from the very first second my real parents approached him." I sigh. "I mean, how can anyone be so incredibly callous?"

He shrugs. "I honestly don't know how to answer that. His treachery goes back a very long time. If you need something to help you explain, though, we've all decided it goes back to losing the woman he loved. A game played by his own father."

"You mean when he took Rebekkah in some stupid arranged marriage thing." It's a statement. Not a question. I know the answer. It's the same thing that's happening to me.

"His father and Ryan's grandfather had a deal. It's typical behavior in the mafia. It's the way alliances are formed. Truces."

"But it was an alliance that never really formed anyway," I point out.

"Well, it sort of did. It started as a truce. The Crane's and Lucinio's agreed not to go after each other. Later, Matthew trusted Alex. Alex didn't want to go after the Crane's because of his friendship with Ryan. Truthfully, though, he knew the Lucinio Mafia would never be able to defeat the Crane Mafia. The Crane Mafia had grown exponentially when Ryan took control and went legal. Alex isn't stupid. Going up against him would have been suicide. Even before he met Ryan, he knew that. Fuck, so did I. And we were right. The Crane Mafia has always been larger than ours. They've always had more guns. Matthew learned the hard way. Every single time he got the balls to attack Ryan, he was beaten. The alliance never really happened until Alex and Ryan became friends. Alex knew he could pull Ryan if he needed him. Ryan knew Alex would maneuver men if Ry needed them."

"It all seems so stupid to me. I mean, the Lucinio Mafia and Crane Mafia are aligned now. And there were no arranged marriages to make it happen."

Josh chuckles. "Ryan has never believed in that. Neither did his father. It's something both me and Alex have been against, too. But we don't run typical mafias, honey. We don't go out looking for wars to gain more territory. Our entire purpose isn't to make as much money as possible while taking down anyone that stands in our way. We cross lines. I won't deny that. But we do it for the greater good. Without us, the entire world would be chaos. As cocky as that fucking sounds, it's the truth. The law can only do so much. Law enforcement can only enforce so much. There are bad guys roaming the streets who have managed to escape the long arm of the law. But not us."

I smile. "You're like a dark superhero."

Josh laughs. "We call Ryan the Dark Knight. He hates it. But when you think about it, we kind of are dark heroes. Can you imagine how the world would be if we didn't catch the amount of drugs and guns that we do?"

I wince. "I'm not sure I want to."

I reach around him for the hiring packet. As I go through it, I sigh. I haven't been able to stop thinking about Alex and the entire marrying thing since we talked about it a couple of days ago while I was trying on that dress. I've been able to avoid the topic since, and he's been sweet enough to not bring it up.

"What's the sigh all about?"

I look up at him then back at the stack of papers in front of me. "Do you think it's wrong that I want to marry Alex? It's been like three months since we've been together. Everything is so great. But…" I trail off and shake my head.

"But…?"

I sigh again and play with a paperclip. "The other day, Alex and I were shopping for some decorations for the employee appreciation party tomorrow. He'll be introducing the new CFO at the same time. At least, that's what the goal was. He wasn't totally sure it would pan out if he couldn't find anyone or if he did find someone and offered them employment, but they didn't accept right away or something. Anyway." I take a deep breath. "He made a comment. I know he was joking, but my mind went straight to marrying him."

"Hmm… What was the comment?"

"I want him to wear a particular shirt tomorrow. I planned on finding a dress to match it. He said something like it starts with me dressing him. Next thing he'll know, he'll be waiting for me at the altar. And I know he was kidding around. I do." I lean back and look up at him. "But I've had fantasies of marrying him before we were even together. Which is stupid and crazy -"

"Raleigh. Stop. Cut off those thoughts now," he commands. "You're not stupid. You aren't crazy."

I look up at him in surprise at his tone. I've only ever heard him sound like that once before. It was when I told him I felt like a completely stupid person for believing Matthew loved me. I had completely forgotten he doesn't like when anyone says that kind of thing about themselves.

"I'm sorry." I shake my head. "I know. I know I'm not. I just feel like I'm so wrong for feeling like that. I mean the first six months of our relationship, he hated me. I was terrified of him. But at the same time…" I trail off again with a whine and put my head in my hands. "Just send me to the funny farm."

Josh chuckles. "Raleigh, I'm not the kind of man who gives a flying fuck about whether you're an adult or not. I swear to God, I will spank you if you call yourself stupid or crazy one more time."

I jerk and look up at him. I expect to see a smile, but I don't. "What?"

He raises an eyebrow. "Did I stutter?"

"N-no…" I stare at him with wide eyes and in disbelief.

"I am not going to tolerate someone I love talking down about herself like that. And if you think I'm joking, ask Alex and Chase about the time Breetana was berating herself and got a spanking after she was warned to stop." He stands with all of the confidence in the world. All I can do is gape at him. "Now, tell me what happened. Because I'm struggling to follow why you're so upset about this marriage thing." He leans against the wall behind me.

I turn my chair and shake my head. "I really don't want to be spanked by you."

He smiles and crosses his arms over his chest. "Then don't make me do it."

I wrinkle my nose. "Done." I lean back in my chair making a mental note to ask about him spanking a grown woman and what caused it. Josh is the type of man who would follow through on that threat.

"Good. Now talk."

I take a deep breath. "It's just that I don't think it's normal for a person to dream of marrying a guy when she first meets him."

Josh chuckles. "You don't believe in love at first sight."

I tilt my head. "Not really. I feel like that only happens in cheesy Hallmark movies and crappy romance novels."

"Yet, what you're describing is just that. You had feelings for him before you knew who he was. They never went away, despite the fact that he was a complete dick to you. Then when he apologized and came clean to you about why he was acting the way he was, you forgave him almost right away. When he kissed you, you told me yourself that was it. You couldn't possibly be mad at him anymore. Even though you weren't entirely certain you ever were. You just didn't understand what was wrong with him, and why he hated you. Hell, you completely disobeyed me and decided to come back here to work after he shoved you against the window in his office. You going to sit here and tell me that it wasn't love at first sight for you?"

I sigh. "Do you always have to be right?"

He grins. "Side effect of being a big bad mafia boss."

I smile and lean my head back on the chair. "So? What do I do about it?"

"Raleigh, I think if you think he doesn't feel the same way, you aren't looking hard enough. Alex adores you."

"Enough to not run for the hills if I say how much I want to marry him?"

He chuckles. "Honest opinion?"

I nod. "Always."

"You only live one life. Why would you waste time? You know how you feel. And if you look closely, you'll see he's right there with you, honey. Why keep it in?"

I know he's right. My heart knows he's right. My problem is my head. I'm letting it get to me. I'm terrified he'll turn away. It would shatter me. Losing Alex after going through everything we've gone through both together and apart would just break me.

But it's not just him. I feel like if I lost him, I'd lose everyone I've come to love. The entire family. Besides Damon, I'm not sure anyone would really want me to stick around. It's just one more thing holding me back from being totally honest about what I want.

I'm also young. What if I have no idea what I want? What if I make a mistake? I trusted Matthew. Obviously, I'm prone to making mistakes. I close my eyes and rub my temples, forcing my mind to stop spiraling.

"I need to be honest. Tell him my fears and feelings."

"And there's the Raleigh I know. Be that fearless, brave girl we know you are."

I smile. "Thank you for talking me through it."

"Anytime." He reaches into his inside pocket as his phone rings. He looks at the caller ID and answers. "Hey, Damon. What -" He stops talking abruptly and looks down at me.

I'm suddenly very uneasy, but don't know why. I turn around and grab Skyla's hiring packet. Alex needs to sign it. She needs to agree. Then I need to get it to human resources so they can do whatever they do.

I take one more look over it to make sure I didn't forget anything and smile. The thought of Alex always makes me smile, but when I think of him in a future with me, I get butterflies and feel weak in the knees.

"This can't be happening. Tell me you're fucking joking."

His tone makes me turn towards him, but when I hear the ding of the elevator door, I plaster on my best smile. I'm not expecting anyone, but that's not unusual. Sometimes other employees come up here to see if Alex is available or to drop something off that needs his signature or something.

"Hey, how can I help -" I cut myself off and let out a strangled cry when I see who it is.

I would crawl under the desk and hide, but I don't have the chance. My chair is jerked so forcefully around that my head actually spins. Josh pulls me up and shoves me behind him so hard, I hit the wall and completely lose my breath. I clutch my chest, still unsure what exactly is happening, and try to breathe.

Like a flash, Josh has pulled the gun at his hip out and is pointing it at the elevator, tugging me down with him as he takes cover behind the desk. He pushes my body against the floor so I'm lying face down.

"Nice to finally meet you Mr. Lucinio. The leader of one of the most infamous terrorist organizations in the world." The deep and dangerous growly voice strikes fear into my entire being.

Josh laughs. "Man, he really had you under his thumb, huh? I'm the farthest thing from a terrorist organization. How about you put down the gun and let me end this the easy way?"

"Nah. I think I'll take my chances. How about you give me what's rightfully mine instead? I'll even be nice and let you have your guard back."

"You mean Raleigh? Not a fucking chance. As for the guard, he's paid to die for me. You think I fucking care if you shoot him?"

I whimper. I didn't get a chance to look, but that must be how he got up here. He took a guard and forced him to scan his card to get up here. Or maybe he just took the card and thought he'd used the guy as a human shield after he got his handprint and card scanned. I know he's paid to protect us all, but I don't want him to die.

"I know more than you think. I know you don't want to see anyone die unnecessarily. That's how I'm confident you'll give me my wife."

"Like I said before. Not a fucking chance. You're not getting near her."

"You won't be able to stop me, Mr. Lucinio." He pauses. "Don't you go everywhere with guards? Where are your lap dogs now?"

Josh chuckles. "Everywhere. Drop the gun. Or I shoot him. Then I shoot you, Mr. Franklin. His death won't be in vain, and he knows that. Yours on the other hand…"

From my vantage point on the floor behind my desk, I can see Chance coming down the hallway from the bathroom he must have gone to. His gun is drawn. I'm thankful he heard what's going on and can help Josh.

A shot rings out. It echoes loudly in the lobby. I scream and cover my ears. Hot tears sting my cheeks as they cascade from my eyes. The shot sounded thunderous. I suddenly feel like I'm deaf. All I can hear is a low ringing in my ears.

The last thing I see before everything goes black is Chance falling to the floor in a pool of his own blood.

Chapter Twenty Six

❦ Alex ❦

"I'm happy you're joining us, Ms. Winters. Really," I say. "I'm looking forward to working with you. It will be a huge weight off my shoulders. Your brother already took a lot of it, but I definitely need you."

"I'm truly honored to have been hired on the spot like this. It's unorthodox, but nothing about this entire process has been anything other than just that." Skyla laughs.

I smile. "Well, Raleigh is going to grab your hiring packet and -" I'm cut off by a sound I never thought I'd hear on the top floor of Lucinio Tech.

Gunshot.

But it's the bone-chilling scream that sets us all into a flurry of motion.

Skyla claps a hand over her mouth to muffle her screams. I send up a silent prayer that she's smart enough to do that. I don't need whatever is going on out there to make its way in here and put more lives in danger.

Without a word, Ryan hands Jason the second gun he always carries. I do the same with mine, and slide it across the table to Chase.

Carrying is a hard habit to break. I haven't been without a gun on my hip since I graduated college.

Jason and Chase lead Skyla to the small kitchen. They close and lock the door as I follow Ryan out of the conference room. We stay low and silent, using the walls to keep us as concealed as we possibly can be. I keep one hand on Ryan's lower back so he knows I'm there. The other keeps my Glock at a low ready.

Ryan holds up one fist, signaling me to stop. I follow the command with no hesitation. I'm sure he knows how grateful I am that he's taking the lead. All I can think about is Chance and Raleigh laying in a bloodied heap on the floor.

I don't even know if Josh is out there with her. I pray to Hell he is, though, because it would mean Raleigh has a better chance at survival. Two people on her side in the fight against whoever is out there is the only thing keeping my heart in my chest.

I close my eyes a moment and force myself to be calm. I can't help her or Ryan, or even Chance and Josh, if I can't focus. I open my eyes when Ryan steps back into me and pushes me backwards a few steps.

Staying low, he shifts so he can whisper. "Franklin. He's got one guard hostage. Josh is behind the desk. Looks like he's probably got Raleigh on the floor. Chance is down."

"Fuck," I whisper back. I run a hand down my face.

"We need to take him down. Once and for all. Josh is in my line of sight. I can signal him. You take the shot. You'll need to go around the corner to get a clear one to the back of his head. Stay low and silent. Watch for my signal."

"Got it." I move around him and quietly make my way around the corner.

I breathe a silent sigh of relief when Franklin doesn't see me. Ryan stands, still using the wall to conceal himself, and uses the overhead lights to refract light from his watch. We're mostly behind Franklin. He wouldn't be able to see us unless he turned his head.

But Josh would be able to. Which is what Ryan and I are both counting on.

Unless a person were truly paying attention, they'd never see the slight flick of Josh's wrist. It's his way of telling us Raleigh is safe. I breathe out quietly in relief and ready my aim, keeping one eye on Ryan's hand. It's the only part of him I can see from where I am. I watch him countdown from three.

"There's no way you're getting out of this one, Lucinio. Just hand her over," Franklin says. "I'm tired of waiting for what's mine."

"I may not have a clear shot, you motherfucker," Josh responds as he stands. He lowers his weapon to his side. "But they do."

As soon as Ryan closes his fist, I take my shot. Franklin drops to the ground before he even has a chance to turn around. Raleigh screams and cries. I waste no time in running to her. I know both Josh and Ryan will cover me if my shot to the back of Franklin's head didn't kill him.

I drop to my knees next to Raleigh and pull her trembling body into my arms. She fights me as she screams and cries. "Shh... Baby, it's me. It's me." I run my fingers through her hair and hug her close to me. "You're okay. You're safe. I'm right here, beautiful." I kiss her neck and try to keep myself from shaking. I need to be her rock.

"Alex!" She throws her arms around me when she realizes it's me. Her nails dig into my back. "I thought he shot you! I thought you were dead!"

"Shh... I'm okay. He's gone. No one is getting to you. I'm okay. Josh is okay. We're all okay." I rock back and forth with her, holding her just as tightly as she is me.

She shakes her head and sobs. "He killed Chance! He shot him! He killed him!" Her body uncontrollably shakes with her cries.

"No. Honey, no. Look. Look, baby."

She shakes her head. "He's dead. He killed him!"

"Shh... Raleigh. Look. Look for me." I tug her hair a little so she looks up.

I make myself let go of her hair so I can turn her face to look at Chance. Chance is groaning and gritting his teeth while Ryan puts pressure on his shoulder. Josh is kneeling in front of the guard Franklin had taken hostage, making sure he's okay.

My heart jumps in my throat when the elevator dings. The doors slide open. Josh, Ryan, and I all immediately point our guns at the doors. Raleigh lets out a squeak and makes herself as small as possible in my arms. We all breathe out a collective sigh of relief when Dane, Cole, and Damon step off the elevator.

"Just us," Dane says with his hands in front of him.

"Go help Ryan. Chance was shot in the shoulder," Josh commands. "Damon, call a clean-up crew. Cole. Jason and Chase are in the conference room with Skyla. Escort Skyla home. Then I need Lance sending out a company-wide email from Alex to all employees rescheduling the party tomorrow. No way that's happening after this. Give it a week."

I hold Raleigh close, soothingly rubbing her back as she cries. I'm sure I don't need to say the words. Everyone here, including her, knows I'm holding her as tightly as I am as much for her as for me.

Everyone follows Josh's orders without a word. My eyes fall on Chance. It scares the hell out of me seeing him like that. If Josh hadn't been here, I wonder if Raleigh would be in my arms right now.

The thought that she may not be stops my heart cold.

Later that night, Raleigh is laying in my lap. I'm thankful that the shock and crying has dissipated, but I'm finding myself beyond terrified. She hasn't talked much since I brought her home. I didn't expect her to. Seeing what she saw had to scare the fuck out of her. I can't blame her. She thought she saw a grown man kill another grown man right in front of her. That's not something the average person sees every day.

I run my hand up and down her back as I have been for the past two hours. I haven't said a word. I've been waiting for her to talk. I know she will when she's ready. I know it will take her some time.

It's given me a long while to freak myself out. There's a very large difference between knowing that the man she's with has taken lives. Knowing the family she's come to love as her own is a mafia family and has done bad things is something she's been able to come to terms with. But seeing it all go down in front of her is something else entirely.

I'm afraid she's going to leave me. I've never been more afraid of anything before. The thought of her walking away from me and this family, though, has me feeling all sorts of emotions I'm not used to. My chest has been tight ever since I got her in my car. She curled into herself and leaned against the door. When I put my hand on her thigh, she jumped.

If I'm being honest, I'm shocked she's laying on my lap right now, given her reaction to my touch in the car. I've watched her go from being terrified I had been killed to being frightened of us all. It's heartbreaking on many levels, but it was her reaction to me that was truly shattering. I'm taking her being this close to me and allowing me to touch her as a sign of hope. Hope that maybe she doesn't plan on telling me to go to Hell.

"I want to marry you," she whispers.

I freeze and look down at her, unsure if I heard her correctly. That's not the words I expected to come out of her mouth. I clear my throat. "What?"

She shifts and sits up on her knees. She folds her hands in her lap and looks at me. Her beautiful eyes are rimmed red from her tears, but it does little to hide the sparkle that shines from them. The pure, unadulterated love.

"I realized…" She drops her eyes to her hands and takes a breath. "When I thought you'd been killed, or I guess that you could have been, that I can't live without you." She bites her lip and looks back up at me. Unshed tears are pooled behind her eyes. "You… said… the other day… about you waiting for me at the altar. I know you were joking, but -"

"I wasn't."

Her pretty mouth falls open slightly. She watches me in wonder. "You weren't?"

I shake my head. "No, Raleigh. I wasn't." I slowly move my hand from her thigh, where it had fallen when she sat up, to her cheek. I tangle my fingers in her hair. She closes her eyes and shifts closer to me. "I want to marry you."

She throws herself at me and hugs me tightly. I feel her tears on my neck. "I thought you'd think I'm too young and insane for wanting to marry you so quickly after we got together."

I take a deep breath and close my eyes. I bury my face in her hair and kiss her neck. I wrap my arms tightly around her and pull her as close to me as I can. All of the tension vibrating throughout my being fades with the breath I release.

"I swear, Raleigh. I thought you were going to leave me."

She jerks back like I slapped her and looks at me with furrowed brows. "Why would you think that?"

"Because of the way you reacted after everything that happened." I pull her closer so she's flush against me again. I don't want her anywhere else. "You were scared. You rightfully should have been. But it seemed like you were afraid of me and Josh. Even Ryan. You were shrinking away from us. You jumped when I got you in the car and cowered from me."

She scrunches her nose so adorably, my heart melts. "I'm sorry. I didn't mean to make you think that was for you." She cups my face in her small hands and kisses me softly. "I was scared, but not of you, Alex. Never of you. I…" She takes a shuddering breath and sniffles. "I… got… a little lost in my thoughts. I didn't know I had jerked away from you. I was just thinking that I could have lost you. Or he… might… have gotten to me. And it would have happened without you knowing how I feel about you."

I nod and hug her close to me as I stand. I lift her with me. She wraps herself around me, soothing the rest of the tension I didn't know I had. "I'm so fucking grateful, Raleigh. I was truly afraid that knowing the things I've done and seeing me kill someone in front of you would make you think I'm not good enough for you. I never want to scare you, baby."

She shakes her head into my shoulder and hugs me tighter. "I don't think that. I'm not afraid of you. You killed him to save me and Chance and Josh and the guard he took hostage. I know what you've done in your past. I know what you sometimes do now. I know it's for the greater good. I was afraid, but not of you. I was afraid that you'd never know how I feel, and that I want to marry you. I didn't know how to tell you. I may have still been in shock. It took me a while to realize Chance was still alive."

I kick the door closed behind me and walk to our bed. I climb in, still fully dressed with her wrapped tightly around me. She settles on top of me. Her hair spreads across my chest. She places her ear just above my heart. I reach over and open the drawer of my nightstand. I feel around for the little black box I've had in my drawer for a couple of weeks now.

"I love you, Raleigh." I kiss the top of her head and close the drawer after grabbing the box.

"I love you, too, Alex," she whispers.

"I was scared to death I'd lost you. Josh signaled you were okay, but… Jesus Christ, I was out of my fucking mind with worry." I open the box behind her head and kiss her shoulder.

I take out the diamond ring on a platinum band. It's simple yet elegant. Just like she is. I can't imagine her wanting to wear a giant rock on her finger. She'd feel like it was just showing off. That's not who she is.

The square princess cut one carat diamond ring sparkles in the low light of the moon streaming through the window.

"When he stood up and put his gun down, my heart leaped in my throat. I was going to tackle him back behind the desk." She kisses my chest and sniffles. "And then when he said that they have a clear shot, I was confused. But when I heard the gunshot, I thought Franklin killed Josh. And then it struck me that you must have been out there. I didn't know who would have been with you, but I thought Franklin killed you."

"No. No, baby." I kiss her head and soothingly run one hand up and down her back again right before tangling it into her hair. I tug lightly so she looks at me. My lips crash to hers.

The kiss is needy because I have to feel her to know she's still here. That she didn't walk away, and that I'm just dreaming she's in my arms. She moans when my tongue dances with hers. I feel her fingertips dig into my shoulders and know immediately that everything I'm feeling, she is, too.

She pulls away slightly and sniffles. I hold her close to me, but release my grip on her hair. I gently wipe away her tears with the pad of my thumb. I kiss her softly and push her hair back behind her ear, holding it there.

"I'm never letting you go, Raleigh," I whisper. I can feel my voice crack.

"I don't want you to," she whispers.

"You're mine, baby."

I feel her gasp out a breath and tighten her grip on me even more. "I've never wanted anything else. Just you."

"Marry me."

She blinks a few times. Her mouth falls open, but no words come out. Her eyes sparkle with wonder. I kiss her softly and watch her close her eyes. I pull back slowly as I move the ring so she can see it.

"Alex?" she whispers.

I gently take her hand and slide the ring slowly onto her finger. She watches my every movement while I watch her. "Marry me," I whisper.

She nods slowly and whispers the word my heart longs for. "Yes…"

I smile. The ring fits perfectly. She can't take her eyes off it, but the smile that begins at the corners of her lips spreads across her face. She sniffles as I wipe tears from her cheeks again. Moments later, she's laughing and hugging me as tightly as I'm hugging her.

"You really weren't kidding," she whispers against my neck.

I shake my head with a smile against her shoulder. "No. I wasn't."

"You really want to marry me." Her lips find my neck. She kisses softly.

"More than anything."

I hug her as close to me as I can. I keep rubbing her back soothingly and hold back my own emotional break until after she's deep into a peaceful sleep. I gently move her to my side and cover her with the purple comforter she bought and begged me to put on the bed.

I quietly climb out of the bed and walk to the balcony off the bedroom. Ending the note happy like that was something I know we both needed, but fuck if I'm still not vibrating with the anger she was nearly taken from me and fear that exact thing damn near happened.

Raleigh, like that purple comforter, has gotten so far under my skin that living without her is no longer an option in my life. I need her more than I need the air I breathe. I take a breath and drop to the ground. I start doing push-ups, hoping they'll use up the extra energy I've managed to build up.

Now that I know Raleigh and I are okay and officially engaged to be married, I can't stop thinking about just how in the fuck Franklin got through my security. Again. The kid from Starbucks got through using Franklin's fucking badge. I changed security protocol and made it so only certain people can get up to this floor without a security escort. He found a weakness and got to her anyway.

I do the pushups until I'm sweating and can hardly feel my arms. I didn't bother counting. I push myself up, panting slightly, and drop on a chair. I take out my phone and dial the number of the only person I know who can solve my security issues. I should have listened to him long ago and let him fully implement everything he wanted to.

"Lucinio. To what do I owe the honor?" my half-brother's deep voice greets me after the third ring.

"Nick." Nick West is Matthew's son and the result of his relationship with Nick's mother before Matthew was forced to marry my mother. Nick is one of the few good things that came out of everything we uncovered about Matthew. "I should have listened to you about all of the shit you wanted to implement at Lucinio Tech when we moved our Headquarters here. Do whatever the fuck you do."

He chuckles low. "I don't mean to sound like a dick, but I knew this call was coming. I've already got a team ready to go. Everything will be set up when you get back to the office on Monday. They'll start tomorrow."

I breathe a sigh of relief and close my eyes. "Thank you."

"Anytime. How are you and Raleigh?"

I sigh. "Okay. Now. I was pretty afraid she'd leave me after this."

"What made you think that?"

"I killed someone right in front of her. I was pretty concerned seeing shit she knew about actually happen in real life would send her running for the hills. I can't say I'd blame her."

"She's not going to walk away, Alex. You have a good one in her. She reminds me a lot of Dani."

I smile a little at the thought of Nick's wife. "Didn't you feel the same way when the mafia life you'd run so far from forced you back into it?"

"Familiar story, huh? I was worried she wouldn't want to stay when she saw the real me. Lesson learned? That you can run from the mafia all you want, but it's part of who you are. Better to make the best of it than deny that part of you exists."

I chuckle. "Little different for me, bro. I tried running from it, but fuck if I didn't miss it. Seeing all the good Josh is doing since he took over... I don't know. Hard not to be a part of that."

"He's going places. I don't doubt he'll surpass Ryan. But don't tell that fucker I said that," he teases.

I laugh. "Secret is safe with me."

"Don't doubt your girl, Alex. I think she's got a few surprises up her sleeve for you. She's a lot tougher than you think."

I smile and glance over my shoulder at my sleeping girlfriend. "Thank you. I don't know why that makes me feel better, but it does. She said yes."

"No shit. You proposed?" I can hear the smile in his voice.

"Yeah." I grin. "You're the first person I told. Don't let Josh know that."

He laughs. "Secret is safe with me," he says, throwing my own words back at me. "Take care of her. Forget about Franklin. He's gone. Focus on Raleigh and you. That's all that matters now. I've got the security in your building covered."

I nod. "You're the man."

He laughs. "Better believe it!" He hangs up.

I stand and walk back into the bedroom. I put my phone on the nightstand and strip my shirt. I climb back into bed and cuddle her as close to me as I can. Sleep doesn't typically come easy to me. I don't expect it will tonight, but before I have time to think of anything other than the woman in my arms, I'm falling fast into a surprising and peaceful slumber.

Chapter Twenty Seven

☙ Raleigh ❧

"Damon? Can you start putting out the chairs? The rental company dropped them by the tent." I point to the far end of the square in Millennium Park.

"On it. You need help with the tent?" Damon asks me.

I shake my head. "Josh and Austin are dealing with that."

"Okay. I'll grab Cole to help."

"Thank you." I move onto the next table and start putting out party favors and arranging my decorations.

Setting up the employee appreciation party is not nearly as fun as I thought it would be. I'm sure it has to do with the fact that it's been just one week since Franklin made his appearance in our lives and lost his. He'll no longer be able to bother us.

I'm still a little shocked that he thought he would be able to take down Josh or the Lucinio Mafia to get to me. I know Matthew had to have done extensive research on how much Josh has grown. He had to have known that the Lucinio Mafia and Crane Mafia had joined forces. Which means, he would have told his associate. Edward Franklin would have known he didn't have a chance.

But something that has been bothering me even more is that I don't feel bad that he's gone. I have no issues with my boyfriend being the one who pulled the trigger. While it's not normal, it doesn't bother me that the police weren't the ones to clean up the mess. They weren't even involved. The fact that none of that bothers me is what bothers me. What kind of woman am I to not have a problem with any of that?

"Lost in thought?"

I jump and spin around, clutching my chest. "Jesus, Dane. You should wear a bell."

Dane laughs. "I called your name a couple of times."

"Really?" I turn to him and rub my head. "I'm sorry. I was thinking about Franklin."

"Fucker is gone. He doesn't deserve your thoughts."

"It's just…" I fold my arms over my chest. "He had to know who he was going up against. Why would he do that?"

Dane raises an eyebrow. "Some people aren't smart. And some are very smart and incredibly cocky. That's Franklin. He believed you were his. And he thought he was better than Josh. I'm sure Matthew told him that Josh and Alex are weak and easy to get through. He killed Ethan Crane. The father of badass Ryan Crane. Ethan and Ryan had always been deemed to be the toughest mafia bosses in the world. He took Ethan down."

I scoff. "By hiring people to ram Ryan's vehicle. He got lucky."

Dane shrugs. "Doesn't matter to him. He did it. If he could take out him and devastate Ryan, why wouldn't he be able to run through Josh and Alex? He'd always viewed them as weak anyway. I'm sure he told Franklin just that."

I shake my head. "It's just so stupid. Senseless."

He chuckles. "Raleigh, let me give you a bit of advice. I've been a cop for a long time. I've learned over the years that if you try and make sense of people's stupidity and actions, you're going to drive yourself fucking insane. You're never going to be able to understand what they were thinking. What you need to do is tell yourself that they fucked up. They paid the price. And put it in the back of your mind. Move forward."

I smile. "Stop obsessing."

He grins. "Exactly." He looks over my shoulder. "You landed yourself in a pretty great family. I'm thanking my lucky stars every single day for the outcomes of the challenges we've all faced. I ended up with a couple half-brothers who I love. I've been reunited with my mom, who I thought was dead. My dad was reunited with the love of his life."

I smile softly. I step into him and hug him. "Thank you."

His arms hug me tight. "You're welcome. But if you need someone to talk to who has an outside perspective? I'd suggest talking to Lyric. Fuck knows she has been in your shoes. Now. How about we finish this up? I think Alex should be here with Skyla pretty soon. Guests should be arriving."

Dane works side by side with me and in silence. He picks up how I want things set up very quickly and mimics what I've done on other tables. Before I know it, all of the tables are finished and look amazing.

In the center of the circular tables is a clear vase filled with silver and magenta rocks and water. I've ordered bouquets of white and pink lilies and arranged them in the vases. The silver and pink confetti I bought is strewn over the tables. Everyone's party favor is a pink or silver box. Inside is a pair of earbuds with Lucinio Tech's logo on the box they come in.

"Damon?" I ask when I see him putting up the last of the chairs.

"Yeah?" he calls back.

"There are some boxes by the SUV that I was driven here in. They have blankets. Can you and Cole set one on each chair?"

"On it, honey!" Damon grabs Cole and heads for the SUV.

"What else do you need from me?" Dane asks.

"Um…" I look around. Josh and Austin have just finished the tent. I'm grateful because the notorious Chicago wind is starting to pick up a little bit. The tent will protect not only the decorations but also the guests. "Oh! We made shot glasses for each employee. They are engraved with everyone's name and the Lucinio Tech logo. I need someone to help me hand them out as guests arrive, but I haven't asked anyone."

"How many people do you need?"

"Well, they'll be going through a security checkpoint as they enter. Maybe we could set up the extra table. I could hand them out as they come in."

"You'd miss the entire party. This is for you, too, you know. Besides, I'm sure Alex would prefer you near him."

I sigh. "Yeah, I know, but I can't ask one of the other employees to do it."

Dane smiles down at me and shakes his head. "You still have a lot to learn about this family." He holds out a hand.

I look up at him, confused, but take his hand. He starts leading me somewhere. "Where are we going?"

"To show you the power of the Lucinio family."

I laugh. "The power of the Lucinio family? I think I saw that already."

He laughs with me. "I also have a surprise for you. Josh just gave me the signal."

My eyes widen. "Surprise?" I ask excitedly.

"Yep."

I practically bounce walk after him. "What is it?"

He laughs again. "I can't just tell you! Close your eyes."

I giggle and close them. "Closed!" I sing-song.

Dane laughs as he stops. "Okay. Ready?"

"Ready!" I bounce on my toes as I wait.

"Open them," he commands.

My eyes fly open. "Chance!" I squeal. I run towards him but stop short of jumping on him. "Oh my God! They said you were okay, but they weren't allowing visitors. Then they said you were back and recovering but needed a little time. They wouldn't let me see you!" I hug him, careful of his sling.

He laughs and puts his good arm around me. He hugs me close. "I know. That was at my request. You'd seen enough. I didn't want you to see me in the state I was in."

"I wouldn't have cared." I bury my face in his chest and hug him as hard as I dare.

"I know, Raleigh, but I did. My job is to protect you. From threats just as much as seeing me hurt like that. I wasn't in the right mind for anyone. I was snappy and being an asshole to just about everyone. I needed a little time to bring myself back. You didn't need that. But I did text you when you checked in. So, you can't hate me too much."

"I don't. I'm just glad you're okay. Hearing from others and reading a text that you're okay isn't the same as seeing it with my own eyes. I really thought he'd killed you."

"But he didn't. I'm okay. The bullet went through my shoulder. I'm not even sure how he saw me. I wasn't in his line of sight. But it doesn't matter. I'm okay. He's dead. You're safe. That's all that matters."

I hug him for a few more moments before feeling brave enough to pull away. I don't let him go, though. I look him up and down to make sure there's nothing else about him that's hurt other than his shoulder.

Since Josh assigned Chance to my personal security, we've become close. I'd say nearly as close as me and Dallas. Chance has become one of my best friends. Almost like an older brother to me like Damon is.

"I didn't realize just how much I needed to see you until now," I say as I look up at him. "I didn't feel…" I pause as I think of the right word. "Complete? Nothing about that day was right, but I've been dwelling on it. I didn't know why until now. I needed to see you were okay. Physically. With my own eyes."

Chance laughs and leads me towards the tent with an arm gently over my shoulders. "I would've sent you a picture if you were struggling that much. I didn't realize my decision was affecting you so badly. I'd have stopped by if I knew. Or let Alex bring you by the guard's quarters." He pulls out a chair for me.

I sit because I've been standing all morning. "Only for a few minutes." I moan and close my eyes as soon as I sit. "Okay, maybe a few more than a few minutes."

Chance laughs. "I just wanted to say thank you."

I open my eyes. "For what?"

"I keep to myself. I'm sure you know that. I wake up. Do my job. Go to bed. I don't have time for friends or anything. Ever since I left the Marine Corps, I've been closed off. I don't plan on that changing." He smiles. "But I can honestly say it's nice having a friend. Even if it just started off as a job."

I smile shyly and lean over to kiss his cheek. "I'm really glad we became friends."

Chance one-arm hugs me again and kisses the top of my head. "Time for you to get ready. Josh said you picked out a dress. None of us have ever seen you wear a dress." He looks down at me. "And you aren't wearing one now, so I'm assuming you need to change."

I laugh and look down at my ratty jeans and t-shirt. "I didn't want to ruin the dress. I brought it with me. I thought I could change in the SUV. The windows are pretty dark. I don't think anyone would be able to see."

Chance stands, shaking his head. "No. They'll still be able to see. I have an idea, though. Come on."

I reluctantly stand and follow him, wincing at how sore my feet are. "To think I need to put other shoes on. Uncomfortable ones. With heels."

He glances back at me and down at my feet. "Why?"

"Why?" I laugh. "Because I can't wear beige flats with it. I'm already a foot shorter than Alex. I do intend to stand near him today."

Chance laughs. "You may not realize it, but men like shorter girls."

I laugh. "Yeah, but I want to make an impression."

Chance shakes his head and takes the tablecloths off the two tables I had set up at the checkpoint. He signals for Damon and Josh to follow him with a jerk of his head as he leads me to the SUV. It never ceases to impress me how they can all communicate with no words at all.

I watch as Chance opens the door and grabs my dress. He hands it to me. I take it while he, Josh, and Damon take the tablecloths and create a makeshift dressing room around me. I can't help but giggle.

Josh winks. "Hurry up. I got word from Alex's security that he's on the way with Skyla." He and Damon pull the tablecloth up so I'm completely covered, and Chance stands guard.

"Can't people see through these? They aren't that thick." I nervously and very quickly start changing, making sure to say behind where Chance's shadow is.

"It wouldn't matter," Damon says. "Chance is in front of you, and Josh and I are blocking, too. You're good."

His words ease my mind. I've definitely come to trust the three men surrounding me. If they say I can't be seen, I believe them. But knowing Alex is coming, I still change in record time. After I have the dress on, I kneel to pick up my clothes and decide to slip my beige flats back on. My feet already hurt. I don't need blisters, and the flats are far more comfortable.

"Okay. I'm ready," I say. They let the tablecloth down. Josh hands them to Chance and Damon while I put my stuff in the SUV.

"People are showing up. I have Dane and Gavin on shot glass duty. Your guests will be going through security then guided to their table."

I nod. "Good. They'll have to show their name to get the right shot glass because they are all customized."

"They're on it. And call me overprotective, but I have some extra people around. I'll be around."

I smile up at him. "Is this you being overprotective? Or would this be you putting mine and Alex's mind at ease knowing you're around just in case Franklin comes back from the dead?"

Josh grins. "It might be a little of both." He looks over my head and nods. "Alex is here."

I turn and see the stretch limo pulling up. I smile. "And it looks like more and more people are starting to arrive."

Josh reaches up and adjusts his tie. "Fucking things are so uncomfortable. Do you know how many times I've worn one of these things?"

I laugh as he walks towards the limo. "Um… I'm going to say eleven."

Josh chuckles. "Close. But before these interviews I got roped into helping with, it was like three. I'm much happier in jeans."

"I think we all are." I look around. "I thought Dallas was coming? She was going to help me set up."

"Right. I didn't have a chance to tell you. Dallas got in a little bit of trouble. She mouthed off to Alec. Said something about him not being her father and not being able to tell her what to do. He didn't take kindly to it as the President of Viper's Venom. But as her brother? Well, it cut him a little deeper than he'd like to lead on."

My eyes widen. "What did she do?"

"I think she called him an overprotective asshole. Then attempted to walk from their compound to ours."

"That's… like… ten miles."

"Yep. He almost let her. I talked him into going to get her. She'd called me to complain about the entire thing. Took every fucking part of me not to go get her."

I shake my head. "I'm confused."

"Well, she wanted me to go get her after the fight. I told her she needed to work it out with Alec. That she couldn't keep running to me when she got into a fight with her brother. She needed to figure it out. She didn't like that answer very well, but agreed. Then told me she was about two miles from their compound. She got a fuck of a lecture on that while I was texting Alec. By the end of it, she ended up grounded to her room."

"I'd…" I tilt my head. "I'd say I'm surprised, but Dallas is a little spitfire sometimes."

He chuckles low. "I know."

I look up at him and smile. I know Josh likes a challenge, but he may have met his match with her. I guess only time will tell. He kisses me on the head and makes his way over to a couple of his guards.

When Alex's driver opens the door and I catch a glimpse of him, my smile spreads wider across my face. I shiver. The butterflies in my stomach take flight just like they always do when he's around.

His eyes meet mine, and I melt. My feet automatically carry me towards him like he's the flame, and I'm the firefly attracted to his heat. The fire he burns just for me. The way his eyes light up when he sees me is heartwarming, but it's the message I see behind them that truly makes me shiver.

I'm his.

All his.

Chapter Twenty Eight

❦ Alex ❦

"There's a lot of security around," Skyla says softly from the seat across from me in the back of the stretch limo we're in when the driver stops at Millennium Park.

I give her a reassuring smile. "When you're the CEO of an international billion-dollar company that specializes in creating security software good enough for the United States and other country's governments, it tends to put a target on your back. Add on the fact that my twin brother is the leader of a very powerful, internationally known and feared mafia, and that my best friend is the leader of another one, it makes my target much larger. Double the danger, double the security."

She nods and rings her hands together. I haven't quite figured out the story of the blonde woman in front of me, but I can't help but think there's something going on with her that she's buried deep. She's a very strong woman, but she'll get brief moments like this one when she seems to be scared out of her mind. Or nervous. Even skittish.

I've only known her for a week. She's proven already that she's an invaluable asset to Lucinio Tech. I don't regret for a second hiring her. After what happened with Edward Franklin, I was shocked she even wanted to still work for me. I'm still pretty surprised her brother hasn't just said fuck it and taken her with him away from all of this. He seems very protective of her.

"Do you think it's necessary for me to have security?" she asks in damn near a whisper. Her eyes remain locked on her feet.

"Do you mean beyond the security I've already assigned you?" I watch her intently for any kind of a sign she's running from something and is scared.

She nods and takes a deep breath before shaking her head. "It's okay. I'm being silly. I'm still shaken from last week."

Before I can say anything else, the driver opens my door. I glance at her once more and slide over so she can get out. I follow her, keeping my eye on the security I assigned to her as they get out of the SUV that was following behind us. While they don't flank her, they are close enough that she visibly relaxes. The smile returns to her face when she sees Austin.

My eyes fall on Raleigh and all else is forgotten. The dress she bought last week looks far better on her than I remember. It hugs her curves, but looks sophisticated enough that I know she's not uncomfortable. The skirt falls to her knees. The navy blue brings out her eyes, but it's the smile on her face that makes it all come together.

She looks happy.

Stunning.

My mouth goes dry. My tongue flicks out and licks my lips as I walk towards her. "You are a sight for sore eyes," I say raspily. I lean down and take her lips against mine. I don't care who sees. I wouldn't be able to fucking stop myself.

She lets out a quiet moan as her arms encircle my waist. It's the sexiest sound I think I've ever heard. I'm instantaneously straining against my slacks, but the sweet taste of her soft, warm lips on mine is far too tantalizing to force myself to back away.

It's only when I feel her pull away a little that I come to my senses. I step back, but keep my arms firmly around her. Her cheeks have turned a gorgeous shade of red. She can't meet my eyes, but she's panting.

I grin and gently cup her chin, lifting her face to mine. I give her a gentle kiss before pulling away. "You're beautiful," I whisper.

She shyly ducks her head. "Thank you," she whispers back.

I take her hand and lead her towards the stairs I'll be giving my speech on. "You're breathtaking. This entire setup is incredible."

"I have us sitting with Austin and Skyla. We're up front. I didn't really want to put us front and center, but Josh said it was okay because there's a lot of security here as well as his team."

I chuckle. "Josh has people around that no one sees. He learned very well from his mentor. Who else is sitting with us? Looks like a table for ten."

"Oh. Right. I have mostly upper management. Security will be escorting upper management to the tables assigned to them. We have the marketing manager, tech manager, and a couple of supervisors with us. The security director is also supposed to be sitting with us, but he's been…" She trails off and gestures around the park. "Directing."

I smile and pull out a chair for her. "Take a load off." I kiss her neck after she sits. I stand and look around. When I see her assigned security near, I start searching for Lance and Josh. When I spot them, I lean down and kiss her lovingly. "I'll be right back, baby."

She looks up at me. "Where are you going?"

"Uh… Skyla. There's just something about her that I can't figure out. I want Lance to check into her."

She nods in agreement. "I feel like she's…" She bites her lip as she thinks. "Afraid of something?"

"Your instincts are pretty good."

"I thought Lance checked into her."

"He did. But we've all caught a few things that throw us. Today, she all but asked for more security. Looking at her now, you'd never guess." I kiss Raleigh's cheek when I see Skyla and Austin walking towards us. "I'll be back."

I give Lance a head tilt signaling for him to follow me. After having someone else take his post, he does. I keep my eyes peeled for Josh, knowing he's around somewhere. I scan the crowd. More and more people are showing up. I love that they're all talking and laughing. It's a heartwarming sight after what happened inside the walls of Lucinio Tech just one week ago.

Everyone here knows the story we've concocted. We said Edward Franklin was embezzling money from the company. After I fired him, he created a plan to get back at me. He kidnapped a security guard and used his credentials to get to my office where he attempted to kill me. He was taken down by Chance, who was shot in the process.

Few know the truth of what happened. Josh had received a phone call from Lance at the right time. Lance was able to complete his track and find Franklin. Unfortunately, it was almost too late. We're grateful it wasn't, and that Lance was able to get the message to Josh in time.

What my employees don't know is what will keep them happy. Happy employees mean good production. Good production means rewards. Like the one I'm about to share with all of them. I didn't gather everyone here just to introduce the new CFO. I brought everyone together to appreciate them and reward them for their hard work.

"What are we doing?" Lance asks.

"Looking for Josh. I have a project for you."

All at once I realize he would want to be near me. I head back towards the tent and see him blending in with practiced ease deep in the shadows. If he wasn't being looked for, no one would have a clue he was there. I walk over to him chuckling. He really has learned well.

"Looking for me?" Josh asks. He remains leaning against a tree with his arms folded over his chest.

"Pretty good position you've taken up. You can see the entire park." I turn and stand next to him surveying the crowd.

He shrugs. "I thought so. What do you need?"

"Well, it's Skyla," I begin.

Lance chuckles. "She doesn't seem comfortable in large crowds."

I watch Skyla's gaze dart all over the place, though she's trying to portray a calm and confident demeanor. "No. She doesn't. But it's what she said on the way over here that throws my hackles up."

Josh raises an eyebrow. "What did she say?"

"She hinted at more security for herself, but quickly backtracked and said it was fine." I nod towards her. "But looking at how uncomfortable and alert she is, though she knows the security I assigned her is near, something just doesn't add up. I want to know everything about her. She's scared. It doesn't take a genius to see it."

"I did a check, Alex," Lance says. "She's clean."

I shake my head. "Dig deeper. Find out more about the company she worked for. I want to know about the entire reason she left."

"I'd say you're fixating on this, but I know you better than that," Josh rumbles. "What are you sensing?"

"I don't know," I say honestly. "She just seems a little too worried about something to me." I glance at my watch. "It's about time for my speech." I look at Josh. "I can't ask Lucinio Tech's security to be her twenty-four seven bodyguard. Fuck knows they deal with enough shit from me. But I think she'd feel more comfortable having security with her."

"You want one of my guards." It's a statement. Not a question. Josh knows what I'm asking.

"I want one of your guards and Lance to dig into her past."

Lance nods. "Nothing I like more than digging shit up. I didn't find anything initially, but that's because I didn't go that in depth. Only enough to know she's a good person. You didn't ask for more than that. Just verification on employment and reasons she's not there anymore."

"I'll get your guard taken care of before she leaves," Josh says. He grins and winks at Lance. "And he'll dig into her. He's bored since Franklin has been taken out."

I laugh and shake my head. "Aren't you monitoring his brother?"

"Monitoring isn't as fun as digging into people's lives and learning about all the skeletons they try and hide." He smiles as Josh and I both laugh.

"You have a speech to get to," Josh tells me after a few moments. "Go. We've got you and everyone else covered."

"Thanks." I take his advice with a smile as I head for Raleigh and our table. It's not that I don't feel safe with my own security or myself. But knowing my brother is watching my back is a good feeling. Especially after all we've been through.

Raleigh looks up at me when I lean down and kiss her. "Hey. Everything okay?"

"It's great. You going to be okay while I do my speech?"

She giggles. "The great Alex Lucinio giving a speech like a real CEO."

I grin and laugh. "Such a brat." I kiss her cheek and walk to the podium in front of everyone.

"You're all set, Mr. Lucinio," the DJ Raleigh hired says to me. "The microphone is good to go."

"Thank you." I nod to him and watch as everyone calms and focuses on me without me saying a word. "Good afternoon, everyone. I hope you're enjoying lunch. I have a few things I wanted to tell you all. It's why I've gathered you all here." I smile at the collective quiet murmur snaking its way through the crowd. Raleigh smiles up at me. "As you know by the end of year report I sent out a couple of months ago, Lucinio Tech had a phenomenal year. Despite some issues within our accounting department, we still managed to come out in the black. Not only in the black, but enough in the black that we've made a huge profit."

Everyone claps at the news. "Whoo-hoo!" a few people yell.

"Yes! Congratulations to all of you for your hard work," I continue. "As a thank you, we've given you each a customized shot glass. There's also a blanket for each of you as well as a few other things with the Lucinio Tech logo. But that isn't all. It's not the type of boss I am. We made far more over the past year than what was projected. I've spent the past week with a few people going over everything just to make sure I'm not wrong. Turns out, I was wrong. But not in the way you think. We made more than what I'd originally thought. And that extra is going directly to you." I pause and watch as everyone murmurs, trying to figure out where I'm going with this. "On Monday morning, you'll all wake up to a nice little bonus." I watch everyone's faces as they register what I'm telling them. I smile a little wider. "Of fifteen thousand dollars," I finish.

It takes everyone a few moments to catch up to me. When they do, I can see a few wipe their eyes. Another starts clapping. Before long, everyone is on their feet joining him in the applause. I meet Raleigh's eyes with a small nod. She blushes. It was her idea to give the extra to the employees. Without them, there wouldn't have been a surplus at all.

I force my eyes away from Raleigh with a lot of effort. My girl is beautiful. I find Josh near the back of the crowd. The next part of this speech involves Skyla. I want to make sure he has her security in place.

When he nods, I continue. "Next, I'd like to introduce to you our new Chief Financial Officer. She's got a lot of experience under her belt, and I know she's going to take us even higher than we already are. As far as I'm concerned, the decision to hire her was a no-brainer. I may have been hesitant about hiring a CFO, but I'm glad I did. This woman is going to take us far. Without anything further from me, I'd like to bring her up here. Give her a warm welcome. Skyla Winters."

She hesitantly gets out of her seat and slowly makes her way to the podium. When she catches her security standing near, she visibly relaxes. But I don't miss how she looks around. I don't know what or who she's looking for, but I'm suspicious as hell about it. I don't think she's in the business of harming me or anyone else. I'm sure as fuck that someone is chasing her, though. Whether her demons are a threat to her or not remains to be seen.

I step aside to let her take the mic, but her eyes widen. I raise an eyebrow and put my hand over the mic. "You okay?"

"Who are they?" she whispers, looking over my shoulder.

I glance over my shoulder, not really needing to, but doing it for her. "They are your new security. They'll be with you twenty-four seven. On each side of the penthouse, there are two smaller rooms. They'll be staying there. You asked me for more security."

She shakes her head. "I -"

"Skyla." I keep my voice low and reassuringly touch her arm. I give it a light squeeze. "You didn't have to come straight out and ask me. I'm a smart man. I don't know where you came from or what you're running from. Maybe you'll tell me when you come to trust me and my family more. Until whatever you're afraid of isn't a threat any longer, they stay with you." I let my hand fall and step aside, but stay close as she steps up to the podium.

"Thank you," she whispers. I nod as she clears her throat. "Thank you everyone for the incredible welcome. A little about me. I'm from New York. Born and raised. Chicago is a bit of a change, but I'm learning the ropes." She smiles like she gives speeches every day. "I started as an accountant in a large firm. T-Rec Merc. I worked my way up to CFO rather quickly and took the company to a new height. Working closely with the CEO, we doubled the company's profit in just over two years. I'm truly excited to work with Mr. Lucinio and all of you to do the same and so much more for Lucinio Tech. I have an open-door policy, so please don't be afraid to pop in or email me if you need anything or have ideas." She smiles again as she steps back. No one else would notice the huge breath she expels if they weren't standing close to her.

I lean down and speak loud enough that she can hear over the applause. "Very well done."

"Thank you."

I lead her back to the table and wait until she's settled before I take my seat next to Raleigh. I let myself relax and enjoy the conversation around me, but after we've all finished eating, I can't wait to leave. Raleigh and her dress are driving me insane.

When I can't take it anymore, I stand and politely excuse us. I take Raleigh's hand and lead her to the limo, hating every second about the quick chats I'm forced to endure on the way. People stopping to thank me for the bonus is nice, but I'm not taking credit for something they've all earned.

Finally, we reach my destination. I guide her inside and turn to the driver. "Partition up. Ignore what you hear, and there will be a huge tip in it for you."

He grins. "Yes, sir."

I duck inside and pull Raleigh onto my lap as he closes the door. She's already blushing. I'm sure she's about to protest, but I cover her mouth with mine and grip the waistband of her panties at her thigh.

I pull back only far enough to talk. "How attached are you to these panties?"

"Not… very," she pants, breathless from the punishing kiss.

"Good," I growl, covering her mouth with mine for another punishing kiss. I rip the thin panties.

Her eyes widen. "Alex!" she squeaks, nipping my lip.

I close my eyes and groan, thrusting my tongue back in her mouth. My cock strains against my zipper, but he'll have to wait. I have other needs. I brush the back of my hand over her pussy and groan again at how wet she is.

"Fuck, baby. You're soaked." I waste no time in ripping the other side of her panties. I pull them off and stuff them in my pocket.

"Only for you," she whispers.

"Damn right only for me." I grip her hips and flip her so she's laying on the seat. I position myself between her legs and wrap them around my shoulders while I push up her dress. Her pussy glistens for me. I let my eyes roam up her body, drinking her in until I reach her eyes. "No one touches you but me. You're mine, Raleigh. You have been ever since I first laid eyes on you."

273

Her tongue slips out and licks her lower lip as she nods. "All yours. And I have the ring to prove it." She holds up her hand, flashing her engagement ring at me.

I grin. I lean down and languidly lick her from her soaked pussy to her sexy little bundle of nerves. I moan low. She shivers at the vibration and bucks her hips into me. I pull back only slightly and run my middle finger through her wetness. I slide it deep inside her and thrust slowly at the same time I take her clit into my mouth and suck while lavishing it with my tongue.

"So fucking sweet." I thrust faster and slide another finger into her wet core. I twist them both and crook them, quickly finding the spot that makes her lose complete control for me.

"Yes! Yes! Don't stop, Alex. Don't stop!" She tangles her fingers in my hair and pulls me closer to her.

I bury my face in her, moaning low and growling while she rides my fingers. Her hips jerk and buck into me. She tightens her legs around my shoulders. Her thighs start to tremble. Her pussy pulses and soaks my fingers impossibly more than they already are.

I thrust a little faster and keep crooking my fingers inside her. She gets tighter and tighter. I flick my tongue rapidly over her clit. She slaps a hand over her mouth and screams when her release gets to the point of no return.

"Fuck, Raleigh. Come. Come for me, baby."

She uncontrollably rides my fingers and trembles as her walls collapse around me. Her pussy clamps down on my fingers. She comes so hard that she almost falls off the seat. I put an arm across her stomach to hold her steady as she rides her release.

"Alex!" she screams behind her hand, thankfully muffling the sound. I told the driver to ignore what he hears, but I don't want him to hear her in her most vulnerable of moments.

I slow my thrusts and licks, bringing her down. She pants and lets her hand fall from her mouth. She loosens her grip on my hair. I slowly pull back with a huge grin and help her put her legs down. She starts to sit up, but I hold her down and kiss up her thigh.

"Not done," I rumble.

"Holy Christ," she whispers.

274

I nip her thigh and grip her hips. I dive back into her pussy, this time with my tongue and only one goal. To see how many times I can make her come before we get home. She bucks into me again and again while I stake my claim.

"This is going to be fun," I growl against her. "So. Much. Fun."

She lets out a guttural moan as she tangles her fingers in my hair again and gives into the pleasure rushing through her and onto my tongue.

Chapter Twenty Nine

❦ Raleigh ❦

I laugh when Alex licks my neck as he stands with me in his arms while he gets out of the limo. I wrap my legs around his waist and arms around his shoulders. My eyes roll back in my head as he starts nibbling his way up to my ear. To anyone watching, they'd think we were drunk. Maybe we are. Maybe we're drunk on each other.

I'm barely aware of anything other than Alex's lips. He adjusts me and releases his grip on me, trusting that I'll grip him tighter. I do just that. Thinking of nothing but him, I begin giving him the same treatment he'd just given me. I kiss his neck and nibble my way up to his ear. The rational part of me is screaming to stop. To wait until we're in the house. The crazy, sexed-up, needy side won't listen.

"Her purse, Mr. Lucinio," the driver says. I can hear the amusement in his voice, but it does nothing to cool me down.

"Your tip I promised. A few hundred good?"

I don't hear the driver's response because everything goes suddenly fuzzy. Alex's hands are quickly back on me, gripping my ass. He squeezes and nips my neck, kissing his way up to my jaw. I cling to him tighter, but not because I'm afraid of falling. It's because I want him to rip my clothes off and make me come again. Selfishly, four times on the way here wasn't enough. I want more. All of him. Nothing but him inside me will satiate me now.

My head falls back when he kicks the door closed and kisses my throat, sucking lightly. "Alex, if I don't have you inside me now, I might die."

He rumbles against my throat and scrapes his teeth lightly across it, sending an earth-shattering bolt of lightning through my entire body. I spasm and moan, nearly losing all control. The cold metal of his belt buckle against my bare pussy when I buck into him is nearly my undoing. I need him more than anything else in the universe.

He chuckles, but I can hear the hint of danger. "Patience."

Desire pools between my thighs. I whimper and moan. Tunnel vision forces me to see nothing around us but him. I don't know if we're in the house, the driveway, or even the limo, but I don't care. I can't wait anymore.

Trusting him to not let me fall, I let go of his shoulders and start undoing the buttons on his shirt, but I quickly lose patience. All rational thought went out the window a long time ago. I love the shirt he's wearing. The rational part of me would keep undoing the buttons like a normal person. But when he sucks on my neck and moans, I grip his shirt and rip it open. Buttons go flying everywhere.

"Fuck, baby. I thought you liked this shirt." He smiles against my neck.

I let my nails scrape up his chest as I tug on his shirt. "I'll buy you a new one." I wriggle against his hard as steel cock hoping to not only relieve the pressure building between my thighs, but also to entice him to drop me on the couch and give me what I crave.

He moans. "Keep that up, we ain't making it upstairs."

I scrape my teeth over his Adam's apple and relish in it bobbing up and down for me. "Good." I press myself more against him and lick his neck. I love the taste of him. Salty and masculine. Something purely, intoxicatingly Alex.

"Fuck it," he growls. He drops me on the couch.

I bounce with a squeak and giggle. Alex's intense blue eyes get darker. Dangerous. Full of primal lust. He yanks at his belt. His piercing stare never leaves me. Getting just as impatient as I am, he breaks the button on his pants. It pings off something while he shoves them down.

"That dress better be off before I sit down or I'm shredding it, just like I did your panties."

His commanding tone leaves no room for argument. I immediately obey and strip the dress from my body. I reach behind me to unhook my bra just as Alex is tearing off his shirt and throwing it into the pile of clothing near us. He sits and tugs me into his lap. I toss the bra over my shoulder not caring in the slightest where it lands. Alex drops me on his dick.

"Oh, fuck, Alex!" I don't swear often. Maybe it's because I was never allowed to. It's something I'm testing my own limits on, but when he slams into me, sinking to the hilt and filling me, all of my inhibitions vanish.

I grip at his shoulders and throw my head back. My release takes over me before I have any chance to stop it. My hips jerk against him, and I writhe as I spasm around him. Wave after wave of ecstasy rush over me until I collapse against his chest.

"Holy Christ," he moans. I can feel his body is coiled and tense. He grits his teeth and stays still as he drops his head back against the couch. "Fucking hell, I didn't know you were that close."

I can't help but giggle into his shoulder. "I told you I'd die without you inside me."

He laughs and grips my ass. "Something about that statement doesn't scream 'I'm going to fucking come right now' to me." He grips my thighs and moves his hands up to my bottom. "But now that you have, you aren't coming again until I tell you to, or I'll torture you all damn night." He slaps my ass.

I jerk into him just as he starts thrusting. "Oh my God."

"I can't believe how tight you are," he whispers in my ear right before he nips just below it. "So fucking tight for me." He starts moving me up and down on him in time to his thrusts. His fingertips dig into my skin.

I tangle my fingers in his hair with one hand and grip his shoulder with the other. I clench around him and moan softly. Each thrust brings him deeper and deeper until it feels like he's pushing against my stomach.

He rocks me back and forth against him as he trusts. I kiss along his jaw, licking at the scruff before meeting his lips.

He nips my lip and sucks it into his mouth before taking me in another searing kiss. One of his hands tangles in my hair. He tugs exposing my throat to him. He kisses it and scrapes his teeth down my chest to my nipples. They ache for him. When his mouth meets the sensitive flesh of my nipples, I have no choice but to arch into him and pull him closer, silently begging for more while I ride him.

I get wetter and wetter for him until I can feel myself dripping with need. His glorious cock, already long and thick, gets thicker and, I swear to God, longer. He sucks and nips at my nipples and slams himself into me over and over again.

He holds me in place and reaches between us. Before I have a second to register what he's doing, he sets his thumb against my clit. My fingertips grip his shoulders harder. The pleasure he'd been working so hard to build reaches a breaking point.

I suck in a sharp breath and tremble. "Alex! Please!" I'm not above begging him to let the release wash over me. My pussy clenches around him so tightly he has no chance of moving. I want him as deeply inside me as he can be.

"Fuck, Raleigh," he grunts. He flicks my clit. I jerk against him with a squeak. His hot breath against my skin as he kisses his way to my lips lights me ablaze.

"Alex!" I'm vibrating. I writhe. I tremble. "Please! Please!" My pussy pulses erratically. My stomach clenches hard. I scratch my nails along his shoulders, unable to control myself any longer.

His lips crash against mine furiously. "Come," he says against them. He tangles his tongue with mine. "Now."

I throw my head back and let the waves and waves of pleasure crash over me until I feel like I'm drowning in it. I can hear his name on my lips, but the animalistic screams coming from me are unrecognizable even to my own ears.

He fills me as he comes with a low growl. Our hips jerk against each other's while we both come. I collapse against him, feeling like I've shattered completely. Like he's the only thing in the world that can put me back together.

Alex wraps his arms tightly around me, and slightly slides his hands up down my arms. He kisses my shoulder. "Beautiful. So fucking beautiful," he whispers.

I blush and hide in his neck. "I can't feel my body."

He smiles. "I can. And it's an exquisite piece of art."

I giggle and blush darker. "I don't think I can move."

He nibbles up my neck to just below my ear. "You don't have to. I'll carry you up to the shower. We do have to clean up, though. Damon's party is tonight."

I smile at the excitement of my brother's birthday party. "I hope he likes what I got him."

Alex laughs. He shifts us as he slides his dick out of me. He stands up with me in his arms. I wrap my legs around his waist. He kisses me and starts walking towards the stairs. "He'll love it. I happen to know Damon is a lover of gifts that have a lot of thought put behind them. Though, he's Mr. Tough Guy. He'll never admit that shit."

I giggle and blush a little. "Really. Do you think he'll like it? It's kind of…" I shrug. "Kiddish?"

He chuckles and shakes his head as he kicks the door to our bedroom closed. "Trust me when I say that Damon will love it. He's a lot like me. Well, our core group. We're all the same. None of us give a shit about money or expensive gifts. We care about heartfelt gifts. Because they are unique. No one else has them."

I smile and kiss him as he lets me slide down his body. "I trust you."

He kisses me again, more deeply, and backs me closer to the large, glass door, walk-in shower. The kiss gets hotter. His tongue meets mine again while he turns on the water. After a few moments, he backs me into the shower under the spray and lifts me once more, pinning me to the shower wall.

Another orgasm later, I've lost count on how many he's given me since we left the employee appreciation party, we both quickly clean up. After drying off, we both find clothing and get dressed. I smile as I'm pulling on my tank top.

"What's that look for, baby?" Alex asks when he sees I'm openly ogling him.

I bite my lip and blush. "I love seeing you in jeans. For a long time, I didn't think you owned a pair."

He laughs. "I prefer jeans over a suit. But I do have a professional image I like to uphold. I don't expect my employees to dress to the nines. But I expect them to look professional. It wouldn't look very good if the boss came to work in jeans and a t-shirt."

I give him an adoring, soft smile. "I love you in them. It's nice to see the ruthless CEO you are to everyone else be this fun-loving man behind closed doors."

He raises an eyebrow. "You think I'm ruthless and some serious asshole all the time?" he asks. I don't have a chance to answer, though.

"Alex!" I squeal as he tugs me into his arms and throws me over his shoulder with such little effort that I'm breathless.

"I'll show you just how fun I can be." He slaps my ass and carries me like a Neanderthal down the stairs.

I laugh and wiggle, trying to get free. I hear that people are starting to arrive to Damon's party and don't want anyone to see me slung like a ragdoll over Alex's shoulder. I squeak and slap his ass in an attempt to get him to put me down.

"Alex!" I laugh. "Put me down!"

"Nope." He slaps my bottom again just as he walks into the living room where people are starting to gather. "Everyone outside."

He doesn't break his stride. He walks past everyone, his grip tight on my thighs. I laugh more. When I see everyone following us, huge smiles on their faces, I feel lighter than air.

I'm so grateful that I'm Alex's, and Alex is mine. But I'm also beyond thankful that I am part of this family. This incredible, strong, and beautiful family. It's all I've ever wanted but never knew I was missing. It's my happy place.

This family, Alex, is my home.

Chapter Thirty

🐚 Alex 🐚

I watch as Damon opens a large gift from Lance. Everyone is full. Happy. The strawberry cream cheesecake Raleigh made last night is damn near gone. The container of butterscotch ice cream Damon loves is empty. Gavin, Josh, Dane, Cole, and Lance are all gathered around Damon. Everyone is laughing. Kent has his arms around my mom. They are standing behind me and Raleigh looking over the entire scene before us.

Raleigh is in my lap. She's waiting until the very end to give her brother the gift she made for him. I soothingly rub my thumb in slow circles over her thigh. Every time she starts nervously chewing her lip, I nip her shoulder.

"It's going to be okay, Raleigh," I rumble against her neck. "I swear he's going to love it."

"I hope so," she whispers.

I chuckle. "Promise, baby. He will."

"Shit," Damon gasps when he gets the wrapping paper off the gift from Lance.

My eyes widen. "Well, that beats mine," I whisper.

"It beats all of ours," Raleigh whispers back.

We're all staring at a seventy-inch painted portrait of Damon and Raleigh. Raleigh is all smiles. A beautiful carefree young woman. The artist captured her innocent spirit with practiced perfection right down to the gold fleck and sparkle in her beautiful eyes.

Behind her, Damon is standing with his arms folded over his chest. He's looking down at her. Anyone who wasn't carefully observing would think the dark look on his face just made him some broody motherfucker. While I won't deny the guy knows how to brood, the look of pure love reflected in his eyes gives him away. It's pretty obvious that he's watching over her. Protecting her like only a big brother could.

"Do you like it?" Lance asks quietly.

Damon looks up at him a moment before standing. "I fucking love it." He pulls him into a hug but quickly clears his throat and glances at us all while he lets go. "I love it." He reaches up and wipes a tear from his eye while he sits down.

Lance's grin could light up the entire backyard if it weren't already lit. Not a single one of us missed the hug or how emotional either of them got over the gift and Damon's reaction, but we don't call them out. Whatever just happened is between them. I smile against Raleigh's neck because I have my suspicions. I have for longer than anyone in this yard knows.

"I'm not giving him mine now…," she whispers to me. She shakes her head. "That was like the highlight. I can't come close to that."

"Raleigh." My voice is low. "It's not a competition. He will love your gift."

She shakes her head. "No. That's the perfect gift. I don't know how Lance did that. We never posed for anything, but that's perfect. Mine won't come close to that."

"I think that about, uh, covers it, right?" Damon is visibly trying to compose himself. "Thank you all. This was the perfect birthday. Thirty-six is sure to be a great year." He clears his throat to cover the fact that he's emotional in any manner. Damon doesn't like showing it in any form.

"Still have one more, brother," Josh rumbles and looks directly at Raleigh. "I think your sister had something special for you." He gives her a reassuring wink. The only people here who know what she made for him are me and Josh.

Raleigh shakes her head. "No. It's okay. I -"

"Raleigh," I growl low and warningly in her ear. "I will take it out of your back pocket and give it to him myself."

She whines and glances at me before taking a deep breath. She quietly stands and walks over to Damon with a seriously furious blush on her pretty face. I can see how nervous she is, but one thing she needs to learn is that no one in this family is going to be judgmental of her thoughtful gift.

I look up at my mom when she lays her hand on my shoulder. She smiles down on me. "Is she nervous?" she asks me in a whisper.

I nod. "She's afraid he won't like it. Think it's too cheap or something." I look back at my girl. "She's afraid it won't compare to Lance's gift."

"That's silly," Kent says with a low chuckle. "It's not a contest."

I smile. "That's what I told her."

I watch her as she hands him the gift. She starts to walk back to me, but he pulls her down next to him. I grin because I knew that's exactly what he'd do. I stand and walk closer. Nick stands next to me when he comes in.

"Sorry, I'm late," he whispers to me and Josh. "We responded to a call, and it went late. What we thought was a run of the mill shakedown, turned into a fucking murder investigation."

"It's alright," I whisper back. "We figured it was something when you texted saying you'd be late."

Damon smiles at Raleigh. "What is it?"

Raleigh looks down and plays with her fingers. "Um… Its… a coupon book… I made it myself," she nearly whispers.

Damon smiles wider. "Like you put things in here you think I'll like, and I get to turn them into you whenever I want to do them?"

"Well, sort of…?" She shrugs. "They're things I thought we could do together. Like to get to know each other better. If you want to, I mean."

"Want to? Raleigh, I'd love that." He opens the coupon book as we all watch. He laughs. "I think this one is my favorite. Adventure. Your choice. Just nothing insane like bungee jumping into a volcano."

Raleigh's smile makes my heart flutter. "Fucking hell, she's beautiful," I whisper.

Nick smiles and shoulder bumps me. "You're fucking smitten."

I smile wider. "Not ashamed to admit it." I can't pull my eyes away from Raleigh's beautiful and happy smile. Damon's admission that he likes the gift is all she needed. I sigh when I feel my phone going off in my pocket. I contemplate ignoring the call, but when I see who it is, I answer immediately, walking into the house. "Hey. What's going on?"

"Sorry to bother you, Mr. Lucinio," my Head of Security says. He has never called me for anything so long as he's been in the position.

"Don't worry about it. If you're calling, I know it's important."

"Yeah." His tone is clipped.

I'm immediately on edge. "What happened?" I close the sliding glass door and watch my family around my pool happily laughing.

"We had a break-in. It's happened once before. Drunk guy thought he'd sleep it off in the stairwell. Security was watching him before the silent alarm even went off. They were already on the way there by the time he got in. Tonight wasn't much different. They were monitoring a girl. She looked pretty fucking suspicious. She was running. Looked dirty. She was outside the building trying to figure out how to get in."

My suspicions are already long raised. "And?"

"She tried opening a few doors. Next thing they know, she's screaming her head off. No one on the streets batted an eye."

I suddenly feel fucking sick to my stomach, but I force my hand to the sliding glass door and open it. I signal Josh. "What happened? Did security go outside?"

"Yeah. They bolted for the door, but by the time they got there, she was gone. They lost her on the cameras. Two of our guys were looking around outside the property. Two more of our guys were on each floor of the parking garage looking for her. It was like she fucking vanished. Thirty minutes later, a silent alarm on the third level of the parking garage went off."

Josh reaches me as I put the phone on speaker. I close the door behind him and hold the phone between us. "How the fuck did she get to the third floor? Where was the guard at the gate of the garage?"

"He was there. Didn't see a fucking thing. I checked the cameras myself. I don't see where she got in. One second the garage is totally empty. No movement. The next second, she appears on cameras on the third floor. Like a fucking ghost, Mr. Lucinio. We checked every single angle we have with cameras. Nothing. Not even a shadow."

I shake my head. "There has to be a logical explanation. I don't fucking believe in ghosts. We have angles we need to cover if they ain't being seen."

"I'm not done."

Josh and I look at each other. "Okay," I say.

"Like I said. We saw her on the third floor. She broke the window of the door. Or at least she tried to. She was smashing a brick against it and screaming. Third floor security heard it at the exact moment the alarm was tripped. Both of them ran for the door. As soon as she saw them, she stopped. Dropped the brick and dropped to her knees. Put her hands on her head and let them cuff her. They brought her in. She begged us not to call the police, and fuck if I understand why the hell I listened. Something about this has a very wang taste to it."

I look at Josh. "What do you think?" I ask, my voice low.

"I think he's right. Something ain't right. I'll grab the boys."

I nod. "We're on our way," I say to my security. I hang up and follow Josh.

Damon watches Josh for a moment and meets my eyes, knowing immediately what he needs to do. "I think I'm cashing in the movie night right now," he says to Raleigh. "What do I do? Rip it out and give it to you?"

She looks up at me in surprise when I kneel in front of her. "What's wrong?" she asks.

I take her hands in mine and lean in. I kiss her, letting her soft lips mold themselves to mine. I pull back slowly and rest our hands on her thighs. "I'm sorry, baby. Security at Lucinio Tech called. I need to go."

She tilts her head and watches the guys behind me moving towards the door. "Is everything okay?"

"I think so. A girl broke in, but it seemed strange. I'm bringing Josh with me to check it out because it seems like she was looking for help. I don't think I'll be long." I lean in and kiss her again. "You won't even miss me. Looks like Damon is already planning your night!"

Damon laughs. "Fuck yes. We're raiding all of your junk food!"

I stand and laugh, throwing Raleigh a wink. "Good luck finding any!"

Raleigh's giggle while she explains to Damon that she has a stamp for the coupons is all I need to stay sane as I follow the guys through my house and out to our vehicles.

But as soon as I jump in with Josh, I can't help but wonder what happened. Why did a woman try to break into my building? And just why in the fuck would she go through great lengths to avoid security if she needed help?

I keep telling myself not to read too much into this. Maybe this girl was terrified. Maybe something happened, and she knew we could help her. The Lucinio name, Josh's name, has been all over the media since he started working with Ryan and making this mafia legal and legit.

So, why the hell am I unable to shake the feeling I have deep in the pit of my stomach that something is off? That this entire thing isn't really just a girl who needs help coming to a building owned by the brother of the man she knew could help her?

Somehow, I know things are going to get far worse. The question I can't get out of my mind is just how bad is it going to get before it gets better?

The End

Next In The Lucinio Family Series

The devilishly dark and alluring Lucinio Family Series continues with *The Player's Rebel*.

Everything has always come easy to me. School. I had great grades. Money. I grew up with it. Women. I met and married the woman I thought I'd spend the rest of my life with when we were in college. After she was killed, I'd vowed never to let another woman near my heart again. But having one to keep my bed warm at night was never a problem.

Enter the beautiful server at Jake's Diner.

After a night of flirting and an exchange of phone numbers that included future dates, I expected Harleigh Harlow to still be in my bed the next morning when I woke up. It was a kick to my ego to find her gone. I didn't expect I'd feel heartsick. I'm usually the one to walk away. Never the other way around.

Licking my wounds isn't simple. Somehow, Harleigh has gotten under my skin. Getting her out of my head is the hardest thing I've ever done. Since she's ghosted me, though, I don't have a choice.

When Harleigh crashes back into my life again, though, I'm blindsided. Protecting innocent lives has never been a challenge, so I know saving her will be the easy part. Keeping her from shattering my heart again when it's all over? That will be a different war altogether.

Order *The Player's Rebel* Today!

The Lucinio Family Series

Available Now

Rising From The Ashes
The Player's Rebel
Encrypting My Heart

Other Books By Melony Ann
The Beautiful Dream Series

Available Now

Loving You
My Love, My Heart
Softening Lyric
Undercover Temptations
Captain Charming
Breaking Boundaries
Crashing Into You
Tactical Inferno
Ravishing Our Queen
Cherished By The Texan
Unveiling Our Passions

Box Sets Available

The Beautiful Dream Series: Box Set: Part 1
The Beautiful Dream Series: Box Set: Part 2

The Crane Family Series

Available Now

The Reluctant Mafia King
Sweet Lies
Billion Dollar Love Story
Be Mine
Protecting Her
Dangerously Forbidden Love
His Heart
Love In The Dark

Box Sets Available

The Crane Family Series

The Deimos Trilogy

Available Now

Connor's Legacy
Aryan's Alpha
Kade's Redemption

Box Sets Available

The Deimos Trilogy

The Forbidden Temptation Series

Available Now

The Detective's Forbidden Temptation
The Running Back's Forbidden Temptation

Multi Author Series
Piper Falls: Firehouse 49

Available Now

Ignite My Fire by Melony Ann
Regain My Fire by Kindra White
Playing With My Fire by D.L. Howe
Fight My Fire by Darley Collins
Against My Fire by Anneke Boshoff
Relight My Fire by Louise Murchie
Harness My Fire by Ayana Lisbet
Quench My Fire by Havana Wilder

Let's Be Friends

Follow me on

Bookbub

Facebook

Goodreads

Instagram

Tik Tok

Visit my website
www.melonyannauthor.com

Subscribe to my newsletter and get a FREE never-seen-before NOVELLA
just for subscribers!
https://www.melonyannauthor.com/exclusive-content

Join my Facebook Reader Group!
Jason's and Melony's Sizzling Book Nook

The official Lucinio Family Series Playlist on YouTube
https://youtube.com/playlist?list=PLGEiD5wbQmDdjFYhMKrFsomQOTr
RK7x9Y

Dedication

When we think we're about to fight the battle alone, you appear like an avenging warrior from the shadows. Your love makes the darkness brighter; the pain bearable. We'll love you until time stands still and beyond.

Acknowledgements

Brad - Thank you so much for being here with me through all of this. I love you so much.

Laura - This will be book number nineteen. And you've been with me through all of it. I wouldn't be here without you and your love and support. I love you more than I could ever say because there aren't enough words in the English language to express the depths of what I feel for you.

Jay - I will forever hate Detroit. But I met you, so I guess it holds one good thing. I love you!

Ayana - The best PA I could hope for. Thank you for not only doing so much for me, but also for becoming like family to me.

Anneke - I really can't wait for you to touch down stateside. You're truly such an amazing human. I'm honored to know you. Even more honored to call you my friend and chosen family.

Jason - Thank you for not ever running away. Even when I think you will.

To the Bookstagram Community.

To my family.

To all of those who believe in me and support me.

To all of those who don't.

Cover by: Carter Cover Designs

Edited by: Alyssa Skaggs

About Melony Ann

Melony Ann began writing short stories and poetry as a child. She continued honing her craft over the years until she took the plunge and began publishing her work, despite having severe anxiety.

Melony writes contemporary romance stories that are full of suspense and a lot of steam.

When she isn't writing, she is loving her family and working to make her life something she deserves.

Melony believes that if her writing can inspire just one person, then all of her hard work is worth it.

Her hope is that her writing allows each and every one of her readers to escape for a little while. To dive into a different world one book at a time.

www.ingramcontent.com/pod-product-compliance
Lightning Source LLC
Chambersburg PA
CBHW070558260626
47161CB00002B/646